Poetry

That Which Already Is (2017)
Into the Nothingness (2017)
Where All the Barren Things Decay (2017)
Lenore and Franklin: A Poem (2018)
Notre Joconde (2018)
Whispering Trails (2018)
Sonnets (2018)
The Collected Poetry of Hue Woodson (2018)
The Remains of What Once Was: Selected Early Poems: Winter 2000 (2018)
From the Other Side (2018)
Past, Prologue: Poems: 2003-2006 (2018)
The Strange Perfection of Hindsight: Poems 2001-2003 (2018)
Leaves, FALL: Selected Early Poems: Fall 2000 (2018)
Collected Longer Poems: 2002-2010 (2019)
In Winter and Discontent: Selected Early Poems: Winter 1999 (2019)
A Thousand Natural Shocks: Selected Early Poems: Spring 2000 (2019)
This Mortal Coil: More Selected Early Poems: Spring 2000 (2019)
Quietus: Additional Selected Poems: Spring 2000 (2019)
Torrents of Spring (2020)

Collections

Two Monsters and Other Dialogues (2017)
Stories for Hemingway (2017)
Angel in the Snow Globe and Other Posthuman Stories (2018)
The Kadena Stories (2019)

Novels / Novellas

Lie Down in Torment (2017)
etc. (2017)
Stormfield (2017)
One Brief Shining Moment (2017)
Mister Sandman (2018)
The Dead Life (2018)
Through Darkened Light (2018)
Blonde in the Halter Dress (2018)
The Jezebel Killer (2018)
Purgatoria (2018)
The Naked Ones (2018)
Harvest Night (2018)
The Dumpster Games (2019)

Also by the author

The Effectiveness of Classroom Seating Arrangements: A Study of Students and Teachers (2018)

Systems of Onto-theology: Towards a Heideggerian Method (2018)

Heideggerian Theologies: The Pathmarks of John Macquarrie, Rudolf Bultmann, Paul Tillich, and Karl Rahner (Wipf and Stock, 2018)

A Theologian's Guide to Heidegger (Wipf and Stock, 2019)

Existential Theology: An Introduction (Wipf and Stock, 2020)

IMPRESSIONS

IN A

WANDERING SKY

Hue Woodson

EREIGNIS Press
2021

EREIGNIS Press

Printed in the United States of America

LIBRARY OF CONGRESS CATALOGUING-IN-PUBLICATION DATA

Woodson, Hue. 1978-

Impressions in a Wandering Sky / Hue Woodson.

ISBN 978 – 1– 7379843 – 0 – 6

1.Title

IMPRESSIONS

IN A

WANDERING SKY

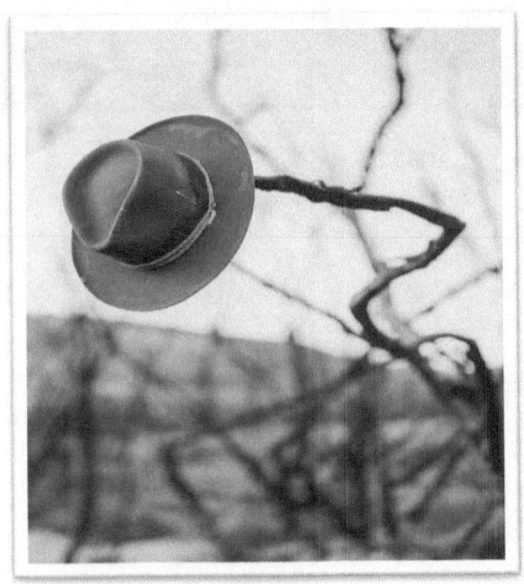

1

You may not know me, dear reader, unless you know of my work. That is, unless you are familiar with the many books I have written over the course of my career, books about the American West and the vast array of personalities bred from that fascinating period in American history. Most of them—my published books, I mean—have been bestsellers, and have sold just as well in the New England states as they have in the most rural territories west of the Mississippi. That means my readership—all you wonderful dear readers—is broad and varied. I don't mean to pat myself on the back, but I was told once by a very reliable source that President Theodore Roosevelt owns a copy of every one of my books and he, being a man that knows the Old West, said my books were better than any other biographer's.

I am, you see, chiefly, a biographer. Though I'd also like to think of myself as a historian, I know I will always be considered as a biographer beyond anything else. And, I suppose that's okay with me, since I have been interested mostly with telling stories about people—people, in my mind, that deserve to have their stories told by someone that knows how.

That, of course, is what this book is about: a man with a story I want to tell.

Sure, perhaps, anyone could write this man's story. I know that. But, I like to think, dear reader, that only one biographer could truly give this man's story justice—and, there's no doubt in my mind that being the writer that I am, only I can truly bring this man's story to life.

As conceded a thing as that may be on the surface, I am confident in my abilities. There is no ego involved on my part, really. Not even in light of knowing that President Theodore Roosevelt felt, as it was relayed to me, that I was the best living biographer in America—a quote that I had my publishers put on the jacket of my last book. So, I have no ego, if you must know. I am, after all, a best-selling author, and, if it had not been for me, many characters from the forgotten West would not have had their stories told as successfully and with the extensive literary treatment I have given them, and might not, for that matter, have had their names enter the consciousness of American life so poignantly and elegantly—that is what I precisely plan to do for the man I am writing this biography about: make him a household name.

That is, I believe, the role of a good biographer: to bring to life the people he chooses to write about, to make them leap from the page as larger than life personalities, to make their readers see them in such a way that they think, through the way he writes, that they actually know the person.

For me, dear reader, that is how I begin researching a subject I want to write about: by knowing the person. I try to find as many documents as I can about them and try to interview as many people as I can that knew them firsthand, so that I can, on some level, I hope, write about my subject as if I actually knew them personally. That, of course, gets passed on to you, dear reader, for you to do with it what you will.

But, what distinguishes my current biographical subject from the other subjects, both men and women, I have studied and written about—and, perhaps, makes it a little more difficult to do my job as a biographer and historian—is that nobody really knows the real name of my subject. What I mean, in particular, is that there is only one name I have ever heard him being called.

They called him Cooley—that's all. Just Cooley—and nothing else.

On occasion, I have found a last name attached to it, and have often found that last name spelled so many different ways that none of the versions seem reliable enough to me to prove worthy of writing about. Only that single name of *Cooley* has remained a constant moniker, nonetheless. That one name, as I have found over the course of my research, seems to stand out like no one single name that I have ever read or heard about has—that single name, you see, is a name that you can ask anyone about and they'd know who you are talking about, a name that is recognizable in various states and territories all over the country, a name that, as I have come to know, seems to evoke a lot of stories, tall tales, memories, and bad feelings.

With all of that, what has struck me as particularly interesting—and, perhaps, a little frustrating, when it comes to writing about this Cooley person—is that I have never found a single document certifying that Cooley actually existed. Not a birth certificate, or deed to a purchased piece of land, or a marriage license, or a death certificate, or a criminal record—nothing, not even a tombstone in a cemetery, for that matter. It is almost as if, without any documentation to back up his actual existence, Cooley was just a ghost floating through people's lives, like leaving impressions in a wandering sky.

I'd be lying to you, dear reader, if I were to say that there hadn't been times when I wondered, myself, if Cooley did actually exist. These were times when I would often find myself thinking, quite frankly, that a person can't exist without any documentation, without leaving a tombstone somewhere, without leaving a paper trail behind them after a life has been well-lived.

But, somehow, I am convinced that Cooley did this. I don't know how, but he did. Somehow, rather than leaving a paper trail, Cooley has managed to exist only in the memories of people he came in contact with, and nowhere else, it seems.

So, dear reader, as you can see, writing about Cooley means depending solely on the memories of others. This makes my job, of course, more difficult. But, mostly, what it does is leave me at the discretion of other people's memories, memories that always fade over time and change shape the more people rely on recollection, and, sometimes, become distorted into different versions of the truth.

I'm afraid that, in depending on different versions of the truth that are based on other people's memories, that leaves me at a huge disadvantage as a biographer, especially when biographers deal with one tangible truth. I know that quite well—the way biographers deal with the truth in its most purist form.

You might even say, since there is no one single pure form of truth about Cooley, it makes Cooley become an undesirable subject of biography—you would have a point that is duly noted. You might even say that, as my dear reader, with me being a person that should write about the truth and nothing but the truth, choosing to write about Cooley compromises my credibility as a biographer and historian—to that, perhaps you are correct. And moreover, it might make you believe, dear reader, that whatever I write about Cooley wouldn't be worth reading and shouldn't, therefore, be classified as biography or history—and maybe you would be in the right to consider that.

Still, what you should consider, dear reader, is that there is no one pure form of truth when it comes to history. History, as I have discovered, is fluid. I had to come to that understanding particularly during the research process of learning more about Cooley. Cooley's history is fluid because that history, for better or worse, means different things to different people. And, when history is in the hands of different people, that history is always interpreted differently. And, rightfully so, I believe.

That means, you see, that my role as Cooley's biographer and historian is to, somehow, bring all those different versions of the truth together into something that you, dear reader, can understand and, in the end, decide which parts of it you ultimately want to believe or ignore.

After that, I suppose I have done my job to the best of my ability. The rest is for you to figure out, dear reader—the Cooley that follows must now be defined by you, because all I can do is tell you what I think.

2

Cooley? Yeah, I knew Cooley. By God, I knew him, once upon a time. That was before I was saved and got filled up with the spirit of the Lord Christ Jesus. When I knew Cooley, I wasn't what I am now, obviously. I was a sinner, then. Cooley was like a vice for me in those days—the thing that dragged me down closer to damnation, I've always believed. I'd be powerfully-happy to forget I ever knew him. But, I know that that's impossible, because he played such an important part in my life before I knew God and got religion.

But, yeah, I know what you're talking about: about Cooley having a kind of fluid history. By God, I don't think the guy really has a history. Not like you and me, anyway.

I don't know where he came from, exactly, in terms of his history.

I mean, I don't rightly remember him ever telling me anything about his life before I met him—he would always say, if I ever asked him, "hey, where did you live before you came here," that he was here and that was all that mattered.

If I bothered to press him a bit further, I'll never forget how mad he would get with me. He'd get irritated at first, and walk out the house, and I'd leave him alone. Then,

I got to wondering about it more and more. This one time, I kept after him, kept asking him stuff like *why won't you tell me where you came from, what's the big deal, why don't know want me to know, what are you hiding anyway,* he charged me, and took me by the throat, and slammed me backward into the wall so hard that the wind got knocked free from me. His face went blank and his eyes were wild, and he choked me until I felt myself getting lightheaded, and, then, I distinctly remember him telling me that he could kill me if he wanted to, and that if I kept asking him he'd make sure I'd never ask him another single question ever again.

When I looked in his eyes that time, I knew he meant it. There wasn't a doubt in my mind that he'd kill me if I asked again. So, I didn't. Not for a very long time, anyway.

I always thought that Cooley was hiding something about his past. Something that I figured must have been pretty bad for him to not want me to ever know anything about it. Something he would kill me over to keep from me ever asking him about—something that was, basically, the one thing that convinced me to leave him for good, in the end.

By God, I loved that man. I really did. I don't mind saying it, now.

But, in the end, you see, love just wasn't enough. Not when I was the only one committed to love, and there wasn't a stitch of love in any of the times he'd beat me or choke me—no, there wasn't enough love in the world to keep me with him.

I know I'd like to believe that he loved me. But, I know that would be foolish. Cooley didn't know how to love. The man was just incapable of it.

If you ask me, I think it was something that happened in his childhood. Something with his mother, perhaps. That's where I think men with problems loving a woman get their problems from in the first place: from their mothers. It's always either that their mothers didn't love them enough, or that they love their mothers so much they don't know how to love any other woman, or that mothers abused them in some way, or that they got taken off the breast too soon, or had been on the breast for too long, or saw something in their mothers that made them jealous of the way their mother loved their fathers, or that they wished they were their fathers so that they could make love to their mothers. I don't know. I'm not one of those mind doctors. Those guys that study your thoughts and dreams and tell you what they mean—learned men with neckties sitting in offices with plush couches telling you to lie down and tell you about what you're most afraid of or ask you if you've dreamed you were falling off a cliff and stuff like that.

All I know, you see, is that Cooley never talked about his mother or father. Not once. Not in the three years I was with him, anyway.

There was just that one time when he told me that something I did reminded him of his mother. I don't even remember what it was that I had done. Probably, it was just something I always did that he just began to notice and think on.

Whatever it was, I remember how we had been in our kitchen and had turned to find him looking at me. Staring at me was more like it. Staring at me so hard that I thought I had done something to piss him off, something would get him riled up enough to choke me or backhand me. But, when that didn't happen, I stood there at the stove and looked back at him.

It was then that he told me that I reminded him of his mother.

I asked him what did he mean, how did I remind him of her.

Cooley looked at me for another long moment. Just sitting there at our breakfast table smoking his cigar, looking at me through the smoke, he never said anything.

I thought to ask Cooley again, but I didn't want to take the chance. I always knew that if I pressed him too much, it was no telling what might happen. A black eye, perhaps. Or, a bruise on my arm, maybe. Getting the breath nearly choked out of me. Sometimes, I found, it just wasn't worth the trouble. But, yet, I remembered not just him saying that about his mother, but the way he had looked at me when he had said it. It was as if he had been there, there whenever, or wherever, that memory actually happened.

I wish I could tell you what it means. But, I don't know.

What I do know, though, is that that was the only time I ever remember Cooley ever saying anything about his mother. By God, I don't even remember him ever telling me what her name was. His father, neither. Somehow, I think that it wasn't that he didn't want me know, but that he wanted to forget.

I guess what I'm trying to say is that Cooley tended to live in the present, not the past. I guess, you could say, he figured that there was no past worth calling the past. If you ask me, I think that he was running away from the past, whatever that past was. Not just his parents, but his whole damn childhood, and everything else that ever happened to him up until the moment we met on that stagecoach—I like to think that the moment we met was the moment he decided that he had wanted to live a new life through me, and through us, and that he wanted that moment on the stagecoach when we sat across from one another and he told me I was the most beautiful woman he had ever seen to be the moment that opened him up to a new world, a world where his past would fade away forever, and that, from the moment we met, he expected me to be his future.

It wasn't much of a future, though—just three years, by God, and that was more than enough for me, Heaven knows.

But, for me, it might as well have been a lifetime. All the terrible stuff Cooley put through in that time made those three years seem like thirty-three. Three hundred and thirty-three, even. All the black eyes and bruises I had to explain to friends in town, all those times I would lay in bed next to him praying he wouldn't ask me for sex, all the times he threatened to kill me, all those instances when I felt he was more of a stranger than a husband, all those times when he would hear him coming home late at night drunk and find myself wondering what kind of mood he'd be in—three years of that was more than enough, and I left him.

I had to do it in the middle of the night when he was gone drinking with his drinking buddies. Since I knew he'd be away until the break of dawn, I knew I had had my chance. You see, I just threw some clothes in a bag, took a little money out of the strong box Cooley kept under our bed, and grabbed the pistol he always kept smashed in between the mattress.

As I sneaked out the house, I had a feeling, a bad feeling.

I don't what it was, or why I had felt it, but I had a feeling that Cooley was nearby somewhere. Something told me that Cooley would hop out the darkness, pounce on me, beat the—Lord forgive me—shit out of me, and drag me back into the house like a bag a horse feed. You might think that that was crazy, particularly since I knew that Cooley had a routine and that part of that routine was coming home at the crack of dawn whenever he was out drinking. But, by God, I guess I was just scared to death of him, scared that he would be a step ahead of me and know what I was up to, scared that I would push him just far enough to kill me like he had always promised. And Lord knows that there was no doubt in my mind that if Cooley found me running away, he would make sure I wouldn't run away again. Probably, if you ask me, he would make sure I wouldn't run anywhere ever again. And that scared me more than anything. It scared me to have that sort of thing hanging over my head. And, anyway, I knew I couldn't spend another night in fear, another night lying next to him in bed wishing he didn't snuggle up to me and grab my breasts, another night hearing him snore like a bull moose.

So, like I said, I sneaked out.

I didn't know where I was going to go. I didn't have any family anywhere nearby. Any of the friends I had weren't my friends anymore, because I lost touch with them through the years. Cooley made sure that I didn't have anyone, and that, like he would say sometimes, *all you need in this fucking world is me and nothing fucking else, because I'm your alpha and omega, don't you forget that.*

And I hadn't.

It always stuck in the back of my mind.

The whole time I sneaked away from the house, the whole time I walked and walked and walked, I thought about it—by God, the thought rolled around in my head so much that it made my head hurt. Even once I had walked for miles and miles and had reached the nearest town just as the sun began to rise, I thought about it—and I began wondering what Cooley being my alpha and omega had to do with anything when he came home and found me gone.

3

Dear reader, I ask that you carefully consider the testimony of Cooley's first wife with a grain of salt. I do not mean to suggest that she isn't telling the truth. As a biographer, it is never my duty to say that someone is lying—I only seek the truth, and nothing but the truth. Facts, in other words. Therefore, my main contention with her story is that many elements of it seem to be slanted too far in her favor and too far against Cooley himself. In this regard, I wonder if her story moves away from the facts and ventures into painting a particular picture of Cooley in Cooley's absentia. What you must remember, dear reader, is, by all accounts, she did not necessarily have a pleasant experience with Cooley and, because of this, I find that she may be prone to make Cooley into a villain.

Of course, I am very much aware that her story is *her story*, and, furthermore, that her story is based on her own perspective. And, to that end, perhaps a great deal of her story is one that features Cooley as the villain and her as the victim.

But, as I am sure you are greatly aware, my undertaking as a biographer is to tell Cooley's story and to present it as factually as I possibly can. I have just as much a duty to the truth as I do to the subject I intend to present to you in as full and as untainted as I possibly can. As I am sure you know, being a biographer is not an easy job and, furthermore, the job becomes even more complicated when the subject of the biography is not available. Given the degree to which I must depend on the interviews and testimonies of people that knew Cooley firsthand, I feel I need to make you aware of what the facts are in an impartial manner and what the facts are when filtered through the perspective of someone such as Cooley's first wife.

As you know, facts are stubborn things—they are unavoidable things, especially when a biographer's purpose is to reconstruct a life. Yet, as you also know, facts are tricky things—they can be slippery, especially when they are far and few in between. You can only do so much with what you have. I am not just speaking here about Cooley, but more generally. When there is little to go on, facts can certainly get in the way—they can become these large, unmanageable things that hinder more than help. Facts can blur what we think we know, until what we think we know—the very thing on which we ground the story of a life—easily becomes a house made of straw. Sure, it feels as if we are constructing something meaningful and something that allows us to build truth, but we always have to ask whose truth is being built? What stands before us, and to what extent can we say—in any concrete way—that the life we seek to describe is a life that can even be captured at all. What can be actually said about Cooley?

It would seem, dear reader, that Cooley's wife would help bring Cooley into view for us. That is to say, for both you and I. But, we have to ask: what comes into view?

4

With an eye squinted open and a finger on the trigger of the Colt six-shooter hidden under the heavy blanket covering him from the cold, I heard Cooley carefully watched his friend Silas's face in the flickering glow of the campfire they lay around.

Though he couldn't tell for sure, Cooley knew Silas was fast asleep right now. He was more than just friends with Silas. I think he knew Silas like the back of his own hand, and certainly, that feeling was mutual. But, the most mutual feeling at this point in their enduring friendship that weathered the storms through the years since they'd been runny-nosed runts in grade school was the knapsack sitting on the ground between them.

Nothing in the whole wide world was more important than what was inside that leather knapsack with the buckle-down strap. As far as Cooley was concerned, that included his two-decade friendship with Silas, too.

Of course, it had been because of their long friendship as to why they ended up here of all places, in the middle of nowhere trying to catch a little shut eye in the warmth of a freshly-made campfire. Though nothing's better than getting warmed-up beside a campfire on a cold night, nothing's really better than catching a few winks in that comfortable warmth. And nothing's better than sharing a good campfire with a good friend. The only problem is that there's always something better, much better.

What was much better than anything else right about now?

Something better than friendship?

Cooley rolled his eyes away from Silas across the way and towards the knapsack sitting on the ground between them. What was inside that knapsack, Cooley knew, was the only thing of real importance.

Though the knapsack had been well-used and well-abused and didn't cost any more than a couple bucks brand-spanking-new, because of what was inside it, that well-used and well-abused knapsack was worth nine thousand dollars. That was the money they'd stolen when they'd knocked over the Carrolton National Bank the day before yesterday.

Cooley could still remember everything about that day, as certainly as he figured Silas himself could, I suppose. And, while he thought about it and imagined it all as if it had happened minutes ago, he thought about how easily the robbery had gone, how well they'd thought out the plans beforehand and how those plans were executed.

Of course, being the friends they were, they'd always wanted to do something together. Ever since they'd been kids, they'd always dreamed of making a name for themselves, of being more than just a couple of back-wood hicks from Carson City, of being more than two of the who-knows-how-many wannabe cowboys struggling to make a living in a world of gunslingers and criminals and unsavory desperados. And ever since they'd been runny-nosed brats knee-high to a June bug, they'd always heard stories about Billy the Kid and Butch Cassidy and the Sundance kid and the Dalton gang and dreamed of being feared and revered like all of them.

Being the criminals they'd become, they'd never ever really planned on making it on profession any more than they'd planned what they were going to do with the money once they'd robbed the Carrolton National Bank. Never did they actually decide to rob the Carrolton National Bank until they'd heard about another bank robbery in Missouri where the criminals robbed the place with guns carved out of lye soap that had been painted black and made away scot-free with all of eight hundred fifty dollars. If you ask me, it wasn't until hearing about that did Cooley and Silas realize that, if those cowpokes in Missouri could pull it off, they most certainly could.

In a matter of hours, after drinking who knows how many shots of whiskey between them in Moe's Tavern across the street from the Carrolton National Bank, Cooley and Silas came up with a plan.

It was simple—simple, true, but, as far as I can tell, still very easy to get fucked up, if not executed properly.

First, Silas had decided they needed to get guns, real guns, preferably Colts, since

Colts were undoubtedly the most reliable firearm on the market at that time. Next, it was Cooley that decided they'd be better off robbing the bank early in the morning right after the bank opened for the day's business. Then, it was the both of them, I think—or, then again, maybe more Silas than Cooley—that came to the agreement that they absolutely, positively, no matter what, wouldn't kill anyone. All they'd do was get the money, scare whoever was there enough to show them Cooley and Silas meant business, and get the hell out of there while the getting remained good.

So, Silas got the Colts at this general store the day before.

Right around that same time, Cooley scouted the bank in order to figure out the banking hours and the bank president's opening procedures and routines of the tellers.

Then, the following day, after building up enough nerve and getting drunk enough to be incoherent and daring—perhaps the only person between the two of them that needed to get up the nerve had been Silas, not Cooley—Cooley and Silas strolled into the bank with handkerchiefs tied around their noses and chins and had their guns drawn.

Though they'd planned everything out carefully in the days leading up to the whole thing—or, at least, assumed they thought everything out as carefully as possible, I think—what they didn't count on was there being a security guard posted just inside the doorway of the bank's main street entrance. Also, what they hadn't counted on was that the guard was older than dirt.

But, what was a surprise, however, was that Cooley and Silas found this guard sitting in a straight back chair taking a snooze—the old security guard had been about as dead to the world at that time as you can imagine.

Cooley knew they could've just as easily held the old geezer at gunpoint after waking the old bastard up, and made the grandpa hand over the revolver strapped in the holster at his side. That, Cooley knew, I think, would've been the most humane thing to do. But, that wasn't what happened, unfortunately.

Being jumpier than he'd ever imagined, Silas helplessly stood by as Cooley shot the old geezer dead right there inside the doorway to the bank—according to what I heard, that old geezer tipped out of his straight back chair and slammed onto the floor like a big floppy bag of birdseed, and had been dead before he hit the floor or remotely had the chance to open his eyes to see who had shot him out of nowhere. Unprovoked, senseless, and monsterish, Cooley shot the old man two more times in the head, and then, stood back and looked down at the deader than dead security guard as if he had been mighty proud of what he had accomplished.

Silas, on the other hand, hadn't been at all proud of that, I suppose. To Silas, I think it made him look at Cooley differently—perhaps, seeing something in Cooley for the first time that he hadn't seen before.

That had been why Silas had wanted to ask Cooley why did he do it—*what gives, what's the matter?*

Yes, I believe Silas had wanted to ask Cooley right then and there, but those two gunshots alerted the whole bank that something was wrong, very wrong. And everything suddenly went into fast forward before either of them knew what was happening.

That was when everything really got fucked up. That was when Silas had to run around behind the bank counter before any of the tellers or the bank president had a chance to sound the bank alarm. That was when Cooley, in the meanwhile, watched over the main entrance, locked the door, turned the OPEN/CLOSE sign back around to the CLOSED side, and pulled the long window-shade down so nobody walking by could see what was going on inside the bank.

And what had been going on inside the bank was, perhaps, nothing short of a kind of hell of earth, I guess.

One of the tellers, a thin blonde with oversized breasts and red lipstick several shades too bright, went charging for the front door like a bull for a matador's red cape. Cooley, standing at that front door as he was, didn't hesitate to shoot that blonde once in the head as easily as you'd shoot some mad dog or a horse with a bad leg. Silas had heard the gunshot from the bank's vault at the rear and knew, immediately, that bad had gone to worse in a hurry, and everything could only get even more worse very soon.

So, Silas hurried in the vault.

He'd loaded the knapsack with all the bundled currency that the bank president could help him with—the bank president constantly asking Silas if Silas was going to kill him. Though Silas, perhaps, would've loved nothing better than to shoot the blabbering blubbery bank president right then and there inside the vault afterwards, he'd decided against it, for some strange reason. It could've been out of pity for the poor slob who knew he'd probably lose his job after this was all said and done with, or it could've been because, subconsciously, Silas knew he and Cooley would eventually be alone with nine thousand dollars and a decision that would likely change their lives forever.

How could he know that?

Maybe it was intuition—who cares, who knows for sure.

The only thing that matters was that Cooley shot off three shots inside the bank killing two innocent people that didn't have to die. And that, because of his stupidity, and the sudden arrival of the town's sheriff and his deputies no sooner than Cooley and Silas emerged from the bank's front door, they nearly got themselves killed.

If you ask me, it wasn't supposed to happen the way it had happened. Just thinking about that, I believe Cooley found himself getting angrier and angrier. In the beginning, I think that anger was nothing more than the sum irritation of the both of them being shot at outside the bank and having to run for their dear lives and ending up leaving their horses behind, their reins tied to the post before the trough outside the town's saloon, and the whole affair not going as smoothly as Cooley had hoped.

But, now the irritation had grown into downright anger, you see.

Cooley found himself angry for a number of reasons, right then. The first and foremost was because he'd had to leave his horse behind and they'd had to walk all this way. Next, was because the last thing he'd expected was to be shot at and having to shoot at the law. And last, but not least, was because Silas had the nerve to lay over there asleep as if he didn't have a single care in the whole wide world.

Ironically, as far as I think Cooley was concerned, Silas had one hell of a problem right about now. In a way, it was kind of ironically funny. It was sort of funny in an ironic sort of way because Cooley and Silas were friends. They'd done who knows how many things together over the years. They'd gone to grade school and played hookie to go out fishing, and now, as adults, they'd robbed the Carrolton National Bank together and had a rather hefty bootie to split between them.

Yet, Cooley found himself increasingly-repelled by the idea. He certainly was smart enough to know that him having a hundred percent of that nine thousand dollars was better than having half—that is, having only forty-five hundred.

But, could he have the whole nine thousand dollars if he really wanted it?

And, what about Silas?

What was Silas going to say about not getting his half, anyway?

I imagine Cooley knew, as he lay there watching Silas sleep in the flickering glow of the campfire, that Silas would rather die than not have his half of his money they'd stolen from the bank. Cooley could imagine Silas, in Silas's theatric, overdramatic way, telling Cooley—no, yelling at Cooley—that he wasn't going to take all the money, and proclaim something about the only way Cooley was going to able to do that was over Silas's dead body.

And, then, what would happen next?

What would Cooley absolutely have to do in order to take all the money for himself?

Well, as far as I believe Cooley could tell, there was only one way to make sure something like that happened. There was only one humane way to ensure that everything worked out specifically the way he wanted it. There was only one way, essentially, that Cooley could be a hundred percent certain that only one of the two of them would walk away from that campfire with all of the Carrolton National Bank money and stroll into the history books as one of the best bank robbers in the business.

Though that might be going a little overboard to say, there is no doubt in my mind that Cooley thought something like that as he imagined what he had to do right then.

Watching Silas sleep with his mouth open and his head craned back over a boulder he was using as a makeshift pillow, Cooley reached out with the Colt he had had hidden beneath his blanket. Cooley, then, leveled the revolver carefully, his finger tense on the sensitive hair trigger. He raised the Colt to arm's length, and looked along his arm and then beyond the Colt's sights until the sights had been squarely on Silas, who had been sleeping and, perhaps, dreaming about all the things he was going to do with his half of the money.

However, Silas would never have the chance to live out those dreams and hopes and aspirations.

That was because, Cooley pulled the trigger—just once.

The gunshot had been loud and quick, full of smoke, instantly making Silas's eyes flash open for a half of a second which was probably the length of time it took for the bullet in Cooley's Colt to open the bloody hole in the center of Silas's head.

Once the smoke cleared, Cooley saw Silas's eyes were wide and gazing fearfully across the way towards him. The campfire flickered an orange glow intermittently across his face enough to make Silas's eyes look ghostly, even shocked.

And, for a moment, just a fraction of a moment, I think Cooley wondered if he had missed. He wondered if the sights of his Colt had somehow been off kilt and, with Silas knowing Cooley had shot at him, there was going to be one hell of a gunfight erupting right then and there. I imagine Cooley didn't have a clue if his mediocre shooting skill could match Silas's sharpshooting prowess.

Then, that was when Cooley saw this little dot of blood in the center of Silas's forehead. From that dot, blood trickled down between his eyebrows and along the bridge of Silas's nose for a moment until it rolled off towards his right nostril. After that, Silas's head tipped over, his eyes blankly staring into the night sky like he was contemplating the constellations and the meaning of our lives underneath them on this earth.

While Silas did that, Cooley got up, holstered his Colt, walked up to the knapsack on the ground between them, and picked it up. He slung the knapsack over his shoulder by the straps and stood over Silas's obviously dead body.

I suppose, he thought about how he didn't want to kill Silas. Not there, not then, and not that way. But, Cooley knew it was probably better for Silas to be killed by his best friend than by some stranger somewhere further down the line. That made sense to Cooley, anyway. And Cooley was, basically, Silas's best friend. That was, of course, until all that money had come between them.

That, by then, wasn't a problem anymore. Not only was Silas lying dead by the campfire not a problem, but Cooley walking away with all the Carrolton National Bank's stolen money wasn't a problem either—it wasn't all that much of a problem at all.

5

Dear reader, Silas is, undoubtedly, a tragic figure. Some would say, judging from what happened to Silas, that it never paid being friends with Cooley and that, being friends with Cooley had just as much capital as being enemies with him. That is the moral to Silas' story. I think, too, that what can be known about what happened to Silas takes us to the heart of the kind of relationships that Cooley had—it tells us, more than anything, that Cooley did not really have any true attachments with anyone in his life.

I have often wondered, still, about the story of Silas. What I mean is I wonder if what happened to Silas is more of a metaphor, rather than something that actually happened. I say that, knowing that there is no evidence that Silas ever lived and, for that matter, that Silas ever died.

As the story was told to me, it is unclear when the story is reported to have taken place and where. It is clear, I think, that the story represents Cooley's early life, long before he eventually settled down into the owner of the bar. Because so much about Cooley centers on the stories that have been told about all the things he did in that bar—the individuals he is said to have killed, the whore-house he is believed to have kept—the story about Silas speaks to something that, in my view, remains an unknown part of Cooley's life. Call it the lost years—the period in Cooley's life when it has been said that he was a drifter, wandering from town to town, living off the land and anybody that helped him make it from one day to the next, and, yes, robbing anyone he saw fit to rob.

There is no doubt in my mind, dear reader, that Cooley robbed stagecoaches in route to places like Arizona, Utah, Colorado, and New Mexico. These trails, you must know, were always ripe for thieves looking to turn a quick profit against relatively unprotected coaches—women visiting families in far-flung territories, or young men looking to strike it rich, but always someone carrying with them large sums of money. There were also the money coaches, carrying decent amounts of funds to small banks.

The point here is that it wasn't a secret that the stagecoaches were out there, sometimes trekking around large, open spaces of land. These coaches made their way through long stretches of valley—often, we know, these stagecoach paths wound through mountainous and, we know too that, sometimes, these paths were frequently monitored by potential robbers. Cooley, for a time, early in his life, was one of men that camped out in mountainous terrain overlooking stagecoach paths, waiting for a ripe one to come into sight. Even so, we have to remember, dear reader, is that those who looked out for stagecoaches tended to work in groups—sometimes, two or three, or a gang of four or five would be on the lookout, eventually descending the hills on any given stagecoach from all angles, and systematically converging on the occupants and drivers like hyenas or buzzards.

But, with anything, dear reader, the larger the group of men involved, the more the bounty would need to be divided. In my view, this is why participating in robber gangs of this sort—or some four or five guys—was probably something unlikely for someone like Cooley. That wasn't something Cooley was ever interested in, as far as I can tell. For Cooley, having just one other guy was the limit—and there is no doubt in my mind that Silas would have been the only kind of guy that Cooley would have worked with, even if I doubt Silas ever existed.

Yet, the story about Silas remains interesting to me. It is interesting, because it is a story that I have heard several times beyond the story I have provided to you. The other versions I have heard place Silas as a cousin, or even as a young brother, and, at times, as Cooley's oldest son—what remains constant, in each case, is that Cooley uses the Silas character's trust to double-cross him. In each story, as far as I can tell, the Silas character falls asleep while Cooley watches and waits—then, in each case, Cooley has no reservations in killing the Silas character, so that Cooley could have all of the money accumulated from various robberies. There is some disagreement over what kind of robberies—the story I have provided to you speaks about a bank robbery, but I do know, too, that Cooley was involved in robbing stagecoaches for a long period of time. I believe that these robberies eventually helped save enough money in those early years to eventually start his bar and whore-house. I can't say this for certain, though. It is impossible to know for sure—even the best biographers have to make educated guesses to fill in where the gaps are, and the story about Silas is just one of the many gaps I have encountered.

So, dear reader, I do not want to say that the Silas story is just fiction. I do think, though, that it is part of the mythology around Cooley—I say that, given the fact that the only Silas that Cooley ever knew was a man named, Silas Rondo. The Silas in this story is surely not Silas Rondo—you need not look any further than the book I wrote on Silas Rondo to know that.

Yet, there is no doubt in my mind that saying the story just didn't happen—or couldn't have possibly happened—is going too far afield. Though I cannot say, for sure, that the story actually happened the way I have presented it to you, I can say, without any reservations, that the way Cooley is depicted is certainly not too far off the mark. In the end, I want you to think not so much about the facts of the story, but more so about what it tells us about Cooley as a person—that's why I think the Silas story, whatever the form, is worth telling, just as the story about Jed, which follows, is.

6

The town wasn't big enough for the both of them. Everyone knew that. There wasn't a person in town that didn't know that one way or another, you know. So, I guess, it was only a matter of time before Jed and Cooley went about settling their differences, even if it was going to happen right in the middle of town at high noon.

It was the biggest thing to ever happen in our town since old lady Smith, living in the house at the edge of town, shot her husband when she found him in bed with another woman. This was a huge thing, you know. Bigger, you could say, than that. This was the thing everybody was waiting for, the thing that had been talked about for the last couple of days since Jed challenged Cooley to a duel inside Cooley's bar.

"I don't think you don't want to do that," was what Cooley had said. He'd been seated at the bar. Drinking, as usual. Taking huge puffs from his cigar in between drinks. His hat pulled down over his eyes a little. "Why don't you just run along? I don't want you momma mad at me for putting you in the ground too early."

Jed didn't like him saying that. Jed was proud and hot-tempered. And, as young as all get-out. Barely seventeen. He was standing there, his hands all shoved his pockets, and his hat tipped back on his head. I guess you could say that all he wanted was respect. Every guy, one way or another, wants respect. Yeah, he was nothing but a kid compared to a seasoned gunslinger like Cooley, who'd probably killed more men than Jed had years on this earth, but, Jed was a man just the same. And a man has to get respect from another man. And when he doesn't—well, he almost has to do something to prove himself a man, especially in a place like Cooley's bar where everybody's got to prove themselves about something.

"Nah," Jed had told him. "I'm not gonna move along. And you leave my momma outta this. This ain't got nothing to do wit her, you hear. You're in my seat. I was sitting here. And you know it."

Cooley chuckled.

He kept looking straight ahead at the wall mirror off behind the bar. "This is a free world, kid. Anybody can sit where they want to." He slowly blew smoke out, and savored the cigar's taste with a smile. "You got up. I came in. You lose your seat. That's just the way it is, kid. You win some and you lose some. And you lost this one, kid."

Jed was kicking mad, "Stop calling me kid. I ain't no kid. I'm a man."

Cooley looked at Jed. What Cooley, I think, saw was what we all saw: a skinny kid with lanky arms and legs and long dirty brown hair, and clothes hanging off him like they were a couple sizes too big, maybe the stuff that belonged to his daddy who got killed a few years back in a duel with—believe it or not—Cooley, himself. And when Cooley looked at the boy, he said, "You just like your daddy. Like him, you don't know when to shut up."

"Don't you talk about my daddy!" Jed was so mad he was practically throwing a fit right then and there. His fists were down to his sides, balled. His baby face was scrunched up in a frown. "You shut your mouth about my daddy."

Then, right out of the blue, Jed did something nobody would've ever imagined, nobody in the right mind would've done, no grown man with any remote knowledge of what sort of gunslinger Cooley was wouldn't have done in a million years: he slapped Cooley's cigar out of his mouth.

Me and Doc Bradley were seated at a table nearby when we saw it. He was just as stunned as I was. And, we exchanged this look with one another that was filled with this mutual fear for the boy. We knew the boy. Watched the boy grow up through years. Saw him shoot up six inches one year like a weed. Felt sorry for his daddy being killed all those years ago. You know, we were even there when that happened. And let me tell you, this was like déjà vu, because Jed's daddy got himself killed for the same thing: slapping Cooley's cigar out of his mouth. That was a no-no if there ever was one.

And to see Jed standing there after he'd done that, and say, "Whatchu gonna do, Cooley? Whatchu gonna do now?" I tell you, it was good to see a guy stand up to Cooley. But, it wasn't good to know that nobody standing up to Cooley ever live very long afterwards.

Doc thought the same thing, and whispered to me, "I wish he hadn't done that." Doc was shook.

And I told him, "Guess he won't see his eighteenth birthday."

You could tell that everyone in the bar that day was thinking the same thing. Thinking that the boy wouldn't see his next birthday. Mostly, I think, everybody was also thinking that maybe, finally, the boy would be able to see his daddy in Heaven.

Well, Cooley was frozen right then and there. It was as if he himself was just as amazed at what happened. He certainly wasn't afraid of the boy, because a guy like Cooley doesn't know the meaning of the word. A guy like Cooley only knows two kinds of feelings: contentment and downright anger. And I could tell, as well as everybody else in that bar that day, that Cooley was downright angry. Somehow, perhaps because he was dealing with a kid and that the kid he was dealing with had a daddy he'd killed a while back, he wasn't letting that anger unleash full blast.

"Look, kid," Cooley said picking his cigar up from the counter, making sure it hadn't been snuffed out or gotten dirty, and put it back in his mouth, and took a long puff off it. "I'ma let you slide, okay. You don't know what you're doing. You're just mad cuz I killed your daddy. That's all. You don't know what kind of trouble you're getting yourself into. So, why don't you just run along, and mind your business, before your momma has to pull that black dress back out of her closet."

Yeah, that was old Cooley. As cool as a cucumber, he was. But, you could tell he was holding back his anger. You could tell he wanted to beat the hell out of Jed right then and there. Cooley had done that kind of thing before to who knows how many guys for an assortment of reasons much less severe than what the kid had just done. And, to know Cooley, you have to know how he's a hot-head. Has a temper the likes you'd never believe. But, to see him there, giving Jed a chance to walk away without feeling the full wrath of Cooley's anger was a strange thing to see. I guess that meant, one way or another, that Cooley had a heart buried somewhere deep down inside. Maybe, you could just as well say he didn't want to hurt the boy after having killed the boy's daddy. Maybe, I don't know, out of compassion.

But, like I said, Jed was only seventeen, and he felt he had something to prove. He wanted to be a man. He didn't care about what kind of horrible reputation Cooley had. All Jed cared about was proving himself a man. There isn't a better way at doing that than with someone like Cooley, and in a place Cooley's bar, in the middle of the day for everyone to see, even if he wouldn't live long enough to enjoy any newfound respect.

So, Jed said, "No." And he slapped Cooley's cigar out his mouth again. And slapped it so hard that it fell behind the bar. "You and me gonna have a duel, Cooley. And that's that."

By then, you could tell Cooley was losing his temper. He was trying so hard to keep it under wraps, and doing his best to take into consideration that this was just a kid and he didn't want to kill a kid. He had a bad reputation, yes, but he'd never killed some kid before. He'd killed an old man once, not that long ago. But, killing a kid put a whole different light on the matter, all together. Killing a kid was like killing an unarmed man, or something. Even if Jed was all of seventeen, it still couldn't be a good thing for Cooley.

But, Cooley had lost his temper. And when old Cooley loses his temper like that, everything gets put into motions like an out-of-control horse-drawn wagon. You can hold the reins all you want to, and you could tell the horse to whoa until you're blue in the face, but you aren't the one in control, see.

Well, Cooley got up from his stool, slowly.

The kid backed off a little to give him room but stood his ground all the same, and kept his eyes gazing into Cooley's face.

And Cooley stood there in front of the boy. He towered over the boy by a good four or five inches, it seemed. Even if Cooley had probably been old enough to be the kid's grandfather, Cooley's size mattered. That, and Cooley's experience.

"You want a duel, kid." Cooley poked Jed in the chest with a finger, and the kid stood his ground with a stiff bottom lip. "Then, you've got yourself a duel."

That was when he turned a shoulder towards where me and Doc were sitting. Cooley's eyes dark under the wide brim of his hat, but brilliant with light, somehow. "Hey, Doc," he says.

Beside me, Doc nodded to him, but didn't open his mouth. Cooley had that kind of an effect on people most of the time.

"You'd better get a coffin ready for tomorrow," Cooley says. "Cuz this kid is gonna finally be able to see his dead daddy." And he brushed pass the boy, and slowly walked out, his boots thudding on the hardwood floor while his spurs jingled at the heels.

Jed stood there with this goofy look on his face. It was as if he figured Cooley wouldn't accept the duel because he was just a kid. That, or the thought that Cooley had been too old to want to bother with a frivolous young man's game. So, the kid stood there all stiff and frozen and looking very much like he was scared out of his mind. If he'd wanted to duel Cooley so badly, he got his wish. And, that was just how he stood there day of the duel: stoic, and blank, and completely frightened. I could see it on his face when he stood at the opposite end of the main street from where Cooley stood. Jed, with his hat tipped back on his head, his shirt and pants fitting too big for him as if they were clothes that once belonged to his daddy. He had this gun belt around his waist. Also something that likely belonged to his daddy. The gun in the holster, too, that holster swinging too far from his hip, even for his hands at the end of his lanky arms to reach. It seemed silly: him standing opposite from Cooley, knowing Jed didn't have a chance in hell to get a shot off before Cooley, with Cooley being the legendary gunslinger he was.

Yet, everyone in town was crowding around the main street to watch. Not really because the duel was between someone like Cooley and a boy like Jed but because it was a duel. Because everyone loves watching a good duel. It's not like there a whole lot to do in a town like ours, anyway. A duel is the only entertainment we have to look forward to, from time to time.

And, going by Doc's count of three, Cooley and Jed drew their guns.

It wasn't exactly at the same time, of course. Cooley was far too quick, and Jed was far too slow.

All that mattered was Cooley drew his gun out first and shot Jed in the chest, sending the seventeen year old kid to the ground like a sack of horse feed. He was probably dead long before he'd hit the ground. Just like what happened to Jed's daddy. And just like when Jed's daddy got killed, rushing out of the crowd crying and screaming, Jed's momma came out to where Jed lay on his back, lifeless. She was screaming, while everyone dispersed, either solemn or shaking their head in dismay. There wasn't anything to see, by then. The duel was over.

Too bad Jed got killed, though. He was a good kid, you know. It's just too bad he was so much like his daddy, though: too headstrong, too stupid, and crossing too much Cooley.

7

The story about what happened to Jed is true, dear reader. Aside from the account I have provided you with, there are at least five other accounts from eyewitnesses to what happened that day between Jed and Cooley—chief among these is Jed's mother herself. I was fortunate enough to interview her in the weeks before she died and was able to corroborate just about every single fact of the story, just as it was told to me, which I have relayed to you in its full measure.

Jed's mother confirmed for me that Jed had had an ongoing dispute with Cooley for some time prior to the duel. She estimated that the feud was over a woman, one of the whores that Cooley employed at his whore-house—the woman in question was someone that Jed, apparently, had fallen in love with and wanted to marry. The whore—the woman, that is—was just as much in love with Jed and, based on what Jed's mother figured, the woman wanted out of whoring.

One of the things I remember Jed's mother pressed was how much she didn't want Jed to marry, let alone fall in love with a whore. She told me that she firmly believed that a whore couldn't be a respectable woman for any man—in her mind, a whore was always a whore, and there was no other way to look at it.

She asked me, I remember, if I felt the same way—if I thought, as she did, that no whore could be made over into a wife. I told her, I remember, that I wasn't there to pass those kinds of judgments on anyone. I told her, just as I will tell you, that a biographer just wants the facts and deals only in the facts, as best as he can. What she was asking me, I believe, wasn't about facts. Sure, the woman was a whore, and yes, there was a difference between a whore and a respectable woman, and yes, respectable women were typically not ever, at any point in time in their lives, whores—so, I told her, logically speaking, that the facts support her view, but I wasn't there to talk about the lifestyle of whores, or to talk about what kind of woman her son Jed deserved to be with, or if Jed had what it took to make the whore a respectable wife. My question, instead, was about how Jed intended to marry a woman that was employed as a whore, when whores were typically the property of their owners. In this case, Jed's whore girlfriend was Cooley's property, through and through.

I remember how she looked increasingly pained when she thought about her son, and thought about the conversations she had had with him about the whore. I remember how she seemed as if increasingly resisted going through those memories, since those memories took her to places that she had chosen to forget over the years. I remember, too, how she seemed to want to block some things out of her mind—perhaps as a way to deal with it, or to minimize the pain.

I remember trying to ask questions—as all good interviewers do—in such a way that didn't make her recoil, but, instead, feel as if she had to tell me. And that she wanted to tell me. I wanted her to see me someone that could help her clear her conscience—someone that was in the best position to tell her son's story.

I admit, dear reader, that my concern wasn't so much with telling Jed's story. Jed was only a means to a particular end for me. I knew that going into the interview with Jed's mother—I knew that full well, I must admit, even though, as a way to get her to talk to me, I told her that I wanted to make sure that Jed's story had more exposure and that the kid wouldn't be drowned under the larger story about Cooley having killed Jed. Admittedly, I didn't tell her I was writing a biography on Cooley, either—I felt that she would clam up, if she knew that. So, I told her just enough for her to trust me, but not enough for her to know what my motivations and intents were.

You may wonder if I should feel bad about that. You may want to know if it would have been better practice to tell Jed's mother—a woman that was still mourning her son's death after all those years, and still found it difficult to talk about—the truth about what I was up to and what I wanted from her. You may think, too, dear reader, that there is no better way to approach an old woman like that other than telling her how I wished to use Jed's story in the end—you may feel that the only way to treat someone is to do so honestly and straightforwardly.

You may think all these things, dear reader, but I know better than you do about these kinds of things. I was a newspaper man for many years. When it comes to reporting a story and finding out the facts, you have to lie a little. That may sound like a strange thing to say—to get the facts, you have to lie. But, it's the truth of the matter—to get what you need out of someone you are interviewing, you need to do so in a way that gets the most out of them. Interviewing is a science, I believe. There's a right way and a wrong way. There's a hard way and an easy way. There's a way to lead who you are interviewing towards where you think the real story is, instead of simply letting the interviewee provide you with things you need to sift through—the latter may be the right way, but it is still the hard way. The easier way is to interview knowing certain answers in advance, so that who are interviewing can simply confirm or deny what you already know—some might say that this is the wrong way to do it. I disagree.

You have to come into certain situations believing you know what the facts already are—you come into it, as a biographer, having particular ideas about how you wish to tell a story, what you think is the best thing to tell, and why certain things are better to tell than others. In my experience, if you don't have some foundation to build upon, you really don't have much at all.

That was why, dear reader, I interviewed Jed's mother, based on a hunch I had about Cooley. It wasn't so much about Jed, or even about what happened to Jed. Those were just things I used to get Jed's mother to sit down and talk to me. You know, sometimes, when you tell people you are writing a book about someone, and you know that this certain person is widely hated, you would be surprised how closed up people can get. Just at the mention of Cooley's name, you would think that Cooley was still alive—it amazed me how scared people would be, and how it seemed to me as if they felt that what they told me would get back to Cooley himself. The fact that there was so much fear about Cooley often amazed me, and yet, it made me all the more fascinated—the idea that Cooley could be dead for years and still cast so much fear on people impressed me, I must say. That's one of the many things that impressed me to write about Cooley, in the first place.

One of the other things, I admit, is not so much what Cooley did to Jed—as terrible as it has been reported to be—but more about what Cooley is said to have done to Jed's father. Some say that that is the real reason behind the dispute between Jed and Cooley—but also, in a way, the real reason why there was so much tension between Cooley and Jed's mother. Getting to the bottom of what happened to Jed's father was the main thing I hoped to get from interviewing Jed's mother. What I didn't know, I admit, was how to get her to talk about it.

The rumor was, as I heard it, that Cooley had had an affair with Jed's mother. Because of that Jed's father had wanted to kill Cooley for revenge—this had all happened when Jed himself was nothing more than a toddler.

Some say that Jed's mother actually loved Cooley and that the affair wasn't exactly an affair at all. Some say, then, that the affair was something that Jed's mother wanted all along, since she would have rather been with Cooley anyway. I don't know if that is true or not. I suspect it may be. Yet, what I do know, dear reader, is that Jed's father confronted Cooley over the affair, Jed's mother tried her best to stop Jed's father from carrying out whatever he hoped to carry out against Cooley, and things ended up going very badly for Jed's father—some say that Cooley killed Jed's father with Jed's mother watching, screaming, and desperately praying to God, all while Jed himself, as just toddler, was tangling from Jed's mother's hip, crying and slobbering, and still wearing diapers.

For the rest of Jed's life, some say, Jed had nightmares about what happened to his father. Jed's mother was traumatized by the experience. Some say her trauma fueled Jed's growing rage towards Cooley until Jed decided that killing Cooley was the best way to solve his problems and his mother's.

Then, there was this thing about Jed's father's death. There has been some talk that Cooley didn't just kill Jed's father, but, actually, Cooley made Jed's father suffer somehow—I have heard too many stories to make any sense of what "suffer" really means. Whatever it was that Cooley did to Jed's father, there is no doubt in my mind that it had a lasting effect on a lot of people and that the story, in itself, spread like a wildfire, as the precautionary tale telling you what would happen if you crossed Cooley the wrong way.

I cannot tell you, dear reader, what it was that made Cooley interested in wanting Jed's father to suffer. I have heard some say that, for Cooley, there didn't need to be a reason. As true as that may be, I don't think it gets anything very far. What I mean is that it is not enough to simply conclude that Cooley didn't need to have a reason to do anything—in my view, there's always a reason, somewhere. I think it is human nature to have a reason—it comes to someone like me, a biographer, to uncover just what the reason is, how the reason manifested itself, and why the reason mattered. So, to me, it is no different when discussing Cooley. There was absolutely a reason behind anything Cooley did, no matter how meaningless it may seem—from what I felt I understood about Cooley, I knew that for sure. Even so, when I reflect on the fact that some say that Cooley cut of Jed's father's head, put it on a pike, and posted it at the entrance to the nearest town, I find myself wondering what reason there could have been for that.

It may be easy to simply say that Cooley did it to make a point, either about himself or about Jed's father. I have heard some make the first argument, and others make the second. Nobody that I have been able to ask about what happened to Jed's father agrees on what it meant.

As difficult as it was for me to ask Jed's mother about it, she wasn't able to provide any real clarity. It wasn't that she couldn't remember. And, it wasn't that all the facts of what happened had become jumbled up after all these years. No, she could remember it all quite well—she remembered in such a clear way that her recollections seem to transport her to that moment in time. Instead, the problem was how much she wished she could block it out her mind, because it remained such a scary thing to think about, even with all the years that went by. When I specifically asked why Jed's father's head, and why on the pike, and why at the entrance to the nearest town, she didn't know.

For me, the scarier thing about it, dear reader, is the possibility that what Cooley did it to Jed didn't really have a reason to it. Indeed, there are facts of the matter and one can certainly collect those facts to make a narrative about what happened, when, where, to whom, and how—when it comes to asking why Cooley did it, why killing Jed wasn't enough, and why Cooley felt the need to do something so gruesome to Jed's dead body, I simply don't know.

8

The gunshots could be heard clear all over the town. From the barber shop across the street, me and Rob knew the shots were coming from Cooley's—if there was anything you could be sure of, when hearing gunshots going off in the middle of the day, it was that something was going down at Cooley's

Me and Rob rushed out of the shop. Business was slow, and when business is slow, we always had a lot of free time on our hands. This was one of those days—seemed like nobody wanted a haircut. Or, even as much as a shave. So, hearing gunshots go off across the way at Cooley's, we knew we had to see what the hell was going on over there—me and Rob knew that if gunshots were going off, that meant somebody was getting killed by someone.

"Come on, man," I told him. "Hurry up."

Rob said, "I'm coming." He was taking just one more squig from his Whiskey bottle before leaving out—he carefully placed it on the bureau just inside the doorway.

I made it across the street before Rob. He was slow and heavy-set and didn't have the easiest time getting that blubber in motion. So, by the time, I made it up to the doorway to Cooley's, Rob was still huffing and puffing his way across the dirt-blown street like a tired locomotive pulling into the last station on the route—this was when more gunshots crackled and flew out the doorway to Cooley's at us like lead mosquitoes buzzing all around us.

"Get down," I shouted at Rob.

And I dived to the hardwood porchway just outside, finding myself cowering beneath the sill of one of Cooley's storefront windows like a baby.

The glass exploded and shattered, and rained glass kernels over me, so suddenly, I found myself shouting, "Oh shit," and closed my eyes.

When I opened my eyes, I saw Rob curled up against the wall on the other side of the main doorway to Cooley's. All I could see was the top of his balding head and his huge mound of body behind it—he had one arm sort of sprawled partially in front of the doorway.

For a moment, I thought about asking him if he was okay. I even thought about telling him that he might want to move that arm out of the doorway unless he wanted to have it blown off to sweet Jesus. But, neither of those thoughts made it down to my mouth—that was when I saw Rob's blood flowing across the hardwood floors, forming a widening red pool that shimmered a little in the sunlight. Not only did I know poor Rob was dead, but I knew that if I didn't figure out what the hell was going on, I'd be dead too—I knew I'd be as dead as Rob.

I sat up on my knees a little, and peered in through the broken window above me—I carefully peeked over the windowsill that had jagged pieces of glass coming up from it like teeth. And I instantly felt more afraid than I ever had at any other time in my life—I felt as if my whole body had turned into a column of shaving foam.

As much as I wanted to think about Rob and how Rob didn't deserve dying like that, not in that way, I knew pondering over such things wouldn't do me any good. Worrying about stuff like that, stuff that far exceeds human understanding that it can only hurt you in the short run. Especially, in life and death situations, where pausing to smell the flowers could have you pushing up flowers in an eternal bed in a grave somewhere. That was the last thing I wanted to have happen to me—the thought of lying in a pool of my own blood like Rob didn't seem particularly appealing to me.

Still, I peered into Cooley's through the broken window just the same. I didn't know what, exactly, to expect, but I knew that whatever was probably happening in there wasn't good. I guess I just had to see it with my own two eyes for that assumption to sink into my mind.

Inside, the first thing I saw was Cooley. He was standing behind the bar with a shotgun in his hands and the blankest look I'd ever seen on his face—Cooley was pointing the shotgun across the bar from the bartender serving area. And when I rolled my eyes towards the person that Cooley was pointing his shotgun at, that was when I not only realized that everyone in the place had cleared away or were on their knees hiding beneath tables or hunches behind overturned chairs, but that there were three men sprawled on the floor dead: one having breathed his last breath just before falling onto a table near this window and collapsing the legs beneath him. You could smell the gunpowder in the air, too—it was a smell I had never ever completely gotten used to, no more than the sight of dead bodies lying everywhere like discarded bags of chicken feed.

"I'm just giving you one more time," was what Cooley shouted across the bar. "before I fill up your chest with lead."

The guy Cooley was shouting at stood on the opposite side of the bar. He was pointing two revolvers at Cooley, and standing next to an overturned table. I could see playing cards scattered over the floor around him and two more men sprawled on the floor, obviously dead or they would have be moving.

"You really think you're tough shit, don't you, Cooley?" That's what the guy I'd never seen before said. His voice sounded a little shaky. "But you ain't shit, Cooley. You ain't never been. You're gonna get what's comin' to you."

Cooley didn't say anything to that. I guess he wasn't going to. He just stood there aiming that shotgun at the guy across the other side of the bar. His face was blank. You couldn't tell what he was thinking. But, I had a pretty good idea, though. I knew Cooley well enough to know that he was probably waiting for just the right moment to do something—Cooley was waiting for an opening so he could blow the guy away to kingdom come.

But, the opening Cooley was looking for didn't come about in the way he looking for it to. I knew Cooley was waiting for the guy to make a move or try to pull the triggers of those revolvers. For Cooley, it was always about the other guy making the move first, so, in killing him, Cooley could call it self-defense. That's just the way old-timers like Cooley look at things, perhaps as a way to justify killing someone else. So, Cooley was waiting for the other guy to do something he could justify killing him for.

That would be the opening, you see. But, that opening wouldn't come because something else happened before Cooley had the chance to shoot the guy right then and there.

One of the guys lying dead on the floor suddenly moved. Obviously, that meant he wasn't quite dead.

So, to hear some half-dead guy groaning and moaning and half-choking on his own blood broke the silence in a way that gave you the creeps.

Cooley's eyes shifted to where the half-dead guy was—the guy was lying face-down in the center of the bar with his hat knocked off and the crown of his head soaked with blood. Maybe Cooley thought the guy was alive enough to make a move for his gun, which was lying on the floor near one of his outstretched hands. Whatever the reason, Cooley looked away for a fraction of a second—it was a fraction of a second too long I suppose.

That was when the guy Cooley had his shotgun aimed at made a move for the door. I guess he thought this was as good a time as any to get the hell out of Cooley's while the getting was still good—after all, I'm sure he didn't want to end up like those other poor bastards scattered over the floor like shit in a shithouse. You couldn't blame him, I suppose.

The guy realized, I guess, that his best chance at living to see tomorrow was in running out of there. It only took him a fraction of a second to come to that conclusion—I could see that realization shining in his eyes as he tuned suddenly towards the door, and made a run for it.

I was squatting outside the broken window, peeking up over the glass chards, seeing Cooley swing his shotgun towards the doorway, and hearing the thumps of the guy's boots coming quickly towards the doorway next to me. Just before the guy reached the doorway, Cooley fired a shot at him—the shot took out a hunk of the doorway overhead in an explosion of wood chips and smoke. And the guy dived out the doorway through the saloon-style half-doors doing an awkward belly-flop on the hardwood porch-way outside—dust and dirt flew up around him, and his hat popped off, and he looked terribly pissed off about it all.

Somehow, his eyes rolled towards me.

In an instant, we were looking into each other's eyes—for that fraction of a second, what I saw in his eyes looked a lot like fear.

But, I guess, eventually, the guy knew he couldn't waste much more time gazing into my eyes. He knew that was a waste of time, in order words. Because he jumped up to his knees, swung his body around, and got to his feet—he left his hat on the ground.

I guess the guy cared a lot more about his life than some dirty hat.

The guy ran towards a horse that was already hitched at a post just across the street, in front of the post office, next door to my barber's shop. I noticed the strange looking flea-bitten horse earlier, and it made sense that a beat-up looking horse like that would belong to a beat-up looking guy like him. But, anyway, the guy climbed up on his horse, grabbed the reins, pulled them towards himself, and jerked the horse around so it headed in the best possible direction to get out of town as quickly as possible.

There were a lot of people peeking out their windows, watching. You could even see a hand full of guys standing around in the street and in front of other business—all of them with their hands in their pockets or smoking their cigars or talking the shit with their buddies on porches. But, none of them did anything to stop this guy—I didn't do anything either, but sit there on my hunches with my mouth hung open.

That was when Cooley ran up to the doorway.

Cooley knocked open the saloon half-doors swiftly with the butt of his shotgun, and rolled his eyes from his left to his right, surveying everything in a way that only Cooley could, trying to figure out where the guy had run off to. He glanced down at me for a moment—though he looked down at me, I don't think he really saw me. He didn't say anything to me. I suppose he didn't have anything to say. Cooley was much more concerned with where the guy went. And when Cooley found the guy, his eyes narrowed—there was this strange smile that came across his face.

The guy swung the horse around rather awkwardly. You could even say, perhaps, nervously. He saw Cooley in the doorway, and panicked in a way that showed. Kicking the sides of his horse, he sent the horse in a kind of quick gallop—the hooves sent up a cloud of dust and dirt, and the horse let out a wheeze that sounded like someone getting a bucket of cold water dumped over their head. The horse started galloping in a good trot for about twenty or so yards—for a moment, I thought Cooley wasn't going to do anything and that the guy was going to get away scot-free.

I should have known better. When it comes to Cooley, I should have figured that Cooley wasn't going to let the guy get away so easily—if Cooley wanted you dead, you were going to be dead, and there was never anything you could do about it, and it was only going to be a matter of time.

"Hold this," Cooley told me. He tossed his shotgun at me and I caught it with my forearms. I almost dropped it. "This'll only take a minute."

Cooley pulled a revolver out from the back of the waistband of his trousers. The barrel of it was longer than normal. The barrel was so long and the revolver looked so strange I couldn't help staring at it for a moment—the revolver wasn't like any revolver I had ever seen before.

With that strange revolver in hand, Cooley cocked himself sideways, held the trigger guard in his left hand, and aimed the revolver over his right forearm. He did this carefully. He held out his right forearm. The guy on the horse was galloping steadily away, and Cooley was taking his time as if he had all the time in the world. Anyway, Cooley carefully positioned the long barrel of the revolver across his right forearm, and steadied it slowly, aiming it in the direction of where the guy on the horse was galloping away in—the long barrel was sleek, and black, and as steady as an arrow as it sat propped on Cooley's forearm.

Cooley squinted his right eye, and cocked his head a little and leveled his left eye along the sights of the strange revolver—that eye carefully measured the guy on the horse.

When Cooley pulled the trigger, I jerked my head toward the direction the guy on the horse went. Sharply, Cooley had shot the guy—it was hard to tell where Cooley had shot the guy, but you could see the guy flinch, bolting upright in the saddle, and lean off to one side, slipping clean off the horse as the horse aimlessly trotted to a stop about five yards from where the guy's body fell to the ground. The guy wasn't moving. He hit the ground too hard and awkward to have not been shot dead before he slipped from the horse.

I looked back at Cooley, and he had this broad smile on his face—this smile that seemed smug.

Cooley looked down at me, "Thanks, kid." He reached for his shotgun, and I gave it back to him. Then, Cooley tucked the strange looking revolver back into the back of the waistband of his trousers, took a look in the direction of where the guy fell, and strolled back into the bar—it was almost as if killing the guy on the horse didn't mean shit to him.

But, believe me, it meant something to the rest of us. It meant a lot to the rest of us, all of us watching the whole thing go down.

All of us carefully made our way from where we'd been watching the whole thing happen to where the guy fell off the horse—all of us coming out in a daze, slowly forming a small circle around the spot where the guy fell. I ended up standing beside Walt, the guy that worked in the post office—Walt was old, kind of feeble-looking, and had a long thin face that came to a sharp point at the chin. Walt rubbed his chin, pondering over the guy lying dead on the ground as if he wasn't sure if the guy was actually dead and didn't want to take the chance by getting too close and finding out the hard way. All the other people that gathered around the spot where the guy fell had the same looks on their faces. Maybe it had something to do with guy lying flat on his face— I guess it was hard to tell if he was dead or faking.

Everyone stood back a bit from the guy, not wanting to get too close. I leaned in closer, squatting on my hunches—I leaned in just far enough to see.

I knew the guy wasn't faking. And it didn't have anything to do with the way he was lying on the ground—it was something I saw that told me.

There was a very small hole at the very back of the guy's head. The guy had a thick head of hair so it wasn't easy to see it—but I saw it. The little hole was right at the lower part of the back of the guy's head. A little trail of blood trickled from the hole, flowing over the guy's thick head of hair, and shining a little in the sunlight. That hole was so narrow, so small, so minute, it amazed me, not only that I could find it at all, but that Cooley had been so accurate—I wondered what in the world kind of revolver he'd used.

"Is he dead?" Walt asked me. His mouth was hung open—that chin of his coming to a point like that always reminded me of a horse's jowls.

I told him yeah.

Walt kept rubbing his chin as if he hoped rubbing it would, somehow, let the whole thing about the guy being dead sink in more clearly. I suppose it was the first time Walt had ever seen a dead body, let alone see someone get shot dead, right out there in the open.

All the other people standing around heard me and were all satisfied enough with it to go on about their business. Someone took hold of the guy's horse and walked the horse away. Two kids stooped down and started going through the dead guy's pockets—they found out pretty quickly that the dead guy didn't have anything worth stealing other than his pistol and his boots. I walked back to Cooley's. The dead guy stayed dead.

When I walked back to Cooley's, no sooner than I got about ten yards from the place, I could hear the music playing inside. It sound like everything had gone back to normal. But, everything wasn't normal—not for me, anyway.

Rob's dead body was still lying where he fell from the shot. His body was crumpled up against the wall to the right of the doorway to Cooley's. In walking up to Cooley's porchway, you could hear people inside singing and laughing and having a good time. It amazed me how quickly everything had continued on as if nothing had ever happened—the man Cooley killed was still lying out there in the middle of the street with his boots now stripped off by those kids, and Rob was still lying on Cooley's porchway with this little pool of blood soaked into the hardwood by his head. Two dead bodies, and the only thing anyone else seemed to care about was getting on with their own lives, and having a good time, and thinking about themselves. It wasn't the same for me. I couldn't think about things that way. Not when my friend was lying dead. There was no way I could just go on after seeing what I saw.

That was why I squatted down to where Rob was lying dead. People coming and going out of Cooley's stepping all around me, looking down at me as if I didn't have a reason to be in the way—it was as if Rob being dead on the porchway was an inconvenience.

I don't know how long I'd been squatted there paying my respects to Rob, but sooner or later Cooley stepped back out onto the porchway. He was smoking a cigar, and took a look at the damage to his store front window. If he saw me squatted there, he didn't say anything right away—Cooley puffed that cigar and went about looking at the broken window. He looked as if he was pretty pissed off about the window being broken, and started telling his waitress Velma to clean it up, because he didn't want all that glass sitting all over the place for people to get cut. Velma brought a broom over and started sweeping, and Cooley stood there outside on the porchway watching her. He stood with his hands on his hips, and that cigar dangling out his mouth, and the smoke lazily wafting up from the lit tip like a snake.

At some point in time, Cooley looked down at me, and smiled.

That smile, somehow, pissed me off a little, and I told him, "What are you smiling about?" I pointed down at Rob's dead body then at the dead guy lying out in the street. "Don't you care?"

Cooley looked at me, at first, as if he didn't exactly understand what I was saying. But, I knew he did. I knew because that smile stayed on his face.

Then, he said, "Care about what, kid?"

"All of this," I told him. I motioned to Rob's dead body again and the dead guy out in the street. "You shot that guy out there. And my friend Rob got killed." I tried to hold back the tears, but I could feel a tear trickle down my cheek—I wiped it away with the back of my hand. "All this death?"

Puffing that cigar, Cooley walked over to me. I didn't know what he was going to do or say. But he leaned over close to me, and said, "Death is a part of life, kid. We all gotta go, sometime. And some people deserve it."

The tears started flowing, and I didn't care at this point, asking, "But, what about Rob? He didn't deserve it."

Cooley said, "None of us do, kid. None of us do."

That smile was still on his face as he went back inside the bar. I wish I could tell you that what he said made everything better or that it, somehow, helped me realize something I didn't realize before, but it didn't. If anything, I suppose, Cooley only made everything all the more confusing—so what if none of us deserve to die, I couldn't wrap my mind around the *why* part.

After a while, I realized that I wasn't going to wrap my mind around anything by standing out there on the porchway holding a one-man vigil for Rob. With all that music and all that laughing and all that drunken singing going on in Cooley's, I knew that was definitely not the best place to be to hold a memorial service. So, I walked back to the barber shop. I left Rob's dead body on the porchway—the town's undertaker had come out and started measuring Rob for his pine box.

When I got back to the barber shop, I stood for a moment in the open doorway. I couldn't go in right away.

I rolled my eyes towards the Whiskey bottle Rob had left on the bureau, and found myself picking it up, and taking the cap off—I took two long squigs from it.

And, before long, after about a dozen or so squigs from the mostly-full bottle Rob had left behind, I didn't care about wrapping my mind around why Rob died or why Rob didn't deserve to die—I was drunk, by then, and when you're drunk, you don't care about anything.

9

What struck me as the most interesting aspect to this interview, dear reader, is that it contributes to the mythology around Cooley. I don't say that lightly, or say that in a way that diminishes what you have just heard—the mythology around Cooley is essential to understanding what people thought about Cooley during his lifetime and, then, what people came to believe about Cooley after his death. Some might say that there is a connection between the two, where the former influences the latter. That is, some might say that understandings of Cooley during Cooley's lifetime directly influenced beliefs about Cooley after Cooley's lifetime. As a biographer—and a historian—I have come to think of the influence understandings have had on beliefs as being, at times, fairly negligible. That's not to say that there aren't some understandings that become the foundation for beliefs—for example, this is certainly true, even for the relationship between the historical Jesus and the Jesus of faith, or what was understood about the historical Jesus in his lifetime and what became beliefs about the Jesus of faith later. What arises, as I am sure you know, dear reader, is the difference between first-hand accounts and stories that have been gradually passed down—it is the difference between what people say they saw and what people eventually believed happened. This difference is often mitigated by mythology, so that there are no blank spaces left behind and all the blank spaces can be filled in—this is certainly true for Cooley.

When viewing things this way, I can't say, with any degree of certainty, if the story about Rob dying actually happened. Aside from the account I have provided, there are no other accounts of what happened to Rob, or anyone named Rob actually existed at all. Even though the account certainly sounds like something that could've happened in Cooley's bar at some point in time—based on all that I know—I'm afraid that that isn't enough to say that this particular one is true. Facts are important here—we have to be careful to not advance hearsay, and there is plenty of hearsay circulating about Cooley.

When we consider, too, that the account is given by someone that was drunk at the time, the narrative itself becomes all the more dubious. Even so, there was no doubt in my mind that the person I interviewed believed what happened actually happened— what this person remembered about what happened to Rob and what Cooley did have remained a potent memory to this day, even if it is highly unlikely that this person actually experienced what they believe happened.

I am generally of the mind, dear reader, that no one's account should be dismissed, and that every experience always matters, one way or another. But, as a biographer, and as someone with an unyielding fidelity to the facts, it is important to place every account in its proper context and make sure that things that need not be perpetuated become further perpetuated—I would like to think, as a biographer, my job is maintaining a boundary that you, dear reader, can depend on.

So, with that said, perhaps you may be wondering why present an account that isn't factual. What benefit would there be in it? By that, the question—and a fair question, at that—would be something like: what benefit is there in providing an unsubstantiated account, if the point, more broadly, is to figure out who Cooley was from what others say about him? If I say, again, that this story about Rob dying didn't actually happen—and say that with a high degree of certainty—what purpose does it have towards coming to an understanding about Cooley? All of these questions are meaningful questions, dear reader, and they are questions that I hope will both lead you away from the larger story which is nothing more than a red herring—by that, I mean that the story about Rob dying, and how Rob didn't deserve to die, or how Rob's death exerted a toll on the interviewee, to the extent that the interviewee, by his own admission, drowned away that pain in alcohol, in its totality, takes us down an unnecessary path. In this sense, dear reader, Rob is only a red herring that obstructs what is more important about the narrative—what supposedly happened to Rob isn't as important as what is said about Cooley's gun.

Indeed, one of the most important parts of Cooley's mythology is what has always been said about Cooley's shotgun—that the shotgun was and remains famous for always being loaded and ready behind Cooley's bar counter. Certainly, there are enough eyewitness accounts to support certain facts of the matter—that shotgun was, undoubtedly, Cooley's desired method of killing, whenever Cooley deemed killing necessary at his bar. Based on what has been frequently said, there wasn't anything particularly special about this shotgun—that is, I can't find anything about any of the accounts of it that makes that shotgun sound any different than any other type of shotgun you might find in anyone's possession, from lawmen to killers to defenders of their property.

What stands out from this account, dear reader, is the description of another gun that Cooley had—a revolver that had been strangely modified. This account isn't the first time I had heard about Cooley having such a revolver. There are plenty of stories circulating in the mythology surrounding Cooley about the existence of a special revolver. What made it so special was that it didn't look like any of the revolvers most witnesses had ever seen. The fact that it had such a long barrel seemed curious to most, since it remained unclear to many, when seeing such a thing, if Cooley had made that revolver the way that it was, or if he had simply stolen it from someone else—in other words, there was always a confusion about where the revolver came from. There was always confusion, too, about what purpose such a long barrel had—some would say that the longer the barrel, the more accurate a shooter could be, and other would say that the long barrel helped with the amount of power such a thing could expend. I can't say if one opinion is more correct than the other. What I can say, dear reader, with some degree of certainly, given that I'm not an expert on firearms, is that a longer barrel would allow for a longer bullet—and there are plenty accounts that say, whenever Cooley shot this special revolver, the bullet always appeared longer than usual. There's even accounts that the bullets shot by this special revolver made a screaming or a whistling sound through the air, and that, once the bullet hit its target—whoever Cooley was shooting—it sounded like a small firecracker popping.

Just as this special revolver contributes to the mythology around Cooley, the special revolver has its own mythology to it. Those that say Cooley stole the special revolver, dear reader, say that the revolver once belonged to a man named Silas Rondo. I don't know what truth there is to that—as you know, dear reader, my previous book was on Silas Rondo and I took great pains to present Silas Rondo's life in as full a measure as I could, doing my best to minimize all the mythology surrounding Silas Rondo's life and death. As I have outlined in the Silas Rondo book, there is no doubt that Cooley once belonged to Silas Rondo's gang of desperados at some point in time, and there is a great deal of evidence that Silas Rondo carried a special revolver which, some say, had a long barrel. Some say, just as I have made clear, that Silas Rondo lost that special revolver running away on horseback from a band of lawmen. These were the days before Silas Rondo formed his gang—it was when Silas Rondo was robbing stagecoaches and trains by himself, and various eyewitnesses noticed Silas Rondo's special revolver during holdups. Yet, no one knows what happened to that special revolver—and I don't know if it is possible to say that Cooley was the one that ended up with it, though, given that Cooley is believed to be the person that killed Silas Rondo, I suppose we can only assume that the special revolver was once Silas Rondo's.

What remains fascinating, I believe, is that Cooley's special revolver is believed to have disappeared at some point in time.

If we are to believe the story about how Cooley came into the possession of the special revolver in the first place, we can certainly surmise that whoever killed Cooley—and I do believe someone killed Cooley, no matter how many theories abound about Cooley eventually dying of natural causes—that person probably took possession of the special revolver.

10

The strange man strolled into Cooley's bar shortly after high noon as if he owned the place. Perhaps, it was something in the way he walked, or maybe the odd way he looked at everyone. Whatever it was, he was trouble—and, I knew, right away, that Cooley not only knew this guy was trouble, but that this was also the sort of guy you put your guns sights on first before you bothered asking any questions.

"What's he doing?" My friend next to me asked. He wasn't talking about the strange man, but Cooley—what Cooley was doing, at that moment, seemed much more interesting than the strange man.

"Looks like he's getting his shotgun," I told him.

And that's exactly what Cooley was doing. Cooley was getting his shotgun. You see, he kept a spare shotgun under the bar—it was always hidden down there with the extra liquor bottles for desperate times as desperate as these.

This was the first time my friend ever saw Cooley get his shotgun like that. At least, not with the intent if possibly using it. Perhaps, somehow, my friend thought Cooley was just a kind old man with a bad limp, a bunch of odd scars, and far too many stories of the things he said he did in the olden days. Maybe, he saw in Cooley all the things he saw in other old fogies that posted themselves up in the bar talking about stuff that happened to them in the past that might not have ever happened to them in the past at all. But, the thing was: Cooley wasn't at all like all the other old timers. I don't think my friend understood that. Few people did—my friend was one of these few.

So, I guess that's why my friend had this surprised look on his face, when he asked, "He's not gonna—" But, he didn't finish that thought. And, I suppose he didn't have to, because I knew where the thought was going.

But, I told him, "I don't know."

And I didn't know. That was the truth. Mostly because Cooley was so unpredictable. You could say he was as unpredictable as the wind—anything was possible. But, no matter how unpredictable Cooley could be from time to time, I knew him well enough to know what he was more likely to do. That is, at least, better than most, since we served in the Civil War together, fighting for the losing cause. Cooley may have gotten a lot older since then, but there was one thing about him that was surely a constant truth: when he grabbed his shotgun, somebody was certainly going to get shot.

Cooley took the shotgun out from underneath the bar. It was already loaded— Cooley always kept it loaded and ready, perhaps out of habit from the war. With that shotgun in hand, Cooley took his time making his way out from around the bar. Not that he did it deliberately, but because of the war, and the time he got shot in the leg by a stray musket shell. I'd like to think that wound slowed him down for a reason—the war, you see, slowed a lot of us down, and not always in the same ways. For me, it was reality that slowed down a lot. Cooley, on the other hand, was slowed down a lot by his bad leg.

But, anyway, Cooley took his time rounding the corner from behind the bar—he held the shotgun down to his side just a little, resting it carefully along the side of his bad leg with the barrels pointed down.

My friend asked, right about then, "You ever seen that guy before?"

My friend was talking about the strange man that had come in—the guy that shuffled to the far side of the bar and took a seat at an empty back table so his back would be to the wall.

I told him I hadn't seen the man before. But, of course, whether or not I'd seen him before didn't matter. If anybody in that bar that day had ever laid eyes on that strange man before, didn't matter, either. All that mattered was that Cooley knew who the strange man was—Cooley knew him and, more importantly, wanted to kill him. And believe me, if Cooley thought the best thing to do was grab his shotgun and ask questions later, then there was something about the man that Cooley would have rather seen sent up to our Maker than have walk the earth among us.

If the guy knew Cooley was coming, I couldn't tell for sure. But, I'd like to think he knew, at least on some level. There was something very odd about how he sat there at the table that let me knew he was expecting Cooley to come to him. Like how a cat lays a trap for a mouse, I suppose. You could say that, maybe, he was baiting Cooley, somehow.

That's when I found myself saying out loud, "Does he got a death wish or something?" If the guy that was, perhaps, baiting Cooley, really wanted to get himself killed.

"Deathwish?" My friend gasped at the thought. "How could anyone have a death wish?"

What my friend didn't realize was that this is a crazy world we live in. it is a world where everyone doesn't have everything fastened down tightly upstairs, a world where everyone isn't playing with a full deck all the time. And, maybe, that was this guy's problem—the strange man that came into Cooley's wasn't playing with a full deck. Maybe that wasn't his problem at all. Maybe there was a lot more to it than that. And, believe me, in a world where the sane are outnumbered by the insane, you're surely bound to find your path crossed with a loon from time to time. I guess that's life. The stuff that makes life all the more complicated. And I suppose that, maybe, Cooley knew all this. At least, I'd like to think he knew, since Cooley was the kind of guy that always knew more than the average guy. After all, for someone to have lived as long as Cooley and survived so many fucked up situations, a lot of common sense is sure to rub off on you. I've always believed that that common sense is the dividing line between normal people and loons, But, then again, Cooley has always been the kind of guy you can't put your finger on—I suppose, if you really think about it, Cooley was a loon more often than not, and perhaps, it takes one loon to spot another.

But, anyway, you could tell the guy knew Cooley was coming. It was in the way he sat there, I think. It was as if he knew something that Cooley didn't—something that he knew that none of us knew.

The strange man sat upright in the chair, his hands hidden under the table. His hat was pulled down low over his forehead so all you could see was his chin and nose beneath the brim's shadow—there was just the faintest trace of a smile that looked like the kind of smile someone would have when they were passing wind. Or maybe, then again, it was nothing more than the smile of someone that was hiding something under the table—that certain hidden something that was surely a revolver.

It was right around this time when everyone in the whole bar knew something terrible was about to go down. And soon. You could feel it in the air, I suppose. It was this strange calmness before the storm. The feeling of something getting ready to happen. And that feeling flew through the bar in a kind of wave. Every eye kept shifting between Cooley to where the strange man was seated at the table alone at the back of the bar. But, mostly, I think a good deal of the attention was on Cooley who was shuffling his game leg, slightly dragging that foot against the wood floor in such a way that it made this weird sweeping sound, and totting that famous shotgun that I know put many a man, woman, and child into early graves.

It was at this time when the piano guy stopped tickling the ivories—he got up from his bench, stumbled a bit over his own two feet, and hurried into one of the back rooms to hide as if the seat of his trousers had been lit on fire and he wanted to hide from the flames. Cooley's waitress did the same thing—she moved behind the bar, and ducked a little as if she thought the gunfire that would start in any moment would fly in her direction. Perhaps, that idea went through the minds of the handful of other people that chose to crawl up under their tables or hurry out the bar all together like loose gooses. Me and my friend just kind of sat there on our stools like two knots on a log. All the other guys in the bar that were used to things like this happening in Cooley's—all of them seated at their favorite tables, some playing cards, others just shooting the shit—sat motionless, their eyes locked on Cooley, all of them pausing for a moment just to see Cooley do what they figured he would do, so they could back to what they were doing.

We all watched Cooley go up to the stranger at that table at the very back of the bar—the strange man at the table didn't seem to move as much as a muscle.

Cooley said something to him, but none of us could make out any of the words. That is, not exactly enough to know the gist of it. But, whatever it was he'd said, you could tell Cooley wasn't wishing the guy a Merry Christmas.

You see, other than saying a few words to the strange man that none of us was able to make completely out, Cooley stood there on the opposite side of the table, with his back so straight and his posture so even you might think, seeing him from behind, that he was a man of half his age, and leveled the shotgun barrels on the strange man.

The strange man just sat there with his eyes fixed on some distant spot on the table. His eyes never looked up at Cooley—his eyes floated transfixed on something as if he was looking into a world far removed from this world that this world didn't matter all that much to him.

That was Cooley said something else to the guy. This time, it was in a slightly raised tone of voice. "I told you—" You couldn't make out the rest. At least, no more than every other couple of words. It wasn't nearly enough to understand anything.

But, whatever it was that Cooley said to the man this time, the man's eyes lifted up from the spot he'd been staring at on the table—if he wasn't all that interested in what Cooley had said the first time, he was definitely much more interested in what Cooley had said the next. His eyes found Cooley's. The brim of his low hat tilted back just enough for you to see his face—his face was lean and narrow and weathered. He wasn't young, but he wasn't all that old of guy either. Beard stubble and dirt darkened his face, and his eyes looked so glossed over he looked like he was drunk. Whether or not, the guy was drunk, I couldn't tell you—but, there was something odd in his eyes that reminded me of a drunkard.

Though he was looking up at Cooley, the man wasn't exactly *looking* at Cooley. It was as if whatever fixed point he'd been staring at on the table now opened up across Cooley's face—the man's eyes looked empty, and emotionless, and lost, and searching for something. What he was searching for, I couldn't tell you—perhaps, if he was looking for something, something like trouble or a shotgun round in his chest, he found it in

Cooley.

And when the guy looked up at Cooley, we could just barely make out the question:

"Why?"

You could hear that question quite clearly from where we were. I'm sure everyone could hear it. Mostly, because the man had mouthed it softly.

My friend looked at me. Just a glance. Maybe he just wanted to pull his eyes away for a moment to kind of touch base with reality. His mouth kind of hung open, like the way a cow's jaw hangs open when it's looking at a new gate.

That's when Cooley raised his voice, shouting, "I said get the hell outta here."

Cooley rarely raised his voice like that. He didn't have to, I suppose. But when he did, that deep voice boomed through the rafters and walls like a rumbling thunderstorm. Like everyone else, me and my friend could feel that voice surge through us like a tidal wave—Cooley's shouting voice boomed so loud it made your stomach turn over.

Though Cooley told the guy to get the hell out of here, the guy didn't seem exactly obliged. Not enough to do as he was told. Not nearly instant enough as most people would, when knowing how cold and callus a killer Cooley could be when he wanted to.

Instead of leaving like he'd been told to do, the guy just stood up. It happened so quickly, everyone in the bar kind of flinched. I guess that was a natural reaction—in a place like Cooley's, any sudden movement like that can make you nervous. But, anyway, the guy stood up so fast, the back of his legs struck his chair, and knocked it backwards into the wall in a deep thud that knocked deep in the pit of my stomach. The chair overturned behind him. The man, long and lean and thin, showed Cooley the sleek steel barrel of his Colt revolver—he held it at his waist and leveled it, from what I could tell, pointed somewhere near Cooley's stomach.

Cooley never flinched though. Cooley wasn't the kind of guy that ever flinched. Especially, not when there was a gun pointed at him. It wasn't as if that was the first time, you see. I'm sure Cooley, in his lifetime, had had a lot of people point a gun at him. Maybe dozens, or hundreds. Maybe more than that. Men, women—it didn't matter. I guess, when a person has lived as long as Cooley, and has been through as much crazy shit as he has, someone pointing a gun at him didn't matter all that much.

That was why Cooley didn't flinch. It was a been-there, done-that sort of feeling for him.

"You think you're all high and mighty, don't you?" The strange man shouted. His thin lips opened to a small sneer. "But you ain't. You ain't shit Cooley. You ain't never been anything but an old son of a bitch bastard that should've been killed a long time ago."

Cooley was used to being called names, too. Like I said, Cooley has been through a lot of shit in his lifetime. And when you've done as much fucked up shit as Cooley has to people that didn't deserve it, that shit always come back to you—they call that karma. Some way, somehow, it always comes back to you. I suppose, no matter how deep you think you've buried away your skeletons from the past, something, somehow, always manages to surface. And it always happens in ways we never expect—perhaps, Cooley just had more skeletons than most. I suppose the strange guy holding the gun at Cooley was just one of them—who knows.

But, Cooley didn't say anything to the guy. Not anything verbal, anyway. Though his back was to us, I was sure Cooley was saying a lot to him with his face—Cooley's face always had a way of saying much more than any words could.

The strange guy stood his ground pretty well. I was surprised. I think all of us were surprised. I mean: about how long he stood there pointing his Colt at Cooley and calling Cooley an old son of a bitch bastard. Anybody else, in the same situation with Cooley, would have been blown away to kingdom come the moment they pointed a gun at him. I've seen Cooley blow a guy's brains out over a table for less. And, now, seeing this strange guy do what he was doing and say what he was saying seemed interesting. None of us could take our eyes off him. Not to say that *he* was interesting, but there was something about him—it was the way he seemed so fearless, I suppose. But if there's anything I know about people being fearless, it is that fearlessness always goes away once you've got a slug in your chest and see your own blood flowing out of you—when you get a warm slug lodged in your chest, a lot of things go through your mind, particularly fear.

But, at that moment, the strange man seemed fearless. He stood there with his feet planted firmly, his stance shoulder-width apart, and the Colt trained on Cooley. It was, actually, somewhat refreshing to see someone stand up to Cooley like that, even if it was a strange guy nobody had ever seen before, even if it was a guy that probably had some kind of death wish or something.

For a long moment, time seemed to stand still. Time stood so still and quiet you could hear the mattress springs squeaking in one of the bedrooms upstairs where someone was getting serviced by one of Cooley's whores—you could even hear one of the whores shouting out for God as whoever kept fucking away on her moaned like a bull moose with its hooves caught in the mud. Otherwise, that silence made the bar seem reduced to a world where there was only Cooley, the strange man, the table between them, and the guns they pointed at each other.

Me and my friend sat on the edges of our barstools waiting—waiting for Cooley to blow the strange man away, and send the strange man to his Maker on a one-way trip by way of shotgun shells.

And just like that, it happened.

The strange man jerked a little. Just a flinch of movement. Perhaps he had just shifted his feet or wanted to make sure his grip was tight on Colt's handle. Whatever it was, he flinched in a way that made it look like he was going to shoot first—it was the kind of flinch that always proved to be the last fraction of movement a person would have before gunfire.

I guess that flinch was exactly what Cooley was waiting for. Perhaps, all along. Because that was when Cooley pulled the trigger.

It wasn't a pretty sight. Not at all. Someone getting killed rarely is. But, sometimes, it can be messy enough to make a man throw up—this was one of those times. Though death is different in many ways, it is, essentially, the same, at least in one important way: the dying part. That is always the ugly part of it, but it is the only thing that matters. And still, it isn't a pretty sight. And, no matter how many times you've seen somebody get blasted away into eternity by a shotgun with such force they get lifted off their feet and go flailing into a nearby wall like a big bag of chicken feed, you never get used to it. No one ever get used to it. I don't think Cooley has ever gotten used to it—if anything, I like to think he's found a way to numb the feeling normal people feel when they've taken someone's life away from them.

This time was no different for Cooley. At least, it didn't seem to be any different for him—Cooley shot the strange man as easily as shooting a rabid dog or into the side of a barn. He took a look at him just to make sure the guy was playing a celestial harp on a cloud in some faraway somewhere, and turned, facing us with a look on his face that nobody could really read, no matter how long you've known him.

I'd known Cooley for a very long time, and it was a look I wasn't all that familiar with—it was a look in his eyes that seemed as empty as the eyes of the strange man that came into the bar.

Cooley rolled his eyes around the bar. With the way his eyes rolled, it seemed as if he was trying to make sure he was where he thought he was, or that, maybe, he wanted to touch base with reality, since, no matter how well you get used to taking someone's life away from them, reality, as you know it, changes. You have to keep checking reality—I guess, for Cooley, it was a lot like how nobody can hold their breath underwater for too long.

But, there was something else about the way he looked around the bar just then—it was this kind of weird thing he did as if he was always surprised everyone was watching. To me, it seemed as if he was not only surprised all of us were watching, but seemed particularly pissed off about it. Through all those gawking stares, Cooley crossed the bar to be back where he served out drinks. His footfalls on the hardwood floor seemed loud—that game leg with the dragging foot making a sound all the more pronounced. Once behind the bar, Cooley placed the shotgun back under the counter.

Nobody moved for another long moment. Maybe we were all trying to make sense of it all or pay respects to the guy that got killed. It didn't last all that long though. That silence never does—everyone eventually makes sense out of it all and moves on. Life moves on, I suppose, when the dead can't.

That's when the piano guy came out of the room he'd been hiding in like a little girl and went back to his piano. Cooley's waitress peeked up from the behind the bar, watched Cooley pass her by, watched him put away the shotgun under the counter, and decided it was safe enough to continue serving customers—though she wasn't exactly scared hysterical because she had been used to seeing people get killed in Cooley's, she was still a woman and women always tend to have a harder time than men hearing gunfire go off so nearby. Everyone, eventually, went about whatever they were doing. Me and my friend turned back to the bar, not only stealing glances at each other to figure out what the other was thinking, but looking at Cooley to get an inkling about what he was thinking.

After putting the shotgun away, Cooley went back to what he was doing just before the strange man walked in: wiping out empty glasses and the bar counter with the same rag you would see him, sometimes, wiping his forehead with or blowing his nose into—looking at him like this, you wouldn't think he had just killed someone barely five minutes ago.

I could tell my friend wanted to ask Cooley the same question that was running through my mind. But, he couldn't bring himself to getting the words out. Maybe, he was afraid of what Cooley might say—perhaps it had a lot more to do with what Cooley might do. What Cooley said and did were often the difference in whether you lived or died. So, whatever the reason, my friend didn't ask it—he couldn't bring himself to take such chances.

I, on the other hand, did—not that I wasn't afraid of Cooley as the next guy, or thought that maybe I would be better off keeping my mouth shut and minding about my own business, but because me and Cooley go back away, I figured what the hell.

"So," I said to Cooley. "Who was he?"

Cooley looked into my eyes for what seemed like a long time. Perhaps just long enough for him to decide if you were worth wasting a shotgun slug on. Since we were pretty good friends, I knew that was what was going through Cooley's mind. At least, not at that particular moment. I was as sure of that as I was of the nose on my face. Yet, somehow, there was still this small degree of uncertainty about him that I had never really been quite able to shake. Sure, we were pretty good friends, but sometimes friendship isn't enough to protect you from someone that wants you dead badly enough.

Anyway, Cooley looked at me for a long time before he told me, "A man with a big mouth." He kept wiping out his shot glasses as if it was more than just something done to maintain cleanliness but more as a kind of way to numb himself to reality.

There was a long silence then. Me and my friend exchanged a glance with each other as if we thought the other person's eyes contained all the answers. Only, the answers were really in Cooley's eyes—his two eyes mostly gazing into mine before he finally said, in a voice that seemed filled with the remorse and consideration he rarely had:

"He was my son," his voice seemed distant, and small.

I looked at him, carefully. Seeing something in him I hadn't seen before. Something that might have been humanity, or a strange degree of weakness. I suppose Cooley had lived his life ignoring that humanity and hardening those weaknesses as a way to keep himself disconnected from all the things that make reality cumbersome. That is, until he killed his own son and had to live with it.

But, then again, who I am to say what a man can live with and what he can't?

Eventually, I guess, we all understood why Cooley had to kill his son. At least on some level, I mean. That still doesn't necessarily make it a pleasant experience or something right. It never should be, no matter how well you disconnect yourself from all the things that make reality humanly-real. The thing is: when push comes to shove, when people change over time, when there is only time between relationships so haunting it destroys them, you have to put all those humanly-real things aside.

So, when someone has a death wish, even if they're your own kid, you have to grant those wishes, somehow, and find a way to move on.

For Cooley, it was a simple thing, and yet quite a complicated thing at the same time—I guess for Cooley killing the strange man that turned out being his son was a necessary thing, since whatever relationship Cooley had had with him died a long time ago.

11

I have no doubt, dear reader, that the strange man that walked into Cooley's bar that day—whenever it was—was actually Cooley's son. I say I have no doubt, because I have no reason to believe that the story isn't a true one. For that matter, I have no reason to believe that what happened didn't happen the way that it has been described, even if the account I have provided you with seems like a tall tale.

I admit, when I first heard this story about a strange man coming into Cooley's one day, seemingly looking to pick a fight with Cooley, I knew it wasn't out of the ordinary. There is plenty of evidence that Cooley was generally targeted by a wide variety of scoundrels and desperados, looking to get revenge on him. Invariably, Cooley double-crossed people, stabbed people in the back, and did despicable things to people to warrant any of them wanting to—needing to—pay Cooley back for what he had done to them somewhere along the way. Indeed, Cooley had many enemies. From what I gather, there were plenty guys in town that hated Cooley for one reason or another—either Cooley had openly made fun of them in front of everybody, or Cooley had embarrassed them with one of the whores, or Cooley had stolen someone's girl from them, or Cooley had had an affair with someone's wife in their home, or Cooley owed someone money and refused to pay it back. Even the town's sheriff hated Cooley for refusing to turn over his firearms, which was the custom, as a way to minimize crime—based on my research, Cooley had been asked by one sheriff after another after another, and in each instance, when the sheriff tried to confront Cooley, Cooley found a way to embarrass whoever the poor guy was, until the poor guy would lose the confidence of the people he swore to protect and, eventually, would resign. To see Cooley walk around town with his revolver holstered at his side only made people hate him that much more. It was an open threat that taunted people, I believe. Someone said—I don't remember who—that seeing

Cooley walk around town was like watching the devil walking around heaven.

Even most of the whores that Cooley employed in the upper floor of the bar hated him. Sometimes, it was about money and the fact that Cooley wouldn't give them the percentage of each trick they felt they deserved. Sometimes, it was about how rough Cooley would treat certain ones—not just verbal abuse, but also physical. Some of them that believed they could talk to Cooley anyway they wished before Cooley would crack their jaw, or swell their eye—then, Cooley would make them turn a trick as damaged goods, when no man would want to have a beat-up whore do anything to them, no matter how much of a discount a returning customer might get.

The point here is that Cooley had a lot of enemies. To the best of my knowledge, I don't think Cooley had any friends—there is no evidence that I could find anywhere that would suggest so. For that matter, there were plenty of people that hated Cooley enough to want him dead and, to my mind, plenty that would have loved to be the one to put a bullet in Cooley's head. So, given that Cooley spent much of his time at his bar later in life, anyone that hated Cooley enough, and wished see Cooley in hell, found the time to come to Cooley's.

Some say that Cooley loved this—that he absolutely loved the idea that someone could come to the bar looking for him and wanting to kill him. Some say that this was something that fed Cooley's ego. It was the danger of it—it was the idea that, on any given day, at any given time, one of many people that hated Cooley could walk in, find him, and try to kill him.

It is probably safe to say, dear reader, that Cooley felt he needed to be armed at all times. Keeping his revolver was about protection—and anyway, by all accounts, there was also was a shotgun stowed behind the bar counter, just in case.

Typically, Cooley kept himself behind the bar, which had the best view of the main entrance. Indeed, Cooley ran the bar and monitored how the booze flowed, but he also liked to make sure he knew who was coming and going—that was the most important thing, if you ask me.

There were plenty of instances when someone got too drunk and needed to be throw out. In those cases, Cooley would make sure the patron knew that they had reached their limit and it was time to go. For the most part, there is evidence that most found their way to the door and didn't need any convincing by Cooley or Cooley's gun. But, there were documented times when things didn't go so smoothly—these were times when a patron didn't want to stop drinking, when the patron wanted more booze, and wasn't ready to leave. Those were the times when Cooley would manhandle whoever the drunk guy was—I found plenty of witnesses that described how Cooley, even in his older years, could lift a grown man up out of his chair, drag him kicking and scratching to the door, and throw out beyond the sidewalk and into the street.

During the best of times, there would be no more to it. The drunk would get thrown out, kicking, cussing, and yelling, and be on his way. But, during the worst of times, things wouldn't transpire nearly that quietly, so to speak. I don't need to convince you, dear reader, that the loudest incidents were generally the most normal. A drunk guy would get mad about being told he was drunk, then become angrier when Cooley had to tell him that he couldn't be served any more booze, then the drunk guy would just refuse to leave, and then Cooley would kick the drunk guy out by force. This sort of scene would capture everyone's attention, but, in fairly quick order, it would all be over—then things would get back to normal. Yet, it was those other sorts of scenes that would draw out longer—though these were certainly quiet, they involve more dire circumstances. This was when it wasn't about the booze, but it was about revenge. This was when it wasn't about a drunk guy that just needed to be thrown out so things could return to normal, but it was about a guy that needed to be killed, in order to remind others who Cooley really was.

Over the years, especially as Cooley reached old age, I believe many of the people that frequented Cooley's forgot about Cooley's past. It was as if, once Cooley became an old man, his past was just some distant thing that matter anymore to the present—even though you would be hard-pressed to not find someone that knew about Cooley's past or had heard through the grapevine about what Cooley did when and to whom, the past remained so distant that it may have well been part of some distant world. Cooley's past, in particular, for those that were in the know, had become like a dirty little secret that became, eventually, tall tales. It was like so many stories about the early days after the Civil War during Westward Expansion—there was always someone that did something to someone somewhere. When it came to Cooley's past, because there were so many things that no one knew for sure, it was easier to forget all the loose ends Cooley left in his life and how, at times, chickens always come home to roost.

There is no better example of this than the story I have provided about the strange man that had come to Cooley's and how this strange man, come to find out, was Cooley's son.

It may be important to note, though, that Cooley had several sons. Exactly how many, dear reader, I can't say for sure. I found evidence that Cooley had at least seven sons all by different women, and all from various states and territories. I don't think it would be too much of a stretch to say that Cooley likely had more children—some say Cooley had as many as a dozen sons and, perhaps, about as many daughters. Also, I don't think it would be too much of a stretch for me to say that all of these children were likely from different women—in other words, Cooley certainly didn't have more than one child from any one woman. There is plenty of evidence, I feel, that certainly supports that fact. Even so, so far, I have only been able to corroborate the existence of at least seven sons—there is no doubt in my mind that most of these sons, if not all, hated Cooley enough to want to kill him.

Essentially, dear reader, it was the same sort of story each time. Each of Cooley's sons hated Cooley for leaving their mother, hated Cooley for not being in their lives, and hated that Cooley didn't care enough to be a father to any of them. Across the board, each of these sons had learned to hate Cooley from their mothers, since it was always the mothers that had come to realize that Cooley had just used them, jilted them, and left them to raise their children on their own—and across the board, too, each of the mothers had sought financial help from Cooley, since, for the most part, each of the mothers had little to no money and little to no family support. In each case, Cooley had been all each of the mothers had had at the time Cooley initially met them. In each case, once Cooley learned they were pregnant—or at some point in time before the baby was born—Cooley would leave. In some cases, Cooley left in the middle of the night when the women were asleep—these women learned Cooley was gone by morning, when noticing he was missing. Others would get the pleasure of being told by Cooley himself that he was tired of them—these women find themselves crying as they watched Cooley pack up his things and leave. Only in a couple of instances could I find that Cooley had been the one that had been kicked out by the women—either from cheating on them, or beating them, or out of simply growing tired of life with Cooley.

What remains similar across all of these relationships with women was that each of them made sure their sons knew who Cooley was. I don't mean that it was about knowing who their father was—as important as that is for any child—but it was more about making sure they understood what kind of man Cooley was and wasn't. Each of these women made sure that their sons had just as much hatred for Cooley as they had—in each case, that hatred was planted very early in each son's childhood, so that, by the time they reached adulthood, each son felt like it was their duty to track Cooley down and inflict the kind of pain on him that he did on their mothers.

In a certain sense, dear readers, it was about revenge. I find that is a bit limiting, though. It is not that none of these sons wanted revenge against Cooley nor that it was that revenge that would, at times, fuel each of these sons into traveling thousands of miles to find Cooley. Revenge was, to my mind, a big part of it all, based on the interviews I was able to get to Cooley's various sons over the years. Yet, what was really at the core of what inspired these sons, in my view, was the idea that they were searching for something about themselves—something, to be sure, that only an absent father could solve.

That was what brought the strange man into Cooley's that day. It was the same thing that always brought other strange men, like the one from the story, into Cooley's— young men that no one had ever seen before in town.

In each case, these strangers were that, at times, would ask around town about Cooley before showing up at the bar. It was always about making sure Cooley was in town and that whatever they had heard through the grapevine was accurate. It was also about determining who was the law in town—always finding out how much of a joke any law enforcement was. They would slowly and carefully survey the outside of Cooley's, in order to determine where Cooley himself was—each time, they could see Cooley standing prominently at the bar. One of the sons told me that, when we saw Cooley for the first time, standing at the bar, he never felt more fear in his life. Another son told me that the sight of Cooley only made him more enraged. The five sons I was able to interview—with two I was never able to track down—all told me that, even when they saw how old Cooley was when they finally found him, they remained focused on wanting to kill him. They were all moved to want to kill Cooley—I guess you could say, when travelling thousands of miles to find someone, there was no turning back on that.

In each case, the son would venture inside and find a seat where they could watch Cooley and, more importantly, make sure Cooley noticed them. Everyone noticed too, since everyone there knew everyone else—generally, strangers always stood out.

I can't say, dear reader, if Cooley always instantly recognized each of these strangers as being one of his sons. I think it is more than likely that he didn't, since Cooley left their lives long before they were born.

Somehow, I do think that Cooley had a certain intuition when it came to who entered the bar on any given day. Cooley always knew who the regulars were, just as Cooley always knew who the guys were that visited more infrequently. So, I would like to think that Cooley always knew strangers when he saw them—and, more than that, I would like to think that Cooley always knew when strangers actually looked familiar and reminded him of someone from his past. I would like to think, too, that, based on the account about the strange man that came into Cooley's, there is no doubt that Cooley didn't know right away who it was. To my mind, Cooley simply waited for the right time for what was, to Cooley, something that had to be done.

I don't know if that completely explains the reaction Cooley had to the strange man that came in that day. I certainly think it explains something somehow. I think if there was something inevitable to what happened between Cooley and the strange man that day—something that had culminated over a long period of time—there is something poetic to what happened. I don't mean to say, dear reader, that killing is poetic. I don't even wish to say that dying is poetic either. Yet, when I make sense out of the strange man that came to Cooley's that day, and how Cooley reacted to the strange man, and what Cooley is reported to have said after shooting the strange man dead, I can't help but find something poetic in the whole thing that, perhaps, speaks to the relationship Cooley had with the strange man, if we can say, of course, based on reports, that it was, indeed, Cooley's son.

12

First off, let me just tell you that Cooley was awfully pissed off that particular day. Whether it had anything to do with stuff at home with his old lady or had something to do with business being pretty slow that day, I couldn't tell you for sure. All I can tell you for certain is that Cooley was pissed off, and when he gets pissed off, you better believe it shows.

From the table me and Rorry and Big Sam were sitting, shooting the shit and throwing back shots of Bourbon, I watched Cooley walk back and forth behind the bar. Every once in a while, he'd shoot a glance my direction, but for the most part he was kind of lost in his own little world. I mean—from what I could tell—he looked to be so troubled with something, that something was the only thing he was able to think about.

"What you figger is wrong with him, anyway?" I asked my buddies.

I wasn't all that drunk yet and I knew they weren't either.

I said, "I mean, look at him. He hasn't as much as said two words to anybody tonight."

"I dunno," Big Sam shrugged his shoulders, poured himself another shot of Bourbon in his little shot glass from the large flask that the three of us were sharing, and gulped it back with a tilt of the head. "Probably's got a lot to do with that rheumatism of his, or something, I guess."

"Naw," I said. I was sitting on the side of the table facing the bar front, and had to look around Big Sam's stout torso and big head to see Cooley. "I don't think so. I mean, normally he's in a good mood."

"Good mood?" Rorry laughed. "Cooley doesn't have good and bad moods. Cooley is Cooley."

"Yeah," I told him. "I know Cooley is Cooley. But, I think something's wrong with him tonight. He looks awfully pissed off about something."

Big Sam slammed his shot glass down on the table, "I'm getting awful pissed myself. You're spoiling my buzz, Hal. Who gives a shit about whether Cooley is pissed off. What are you? The old man's keeper, or something?"

"Yeah, Hal," Rorry jumped in. "Don't worry about Cooley. He's been living longer than the three of us put together. If he's pissed, he's got a right to be pissed. After all, if I was his age and had seen all the fucked up shit that he's seen in his life, I'd be pretty pissed off, too."

Rorry reached for the large flask of Bourbon around the same time Big Sam was reaching for it. The both of them looked at each other with surprise, then that surprise changed in a curiosity. Before I knew what was happening, the both of them were tugging on the bottle as if it was a rope and they were playing some childish game of tug-o-war.

"Gimme," Big Sam said.

"No," Rorry said. "Gimme. You're drinking more than your share, anyway."

"More than my share?" Big Sam looked thoroughly pissed off. "I paid for this fucking bottle, you son of a bitch."

"Oh," Rorry said. "I got your bitch, alright, you big galoot."

After Rorry said that, something in Big Sam snapped, and the big man shot straight up out of his chair and grabbed Rorry by the collar of the shirt. Rorry, probably weighing no more than a buck and a half soaking wet, got pulled up out of his seat as limply as a sack of horse feed.

"You put me down!"

Big Sam just looked at him, pulled the little guy into his big barrel of a chest, reminding me of that fellow Gulliver and all those little people whose island he got stranded on.

"I oughta kick your ass, Rorry."

"I ain't afraid of you," Rorry said, his voice shaky, something looking a lot like tears forming in the corners of his eyes. "Tell him, Hal. Tell him that I ain't afraid of him. Tell him I've licked bigger fellas than him before."

As much as I wanted to say that, I found myself unwilling to get in the middle of their petty little argument over something as insignificant as who's drinking more than their share and who paid for the bottle. I would've liked nothing more than to go about drinking, and minding my own business. But, I couldn't let Rorry get his ass beat, even if his mouth wrote a check his fists couldn't cash. Even if, for once, I would've loved to see that loud-mouthed Rorry get one of Big Sam's big fists jammed in his mouth, there was no way I could let it happen.

"Com'mon, Sam. Put him down."

Big Sam rolled his eyes towards me as if to say, wordlessly, how much he really wanted to pound Rorry into powder right here and now, even if the little squirt was my brother's best friend and the fight wouldn't be a fair one.

"Yeah," Rorry ran his mouth again. "Put me down, Sam."

Big Sam's eyes rolled towards the little squirt again. This time, in his eyes, you could tell he really wanted to do it, even if, with one punch of Big Sam's punches, Rorry's whole face would probably cave in. "Just let me hit him once, Hal. I won't hurt him too bad. Just once, okay."

"No," I said.

Sometimes, I've always found, you have to talk to Big Sam like a kid. It's not really because he was slow-minded or anything, but because, whenever the big man got worked up about something, you have to handle him with care.

I said, "Put him down, Sam. He ain't worth it. I'll buy another bottle, okay?"

"Of Bourbon?" The big man asked, glancing at me out the corner of his eye. The thought of a new bottle seemed very interesting to him, especially if that bottle was going to be a free one. Nothing's better, I think, than having something free, you know. "You're buying?"

"Yeah," I told him. "The bottle's on me. Just put Rorry down."

Big Sam thought about it for a moment, looked into Rorry's scared eyes that were slowly but surely filling up with tears even if Rorry was trying his best to hold them back, and threw Rorry right back into the chair he was sitting in. Rorry sat stiffly in the chair, looking up at Big Sam. The collar of the little guy's shirt all scrunched up around his neck and he looked like someone so scared, they couldn't move a muscle for fear they'd shit in their pants.

"Just sit back down," I told Big Sam. "Calm down. And I'll get Billie over here and order another round, okay."

"Okay," the big man said, sitting back down, and shooting a glance at Rorry as if to say: *You're lucky this time, but you might not be the next.*

"Hey, Billie," I yelled across the bar.

Billie, Cooley's waitress, looked up from a table to the immediate right of the main bar where she went about counting the tips she'd received from customers, Whatever she got in tips never amounted to very much by the close of a given work day, but for Billie, something was much better than nothing.

Looking up as she did, Billie had a blank look on her face—come to think of it, Billie almost always had a blank look on her face. Don't ask me why.

I told her, "Another Bourbon over here, will ya."

Billie nodded, got up from the table, stuffed the tips she received away in her front apron pocket, and walked over to the bar. Cooley was wiping out some glasses and didn't seem to mind that she went ahead and came behind the bar. Under normal circumstances, if Cooley hadn't been in such an awful mood, he probably wouldn't have let her do it. Cooley didn't believe Billie or anybody else had any business being behind his bar—only him—since he was, after all, the bartender. But nevertheless, Billie went back there, and selected a Bourbon bottle from the broad shelf running along the wall back there, put that bottle on a tray, and proceeded to bring it to our table.

Rorry leaned towards me, "Who the hell is that?"

"Who?"

"Her?" He nodded his head in Billie's direction as she made her way across the bar to where we were sitting. "What's her story?"

"She's outta your league, pipsqueak," Big Sam grunted with a smile. By then, the big guy had pulled out a match, flicked it against the heel of his boot, and navigated the modest flame up to the end of one of those stinky, slim cigars he always loved to smoke. "She don't like runts like you. What she likes is real men like me, guys that can fuck the ghost out of her."

"Shut up," Rorry told Big Sam, perhaps knowing full well about Big Sam's repetitive sayings. Then, looked back at me, "Introduce me to her, okay?"

I didn't want to tell Rorry that Big Sam was probably right about him being out Billie's league. Billie was, after all, a pretty good-looking woman in comparison to most of the women we had there in our little town. She could probably have had her choice of any guy, so why in the world would she waste any time on somebody like Rorry who probably had more hair on his head than over the rest of his body? Rorry, who was only seventeen, couldn't shoot a tin can off a fence post at fifteen yards, for that matter—Billie was just too much woman for a guy like Rorry.

Though I didn't want to introduce him to her, for fear she'd bust his chops with a healthy dose of reality, since he was my brother's best friend, I figured no other way would be better for him than to hear Billie tell him out of her own mouth that she wasn't interested in him, and would never really be. It didn't really have anything to do with Billie not liking squirts, but had more to do with her being Cooley's girl.

Sure, Billie was a big-breasted, blonde that seemed far too young for an old fart like Cooley—Billie probably coming in somewhere around a third of Cooley's age—but, who am I to say anything about love, since I've been married twice and divorced twice? Who am I to say that Cooley shouldn't be with somebody like Billie, even if he is old enough to be her grandfather, even if, as far as I'm concerned, there's no way in hell Cooley could ever really, completely, keep someone as vivacious as Billie happy?

So, anyway, I didn't say anything to Rorry about it. I didn't say anything about Billie being Cooley's girl. I guess, in a way, I didn't think I needed to, since I'd thought Billie would just blow Rorry off if Rorry said anything, and Rorry would go on about his business.

That's what I'd thought. But, that isn't what happened.

What happened was this: Billie walked over to our table with the new bottle of Bourbon on a serving tray. She came to the side of the table between Big Sam and Rorry. She took the bottle off the tray and sat the bottle on our table while the three of us looked on. I had a couple silver dollars that I was trying to hand her across the table as she'd leaned forward to reach for them, and it was, at that moment, when something I would've never imagined happening actually happened.

Billie jumped at something, startled with a squeal, just before she could take the two silver dollars from me, and stood back from the table a bit, immediately hitting Rorry across the shoulder.

"Was that my hand that did that?" Rorry smiled so devilishly I thought Billie would slap him across the face next. "Pardon me."

Though he said that, you could tell by the expression on his face that he didn't mean it. Billie could tell he didn't mean it, and the mere thought of a man pinching her ass like that completely repulsed her beyond words. So, Rorry's "pardon me" didn't mean shit.

But, somehow, after being flabbergasted at first, she said,   "You had better keep your hands to yourself, fella."

"Is that so?" Rorry smiled. "I'd rather have these hands all over you."

Big Sam might as well as been in another world all together because he just went about smoking his cigar, inhaling with pleasure and exhaling in this kind of ecstasy where he'd close his eyes and crane his head back and blow the smoke up toward the ceiling. Big Sam didn't care about anything else but his cigar. So, in other words, the big man wasn't really paying much attention to what was happening. If he was, he didn't care, perhaps wanting nothing better than to see Rorry get slapped, or worse.

Even if he was my brother's best friend, I would've liked nothing more than to see Rorry get slapped. Rorry was arrogant, a loudmouth, and had an ego as inflated as a hot air balloon. And, if there was anybody that had a slap coming, it was him. Call me sympathetic, but though I didn't particularly like Rorry, and would've loved to see Billie slap him, I didn't want it to happen.

"Hey, Rorry," I told him. "Knock it off, okay."

Rorry looked at me as if he didn't understand the words coming out of my mouth, then gazed up toward Billie, "Oh, I'll knock it off, alright. How about you let me knock it off upstairs."

"I don't do that sort of thing," Billie told him, growing more repulsed by the moment. "I'm a waitress. We got whores upstairs."

"I don't want no whore," Rorry said. "I want you."

"Well, you can't have me. I'm spoken for."

"Spoken for?"

"Yeah," I told Rorry. "She's Cooley's girl."

Rorry glanced towards the bar over a shoulder, saw Cooley across the way pacing back and forth in that feeble manner he always moved around in, and looked at me, "Cooley's girl? You gotta be kidding me. That old fart? He can't know how to love a woman like this. Not like I can."

"Better keep your voice down, Rorry," Big Sam said. "If you know what's good for you." I didn't think the big man was paying attention to what was going on, but, believe me, that wasn't the first time I'd ever mistaken Big Sam's attentiveness. "That old fart, as you call him, might come over here and show you and thing or two, squirt."

"Show me a thing or two?" Rorry laughed. "I'll show this bitch here a thing or two." He grabbed Billie around the waist with one of those pipe arms of his, and pulled her into his lap before she had as much of a chance to put up a good enough fight against it. "You know you want me, Billie. You know you want a real man to show you what it's all about."

"No!" Billie squealed like a trapped pig in a slaughterhouse. "Leave me alone! Let me go! No! Stop! No!"

But, being the young guy that he was, being the young guy that was as sexually hungry as a dog in heat, Rorry didn't stop. He held her down in his lap, and began groping her all over her breasts, and managed to get a hand up underneath her dress. Billie squirmed, but Rorry held her down, laughing and hooting and hollering and having a grand old time at Billie's expense.

"I don't why you're fighting me, sugar," Rorry told her leaned in close to her ear while he kissed her on the neck. "You know that old fart can't do nothing for you. You know you want a real man. A real man like me."

I remember thinking about how Cooley was much more of a real man than Rorry could ever be. I remember watching him grope Billie and laugh up to the high heavens as she squealed and squirmed. I remember, then, lifting my eyes beyond them and peering across the way towards Cooley was, who was already looking our way. I remember the look on Cooley's face just then—I will never forget it, you see.

Let me tell you, Cooley wasn't wiping out any glasses anymore around this time. His eyes looked like they were practically on fire. His face scrunched up in the kind of grimace I'd seen before, the kind of grimace that more often than not meant something terrible was about to happen.

What was about to happen, exactly?

I didn't know. I knew Cooley for all these years and had heard about all his exploits, both the good and bad, and still I wasn't entirely sure what was about going to happen. All I knew with any shred of certainty whatsoever was that Cooley was pissed off. Add how pissed off he looked now to how he'd already been pissed earlier, and you have the potential for something terrible to happen, one way or another.

Big Sam, though he didn't say anything else, looked as if he'd thought the same thing I thought. He shot these curious glances over his shoulder to see what Cooley was doing, and looked at me as if to ask: *Something very terrible's about to happen, Hal, isn't it? And I can definitely feel it.*

And, as far as I was concerned, he was right.

Cooley disappeared from behind the bar for a moment. Where he went I didn't know, but had an inkling, just the same.

Then, just as quickly as Cooley had disappeared, he reappeared from a doorway to one of the back rooms where he had this makeshift office. He was holding a shotgun at port-arms, and he was charging towards the table where we all were—he looked like a madman.

"Cooley," I shouted across the bar to him. "Whatever you're thinking about doing, don't do it. He's just a kid."

That was when Big Sam turned around, saw Cooley coming with the shotgun, saw how angry Cooley was, and jumped up out of his seat, as if it was on fire. That was a lot of Big Sam moving quite fast. That was because, even Big Sam, knew that the last thing any rational-thinking person wanted to do was mess around with Cooley whenever he had any kind of gun in his possession. Big Sam may have been a big man with his own reputation that preceded him, but Big Sam was small potatoes compared to Cooley and all the stuff Cooley had done, and the kind of reputation Cooley for himself.

For whatever it was worth, Big Sam jumped out of that seat of his, and hurried over to a neighboring table, just as Cooley hurried over to our table. I couldn't do anything but watch as the old man kicked the chair Big Sam had been sitting in out of the way, grabbed Billie by an arm and yanked her up out of Rorry's lap, and pointed the two barrels of his shotgun into Rorry's nose.

"Cooley don't do it," I found myself screaming, not because I didn't want to see Rorry get what he deserved, but because I didn't believe the kid deserved getting killed over being a jackass. "He's just a kid."

"Yeah," Billie said. I think she felt the same way that I did.

Cooley snatched her so hard out of Rorry's lap, the momentum took her a good ten feet away, I think—which says a lot for Cooley's strength, even if he was an old man. Some would call that old man strength. Cooley had plenty of that, you know. It always tricked you. I mean, you would fool yourself into thinking that, as an old man, Cooley wouldn't do this or do that, or couldn't do this or do that—then, you would realize how wrong you were. This was one of those times. For me, of course, no matter how many times I had watched Cooley do things that an old man shouldn't be able to do. But, also for Billie—she rebounded, and started tugging at the back of Cooley's shirt. I guess she thought that would help.

She told Cooley, "He ain't worth the trouble. He's just a kid."

But, if she actually didn't want Cooley to kill Rorry because he was just a kid or because she didn't want to see any bloodshed, it's hard to say.

"I don't give a fiddler's fuck, if he's just a kid," Cooley said, leveling the barrels of that shotgun carefully, then cocking the hammer. "That don't matter to me. He's got a mouth on him like a man, and he can die like one."

I thought, being that Rorry had a big mouth, that he'd be able to stand up for himself. After all, he'd stood up to Big Sam, and Big Sam was at least three times Rorry's size. And, I'd seen Rorry stand up to guns he was staring down before, on countless occasions. But, this was an occasion, when Rorry was at a loss for words, for a change. All Rorry did was just sit there with his eyes crossed onto the shotgun, sending glances up into Cooley's face every once in a while.

"Please don't do it, Cooley," I found myself speaking for the kid since the kid wasn't speaking for himself. "He ain't mean no harm, okay. Can't we just forget it? Whatdooya say?"

Cooley didn't say anything to that. It was almost as if he hadn't heard me.

I watched as Cooley looked deeply into Rorry's eyes, as if he saw something in them that none of us could see.

As far as anything I'd said, I might as well have been talking to a cow or something. You see, if there's anything I know about Cooley, I know that, when he gets his mind set in a direction, he won't take himself off that train of thought. But, I wanted to believe that there was a warm heart somewhere in there, that Cooley wouldn't kill an unarmed kid even if I knew Cooley was as coldhearted as the devil himself. I wanted to believe that, maybe just this once, Cooley would let the kid slide, even if I'd never known Cooley let anybody slide once he had a shotgun up to their heads and the hammer cocked. From what I'd always known of Cooley, if he had his hammer cocked and his finger on the trigger, he meant to shoot.

And hadn't he gave me advice once, a very long time ago, about never putting your finger on the trigger unless you plan on shooting somebody?

And that's when it happened.

Right there before my eyes, without another word, while me and Billie and Big Sam, from a distance, looked on, with Rorry looking up into him with two of the most frightened eyes I ever saw, Cooley pulled the trigger.

Just one shot.

That one shot, being as close to Rorry's face as it was, blew Rorry's face off in a splatter of blood and bits and chunks of flesh. I'll never forget it for as long as I live, you see. It was like Rorry's face had been made of clay or something. And, the power of that one shot knocked Rorry's body backward out of the chair. His body crashed to the floor in this terrible thud.

Billie let out this scream and went running in the direction of the main bar, crying, and making these frantic hand gestures as if she was about to lose her mind.

Big Sam, though, let out something that sounded like an odd cross between a laugh and a gasp. I heard a cow make a sound like that once. What that sound meant coming out of Big Sam's mouth, I wasn't sure. Though I couldn't see Big Sam's face, I was sure Big Sam was thankful it was Rorry getting the business and not him—Big Sam wasn't especially bright, but he was smart enough to know the fair side of the buckwheat.

I remember looking at Cooley who just stood there, shotgun still in hand, with this crazed look on his face.

"Why did you do it, Cooley?" I asked him. "Why did you have to kill the kid like that?"

Cooley looked at me in a way that seemed as if he was looking through me. And for a moment, before he opened his mouth, I thought he was about to shoot me like he'd shot Rorry. That was when he said, plainly, simply, in a voice that sounded intoxicated, "Because she'd said no."

I just stood there looking at him, slightly frozen, "Because she'd said no?"

Cooley looked at me, nodded, looked down at Rorry's dead body just before he walked back to the bar, and he never said a word about it since.

Even to this day, he hasn't talked about it. I guess I'm afraid to ask him, not because I'm particularly scared of what Cooley might do if I bring up the subject, but mostly because I'm not particularly fond of dying over bullshit, like the kind of bullshit Rorry got killed over.

13

What happened to Rorry, dear reader, is undoubtedly a tragedy. But, I will say, it is a tragedy that was a common occurrence, with respect to how Cooley did business at his bar and how, for that matter, Cooley established the reality of the world around him—in a certain sense, Rorry represents, on one hand, the boundaries in which Cooley functioned in his life and, on the other, an encapsulation of his past.

Typically, there were plenty of Rorrys that confronted Cooley from time to time. Most notably, once Cooley reached a certain age and had all of that history behind him, there was always a Rorry-type that wanted to test Cooley—always wanted to see if all the stories were true, if there was anything to the legend, and if it was possible to be the one that would make history. Essentially, Rorry was one of many that always wanted to be the one that killed Cooley—after all, dear reader, I do not have to tell you that it was not lost on anyone that killing Cooley would make history and any potential killer wanted their name in the history books.

The thing with Rorry, I would argue, is probably no different. From what I know about Rorry, he was ambitious and brash. Rorry was young, true, but there was a worldliness to him. Some have told me that, from the time he was very young, Rorry has always wanted to kill Cooley. Some say that, when Rorry could barely hold a gun, he expressed how much he wanted to rid the world of Cooley—anyone that knew Rorry knew that this desire was an important part of his life.

I think it is safe to say that Rorry visited Cooley's so much, with the hopes that the moment would present itself—that, at some point in time, something would happen that would allow Rorry to carry through with what he wanted to do. Sure, there is no doubt in my mind that Rorry enjoyed drinking and playing cards, which a lot of men did at Cooley.s. I also think that Rorry enjoyed having his turn with Cooley's whores—just as most men did in town.

To a certain extent, there was certainly something there between Rorry and Billie. Some say that Rorry liked Billie, and that he had liked Billie from the time when the two of them were small kid—but what Rorry felt for Billie was always more than what she felt for him. Some say that Rorry and Billie were friends, but something went wrong at some point in time—then, things went sour. Some say, too, that Rorry had asked Billie to marry him, she turned him down, and that was why he spent so much time at Cooley's—he had hoped to convince her that he was man enough for her. Some say that Rorry and Billie actually didn't know each other at all and that—on the day Rorry was killed—that was the very first time Rorry and Billie interacted the way that they did, other than that of a customer and a waitress. Those that say this say, too, that Rorry had simply used Billie as a way to get Cooley's attention—it seems that those that believe Rorry coaxed Cooley into a confrontation think that Rorry had something of a death wish.

In my opinion, dear reader, it remains impossible to know exactly what compelled Rorry to do what he did. Indeed, it is easy to figure out what drew Cooley into the matter, but this thing with Rorry still remains more difficult to ascertain—yet, I think there may be something to the idea that, perhaps, Rorry had a death wish.

Dear reader, I certainly don't like interjecting my opinion. I have always felt that, as a biographer, the best practice is to give the facts and let the facts speak for themselves. From the facts, dear reader, you can draw your own conclusions. You certainly don't need me to be in the way—a historian gives his audience what history is in terms of facts, in terms of what happened and what didn't, and the audience, then, makes meaning out of those facts, and out of what happened when compared to what didn't. So, I can only tell you the facts, as I know them to be. Even so, when speaking about what happened and what didn't, all one can hope to do, in making sense out of it all, is what is made meaningful by what happened and what is made meaningless by what didn't. However, in this case, when there are so many facts are absent, all I can do is provide you with the best account that I can, with the hope that all the accounts you have collectively bring something into view for you. In this case, Rorry's story becomes important—it gives you an account that brings something about Cooley into view for you.

That was the reason why I interviewed Rorry's younger brother, Hiram. My hope was that Hiram would shed some light not just on what happened to Rorry—and what didn't take place—but also shed light on something about Cooley, since Hiram knew Cooley very well.

I remember meeting Hiram at the little house he and Rorry shared just on the outskirts of town where Cooley's bar was. I would say that the house is about a couple miles away from town. The house had once belonged to the brothers' parents—in fact, it was Hiram's and Rorry's father that built the house from the ground up. Hiram and Rorry had been raised in the house and, once their father passed away and their mother passed away not long afterwards, the brothers lived in its together, since it had been the only things that their parents left to them. There was a barn erected just behind the house— this was where Hiram and Rorry, as adults, stayed from time to time, when they had either nowhere to stay or were just passing through the area on their way somewhere else. It was only after their father died when Hiram and Rorry permanently lived on the property—they had done this, Hiram told me, to take care of their mother.

Their mother had been sick for some time after their father's death. Some say she lost her mind—Hiram simply told me, in a rather flat way, that their mother lost the ability to care for herself. Whatever the reason, once she died, the two brothers took over the property—the small house was divided in two, so Hiram and Rorry could have their own space, and the barn outside was used to keep livestock.

According to Hiram, Rorry spoke about Cooley frequently. Indeed, they both grew up hearing stories about Cooley from their father, who had known Cooley himself. But, Hiram makes clear, Rorry was the one that became obsessed with wanting to know more about Cooley, with tracing Cooley's history, with figuring out who Cooley killed and where, and with the idea that Cooley needed to be brought to justice, somehow.

Hiram told me that some of this obsession was also their father's. Their father had had this friendship of some sort with Cooley—that is, if it is even possible to say that anyone could be friends with someone like Cooley at all—and would tell these stories about who Cooley killed in Kansas, or who he killed in Texas, or what Cooley is said to have done to a man in Oklahoma.

I remember how general Hiram had been with me. What I mean, dear reader, is, at first, Hiram talked about Cooley in a way that seemed too artificial and cold. It was all about facts—people and places—but it was never really about anything you could really feel. I don't know if it had been because he had had his guard up. Maybe so. I often find that when you ask specific questions about specific things, people tend to clam up. Maybe, it's because they are afraid of what to say or how what they say might be perceived—maybe, it's because they don't want to be on the record as having said things, with which their name could be attached. There is always this resistance sometimes, especially when the person I interview knows my work and knows what it means to be a biographer. I can't say if Hiram for sure if Hiram knew of my work or my reputation— he, in fact, said he had never read any of my past work and, for that matter, didn't read at all—so, perhaps, he just wanted to protect his brother, Rorry's memory, as well as his father's.

So, it took me a while to gain Hiram's confidence. I talked with him about his dead wife, who had passed away just a few months before my talk with him. We talked about how much his wife meant to him, especially after Rorry died—he spoke to me about how his wife saved him from a deeper depression, and from wanting to kill Cooley himself.

It was then that I pressed him about how he felt about Cooley, and about if he really intended to kill Cooley as revenge for what happened to Rorry.

Hiram said, yes.

He told me that he began to obsess over Cooley in much the same way that Rorry had before. It had happened rather suddenly for him—he told me, when Rorry was killed, he didn't initially think about wanting revenge. He said it was never something on his mind at the time. He had just wanted to give his brother a decent burial and figure out what life thereafter was going to be without Rorry. He told me that he often thought, at first, that he was to blame for what happened to Rorry, and that, maybe, if he had talked Rorry out of it, Rorry wouldn't have gone to Cooley's looking for a fight. He told me how often he tried to convince Rorry about trying to kill Cooley would be nothing more than trying—that, in the end, Cooley always find a way to kill whoever wanted to kill him. He told me how he told Rorry that all of this—this whole Cooley thing—would never amount to anything, and that none of it was worth anything in the end.

I asked him: did Rorry really believe that he could kill Cooley?

Hiram told me that Rorry did believe it. Somehow, Rorry believed, Hiram said, that he could succeed where others had failed. For Rorry, Hiram said, it was a matter of catching Cooley off-guard.

I asked: so, was that what Billie was for?

Hiram said, yes.

Hiram told me that Rorry had planned the whole thing for days. He said that Rorry would talk it through out loud—Rorry would reenact what he thought Cooley might do if this or that happened, and about how Rorry figured Billie would be a good distraction. Rorry felt, Hiram said, that it was impossible to just square up to Cooley one-on-one— Rorry knew that he wasn't that good of a gunfighter as much as he knew that Cooley was. So, Billie, Hiram told me, would be something that could lure Cooley into a confrontation.

I asked: did Big Sam know anything about what Rorry was planning?

Hiram told me that he didn't think so. If Big Sam had known, Hiram told me, Big Sam would have certainly tried to stop Rorry. Big Sam would have talked Rorry out of it. Big Sam was the kind of guy that knew how to talk reason into Rorry's head in a way that even Hiram himself couldn't. So, Hiram was sure that Big Sam didn't know—for that matter, Hiram told me, Big Sam took Rorry's death pretty hard, and Big Sam was never the same after that.

I asked: what do you mean?

Hiram told me that Big Sam blamed himself for what happened to Rorry. Big Sam felt that he should have known what Rorry was planning to do, and, because he didn't, Big Sam believed he had let Rorry down. Big Sam felt that he hadn't been a good friend, since a good friend would have known—even if Rorry didn't voice anything—what Rorry could have been up to. Then, Hiram told me, there was the shock of seeing Rorry get killed the way he had—that, Hiram told me, was something that Big Sam couldn't' get out of his head. Big Sam, Hiram told me, took that memory all the way to the very end.

I didn't know what he meant by that, so I asked him: to the very end?

Hiram told me, yes. Big Sam hung himself from a tree behind his mother's house. Big Sam's mother found him hanging there from that tree—the same tree Big Sam used to climb as a kid—one morning barely a week after Rorry was killed by Cooley. Hiram told me that Big Sam didn't leave as much as a note or anything. In fact, Hiram told me, he and Big Sam had had drinks the night before.

I asked Hiram if he remembered seeing anything about Big Sam that night before, which, in hindsight, told him, now, that Big Sam was thinking about committing suicide.

I remember how Hiram looked at me. It was the look I often get when I realize that I have asked too many questions and pushed too far. It was the look that I always tried to prevent, because I know that it prevents me from having the access that I need to the facts I require. In this case, Hiram told me something that was quite profound—it was so profound that I never forgot it.

Hiram told me that death doesn't work that way. Hiram told me that death is like everything else: it just happens. Either it happens to you or to someone else. It's always about who is doing the living or who is doing the dying—that was what kept Cooley going, Hiram said, all Cooley cared about was who was doing the living and who was doing the dying. For Cooley, those that do the killing take themselves out of it—those that do the killing decide who is doing the living and who is doing the dying. That was

Cooley's way, Hiram told me—it was this kind of way that kept Cooley above everyone and everything else. It was the thing that made Cooley a God and all the rest of us spending our days wondering who would be doing the living and who would be doing the dying. It was just that, Hiram told me, that moved Big Sam to commit suicide—for Big Sam, Hiram told me, it was about snatching that power away from Cooley somehow, so that Big Sam wouldn't be just either doing the dying or doing the living. For Big Sam, the idea of killing himself—the thought of being the one doing the killing—was probably the happiest feeling in the world. When Big Sam set his mind on hanging himself, Hiram told me, it was probably the moment when Big Sam believed he was doing what would bring him more peace than getting revenge.

I could tell, dear reader, that Big Sam's death still affected Hiram. Maybe, it was the thought of what Rorry's death did to Big Sam, or the idea that Hiram himself could have done to himself what Big Sam did to himself. There was certainly a deep regret there, I will say. I remember how Hiram shook his head, thinking about how much Rorry meant to Big Sam—but I think, too, he was thinking about Rorry.

It was then, when I thought to ask Hiram about Billie, since I began to wonder whatever happened to her, particularly after Rorry's death. It occurred to me that Billie had disappeared from this whole story about Rorry—so I asked Hiram if he knew anything about Billie.

Hiram told me, dear reader, that Billie was his deceased wife.

I thought to ask Hiram more about that, since I didn't know that Billie had married Hiram somewhere along the way. It made sense to me, true, given how much of an effect Rorry's death had on Billie—some say that Billie never forgave Cooley for what he had done to Rorry and that Billie cussed Cooley out over the whole thing later the same day of Rorry's death. It is my understanding that Billie quit working for Cooley, too—the story is that Rorry's death had been one too many for her, after all the years she had seen Cooley kill others at the bar. Rorry had been the last straw for Billie, I suppose. I guess it is safe to say, then, that Rory's death brought Billie and Hiram together—I don't have to tell you how grief brings people together.

Still, I thought to ask Hiram about how he and Billie got together after Rorry's death. I thought to ask, then I changed my mind. I saw the pained look on Hiram's face, since, after all, his wife's death was still fresh and raw. So, I decided to not go there with him.

14

Actually, the reason why everybody was staring at the guy that came into Cooley's Bar that rainy night wasn't exactly because any of us were scared. It wasn't even about thinking we'd seen a ghost risen up from the grave as a spook of the past haunting the people of the present.

You see, we all stared on account of the fact that the guy that came waltzing into Cooley's that rainy night, wearing a long black overcoat and a hat with the brim pulled down low over his eyes, was an Indian.

Don't get me wrong, it wasn't as if none of us had ever seen an Indian before— because, I think, we all had, and probably, for that matter, too many times to count. It was because we'd never seen one come into town before. And it wasn't on account of seeing one come into an establishment as trafficked as Cooley's—Cooley's being a bar where there are more drunks with hot heads that would love to be cooled off by putting a few bullets into some wandering Indian than you could possibly shake a stick at. Just for the hell of it.

I can't really speak for everyone else that was in the bar that night, but I know all of them, one way or another, well enough to know that none of them hate Indians or anything. They're not prejudice, I mean.

It's just that when you have enough run-ins with blood-thirsty Indians, it's hard not lumping them all up into one big fat group. Maybe that's what being prejudice is—I don't know. But, it's probably easy to make them into one big fat group of yelping monsters riding horses bare-backed, shooting bows and arrows with their faces painted and their hair all grown girlishly long.

But, this Indian that came into Cooley's that rainy night didn't look at all like any of the typical Indians we'd happened to run into from time to time out in the prairies or in the mountains. This Indian was different.

Like I said, for one thing, he was wearing regular clothes instead of the buffalo-skinned boots and a customary flimsy loin cloth over his groin we'd normally them wear. This one had gone up to the bar where Cooley stood behind wiping out a glass as usual—Cooley watched the new customer with a curious, kind of suspicious eye. The Indian climbed up on a vacant stool directly in front of Cooley and asked Cooley in the most proper English—and probably a lot better brand of English than any of had ever used ourselves—I'd ever heard, if he could have a shot of Whiskey.

Me and my buddies Buck and Ford were sitting at a table nearby when we'd heard the Indian ask Cooley that question, and saw the look Cooley shot at him. It was the kind of strange look none of us had ever really seen before. It was the kind of look that told all of us—if it didn't exactly tell the Indian anything—that there was probably no way in hell that nicely-dressed, civilized Indian was ever going to get a shot of Whiskey from Cooley in a million years. It was the kind of look that said that the only way the Indian was going to be served as if hell froze over and pigs decided to sprout wings and fly, that is.

"I think you'd better turn yourself right back around," Cooley told the Indian, still wiping out the glass he'd been wiping when the Indian had come in.

I remember how Cooley's voice being more sarcastic than ever.

Then Cooley said directly, "And get the hell outta here. We don't serve injuns in here, injun."

Me, Buck, and Ford all glanced at each other, the three of us knowing that, eventually, one way or another, that Indian—*injun*, as Cooley pronounced it in his sometimes slurred English—sitting up there on the stool believing he was going to get a drink was going to get a drink alright, not any Whiskey, but from the dirty trough out front more than likely.

And, since the Indian kept sitting there like he was, all three of us had a feeling something bad was about to happen. We could feel it—the fancied-up Indian was about to be roughed-up and thrown out, if not killed first out right.

Because, if there was anything the three of us knew, as we got up from our table in a hurry and cleared out of the way just as everybody else in the bar had done, it was that Cooley had quite a temper if you riled him up enough. We knew that if Cooley told you to get out and you didn't, then something dreadful was bound to happen.

But, apparently, the Indian didn't see the potential of trouble happening.

I guess the only thing that probably crossed the Indian's mind was that a guy as old as Cooley—pushing at least sixty at the time, and so feeble-looking you'd think, if you didn't know any better, that a stiff wind would blow him away—couldn't hurt a fly.

It was kind of funny, I remember thinking, how the Indian looked across the counter at Cooley and said:

"Get outta here?" What? Are *you* going to throw *me* out, old man?"

When I say that was funny, I don't mean what the Indian said was exactly funny. It wasn't even funny to see the expression of rising horror I'd glanced on Alice the waitress's face. What was funny, I think, was the expression Cooley had on his face—it was an expression that told everybody in the place that knew Cooley and his exploits well enough to see Cooley temper was about to reach the critical point, and that that Indian was going to see just how un-feeble a guy as old as Cooley really was.

That's when Cooley started laughing. At that time, Cooley turned his back on the Indian sitting on the stool at the counter—Cooley put the glass he'd been wiping out down on the little table behind the bar.

It was then that the Indian looked around the bar, once over each of his shoulders, seeing how everybody had cleared out of the way, seeing that everybody—including me and Buck and Ford who looked downright scared enough to make me wonder if the dark spot spreading on the crouch of his jeans was on account of him peeing on himself in fear—look ghostly scared, badly frightened, and downright mortified.

I remember how the Indian swung his confused stare in my direction, locked his eyes on mine. He saw something in my eyes, I suppose—whatever it was, it scared him enough to make him look back around at Cooley.

It was then that Cooley brought out the shotgun that he always kept behind the bar. Quickly, Cooley leveled the two barrels on the Indian's two eyes, and the Indian froze where he was seated. Everything went so still, I'm sure the toes of a rat could be heard scurrying over the floorboards.

"Either you leave now," Cooley told the now terrified, but well-dressed Indian. "Or, I'll blow your goddamn head off, you damn injun."

Cooley couldn't see what we could see just then, which was the Indian trying to slowly, gradually, carefully, nice-and-easily reach for a gun holstered at his hip somewhere beneath his overcoat—but, I suppose, Cooley surely knew this, at least enough to say what he ended up saying, I mean.

"Don't even think about it, you filthy injun," Cooley barked in a calm voice, one eye closed and the other squinting down the length of the shotgun sights. "I swear by sunny Jesus, I'll blow your fucking head off, right here and right now."

But, I suppose, either the Indian didn't believe Cooley was serious. I guess the Indian, somehow, thought, one way or another, that he was quicker on the draw than Cooley would be. With Cooley being such an old man, the Indian probably believed that he had Cooley outmatched—the Indian was probably half of Cooley's age, at least, and probably believed that that difference mattered quote a lot. When it came to who could draw the fastest, the Indian probably believed there was no way it wouldn't be him—I say that, because the Indian went for his gun.

Drew his gun, the Indian did, probably about as quickly as any man could hope to draw his gun.

But, it wasn't as quickly as Cooley pulled the shotgun's trigger, though.

I wish I could tell I was surprised. But, I wasn't—not in the least. I guess, if there was anything that surprised me was how much the Indian over-expected what he could do and under-expected what Cooley could do. It surprised me, too, that Cooley even let the Indian draw his gun at all—I don't know if Cooley either over-expected or under-expected what the Indian could do, because all I knew, at the time, was that clicking sound.

That's when Cooley blew the nicely dressed Indian's head off his neck and shoulders, when the Indian's head exploded in a way that reminded me of what happened in the warwhen we were kids and used to put firecrackers inside pumpkins we'd partially hollowed out, so the pumpkin would explode from the inside out. It made me think about the war when I saw, on the battlefield, a man's head get blown to bits by a cannonball.

Bits of bloody flesh and dust from shattered skull sprayed everywhere, smoke from the barrels of Cooley's shotgun hovered like a thick fog over the Indian's stub of a neck and the blood-soaked shoulders of his black overcoat. The Indian's hat flew across the bar and landed near where me and Buck and Ford were all squatting behind a table we'd turned over to protect ourselves, just like everybody else in the bar did at the time.

Alice, Cooley's waitress, let out a shrieking sort of scream that made my ears pop so loudly I thought I was going to lose my hearing or something. Alice was screaming, as if it was the first time she'd ever heard a gunshot, when, I knew, she'd probably heard more than her fair share working at Cooley's over the years.

Ford, seeing the cowboy hat that had been on the Indian's head land near us with its inside full of blood and a crescent shaped hole blown out of the front brim, yelped something about being tired of Cooley and Cooley's temper. Ford had had enough of Cooley and the thought that Cooley killed so easily. Ford had a point, you know. Ford understood, I think, that, even if Cooley was the law of Sleepy Eye, there was a line that shouldn't be crossed, which Cooley crossed all the time. There was this sense of what should be right and what should be wrong, which Cooley didn't care about—Ford had come to the point, just as I had, that Cooley was playing god. Cooley was always doing the killing, another friend of mine would always say, while the rest of us is either doing the living or doing the dying. In the end, it wasn't enough to simply hope you weren't the one doing the dying. For Ford, that wasn't enough—it wasn't just about making sure, when it came to Cooley, that someone else was doing the dying. Ford didn't want to live like that, I guess. That was why Ford went on and on, just then, about how he was never ever coming to Cooley's again, even if Cooley's bar was the only place in Sleepy Eye where you could go to have good drink and a good lay with a whore under the same roof.

I guess, for Ford, even if he was fed up and realized that Cooley's killing of the Indian was going too far, he had to figure out what was it worth to make sure you were always the one doing the living.

Buck, on the other hand, let out a laugh that both surprised me and made me suddenly start laughing myself, even though there was nothing to laugh about. Once the smoke cleared, we both stopped laughing—I don't even know why we were laughing at all. I guess laughing was a way to make everything seem less real. I don't know. I remember how the Indian's now stub of a neck and the blood-soaked shoulders of his overcoat was there for everyone in the whole bar to see in all its ghoulish horror—I knew none of us would ever unsee that.

You see, everyone could see that Cooley had, in fact, literally—though we all wished to God it would've only been figuratively—blown the Indian's head off.

I know what you're thinking. When you hear something say that—that someone's head was blown off—it's easier to think that all of that is just made up. It's easier to think that something like that couldn't happen—or that, even, something like that can't happen. I guess what I'm saying is that, yes, it does happen—things like that happened more times than I care to remember, during the war. I guess, for me, it was about believing that only in war do things like that happen—when you see a man's head get blown off. For me—and for Ford and Buck, who had both fought in the war, but on the other side from mine—you don't expect seeing it in a place where you are supposed to have a good time, a good drink, and a good whore. I always came to Cooley's to forget about all the memories—all the bodies piled on the battlefield.

Speaking of bodies—the Indian's body kept sitting there on the stool facing the bar counter. It was, I remember wondering, as if it didn't know it was headless and was, now, supposed to fall over to the floor like headless bodies are supposed to do when they're disconnected from the brains that control them. But, then again, having seen the strange things that dead bodies do, it's impossible to make sense of any of it. Given that the head was gone—which I saw a time or two on the battlefield—bodies can have a mind all their own, I suppose.

Cooley lowered shotgun—it still smoked a bit from the barrels. He gawked at the body with the same kind of horror the rest of us had.

Though Cooley's eyes were as wide as two saucer plates, I knew he wasn't as scared as the rest of us. Cooley wasn't the kind of guy that got scared of anything, I suppose. If anything, Cooley was probably wondering how long the body would stay propped up on the stool the wat that it was—I was sure Cooley, despite all the experiences he had had doing the killing and had always been the one doing the living, had never seen anything like that. That surprised me—to think that, despite all the things Cooley had done in his life, and despite how he had done all that living by doing all the killing, this was new to him.

That's when Cooley saw, just like we all could see—and sometimes, the whole thing seems more like it was nightmare than it was actually something that really happened in real life—the Indian's headless body get up from the barstool. I shit you not. The body stood up and turned shakily towards the doorway—the same doorway the once-headed Indian had come in not ten minutes before. The body, you see, turned towards that doorway with, the jagged nub of neck glistening with blood from the stump—it took a couple of steps, the headless body did, in the direction of the doorway, as if there was still a head with two eyes on it that could see where it was going.

But, the thing was, we all knew it couldn't see where it was going. We all knew that headless bodies aren't supposed to walk on their own if there's no brain to direct them and if there's no eyes in front of that brain to see where in the world they're going. We all knew that, you see. But, you'd be surprised what dead bodies can do, even the headless ones.

That's when Alice suddenly screamed again.

But, it wasn't because she had looked down and saw blood from the Indian's blown-off head splattered all over her dress—since she chose to just stand there instead of duck behind an overturned table like the rest of us had wisely done—but because the headless Indian's body had raised its arms up shoulder-high and the fingers on the hands splayed-open, and it began reaching for Alice.

Alice stood there—it was if her feet stopped moving.

Cooley re-cocked the shotgun again right around that time.

I shot my eyes at him towards Cooley, watching Cooley aim somewhere at the legs of the headless body. Cooley aimed carefully, as the body slowly walked toward Alice, who kept screaming all the while still standing in the same place where she'd stood in the moments before the Indian's head had been blown off.

Cooley, then, shot the headless body's right leg out from under it.

Blood and fragments of flesh and who knows what else sprayed across the floorboards of distance between the headless body and where Alice was standing frozen and screaming.

A nub halfway up the thigh was left behind.

The headless body just toppled over to the hardwood floor on its side—it went down hard and fast, with a thud.

With most of the right leg from a little above the knee down blown completely off—only flecks of leather from the boot and material from the pant leg and bits of what was probably bone and red matter likely flesh all littered over the floor beneath where the body fell--you'd think that the body would stop moving. At least, that's what I thought, anyway. I thought that it would die once and for all, done and done you might say.

Right?

But, we couldn't have been wrong about that—especially me.

Sure, the Indian was dead—and had been dead, as far as I'm concerned, from the moment Cooley had blown his head off—but the headless, and now right legless body kept, somehow, moving.

Kept twitching, kept convulsing, kept shaking, and kept vibrating like a person going into shock or something—minus that right leg and the head of course.

But, eventually, as we all hoped, as we watched on in silent but rising horror, the dead Indian's body stopped moving.

That was around the time Alice finally put a cork in her high-pitched, annoying screaming enough to see that the body wasn't coming for her anymore. That was when we all were glancing at her as if she was the stupidest broad in the whole wide world, because she was scared of a headless and right legless body for no reason. Sure, we were all scared, I think. I don't mind saying so, even if none of the other men that had been there would admit it. Yes, I was quite scared. Even though I saw a lot of shit in the war, I was still scared. I'd like to think Cooley was, too—but, I think Cooley was taking it all in, somehow.

Indeed, we were all scared. We were just not scared enough to scream out loud, like Alice had. We screamed, I think, only in the inside where most men bury away all of their emotions and true feelings, so other men won't think they're pussies.

And, if there were ever any man that I would've thought would've surely been the rock while everyone else was falling all to pieces inside, probably so scared they were looser than the cunts of the whores Cooley kept upstairs, I would've figured Cooley would be the one.

Cooley was the one that wasn't scared at all—I remember how he wasn't of any of what happening.

I figured Cooley would just say something sassy, maybe do one of those one-handed cocks of his shotgun, and wink an eye at us and at the eliminated danger he'd just come face to face with. I figured Cooley would, perhaps, go right back to what he was doing, as if there wasn't a headless and right legless Indian dead on the hardwood floor just then. I figured, you see, that Cooley would just tell Alice to clean up the fucking mess.

But, I couldn't have been more wrong, I suppose. Even if I had known Cooley like I knew the back of my own hand, I was wrong. As much as I knew that the whores he kept upstairs had loose cunts, I was wrong about how Cooley was taking it all in just then.

Because that's when I could see—nobody else, I don't think, only me—this completely horrified expression stamped across Cooley's face as he looked down towards the floor towards the Indian's body. He was gawking at it as if whatever it was he could see it frightened him so badly that he couldn't take his widened eyes away from it and left his mouth all hung open in awe.

That was first time I'd ever seen Cooley so scared, so mortified, so utterly frightened, so completely horrified. As long as I'd known him, I had never seen like that.

But, once Cooley realized that I was watching him just then, seeing that very understandably human side to him that had otherwise been hidden behind a thick, coarse mask of courage stiffened in the face of more danger than any man could ever hope to see in their lifetimes, he got angry, I think. He was angry at me. So, he raised his shotgun back up, and pointed it at me.

"U gotta problem or sumthin, Hal?" was what he mouthed as clearly as if he'd spoken it out loud.

I glanced at Buck and Ford who were already looking at me, then at Cooley, then back at me again. I shook my head to what Cooley had asked, and mouthed, no, I didn't have a problem, didn't have a problem at all. What I knew, as easily as the Indian had known when he'd heard Cooley cock his shotgun and level the two barrels on the Indian's two eyes, was that Cooley would have not problems shooting me. Even if I was his friend, none of that mattered anymore—it probably never mattered to him.

I knew that, even if I'd known Cooley and he'd known me for a while and that I considered us to be pretty good friends, Cooley had no problems blowing my head off too. It didn't matter to Cooley. Even if it was just to keep anyone from knowing that he'd ever been scared of anything—even if it was of an Indian that had kept moving after his head had been blown off to smithereens—Cooley was more than willing to kill me.

You see, when you're like Cooley and you're not only the best damn bartender in the whole world, but you're also the only law in a town as small as Sleepy Eye, anyone knowing that something frightened you—even the least little bit—could make everyone eventually lose any confidence they might've had in your authority. And, you know, for Cooley, authority is everything—his authority, I think, is built on Cooley's history of always being the one doing the killing.

The same authority that the Indian came face to face with that rainy night, even if it was over something as stupid—I realize now, you see—as not serving him, the Indian, any Whiskey just because the customer asking for it was an Indian, just for the hell of it, and just because Cooley could, I guess.

You see, in a town like ours—this one-horse kind of town that Sleepy Eye was in those days—Cooley could do absolutely anything he wanted to do. That meant that Cooley could do all the killing he wanted to, even if that also meant being scared every once in a while.

15

Dear reader, there is certainly plenty to discuss about the account of Cooley killing an Indian, if for no other reason than because it displays, in an explicit way, a racist streak in Cooley's thinking. I don't think we can go too far in saying—even if by only surmising something broader from this incident—that Cooley's racist ideas were behind his not wanting to serve the Indian. Coming to such a conclusion seems obvious, as far as I am concerned, and, for that matter, it is safe to conclude that the incident doesn't represent an isolated incident, either. Though I can think of only one other account of Cooley rejecting serving a customer that happened to be non-white—this incident being a time when, some say, Cooley threatened to kill a free negro slave that came into the bar—it is clear to me that Cooley was what he was: racist.

I don't know what more I can say about that, given that Cooley once belonged to Silas Rondo's gang, and Silas Rondo's gang, as I write in the book on Silas Rondo, carried out a series of raids targeting Indians and free negro slaves, with the intent of exterminating them from various territories.

Just as I make clear about Silas Rondo, it is no secret that Silas Rondo saw himself as someone hoping to avenge the South after the war—for Silas Rondo, the best way to make things right was to get rid of the free negro slaves, wherever they didn't belong, and, for good measure, get rid of any Indian, wherever they didn't belong. If Cooley was part of such an enterprise—and, indeed, he was—we can certainly assume, dear reader, that Cooley believed in the same things that Silas Rondo did.

Still, there are plenty of rumors about Cooley participating in other aggrieved groups of men interested in rounding up Indians and free negro slaves attempting to settle families in particular territories, such as Arizona, Oklahoma, and Texas. Some say that Cooley personally killed an Indian family, shooting them one by one, including some very young children—the children, they say, had been saved for last. Others say that Cooley, along with two other aggrieved men, chased down a free negro man for dozens of miles across Nebraska, until the three of them caught the unknown negro, who had been on foot, and shot and killed him—those that tell this story also say that the three men used the dead negro for target practice, before they cannibalized the body and burned the body parts in a bonfire.

I wish I could tell you that what I heard about the unknown negro is just rumor, and that the whole thing is nothing more than part of a mythology about Cooley.

But, I'm afraid it's not—that's because Cooley, some way, was proud of telling the story himself and always claimed that what he had in a large jar proudly displayed behind the bar was that unknown negro's right hand. Cooley had had the hand preserved with embalming fluid—it was preserved and put on display like a monument to something. I can't see it as anything else than a monument to a killing—and not just any killing, but a killing that Cooley was proud of.

I wish I could tell you that those that gave accounts of seeing that hand in a jar found what they had seen morally reprehensible—or even that remembering what they had seen was morbidly appalling.

The fact that none of them—any of the individuals that recounting what they had seen, who the hand once belonged to, how Cooley had come into the possession of it, and why it was in a jar—saw anything wrong with it says just as much about Cooley as it does the world we are living in, if we can say that it is a world that hasn't improved since the war, particularly in the regions of America that build on Cooley's mythology and always refer to the war to preserve the union as the war of northern aggression.

16

"Is this Cooley's bar?"

Since I'd been taking a nap in the rocking chair out front, I had my hat pulled down low over my eyes to block out the glare of daylight when the kid walked up. So, the first thing I'd noticed about him was how dirty his boots were. But, if that alerted me to anything, all it told me was that he'd traveled a lengthy, hell of a distance to get here.

"Yeah," I told him, rather curious why he couldn't see the big sign out front proclaiming this place as Cooley's bar, which was probably why I had a little too much sarcasm in my voice. "Can't you read, kid?"

Seeing him only from the knees down, I noticed he'd shifted his feet a little, almost as if he were pulling something out of his pocket. That's when I heard this clicking sound. Not only was it unmistakable, but it was something I'd heard enough times in my life to know exactly what it was without having to look up to be sure. Yet, I found myself looking up just to be sure, anyway. And when I did, let me tell you I was so shocked beyond words that I found myself shoot straight up in the chair as if I'd been struck with lightning.

"Can you read this?" the kid, looking no older than thirteen, asked me.

And, I *could* definitely read what he was showing me better than you could possibly imagine. You see, as I've always found things, whenever you got somebody pointing a gun at you that's got its hammer cocked, it's pretty hard not to read it for what it means, you know. There's no way you can possibly confuse what that obviously means with anything else.

"Hey," I told the kid, showing him my hands and hoping to convey the message that I was unarmed, finding my eyes glancing up and down the main street with the hope that somebody would see what was happening. But, what I realized was that, at this time of the morning, very few people were moving about. "I don't want no trouble, kid."

I showed him my hands. It was a customary thing to do. And anyway, I wanted to show the kid some respect, you see, even if he was nothing more than a kid. Because I was on the wrong side of the gun, and he was on the right side, that made all the difference.

"What's this all about?"

The kid said plainly, "Cooley."

"Cooley?"

"Yeah," the kid said.

He kept the gun pointed at me, just as steadily as he kept his finger on the trigger. He was cool.

The kid said, "This is about him. That is, unless you want this to be about you. We can make it about you, you know."

I kept showing the kid my hands, palms facing him, "I told you I don't want no trouble, didn't I?"

"Nobody ever really wants trouble," the kid said, beginning to start off on something that seemed far too philosophical for his limited years of life. "But they always get it just the same. And Cooley's gonna get his. And you just might get yourself in trouble, if you don't pay attention."

If I don't pay attention? How could I not be paying attention when I'm the one on the wrong end of a gun?

I just looked up at him, wondering what kind of grievance he had with Cooley, anyway. That, of course, and if he actually had the wherewithal to put a bullet in my head all because I might have smarted off to him. As much as I liked Cooley and thought of him as something of a close friend, perhaps a good enough friend to not wish he got a bullet put in his head, I had to think about myself. I had a wife and three children to worry about, and I knew my wife would be pretty pissed off if I messed around I got myself killed in front of Cooley's so early in the morning by some kid no older than thirteen.

"I'm paying attention," I told him.

My voice was about as shaky as the two hands I held up palms facing him.

I told him, "Just don't hurt me, okay?"

That's when the kid smiled for the first time. If he smiled because he'd thought about how much control he'd had over the situation between us or if it had been something else entirely, I couldn't tell you for sure. All I can say is he smiled. Though there were a couple front teeth missing, the kid, otherwise, had a swell smile. As swell as it was, he was still holding a gun up to me, and that made the smile all the more spookier than anything else.

"You know what?" the kid said. "I like you. You're alright. I guess I might just let you live for the heck of it."

Though I didn't say anything, I thought to myself: *Gee, kid. So glad you're being so fucking gracious to me.*

"You know why I'ma let you live?"

"Why?" I asked the kid.

"I'ma let you live because I need somebody to live on to tell my story. To tell everybody about how I'd killed Cooley," the kid said, still smiling, still showing all those missing front teeth as proudly as anyone would show off a mouthful of pearly-whites. "That's what's gonna make me famous all the world over. Maybe even more famous the Wild Bill."

"I wouldn't put the carriage before the horse, kid," I told him. "You gotta kill Cooley first. And it ain't like he's gonna let you just walk up in there and shoot him dead. Cooley's an old fart, but he's a smart old fart. He's got a hell of a lot more experience with a gun than you do. And, believe you me, kid, you aren't the first somebody to come here looking to send Cooley off to his maker. Every man that's ever tried at one time or another have all ended up getting sent to graves earlier than they would've liked."

The smile slipped away from the kid's face as easily as I've sometimes seen the nightgowns whores wear slip from their bodies to the floor once you give them however much they cost for one night of fun. What replaced it was this stark, almost disgusted look, the kind of look someone would give you if they thought the world was flat and you told them it was round.

"Feller, that's before I done come along," the kid told me. Without that smile, his face looked older than his years, and said, "And you're gonna help me."

"What if I don't wanna?"

"Then you'll die right here and now," he told me, and though I wanted to keep telling myself that this was just a kid, that this kid couldn't possibly have any balls to actually shoot me if need be, that this kid probably didn't even know how to use a gun whatsoever, I found myself all the more scared just the same. I found myself so scared I didn't say another word.

"Unless you don't wanna die," the kid told me. "then you'll take me to Cooley, alright."

"And what do I say, if he asks me who you are?"

The kid smiled, "You seem like a smart, learned feller. I'm sure you'll think of something smart and learned enough."

I sat there looking at him as if he'd spoken Spanish instead of English. You could say that I was probably more scared at that particular moment than I'd been thus far. And, I think I was much more scared about who I was going to tell Cooley this kid was than I was about the chance of getting shot dead.

"So, you lead the way," the kid told me, making a subtle gesture with his gun that subtly meant he wanted me to get up out of the rocking chair now, which I did. "Good. Now you go on ahead, alright."

Rounding the rocking chair once I stood up out of it, I headed toward the doorway that went into Cooley's bar. Just before I walked through those double doors, I stopped for a moment, thinking about what kind of chance I had at making a dash for it and exactly what kind of aim the kid was capable of if I did.

"Don't even think about it, feller," the kid said, poking the end of that gun of his into the small of my back. "Let me assure you that, though I look young, I don't shoot like no young'un."

He didn't have to assure me anymore. I was certain, somehow, that he was one of those kinds of gunslingers that could shoot a tick off the ear of a horse running at fifty yards. Why did I think him to be that good? I don't know. I guess you just feel things like that in the pit of your stomach until you're sure what you're feeling is much more than just butterflies, until you're absolutely certain that what you're feeling isn't just some petty inkling.

So, I went on through the double doors, and inside Cooley's bar with the kid close on my heels with his gun pressed into the small of my back.

This was early in the morning, you see, and Cooley's bar was pretty much deserted. Cooley's bar wouldn't be packed with customers until sometime around noon. So, at this particular time, the bar was empty except for Billie, Cooley's waitress, who was walking around wiping tabletops. The old man himself, Cooley, wasn't behind the main bar cleaning out glasses, or even sitting at the piano on the far side of the bar playing tunes.

"I don't think he's here," I told the kid.

"Don't gimme that," the kid hissed in close to my ear. His breath stiff with alcohol of some sort. "I know for a fact that he's here somewhere. He's here. Take me to his back office."

Back office? I found myself wondering how in the world did the kid know Cooley had an office in the back. Did that mean that, somehow, the kid had been here before? Did it possibly mean that the kid was much more to Cooley than just somebody with a bone to pick, someone with a grudge that they needed to have settled one way or another?

I didn't know. I just did as I was told.

With the kid huddling close behind me, we walked further into the bar until Billie noticed us. She looked up from the table she'd been wiping, threw me this warm smile as warm and friendly as the smile she threw to the kid just over my shoulder.

"Hey, Hal," Billie said. "Who's your friend there?"

Though I knew Billie would ask me about who the kid was before she even as much as opened her mouth, but I found myself just as unprepared as if she'd completely blindsided me with that question. I found myself between wanting to tell Billie that this kid wasn't any friend of mine and that he wanted to kill Cooley and knowing that, if I'd said what first came to mind, not only would I get a bullet in the back of my head, but Billie would get killed as well.

Hedging a little at my words, I told her, "This is my little cousin. He's looking for a job. And I told him and take him to see if Cooley had anything."

Billie said, "Oh."

There was this look on her face that told me that she didn't believe me. It was this skeptical look telling me she figured something was wrong in the way the kid was hugged close into the back of me, and how I probably had a nervous, uncomfortable expression on my face.

"He's in the back, isn't he?"

Billie looked from me to the kid, then back to me again, "Yeah. He's back there. Counting the money from yesterday."

When she looked at me, I could tell she was asking me with her eyes if everything was okay, if I was in any kind of trouble, and if there was anything she could do to help.

"I'll just take him on back there," I told her, using my eyes to tell her, subtly, that she'd be better off not getting in the middle of any of this. "You can go on about your business, okay."

"Yeah," the kid said. "go on about your business, bitch."

If there was anything Billie hated more, she hated being called a bitch. It was uncalled for, very tacky, and ungentlemanly, and there wasn't a single time that went by, as far as I knew, when she didn't tell whoever had called her that to fuck off. This time, however, was the only time when Billie stayed silent, perhaps because she knew the situation at hand was a touchy one.

So, Billie just went about her business. Well, not completely and not all that quickly because she watched me and the kid walk around to the back of the bar to Cooley's office. She stood there at the table she was wiping about as frozen as a statue.

Heading to the doorway to Cooley's office, the door was cracked a bit and I could see inside just a little. He was in there, alright.

"You're going in first," the kid told me, pushing me lightly ahead. "You introduce me to him the same way you did to that bitch out there, okay."

I nodded

I drew my hand ahead and knocked on the door.

"Yeah?" came from inside. Cooley's voice thick and hoarse from the many years he smoked cigars and drank whiskey straight out the bottle.

I pushed the door open. There, behind his desk, Cooley sat, counting money just as Billie had said he'd be doing. The old man looked up at me, threw a look over my shoulder at the kid, and looked back down at what he was doing, completely unfazed by the stranger.

"How's it going, Hal?" Cooley asked me, briskly thumbing through the bills like a bank teller. "What's on your mind? Who's your friend there?"

"Um," I started with this frog momentarily snagged in the wall of my throat. This frog I had to clear out before I could continue with what I wanted to say. "This is my little cousin, on my wife's side. He's interested in seeing if you got any jobs available."

Cooley looked up at me again, glanced at the kid just over my shoulder whose face had completely come into the light by then, and looked right back down at what he was doing.

"Is that right?" the old man asked. "He's looking for a job, is he?"

"Yeah," the kid said, moving around from behind me to beside me.

Cooley asked him, "What's your name, kid?"

That's when the kid chuckled for no apparent reason just before he'd pushed me aside, charged toward the front of Cooley's desk, leaned over his desk, and pointed his gun into Cooley's calm and collected and unfazed face. "I'm the Grim Reaper. I've come to collect, you son of a bitch."

Cooley calmly set down the money he'd been counting, and one of his hands disappeared into his lap underneath the desktop. He looked up into the kid's dusty face smeared with dirt such that it looked like he'd had a five o'clock shadow of a beard. If Cooley recognized the kid from the past, one way or another, he didn't particularly show too much recognition in the expression on his face. If anything, Cooley acted so calm, and collected, and unnerved that I wondered if he recognized the kid at all.

"I must say," Cooley said, cracking this smile that seemed about as out of place at this particular moment as the town pastor paying a visit to the whorehouse. "I thought the Grim Reaper would be a hell of a lot older."

As much of a joke as it was, the kid didn't think it was all that funny.

With the hammer still cocked back, the kid said, "This is for what you done to my momma."

And, before I knew what was happening, there was the explosion of a gunshot, throwing thick white smoke everywhere, concentrating between the length of space from where the kid was standing and Cooley was seated.

I blinked my eyes, covered my ears with my hands, and huddled over a little in the corner of the office. When my eyes opened up completely and I peered toward the fading smoke, just as I was beginning to think that Cooley had got shot dead the kid just as the kid had told me he'd wanted to do, the kid's body fell to the floor across this broad space in front of Cooley's desk.

Immediately, I saw this spreading spot of blood right smack dab in the center of the kid's chest, soaking through his white shirt.

Billie came in screaming from outside, and stood in the doorway, "You okay, Cooley? Everything all right?"

Cooley stood up from his desk. The smoke was clearing quickly and I could see he had a revolver in the hand that had disappeared into his lap. He came around to the front of his desk, stood there for a moment at the feet of the kid dead on floor, and looked down at the body.

"Yeah," he told Billie. "Everything's fine. Just go back to work, okay."

Billie shrunk away from the doorway.

Cooley stopped her, "Wait. Go get Hank, will ya?"

Billie's eyes were large. You could tell she didn't want to go get Hank—nobody liked talking with Hank, the undertaker, mainly because Hank was so creepy, and he was always more concerned with business than the respecting dead.

Yet, Billie did as Cooley asked.

I could hear Billie walking away, nervously. Someone asked her what happened in there, and what those gunshots were all about. Billie told them it was none of their business.

Then, me and Cooley were alone, with the dead kid on the floor—I remember how his eyes were staring into that great beyond. I wondered, then, what the kid was seeing then, and that, since he was just a kid, he would never see anything else in this world ever again.

"You know him," I asked Cooley. "I mean, you knew him?"

Cooley looked up at me, "Yeah. I guess you could say that."

"What does that mean?"

Kneeling down beside the kid's dead body sprawled on the hardwood floor, leaning over the body, and reaching over the kid's face to gently close the kid's wide-open eyes, Cooley told me, almost sadly: "He was my son."

17

Unfortunately, dear reader, I have found that there are quite a lot of stories about men coming to kill Cooley. There are so many stories that it is impossible to know if any of them hold true—in other words, based on the sheer number of times I have interviewed witnesses that say that someone came to kill Cooley one day, it remains largely difficult for me, as a historian and a biographer, to make any sense out of it all. There remains only this word of mouth about it—still, I haven't found much evidence to support it.

In a way, it seems to me that there were plenty of people that would have wanted Cooley dead. There were plenty of different reasons, yes, but there is no doubt in mind that Cooley always had a target on his back for most of his life—if it is possible to say that Cooley probably made someone angry enough to look for him, I can only assume so, dear reader.

Some say that Cooley lived the kind of life where he was always the one doing the killing and others were generally doing the dying—that brought Cooley a lot of enemies. I have tracked down a lot of stories about Cooley's exploits—stories about men gunned down, incidents when women were shot dead, and even rumors about children being shot in the head. With so many of these stories out there in the ethos-sphere, dear reader, I must say that I wonder which ones are true, which are simply embellished, and which ones are totally false. Those are the only three options, since, I admit, I have found it very difficult to believe that Cooley has killed all the people he is said to have killed—for me, as a historian and a biographer, as someone that is deeply interested in the facts and finding out where the facts will lead me, I wonder how much myth has found its way into the larger narrative about Cooley.

I don't have to tell you, dear reader—especially if you have read my previous work—how easily truth can be blurred by myth. Everything always begins with truth, and that truth becomes the foundation for any narrative, and that narrative becomes what others tell others about, as a way to not just capture what the narrative is, but also what is at the very heart of that narrative: truth. That's why we—as humans—tell stories. We want to—as humans—make truth transactional, so that truth can be experienced by everyone equally. We want—as humans—to feel the same truth that someone else once felt. We want others to experience the potency of that truth that lies at the heart of a narrative, with the hope that that narrative can be packaged and shared easily—the whole purpose, I believe, is to tell stories that can effectively bottle an experience in such a way that the truth in it is clear. But, often, things are not as clear as we wish them to be— often, what we experience becomes these murky things that will not allow themselves to be explained in a way that makes sense. Often, what is experienced will not translate into the kind of narrative that we think will completely represent what must be represented— in this case, what is experienced is not always what is represented, and what is represented is not always the truth.

It is here where I think myth comes into the play—it is myth that fills in the gaps in what is experienced, what is represented, and what is rendered possible in a narrative, so that mythology itself becomes a stand-in for truth.

Every historian and biographer—including yours truly, of course—tries to strike the best balance between what is truth and what is myth. Some might describe it as a delicate calibration between truth and myth—the way to measure which historians and biographers are successful is with respect to how well one handles the ambidextrous demands of both truth and myth. Both are important to what it means to tell the story—there is always some form of truth and some form of myth that informs any subject. If we are each the subject of our own narrative, we deal in truth and myth all of the time, dear reader. Because of this, truth and myth become interchangeable ideas—it is not so much about the truth being what we tell ourselves and myth being what others tell us, but it is also, perhaps more importantly, about how myth becomes what we tell ourselves so that truth becomes what others tell us.

One of the tasks of any historian or biographer—with present company included, of course—is not allowing myth to overshadow the truth. That is actually more difficult than you think, because it is easy to enhance myth for the sake of making a narrative sound better than it is to handle truth in all its messiness—that is why, I believe, myth is tempered by truth, but truth does not, if you will, completely overshadow myth.

I have often believed that myth plays a role in storytelling. That is what I do—I am a storyteller, just as any historian or biographer will tell you. Writing any narrative about people and the events of their lives requires understanding where the line is between myth and truth—if you want anyone to read what you write, you see, it becomes imperative to know what that line is, and know, dear reader, how to balance between the demands of the two. Indeed, it is easy to simply write about every single salacious thing about any given person's life and embellish every subsequent event, for the sake of making sure your audience is firmly enthralled. I know this too well. There is always this seductive quality to myth, which any writer—worth their grain in salt—would love to exploit. I am sure you would agree, dear reader, that a narrative is more interesting the more exclamatory it is—in other words, I am sure you wouldn't want to read about the mundane day-to-day drone of someone's life. You wouldn't care to know about the monotony of daily life, and about the human experience in all its boredom and blandness, and about the thousands natural shocks, as Hamlet says, that flesh is heir to—if I am to accomplish anything, it would be to present you with the best illustration of what can be known, why certain things are important to know, and how you are to absorb what is given in its totality.

I say all this—and forgive me for not arriving at the point sooner—to say that, regardless of where one places the line between myth and truth, everyone must negotiate a set of facts. Every life lived is comprised of facts—these little stubborn things that accumulate over time. President John Adams was the one that said that facts are stubborn things. What makes them so stubborn—facts—is that they are unavoidable. Facts are the building blocks of life, you could say. Facts, once they are collected, have a way of helping us locate the line between myth and truth, because facts only take us so far from the truth and only reach so far into myth—facts are the great equalizers for any historian or biographer, since facts, dear reader, become the great compass that leads all historians and biographers. Essentially, because facts guide us like a great compass, facts are things by which we measure what a life was, how a life is understood, and why a life mattered.

In my experience, dear reader, those three questions must always be posed, if any historian or biographer, not just present company included, wishes to investigate any particular life—in this case, Cooley is certainly no different.

It seems to me, then, that the best way to sum up Cooley in terms of what his life was, how his life is understood, and why his life mattered is through the notion that he spent his life making sure he was the one doing the killing and others were the ones doing the dying. That is one thing I know for sure—in making sure that Cooley was always the one doing the killing, his life, as best as I can determine, was defined by those that were doing the dying. That was, I believe, all that mattered to Cooley: who was doing the living, who was doing the killing, and who was doing the dying—nothing else mattered.

When you narrow down what can be known about Cooley—rather than what remains impossible to know for sure—to what his life was through killing, and how his life is understood through killing, and why his life mattered through killing, it becomes possible to develop a composite of the man. I admit, it is difficult. I admit, Cooley, as a subject, is extremely elusive. There aren't very many facts, to which a biographer, such as myself, can use to construct a meaningful biography—there aren't very many of the meaningful facts, to which a historian of any dexterity, can outline a meaningful chain of events. The problem, dear reader, is that the kind of facts that historians and biographers work with are missing when it comes to making sense of what Cooley's life was, how Cooley's life can be understood, and why Cooley's life mattered—these three questions, dear reader, remain difficult to answer. I don't say that simply for my sake, but anyone interested in Cooley as a subject—perhaps, that's why all histories can't be told any more than all biographies can be written.

I'm sure you are wondering, dear reader, why would I focus on a subject that defies biography? If there aren't many facts about Cooley's life—such as when he was born, where he was born, who his parents were, and so on—what reason would there be to continue with such a project? You might wonder, too—if I can imagine what you are thinking, dear reader—if there are certain subjects that are better off defying biography, if there are basic facts that remain unavailable?

If you are asking these questions, do know, dear reader, that I have asked myself these same questions—without facts to strike the necessary balance between myth and truth, how can someone like myself continue?

I know that one can glean only so much for interviews. I don't have any delusions about that—I never have, particularly when considering what the interviews say or do not say about Cooley. I know that what someone says about Cooley may be more myth than truth—I am aware, too, that I may be chasing someone that may not actually be real. Allow me to re-phrase that thought. For all I know, though I have no doubt that Cooley is a real person—that is to say, Cooley was born, lived, and died—there remains myth about Cooley conflicting with the truth of who he really was, which makes my mitigation of what really matters all the more difficult.

Indeed, though it remains impossible to precisely when Cooley was born or where he was born, and, even if it remains impossible to know precisely when Cooley died, there is no doubt in my mind that the events of Cooley's life exacted an influence on how Cooley died—in other words, the way that Cooley lived his life, as someone that spent a lot of time being the one doing the killing, certainly had a significant bearing on how he died.

It is this fact, dear reader, that makes it possible to continue with this project—it is the idea that, if I can trace all the various killings Cooley is said to be responsible for, there arises the possibility of separating the myth about Cooley from the truth of who Cooley really was.

One of the very first things I had ever heard about Cooley was, one day, a man came into Cooley's bar, wanting to kill Cooley—apparently, the man wanted revenge against Cooley for something Cooley had done in the past, during all that time when Cooley was always the one doing the killing and so many were the ones doing the dying. The story goes on with Cooley killing this mysterious man—a man that no one had ever seen before in town—with the mysterious man being identified as Cooley's son, by none other than Cooley himself. That was what Cooley is said to have done: he identified the dead man—the man he had just killed—as his own son.

In my view, though I have one person, on the record, stating that Cooley said this—that the man he killed that day was his son—I believe such an account is dubious. Granted, I don't mean to say, dear reader, that this report is intentionally untrustworthy. In fact, there is no doubt in my mind that the individual that told me what Cooley said certainly believed it to be true—that is, if this person claims that Cooley said that the man that he killed that day was Cooley's son, I don't doubt that this individual isn't telling the truth. My guess is that Cooley actually said this to this individual—what is dubious about it all, then, is that I don't believe Cooley was telling the truth at the time.

18

Nobody wanted to say anything about it, I think.

I mean, after all, it wasn't as if no one had ever heard one of the whores in Cooley's upstairs row of bedrooms, where you could buy a girl for a dollar-a-turn, go yelling out for God before.

So, it wasn't as if any of us had the slightest notion that what we'd heard wasn't a whore getting fucked three ways from Sunday. What I mean is, nobody imagined that a whore was getting killed up there.

I had been at the bar talking to Cooley about whether or not he thought it was going to rain. The sky was all cloudy and dark and the wind was kind of picking up—so I wondered if Cooley had any thoughts on it, since Cooley would always tell me he had a bad hip that would tell him if raining was coming. Then, that's when all hell broke loose—that was when I heard one of the whores up there screaming for God, just yelling out for God's help.

And, like I said, probably like most everybody else, I figured it wasn't anything to get all worried about since there would just about always be a little screaming up there. I mean, what do you expect? It wasn't out of the ordinary to hear a little shouting out for God Almighty going on upstairs, at least every once in a while, depending on how brisk the whore-and-hump business was.

Because, sometimes, there would be a lot of screaming and yelling and moaning and groaning and carrying-on, especially if the Beaumont Brothers came into town and spent sometimes as much as a hundred dollars between the three of them, taking three of Cooley's best whores out of the lot of eight, and go behind the doors of three of Cooley's five upstairs bedrooms, and sooner or later, that's all you were liable to hear—that screaming and yelling and moaning and carrying-on.

But, the thing was, the Beaumont Brothers weren't up there this time.

Instead, it was someone else. It was this quiet sort of guy with a hump in his back like Quasimodo—he shuffled his way into Cooley's without as much as saying any more than a few of words. Maybe he was shy—I don't know.

All he did was cross from the saloon doors, glance left and right, then make his way up to the bar. He asked Cooley something, Cooley pointed upstairs, and the goofy-looking guy shuffled his way away from the bar, glancing left and right again, maybe wondering if he was being watched or not, seeing he wasn't—or at least thinking he wasn't, even though I was watching him—and continuing to the foot of the stairs and carefully going up.

He kept taking all of these sideway glances out of the side of his eye. I saw him—his eye in one of those sideway glances found me over at a table drinking whiskey with

Dudley, one of our town's two dimwitted but often loveable deputies.

"Whatz dat fella lookin' at anyway," I say to Dudley, who just kind of shrugged his shoulders as if to say he didn't know and didn't care and didn't bother to see who or what I was talking about either.

Maybe it was the whiskey, or maybe Dudley had gone a little yellow, I wasn't all that sure right away.

But, what I was sure about was that it didn't take being a deputy to know when you see a fella all sleazy-looking watching everyone to see if anyone was watching him that something wasn't right about that, or about him, and that something bad might happen very soon.

"Don'cha think that fella looks right peculiar, Duddie?" I ask.

Dudley gazed up at me from across the other side of the table through a pair of drunkenly-hazed over eyes—he looked at me as if he saw three of me.

Dudley goes, "What fella?"

"The humped-over fella dat just come in," I say to those glazed-over eyes looking through me. "Went up and asked Cooley something and went upstairs. Kept looking all over the place as he did."

Taking another sip from the whiskey bottle Dudley had in his hands, his voice slurring as he asked, "So whut? He looked 'round a little bit."

"Don'cha think that's mighty strange?"

"No more strange than any of da other fellas dat go up there," Dudley said in a clearer voice, swaying from side to side in his chair. "What fella ain't a little embarrassed? After all, he'z buyin' hisself a whore, ain't he?"

I wasn't all that sure about whether or not the guy I'd seen go upstairs was actually upstairs to buy himself a whore or not.

True, he'd asked Cooley something and Cooley pointed upstairs, and that's normally how guys that have never been here before usually act, and a guy looking like him, a Quasimodo-type, a guy that probably couldn't get a girl on his own without buying himself one, certainly would be the type of guy looking for a respectable whore to let himself loose in.

But, there was the way he kept looking around the bar as he headed upstairs that bothered me. There was something about it—how he kept his hands in the pockets of his large overcoat, how he looked as if he was up to no good, as if he might be going upstairs to see a whore but probably wasn't going upstairs to actually buy a whore for an hour like anyone else that might go up there.

"I don't think he'z buyin' a whore, Duddie," I told Dudley, who right about then had stepped both of his feet across the threshold of drunkenness, still swaying back and forth in his chair, holding onto his bottle of whiskey, and banking harder to one side until I knew what was about to happen.

Dudley fell out of his chair and landed on the hardwood floor with a thick thud. His bottle of whiskey—only a third left—was still clutched around the neck and spilling over his chest. Dudley was laying there passed out.

"Duddie?" I asked, standing up and gazing at him lying on the floor, looking at his eyes flustering half-staff and all the whiskey soaked through his shirt. "Duddie?"

But, Dudley was passed out cold. He was never much of a drinker as long as I'd known him—he couldn't hold his liquor even if his life depended on it. And now, the same thing was true: he couldn't keep himself sober and on the job any more than he could see that the guy I watched go upstairs to see a whore wasn't going up there to buy a whole but to probably hurt a whore, maybe a whore that had laughed at him because he couldn't stay up or his penis was too small or something.

That's when I and everyone else in Cooley's heard the whore upstairs scream out for God to help her.

I looked around the bar, wondering if anyone else figured that maybe the whore was in trouble up there, and that the whore wasn't screaming out from ecstasy's pain but was actually screaming out the pain of being punched or kicked or maybe having a gun poked into her face or something. What I mean is, it wasn't a good kind of screaming.

Like I said, nobody wanted to say anything right about then, everyone just went about minding their own business, playing their card games and drinking their liquor and talking amongst themselves, acting as if they didn't hear the whore screaming upstairs, acting as if they wanted to ignore what was going on upstairs, acting as if they were more than comfortable in their own little worlds without wondering what was going on inside the world of that upstairs bedroom between the whore and the Quasimodo-looking fella that had gone up there moments ago.

Except, Cooley.

Cooley was standing behind the bar, I remember seeing, but had his eyes looking towards the stairwell that led up to the upstairs bedrooms.

Having set aside the shot glass he'd been wiping out with a handkerchief, Cooley leaned over and grabbed something from behind the bar. But, before he brought up what I knew he kept behind the bar in the case that some cowpoke with a chip on his shoulder decided to come into his bar and start trouble, I had my revolver drawn from the holster I always keep strapped at my side—I had that revolver not because of the possibility of trouble going on in Cooley's, but on the account of trouble in general.

Cooley chambered two slugs into the shotgun and walked out from behind the bar heading to the bottom of the stairwell.

I met Cooley there and asked him, "Whutchu gonna do?"

Cooley looked at me with those old eyes of his that had seen all sorts of things in his past probably dozens of times worse than the Quasimodo that had gone upstairs.

"Preteck my investment," was what Cooley said, giving me a wink of the eye, the Winchester shotgun he'd had for years with its barrels up. "Kan come along if U want."

And, I did want to come along, not because I wanted to help Cooley, as he said, protect his investment—his investment being all the whores he kept upstairs and sold for twenty dollars and go—but because I didn't particularly like the jib of the fella I'd seen go upstairs, and certainly didn't like the thought of him hurting a whore, even if she was a whore.

Cooley hurried up the stairwell with me right on his heels, while all of the other people in the bar—and Bille, the waitress—kept minding about their own business, as if the scream they'd heard upstairs wasn't anything to get worried over, and as if a scream like that was the same kind of scream that you'd always hear up there from time to time.

But, just like Cooley, I knew this scream was different. I knew that the whore wasn't screaming out in ecstasy—she wasn't screaming out because old Quasimodo was really banging her three from Sunday up there, but because she was actually in distress.

When we'd made it up to the top of the stairs, the whore stopped her screaming and there was nothing but an odd kind of silence that worried me, and probably worried Cooley too, since Cooley stopped at the head of the stairs and looked back at me as if to say *I hope she ain't dead, I hope he ain't killed her.*

All I could think about, looking into Cooley's eyes, was that if he had killed her up there. I thought, he didn't use a gun, because there hadn't been any shots, and there was only the sound of her screaming. That probably meant, I figured, that if he was killing her up there, Quasimodo was using his hands, or maybe a knife.

Cooley continued on, following along the banister railings running by the row of upstairs bedrooms—all the bedroom doors were open except for the one at the very end of the walkway. Me and Cooley passed each of the open doorways along the way, glancing inside each.

But, it was hard for me to just glance inside the open doorways of the bedrooms along the way, because inside every bedroom we passed, a whore was inside, either half-naked or completely naked, and making eyes at me as if they wanted me to come inside, puckering their lips at me.

You can bet that a large part of me wanted to go in any one of the those bedrooms, and wanted to lay any of those whores down on the bed in the center of those rooms, and have a go at it in there, even if I'd have to pay Cooley twenty bucks and know inside that whichever whore I ended up with had probably been with dozens and dozens of guys and that all I'd ever be to the whore I was with was a customer.

It was thinking about all those things that kept me focused on the task at hand, which was seeing what was going on in the bedroom at the end—it was the bedroom that had its door closed and had fallen silent inside, a bedroom where a whore and Quasimodo were inside doing who knows what.

Cooley, in a shooter's crouch, eased his way up to the outside of the bedroom door. Even though Cooley was at least fifty—or maybe older than that, I can't for sure—probably suffering from rheumatism and arthritis in his hands and knees, he could still handle that shotgun of his as good as any man half his age, and he was just as fearless nowadays as Cooley had been when he was younger, when Cooley had been one of the baddest cowpokes that always, somehow, ended up as the one doing the living while others were doing the dying.

I can't say the same about myself, though, even though I've been in a few fistfights here and there in my day, and broke a few bottles over a few heads every so often, and maybe shot my gun at somebody to keep myself from getting shot. What I mean is, Cooley had a lot more experience than I did.

But, unlike Cooley, I never killed anyone before.

Cooley—well, I don't think Cooley knows for sure how many men he's killed before, but I'd like to guess that it's probably somewhere up there with the number of guys any one of his whores have had sex with over their lifetime of whoring around.

So, standing outside of the bedroom at the end, I knew that Cooley was probably going to rack up another notch on his belt in a few moments, and that whoever the guy was that was inside the bedroom with the whore had better be good with the big man upstairs because he'd likely be playing his harp pretty soon. I could feel it—knowing Cooley as well as I did, I knew for sure who would be doing the dying that day.

Cooley knocked on the door to my surprise—just twice.

There was no answer inside, not from the whore or Quasimodo.

Cooley looked back at me as if to say *what do U think's goin' on in there, Buster?*

I shrugged my shoulders at him.

My eyes were probably as wide as saucers, just then. I know my heart pounding away in my chest hard enough to make me wonder if, even if I was only eighteen at the time, I was going to have a heart attack and just die right then and there, keeled over on the hardwood floor.

To say that I was scared is probably the biggest understatement in the whole wide world right at that moment. To say that I wasn't sure if I'd even be able to shoot my revolver if the chance presented itself is also probably the largest understatement ever. And, to say that I'd probably pee in my pants before I'd pulled the trigger—well, that's an understatement too.

But, Cooley on the other hand, he was cool and calm and collected as always. He was no more scared at that moment than I'd ever seen on any number of occasions when some cowpoke would walk into his bar looking for trouble.

Cooley knocked on the bedroom door again, harder—three times, this time.

This time, there was the sound of a gun chambering inside—just the soft click of a hammer being pulled back.

Cooley waved at me to stay back, or maybe his wave of the hand meant he wanted me to get ready—I don't know.

I wasn't completely sure what his wave of the hand meant, so all I did was stand where I was in my own shooter's crouch. I made sure I just a little back and away from the doorway, but not too far back. I was scared, but I wasn't yellow, if you know what I mean—my main thing was I liked living and didn't want to do any dying that day.

That's around the time when Cooley got impatient and, before I knew what was happening, he kicked the outside of the door so hard that the door crashed open in splinters, breaking away.

Cooley jumped into the doorway with his shotgun drawn and aiming inside where he shot off a slug that licked a brief flame out of the end of the barrel—the gunshot popped like a firecracker, smoke immediately filling up the doorway and wafting out just above Cooley's head as he squatted down, and looked inside.

He hurried in once the smoke cleared a little

I followed in behind him, wondering what was happening, and wondering if Cooley had shot the guy that had a hump in his back like Quasimodo—knowing that there couldn't have been anyone else inside that he could've shot.

Through the doorway, coughing at the smoke, peering inside at the little bed in the center of the room, I saw the whore laying naked on the bed. Her throat had been slashed so deeply from ear to ear that she was may as well have been decapitated from the way her head was awkwardly-angled backward into the pillow—that pillow and the sheets were soaked full of blood.

My stomach gurgled and I could feel myself almost throw up, but, somehow, I held back what wanted to come back up my throat.

Cooley hurried around the bed, giving the dead whore laying there a curious but not quite investigative glance, and squatted down to the floor on the other side of the bed.

It was right about then when I looked up at the window on the other side of the room from the bedroom doorway, and saw the broken out hole in the window that had blood splattered over what was left of the windowpane.

On the shakiest pair of legs in the whole wide world, I walked inside, and walked around the front of the bed. For a moment, I couldn't take my eyes off of the dead whore laying in the bed with her neck slashed and her eyes gazing lifelessly up at the ceiling— she looked like she seeing the great beyond, for all I knew. Then, saw the whores clothes littered on the floor at the foot of the bed—just panties, some frilly-laced bloomers, a petticoat, a pair of stockings, and stuff.

Then, on the floor on the other side of the bed where Cooley squatted, I saw the guy that had come in Cooley's—yes, there he was: that Quasimodo that had had his hands in the pockets of his overcoat and kept looking around the bar as he made his way up the stairs after asking Cooley something at the bar.

Cooley had shot Quasimodo right through the center of the chest, and the revolver Quasimodo had chambered a bullet in before Cooley kicked the door open had been thrown off to the side. The knife he'd used to cut the whore's throat sticking its handle of out his inside overcoat pocket.

I didn't know what to say as I looked on, watching Cooley search the dead guy's pockets. I didn't know if there was anything that could be said at a time like that. But, somehow I ended up asking with something caught up in my throat, "Why would he kill a whore, Cooley?"

Cooley, still rummaging through the dead guy's pockets, said, "Can't say. Guess he wuz an unsatisfied customer."

I don't know if it was what Cooley said that made any difference. What I mean is, with the dead whore and the dead Quasimodo guy, what Cooley said didn't make me feel any better. It told me, I think, that Cooley didn't care about the dead Quasimodo any more than he did about the dead whore—I think, for Cooley, it was always about who is doing the living, who is doing the killing, and who is doing the dying. That was always the only difference that mattered to Cooley—everything else was meaningless.

19

Dear reader, if you have heard of the book, *The Hunchback of Notre-Dame* by Victor Hugo, you will have certainly heard of the name "Quasimodo"—just as Quasimodo, the main character of Hugo's novel, was shunned due to his deformities, so, too, was the life of the man that everyone in Cooley's place called "Quasimodo." Some say, of course, that the name was given to the man—who's name remains largely a mystery—by someone that had read Hugo's book, given that the man is said to have had a hunchback and one eye larger than the other.

When I first heard about this Quasimodo person, I admit, I wondered if the descriptions of his appearance were just exaggerations. I don't know about you, dear reader, but I have never seen anyone with Quasimodo's characteristics in real life. A novel is one thing—it is an entirely different thing to say that it is possible for someone with Quasimodo's description to exist beyond the pages of fiction.

Yet, the fact that the Quasimodo story—and how his appearance has been frequently described—came to my attention in several interviews, beyond the account I provided, leads me to conclude that there was, indeed, someone fitting that description.

Why he was in a town like Sleepy Eye remains unknown—that is, I was unable to uncover what precisely brought him to the town in the first place. It's also unclear, dear reader, if the man they called Quasimodo had a family, or if he had any friends—I would assume he had neither, given that, according to various accounts, he frequented Cooley's bar everyday—all day, in fact—seemed like a loner, and stayed in the town hotel on something of an extended-stay agreement with the proprietor. Just how long he stayed there, I can't say—some say the man called Quasimodo stayed in the hotel for months, while others say it had been for years. However long the man called Quasimodo stayed there in town, I haven't been able to determine it precisely—what is clear, dear reader, is that, though the man called Quasimodo was well-known around town, he remained a complete mystery to everyone. It had been said, too, that he mostly kept to himself, and that he wore the same black suit, black boots, and black Stetson, and that he charged the same items from the general store on his account the beginning of each week and promptly paid-off his store account at the end of each week, and he would pay his hotel bill weeks-in-advance. No one ever came to visit him and, from what I was told, the man they called Quasimodo never received any incoming mail from the regular stagecoach— yet, it has been said that he routinely sent telegrams to someone in New Jersey, though it is remains unclear who the recipient of those telegrams was. There were plenty of rumors circulating, at the time, about the man they called Quasimodo possibly coming from a wealthy family back east—in New Jersey, as it has been claimed—and that was the source of man's money. Having that kind of money, you can imagine, was notable at the time—and it was especially noted by all the customer's that frequented Cooley's, because the man they called Quasimodo liked buying Cooley's whores, typically on a charge account.

From what I have been able to determine, Cooley wasn't the kind of proprietor that worked on credit, nor had charge accounts. That wasn't Cooley's style. For Cooley, generally speaking, it was always about having the money at the moment that services are rendered—that was how Cooley ran the bar and how he ran the whore-house.

So, the idea that the man they called Quasimodo had a charge account with Cooley was highly unusual—what was even more usual, dear reader, is that Cooley kept that particular charge account a secret, even from most of his whores. The only way I found out that Cooley had had such an arrangement with the man they called Quasimodo was from papers "Quasimodo" left behind—Quasimodo kept detailed notes about who he paid, when he paid them, and how much—in which "Quasimodo" writes how much he owes Cooley at the end of each week for the whores. Apparently, from these papers, it seems that "Quasimodo" only paid Cooley for whores, and never for anything from Cooley's bar. "Quasimodo" even made it a point to name each whore and how much each whore charged, and how many times each week "Quasimodo" visited each given whore—like I say, dear reader, the man they called Quasimodo kept very detailed records and not just about Cooley's whores, but also about everyone else he owed money to, and when he paid them, and how much it was at the end of the week.

The arrangement the man they called Quasimodo had with Cooley was obviously different. I don't have to tell you how different it is to pay for a room at a hotel, or pay for things at the general store, or pay for an occasional shave—paying for whores is altogether different.

One of the most important things that made the arrangement different is that, as I have mentioned, Cooley never told most of the whores about this arrangement beforehand. There is no doubt in my mind that Dolly—Cooley's main whore, or what you could call the head of all of Cooley's whores—knew about the arrangement. It was Dolly that the man they called Quasimodo generally visited two to the three times a week, according to those detailed records from "Quasimodo"—because "Quasimodo" wasn't paying Dolly directly, and since customers always paid their whore directly, Cooley would give Dolly her cut of the trick. In Dolly's case, though, Dolly, I am told, worked out a side arrangement with Cooley, so she could get a larger cut for doing "Quasimodo"—this, too, was kept a secret from the other whores working for Cooley.

As you can see, dear reader, not only was it a secret that the man they called Quasimodo had an arrangement with Cooley, but it was also a secret that Dolly had her own arrangement with Cooley on the side—all of this became a problem the day the man they called Quasimodo ended up being the one doing the dying.

"Yeah," Dolly once told me. "It became a big problem."

I was interviewing her, once upon a time, at her home. We were sitting in rocking chairs on her front porch, and the porch overlooked a fenced-in area where Dolly's husband—a guy that had once been a regular trick himself, and wasn't much of a talker about Dolly's past—was tending to the cows. Dolly had a couple of small children running about—both were probably no older than five, and both looked like they hadn't had baths in a long time. As for Dolly, I remember looking at her and wondering how someone like her—a fairly decent-looking woman, though her appearance, at the time of our talk, told me that she hadn't always been a house wife—spent so much of her time whoring and, in particular, whoring for Cooley.

I asked, "Because of the arrangement Cooley had with him? Was that what the problem was?"

"No," she told me. "Cooley and I had arrangements like that, from time to time. Not all the time, you know, but sometimes."

I nodded.

"You see," she went on. "there was a reason why the guy was called what he was called. You know what I mean?"

I told her, yes, I knew what she meant. But, I wanted to make sure we were om the same page on that account. "The hump he had?"

Dolly laughed.

I didn't know what was funny. What I mean, of course, was that I knew what it was that she found so funny, but I knew that the fact that the man they called Quasimodo had a hump like the Quasimodo from Hugo's book wasn't something humorous. That hump, I had discovered, was a source of ridicule for the man, according to his writings. How he was physically was what, I believe, brought him to Sleepy Eye—it seemed to me that he was hoping to get away from that same laugher Dolly had.

"The hump, sure," Dolly said. "But, so much more than that."

I knew what Dolly was beginning to speak about, because I knew there were a lot of reports about Quasimodo's appearance. Some say he wasn't fully human—and that he was part-beast of some sort and kind. Some tended to make even wilder claims about what Quasimodo's hump was religiously and what his appearance meant theologically—perhaps, it is best to not give these more fanciful and creative assessments any more credence than I already have. Suffice it to say: the town pastor thought Quasimodo looked the way he looked because he was cursed by God—the thought was, you see, that Quasimodo had and was the biblical mark of the beast.

"Do you mean about Quasimodo being damned by God?"

Dolly looked at me, with a dry smile, "Mister, do I look like I give a fuck about God?"

I can say, with some certainty, that Dolly certainly didn't look like someone that cared about God, or about the Bible, or about church, or about piety.

Dolly went on, "Lookie here, Quasimodo was the ugliest guy I ever did see. That hump wasn't half of the problem. The man smelled like shit. His breath, his dick— everything smelled, you hear me? He smelled like complete shit. Horseshit, you know? Have you ever smelled a horse's shittings? You know what I mean? What that smells like? You know, right? Well, that's what Quasimodo smelled like—like horseshit. The moment he took his pants off, you could smell it. You know what I mean? Like a complete shit, you hear me?"

I remember listening to her and watching her variety of facial expressions. I remember marveling at how moderately beautiful she looked, and how disgusting her mouth was—I don't know why I expected more from her, given her long career as a whore, and yet, I was taken aback.

So, I nodded—I nodded to what she said about how horrible horseshit smelled like. But, mostly, I just let her ramble, with the hope she would say something interesting and useful.

One of the most important things I learned as a biographer, dear reader, is to listen. I have often found that if you give an interviewee just enough space and time, they will say something more profound and significant than anything you can imagine asking them. Sometimes, letting them talk gains insight—Dolly was the kind of person that needed to talk, since I knew right away that she didn't have the faculties to answer any complex questions.

I listened as Dolly went on and on about how horrible Quasimodo's body odor was, and how she had felt like she was going to throw up the first time she gave him oral.

She talked about how Quasimodo's face was uneven, like one side had melted down, while the other remained fixed in place. She talked about how Quasimodo would smile at her—he had teeth missing in the front. She talked about how he had long hairs dangling from his nostrils and out from his ears. She talked about how his clothes were always nice and his shoes were always shined to a high gloss. She talked about how Quasimodo's eyes would attentively watch her whenever she did whatever she did for him on any given trick—his eyes always looked like the trick was more than just a trick to him. She talked about how Quasimodo told her he loved her during that very first trick, and that he managed to say it each and every trick thereafter.

"It was creepy, you know," Dolly said. "I didn't know what to make of it."

She paused for a moment, looking at her husband across the way.

I did the same.

She pointed to her husband, "He's the only other man that ever told me anything like that. You know?"

"Do you mean during the trick? Or, after it was all over?"

"During," she told me. "I guess that's why it's so creepy." She pointed to her husband again. "He's the only other man that did that. It was a nice thing, then. But, when he did it—" This time, I could tell she had shifted to talking about Quasimodo. "It creeped the shit out of me."

"Why?"

Dolly said she didn't know—that it was hard to explain.

"Is it because you didn't think Quasimodo meant it?"

Dolly shrugged her shoulders—for a moment, she fixed her eyes on one of her children running by, watching the child trip over their own feet, fall awkwardly, then rebound. "I'm not sure. Maybe that was the creepy thing: that I knew he did mean it."

It seemed to me, dear reader, that Dolly felt ashamed of something. I couldn't put my finger on what it was—but I could tell that it was something about knowing that Quasimodo loved her, however he did, which made her feel uncomfortable about it, somehow.

Dolly went on to explain how, once Quasimodo told her that he loved her after that very first encounter, she could tell that he was only falling deeper and harder for her as time went on. She could tell all too well—and, given that she never saw him as anything more than a customer, it only made things more uncomfortable for her. But, as Dolly said, money was money. And, Quasimodo was a good paying trick—Cooley was getting his, Dolly was getting hers, and, at the end of the day, Quasimodo was getting his, too. For Dolly, everyone was getting what they were getting, so she tried to not think too much about whatever feelings Quasimodo had for her.

"I think it was better that way," she told me. "I just didn't want anything to get in the way of the money."

I wanted to ask her, now, in retrospect, if she felt as if she had been more concerned about Quasimodo's feelings. Sure, maybe at the time, when all she was concerned about was, as she said, getting hers, Quasimodo's feelings didn't matter all that much—I guess, frankly, in that kind of business, generally speaking, feelings are never a part of the broader equation. But, now, I wondered if she thought of things differently—I wondered if hindsight, as they say, was clearer, especially after what happened to Quasimodo.

I decided not to ask any of that.

"But, eventually," I asked. "it did get in the way of the money, right?"

Dolly's face went flush, just then. I knew that she knew what I was talking about—somehow, even if I didn't specifically ask what I wanted to, I knew I had asked the right question to get Dolly where I wanted her to be.

I asked, "Was that what caused a problem?"

Dolly's eyes avoided mine.

"Did Cooley know about Quasimodo's feelings for you?"

Dolly's eyes shifted towards her husband's direction. Her husband, who made it clear from the very beginning—from the moment I arrived—that he didn't want Dolly to talk to me, was watching. He was making his way towards us slowly, but methodically—the look on his face never changed, and that was that he didn't want me there. His reasons were a bit murky, but the most I could make out of it, dear reader, was that he didn't want Dolly to be a part of anything that had to do with Cooley, even if Cooley had been dead for some time now.

Instead of answering me, Dolly threw my question at her husband. She shouted to him, with a point of the thumb at me, "He wants to know if Cooley knew about Quasimodo's feelings for me?"

Of course, I was taken aback. I had come there to interview her—and her husband wasn't part of the interview process. But, I went along with it.

I suppose I figured something good would come of it, since, as I have often believed, when gathering information about a subject, there are always things you plan for and things you do not. Indeed, there are always particular questions that you wish to ask a specific person with the hope that the answers you get are meaningful, and there are always unforeseen questions that are asked of people that you believe can't possibly contribute anything meaningful. These were the things that went through my mind, as Dolly brought her husband into our discussion.

"Quasimodo?" He asked.

"Yeah," Dolly told him, glancing at me. "He wants to know about Quasimodo, and what Cooley knew about it all. You know what I mean?"

Her husband drew closer to where Dolly and I were sitting. I saw a smile break across his face, and his eyes peered carefully at me.

He asked me directly, "I thought you said you wanted to talk to Dolly about Cooley. That you are writing about Cooley, right? But, Quasimodo? What's he got to do with anything?"

I told him that I was trying to collect some facts about Quasimodo's death and figure out why Cooley killed Quasimodo.

"Yeah," Dolly's husband laughed, and squatted on his hunches on the far side of Dolly's chair. "Cooley killed him alright. He sure did. Shot that poor man dead, for no reason."

Dolly interjected, "Murdered Quasimodo, he did."

Her husband said, "Yeah, murdered him. That's what it was—in cold blood."

"Yeah, in cold blood."

"It was always in cold blood," Dolly's husband said. "Cooley never had a good reason for killing—I mean, murdering anyone."

I asked Dolly's husband if he had been there when the incident happened.

"Yeah, I was there."

Dolly interjected again, "Yeah, he was there."

"I was in the room next door."

"Next door?"

Dolly jumped in again, "He was in the room next to the one that me and Quasimodo were in. He was with Amanda, at the time."

"Yeah, that's right," her husband said. "I was with Amanda, at the time, when it happened. Amanda was the big-breasted one."

"But, you ended up with me, though," Dolly interjected, with a smile.

"Yeah, I did," her husband said. "But, I was one of Amanda's regulars. I had Amanda two or three times a week, back then. It seems like every time I was making my Amanda-visit, Quasimodo was making a visit to Dolly."

Dolly looked my way, "Every time."

"So," her husband said. "I saw Quasimodo quite a lot. I never really said anything to him. I didn't want to, you know. I was there to get my rocks off, so I didn't care who else was there to get theirs."

"And with Amanda, too," Dolly laughed.

"I didn't know you then," her husband said. He turned to me, "I didn't know anything about Dolly for a long time, you see. I had known Amanda for quite a while. I'm talking way before she started whoring for Cooley—I knew Amanda back in Arizona. Anyway, me and Amanda had a deal—just basically a business arrangement, I guess."

"That's what he says," Dolly interjected to me, "I think it was more than just a business arrangement."

"Well, it was—that's all it was."

"Amanda told me herself that they planned to get married one day."

"She did not."

"Yeah, she did—she told me that."

"Well, that ain't true, and you know it."

Dolly looked at me and rolled her eyes.

I decided to jump in, so I could redirect the discussion to what I wanted to know more about—I wanted to know what Dolly's husband witnessed, with respect to Quasimodo's death.

"You were saying you were next door, when it all happened?"

Dolly's husband paused, and then said, "Oh, yes. That's right. I was next door with Amanda. That's when all it happened."

"That was when Cooley came upstairs," Dolly said.

"Yeah," her husband said. "And, you know, Cooley never came upstairs like that. And not when the bar was packed—and it was packed that day."

I asked why Cooley came upstairs.

Dolly and her husband glanced at one another, sharing a look that I couldn't completely read.

"Because of me," Dolly said. She was looking down in her lap and at her hands, as she kneaded them. "Because of me," she repeated.

I told them that I didn't understand.

"Let me," her husband told her. "You see, Quasimodo didn't have the money that day, right? Right, Dolly?"

Dolly nodded her head.

"Quasimodo wanted Dolly to let him pay on the next time."

I remember thinking that I knew what he meant. Still, I wanted to be sure, so I asked, "What do you mean?"

Dolly's husband shared a look with Dolly, and he said, partly to her and partly to me, "Like—what do you call it?"

"One on the house," Dolly said.

I asked them, if Quasimodo wanted a charge account like the others he had with the hotel, the general store, and the barber—Quasimodo kept records of all of these, detailing how much he owed which place, writing when he promised to pay back which people, but never noting if he had actually paid them back. My instincts, dear reader, was that Quasimodo never paid his debts. It seemed to me that, though Quasimodo had the money to pay his change accounts, for some reason, he didn't always do so.

Dolly nodded, "Yeah."

"And Cooley wasn't having that," her husband said. "Cooley wasn't having any of that, at all."

"But, I had to tell him," Dolly said. "Cooley told me to."

"Cooley?" I asked.

"Yeah," Dolly said. "Cooley told me to let him know if Quasimodo tries to pay later, like he done with everybody else. If he—Quasimodo—asked to pay later, Cooley wanted to know."

"That was when it happened, you know," her husband interjected.

Dolly nodded to that, and said, "When Quasimodo didn't have the money, I had to let Cooley know."

"She had to."

"I wish I had made sure before," she said. "You know, I should've made sure before. But, I didn't think about it. He had never asked to pay later before—he always had the money when the trick was done."

"It's not your fault," her husband said, then looked at me. "It's not her fault, but she blames herself sometimes. She thinks, if she had known Quasimodo wasn't going to pay when the trick was done before the trick got started, she could've told Quasimodo that Cooley wasn't going to let him pay later. She thinks she could've warned Quasimodo, and could've kept what happened from happening."

She paused a beat or two.

"I know I could've," she said—I will never forget how sad she looked.

She paused again.

"I could've warned him," Dolly said. "I know I could've told Quasimodo that there was no working it out with Cooley, once Cooley had his mind set."

"Yeah," her husband chimed in. "Once Cooley had his mind set, there was no changing it."

Dolly said, "Quasimodo thought he could work it out with Cooley. That he could change Cooley's mind, I guess. That Cooley would just let him pay later."

According to Dolly, once the trick had finished and they—her and Quasimodo—were redressing, and once Dolly realized that Quasimodo wasn't going to pay for services rendered, as he had successfully done countless times, Quasimodo stepped out of the room.

"He was getting ready to leave," Dolly said. "And Cooley was already watching from downstairs."

"Cooley was always watching," her husband said.

"Yeah," Dolly said. "Cooley was always watching from somewhere."

"He was at the bar, right?"

Dolly glanced at her husband, then said to me, "This time, Cooley had been at the bar—from there, he was watching when Quasimodo stepped out. I was right behind him."

She, then, began to describe the hand-signals that she and Cooley had with one another, which would let Cooley know that payment had been made and the trick was done. Apparently, this was a hand-signal that Cooley had with all of his girls—there were hand-signals letting Cooley know about payment being made, but also hand-signals letting Cooley know if there was a problem.

Dolly said, "I signaled to Cooley that there was a problem."

"And I was finishing up with Amanda at the time," her husband said. "I stepped out the other room just after Quasimodo stepped out of his. Of course, Amanda signaled to Cooley that I was good-to-go, you know."

"Yeah," Dolly said to her husband. "You stepped out and blocked Quasimodo's way."

"I nearly ran right into him."

"Yeah, you nearly ran right into him."

"That's right," her husband said. "So, I say—to Quasimodo, I say—pardon me, mister. My fault."

"And Quasimodo didn't say nothing to you, did he?" She asked him, though it was clear to me that she already knew the answer to that question.

"Nothing," her husband said. "Just nothing is right. The bastard just looked at me. Just looked at me, he done. Didn't say shit."

"I don't think it was on account of you," Dolly told me, but glanced my direction. "He heard Cooley move, remember. That click, when Cooley moved out from around the bar—when Cooley grabbed his shotgun, remember?"

I could tell, just then, when Dolly's husband began to remember the sequence of events. He said, "Ah, that's right. I forgot about that."

Dolly turned to me, "Yeah, Cooley got his shotgun. You see, Cooley always kept a shotgun behind the bar. It always there just in case—that shotgun. Did you know that? You know that already?"

I assured Dolly that I knew about Cooley's shotgun behind the bar.

Dolly continued, "Okay, well, anyway, Cooley grabbed his shotgun. It clicked, whenever he did. You know what I mean? That clicking sound?"

I nodded.

"That was how you would know, you know," Dolly said. "That when you would know Cooley was coming."

Dolly's husband nodded. "I heard it and I knew too."

Dolly explained that, upon hearing the clicking sound of Cooley's shotgun, Cooley made his way quickly from behind the bar, through tables and chairs with people drinking and carousing, and over to the stairs that led to the upper floor with the row of rooms where the whoring took place.

"Everyone in the place knew something was about to happen," Dolly said. "Guys were dropping to the floor, ducking behind tables overturned."

Dolly's husband said, "I ducked back into Amanda's room."

"Amanda screamed, too."

"She surely did," her husband said. "I pulled her back into the room. I told her to shut the fuck up and get out of the way, so I could close the door."

"I ducked back in my room, too."

I asked, "What about Quasimodo?"

Dolly shrugged, "He just stood there, like a knot on a log."

"So, he didn't try to get away?" I asked.

"Nah," Dolly said. "I suppose not. When I closed my door, Quasimodo was still standing there. Like a knot on a log, you know. I remember how he turned towards Cooley, just as Cooley topped the stairs. He—Quasimodo—tried to say something to Cooley."

I quickly jotted down some notes.

"Then," Dolly said, taking a hard swallow. "Just as I closed the door shut, Cooley fired the shotgun."

I watched Dolly's face carefully.

"I'll never forget it, you know," she said. "What Quasimodo's face looked like, when Cooley blew his head off. I'll never forget that—not as long as I live."

"She has nightmares about it, still," her husband told me. "Just about every night, too."

"Yeah," Dolly said. "Just about every night. That's right. I just can't get it out of my head, you know—Quasimodo, trying to say something to Cooley, and then the sound of Cooley's footsteps rushing right up to where Quasimodo was standing, and then the shotgun barrels getting shoved right up into Quasimodo's face—and then hearing that loud pow."

I could see tears filling up in her eyes.

Her husband told me, "Amanda was screaming her head off."

"All that blood," she said. "If only I had closed that door sooner—all that blood. I can't forget how all that blood spattered everywhere."

"Everywhere," her husband chimed in. "All that blood ended up all over the walls and the floor. She and Amanda had to clean it up, too."

Dolly said, "Yeah, with Billie, too. Cooley made the three of us clean it up."

Though I didn't doubt that Cooley made Dolly, Amanda, and Billie clean up the mess left behind from Cooley having shot Quasimodo, or even that there was probably—more likely than not—a great deal of blood that required cleaning up, what I wondered, nonetheless, was why Dolly's story was so different from the other account I had already heard about the sequence of events leading up to the incident. For that matter, Dolly's husband had the same story. For both of them, they seemed to have a shared understanding about how Quasimodo was killed—I wondered, then, what the real story was, if theirs was so fundamentally different from what I had already heard.

I am afraid, dear reader, I don't know what to make out of it—I can't say for what exactly happened, particularly diverging with respect to where Quasimodo was shot and why. More specifically, what remains unknown, I feel, is if Cooley shot Quasimodo in the face, as Dolly claimed, or in the chest, as the only other account claimed, and what the reason was behind it all—if Cooley killed Quasimodo over Quasimodo wanting a charge account for the whores or if Quasimodo was killed because he killed a whore. In both cases, you see, whether we are talking about where Cooley is said to have shot Quasimodo, or why Cooley is believed to have done it, the two accounts are far apart on two fundamental points. Sure, it would be easy to just say Dolly's account is correct, or that the other account is correct, but that would be doing a disservice to one over the other.

As a biographer—one that is always interested in all the facts and where all the facts go—it would be unhelpful for me to say that Dolly's account is correct, or that the other account is correct. It would be unhelpful, too, to say what I think about Dolly's account, or even the other account—indubitably, it is best to let the two versions stand as they are, much like, frankly, how the four gospels present four versions of the Jesus's story.

The only thing that can be remotely certain, not just for me but for anyone interested in seeking the truth about what happened to Quasimodo, is that Cooley killed Quasimodo, and that the killing was just as violent as any of other people that Cooley killed, and that it was just as unnecessary as any other killing.

20

"Which one you say he was?"

"That one," I pointed. "The old man."

Frank asked again, following where my finger was pointing as best as he could. "Half the guys over there are old men. Which old man?"

"The one with the thin white beard," I told him, leaning in closer to him so nobody at any of the neighboring tables would catch a listen to what I was saying. "He's got his back to the wall. He's got a cigar in his mouth, too."

"Oh. That one."

"You see which one I'm talking about, now?"

"Yeah," Frank said, though there was a layer of uncertainty running just underneath the certainty he did his best to show me. "But, are you sure?"

"About what?"

"That that's really him."

I told him, after taking a drink from the bottle of whiskey I'd brought for myself, mostly to get the nerve up to do what I knew me and Frank were there to do, "I'm about as positive as I can be. That's him, alright."

"He's nothing but an old fart," Frank laughed, sipping from the bottle of rum he'd brought for himself. "That can't be Cooley. There's no way that that's Cooley. Why, that old, washed up fart over there probably couldn't hurt as much as a fly, even if he wanted to."

That was when I drew a couple chuckles of laughter under my breath.

"What? What's so darned funny?"

"Believe me," I told him, keeping my voice down low, even though I could feel all the whiskey really taking its toll on me. "Cooley's probably hurt just about any and everything that's done lived and breathed air on this earth at one point in time or another, other than our mama and daddy."

Frank went quiet for a long moment. For as long as I'd known him, I knew that whenever he went quiet like that, for any length of time, he was just about always thinking heavily about something. And, at that moment, while he took long sips from his bottle of rum, I could tell Frank was more than just thinking about something heavily but was, though I hated to admit it to myself since Frank was my brother, on the verge of losing his nerve.

"You ain't scared, are you?" I'd asked him flat out, taking glances in the direction of the old man with the thinning white beard that we'd come there to kill. "Because you had better not be, bro. That's all I know. Not after we'd come this far, you're not."

"I ain't scared," Frank told me, "I was just thinking. That's all. I was thinking if that guy is as bad as they say he is, what makes us think we can just mosey up there to him and kill him. He may be old, but he's dangerous. That's what they say, you know. I heard he's fucking dangerous."

I looked at Frank, as if he grew another head.

For the first time, since we embarked on this mission, I think, without question, he was losing his nerve. I was sure of it this time, even if I hadn't been before. Though I'd never seen him lose his nerve like this, I was positive it wasn't something I was imagining. And, as far as I was concerned, we'd come too damn far for any of that. We brought our guns, gone through the trouble of hunting Cooley down for the past two years, and had finally found him here in a one-horse town named Sleepy Eye running some two-bit bar. The longer I looked at Frank, the angrier I got knowing that the bastard that killed our parents didn't deserve to live, even if he was running a bar, and even if we'd have to kill him right in front of all his friends and customers. We were here on an even kill, and that was all that mattered to me, and nothing else.

"I don't give a rat's ass if they say he's dangerous," I said, my voice raising a little above a whisper to the point I drew glances from customers at nearby tables. "He's still a fucking man. He bleeds like we do, you know, and he's got to put his pants on one leg at a time, don't he?"

Frank didn't look all that sure.

"Well, don't he?"

Then, Frank said, "Hell, I know that."

"Then, why are you turning yellow on me?"

Frank slammed his mostly empty bottle down on the table, "I ain't turning yellow."

I could see, for the first time since we found out who killed our mama and daddy that he was really starting to get mad. Not angry, but downright mad. And that was good, even if I had to push him by calling him yellow. Though, I hated to play on something like that, something that you could trace back to when we were kids, I had to do it. I knew there was no better way to encourage him than by calling him the one thing he hated more than anything else.

"Okay." I told him. "Then after we finish drinking, we'll do it, okay? Whatdooya say?"

Frank nodded and downed another mouthful of rum. The rum was helping him get his nerve.

I did the same with my whiskey, and the both of us sat at our table watching Cooley ham it up like the bastard he was by laughing and yucking it up, and carrying on with his table of buddies. They were playing cards, drinking, and generally being assholes. But, even if you didn't know anything about Cooley, you could see he was the bright light among a constellation of dim stars. You could tell he was the loud-mouth of all loud-mouths, the kind of guy all the attention moved towards like he was the center of the whole fucking world or something.

As far as I was concerned, though I can't speak for Frank, Cooley looked like the kind of asshole that needed to be dead, the kind of creep that didn't deserve to be anywhere except in Hell, or worse. And, as much as I would've liked to kill him right then and there, as much as I would've liked to just go running up there to the table he was at and start gunning away like a madman, the best thing to do was wait for just the right opportunity.

Me and Frank sat there for another half hour, long after we'd finished our individual bottles of liquor, when just an opportunity presented itself. And that opportunity couldn't have presented itself in a better way than the way things were turning out.

"Ready?" I asked Frank as we watched Cooley get up from the table he'd been at, hem-haw with his buddies for a moment, and walk off in the direction of some back room tucked in the far corner of the place, beneath this staircase ascending to an upper floor where me and my brother heard Cooley kept whores you can fuck for the right price. "It's either now or never, Frank."

Frank looked at me, threw me this smile, and said, "Let's do it, bro."

The two of us got out of our chairs immediately, but not too abruptly as to not draw any attention to ourselves. That was the last thing we needed to have happen right about now—not now after we'd come so far. So, I think, though we didn't talk about it beforehand, me and Frank were in the same frame of mind, knowing just how important this was and how we absolutely couldn't afford to fuck anything up.

On our way across the bar to the backroom Cooley disappeared into, Frank asked me, "So, how are we gonna do this, anyway?"

Though there was this small hint of uncertainty in his voice, there was no fear in it whatsoever—and that was a good thing.

"I figure," I told him, shooting glances at everybody in the bar to see if anybody was watching us and what we were doing. Of course, nobody was. "We knock on the door, wait for the old fart to tell us to come in, bust the door open, and start blasting away until our guns go empty."

Sure, the moment I'd told him that, the moment I let that plan roll off my lips, I knew full well just how bad of an idea it was. I guess, in hindsight, since I was pretty young at the time, I figured nothing bad could possibly happen and that we both could barge in and send a hail of gunfire in there and all of it would be over with in no time. But, if there's anything I realized in life since, I think I've realized you can't take anything for granted, even if you believe you've got the upper hand in something.

That's what me and Frank believed—that we had the upper hand—as we navigated our way through all the tables and made it to the outside of the door to the back room Cooley had disappeared into the door was closed shut.

"You sure that's gonna work?" Frank asked me.

"Why wouldn't it?"

With his two revolvers already out just as I'd had my two already out and partially obscured by the oversized lapels of the knee-length overcoat I'd been wearing, Frank asked, "I mean, they say he's dangerous, you know."

"Who gives a flying fuck?"

"I heard he once killed ten men single-handed," Frank told me. "That was back when he was marshal down in Kansas."

"Well, he ain't no marshal now," I told him, finding myself more and more anxious to kill Cooley now that we'd arrived at the moment of truth. "He's just a murdering son of a bitch that killed our mama and daddy for no reason."

Frank went quiet in thought for a moment.

"Ready?"

Frank nodded, but I could tell he was really ready.

I told him, "Now, you knock on the door, okay."

Frank looked at me with a pair of the most unsure eyes I'd ever seen in all my born days. You see, it's those eyes, more than anything else I think, that always stand out in my mind somehow. Those eyes always find a way to haunt the worst of my nightmares, especially in the weeks after we confronted Cooley.

But, even though Frank's eyes told me, without words, how much he didn't want to do this. Though he probably wanted some form of revenge, I could still see how much he would rather be back on the farm our parents left us after their deaths—I was sure Frank wanted to be anywhere else in the world, but there.

Still, Frank went ahead and knocked on the door, rather reluctantly.

Just three times, and that was it.

There was no answer inside.

Frank glanced at me, questioning with his eyes, and I nodded for him to go on, and to knock again.

I remember how tense I was at that particular moment. I remember wondering if I'd really be able to shoot Cooley at all, since I'd ever shot anybody before, let alone, killed anyone. And, most of all, I found myself wondering why there wasn't an answer inside when Cooley had gone in there only moments ago. That made me uneasy—I kept thinking about what Frank said: that Cooley was dangerous. Thinking about that, I began wondering if Cooley knew me and Frank were here to kill him—a dangerous guy like Cooley always knew, somehow. In a way, I couldn't imagine he would know, since it had been two years since he'd killed our parents and I would sure he had probably killed who knows how many more people since then—yet, a guy as dangerous as Cooley always remembers things, somehow.

No matter what may have crossed my mind, Frank went ahead and knocked again—Frank's face was practically pale.

Once again, there was no answer inside.

Though I know myself I could hear something inside, I knew it wasn't enough of something—or so I thought at the time—to matter worth anything.

"What do we do, now?" Frank asked me.

I told him, "We go in, that's what."

"Okay," Frank said, though he didn't particularly look okay. His eyes were telling me that he didn't want to go in any more than he wanted to be in the bar. I remember how he looked as if he wasn't okay but would be okay as long as I was leading the way.

And, that's exactly what I was doing: leading the way.

So, after taking in this long, broad, involved breath, I charged towards the door shoulder-first. Instantly, the door blew open and I lunged inside to find a rather small office with walls shotguns hanging displayed and another with a moose-head. A desk was in the center of the room, not particularly neat but not particularly cluttered. The only thing that really mattered, I guess, is that there was nobody was behind the desk—me and

Frank were aiming our revolvers at and were ready to shoot someone that wasn't there. As far as I could tell, at least at first, nobody was inside the office whatsoever.

How in the world could that be possible?

Right behind me, Frank asked, "He came in here, didn't he?"

"Yeah," I told him. "I could've sworn he had." My eyes scanned the empty room in disbelief.

"Then, where the hell is he?" Frank asked—he was frantic.

I started to tell Frank something. I say I started to tell Frank something, because I never had the chance to actually tell him anything that might have been on my mind in that fraction of a second. You see, in that fraction of a second, there was this clicking sound that clicked twice just before I caught movement coming from the left side of my eye in the darkened area behind the opened door.

"What the fuck?" I found myself shouting, and flinching without really realizing I'd flinched, and throwing the revolver I had in each hand up in front of my face to, somehow, shield myself. What exactly I was shielding myself from, I couldn't tell you.

All I know is that Frank shouted to me, "Look out! Behind the door! Oh shit!! Shit!!"

It's kind of a shame, I think, at least when I look back at it all in hindsight, to know that a curse word like that was the last word Frank would ever say. I say that because, no sooner than those words left his mouth, having ended with *shit*, whatever jumped out from behind the opened door, shot Frank twice—both times, directly in his face.

Immediately, blood exploded from Frank's face in a kind of dark red plume of a cloud that splattered speckles on me just before he fell backward to the hardwood floor. Frank's body fell outside the room. The heels of Frank's booted feet landed on the threshold. His hat was knocked off, rolling somewhere outside.

That was when I looked back and down at my brother laying dead only inches from where I was standing. Frank's eyes were wide open. Glazed, and his mouth was gaped, and he seemed as if he was staring through the ceiling hoping to get a good look at

God's face in Heaven. As far as I could tell, he'd died before he'd hit the floor, and I hoped to God he was there in Heaven instead of making his way down towards Hell.

"Tell me who the hell you are," a voice told me. "and I might let you live."

When I turned back toward the voice, I found myself face to face with Cooley. I found myself staring into his eyes and him into mine. For what seemed like the longest moment of a few seconds of my life, I remember standing there, frozen, unable to speak, let alone tell him who I was. With the two revolvers he had pointed up into my face, I found my own revolvers falling down to my side as if they'd turned into solid stone far too heavy to hold up anymore.

Cooley looked deeply into my eyes, carefully studying me, "You and your friend came to kill me, did you?"

My head nodded slowly, almost child-like.

Cooley laughed.

I didn't think there was anything funny.

"You thought you could just come in here, did you?"

Something wanting to come out my mouth remotely resembling a yes dried up on my tongue as quickly as a drop of water on the hot ground out in the Arizona desert. I'd found that I couldn't do anything other than stare into his eyes and hope for the best.

If hope for the best included Cooley not laughing at me and taking those two Colt revolvers out of my face, I guess I couldn't ask for anything better. But, to see that broad smile and hear his throat-heavy chuckles, I remember this cold sweat breaking out all over my whole body in this one long wave flowing from my head to my feet and back again. The next thing I remember is how he glanced down at Frank dead on the floor, then up toward me, but a little beyond me at something not far behind me.

"There ain't nothing to see here, guys," Cooley said.

I turned around to see what looked like just about everyone in the bar that night crowding around in that nook of a corner to see what was going on. Obviously, they'd all heard the two gunshots and, with a dead body on the floor with its face mostly obscured in thick wet blood, they all gasped and sighed. The women hugging the men beside them and hiding their scared faces in those men's chests and shoulders. All the men looked shocked and astonished.

"Just go back to what you were doing, I said," Cooley told the crowd in a much more serious tone of voice.

The crowd dispersed at the sound of that more serious tone of voice rather quickly—I guess each of them realized that they didn't want to be like Frank.

"Go on," Cooley said. "There ain't nothing to see here, okay. Go on. Get outta here. Go on."

Cooley waited until the entire crowd was gone, including any curious stragglers before he walked right up in front me. There was probably no more than six inches between our noses. Being as close as he was to me, I can't help remembering how immediately intimidated I was by him, how I felt as if I couldn't do anything but stand there like a knot on a log and just let him do it. In hindsight, I suppose, that was what Cooley was good at: intimidation.

He looked into my eyes and asked me, "Why did you come here to kill me? You and your friend?"

Somehow, I found a way to tell him, "You killed our mama and daddy, that's why." I'd kept my eyes steady on his eyes, and I remained as calm and cool as I possibly could, even though I could feel my eyes watering up with tears and couldn't do a damn thing about it.

Cooley saw the tears filling up in my eyes, "I killed your ma and pa?"

"Yeah."

Rolling his eyes in a sideway glance towards the floor behind me, "I take it that was your brother, right?"

I nodded.

"And you and him wanted to get even with me for killing your parents, right?" He looked deeply and long enough into my eyes to watch this single tear roll off my right eyelid and roll down that right cheek and roll into the right corner of my grimaced mouth. "How old are you, kid?"

"Fifteen."

"And your brother?" Cooley asked. "How old was he?"

"Thirteen."

He shook his head in this kind of baffled ecstasy—that's the best way I can describe it—as if something he hadn't remembered before was something he was remembering now, "Out of Kansas, right?"

I nodded.

Cooley flashed me this smile, "Your ma was Sue Ellen. Your pa was John."

Just as I'd done so far, I only nodded as if my voice box didn't work.

"I remember," Cooley said, not really to me I don't think, but to more himself. "I remember. Kansas. On a little farm, out in the middle of nowhere."

I found myself looking into his eyes as he remembered and looked off to the upper right. When his eyes found mine again, he told me something that I don't think I'll ever be able to forget for as long as I live and breathe.

"I don't kill nobody that don't deserve to die," he'd told me. "I don't reckon you're old enough to understand but your ma was a wonderful lady who just had the misfortune of marrying an asshole. Your pa—he was the asshole. And I've made a living killing assholes, even if that asshole is a dog gone mad. Do I need to explain myself any further, kid?"

Just by the look in his eyes, I knew he didn't have to explain anything to me any further. I knew, somehow, that if I let him explain anything further than he already had, I could very well end up with a bullet in my face just like Frank spread out dead on the hardwood floor. So, I didn't say anything. That may not have been the best choice I've ever made in my life, considering the old man had killed both my parents and now my own brother, but if I didn't make that choice I surely wouldn't be here to tell you about now, would I?

For whatever it was worth, Cooley somehow saw fit to let me leave the bar with my tail between my legs, instead of leaving the whole world, like my brother had with two bullets in his face.

I never looked back. No, I didn't look back because I was scared or anything like that—it was because I couldn't bring myself to look back.

Though I find myself, ironically, looking back after all these years, let me tell you that—now that I'm older and wiser, I think—if I ever had the chance to run into that old fart again, I know I'd make good on what I didn't do all those years ago. I know I would, since me and him aren't even yet—and I want to get even.

21

Here, dear reader, there is quite an interesting story to tell, which I hope will give you some context to what happened long before Frank and his older brother, James—he is the one that I was able to interview—decided that they would find Cooley and kill Cooley for killing their parents, John and Ellen.

There is no doubt, as I am sure you can tell, that James, even as an old man, has never completely come to terms with what happened to his little brother, Frank. Indeed, just to think that Frank was only thirteen at the time, and James, at fifteen, watched it happen—suffice it to say, even as an old man, pushing seventy, by the time I interviewed him, that's the kind of thing that is impossible to forget.

I knew, you see, that it would be difficult for James to share with me what happened the day that Frank was gunned down by Cooley. Knowing that as I did, I second-guessed myself, wondering if it would be worth it—and wondering if interviewing an old man about what he experienced in his childhood would be too traumatic to re-live. I knew, too, that James wouldn't want to talk about Cooley—and that talking about Cooley and what happened could just as easily get him so worked up that James, as an old man, wouldn't be able to take it. That was the last thing I wanted to have happen—I didn't want to send him to an early grave, just because I wanted to connect some facts and get some details about something that remained so painful for him. I knew, you see, that James was in a lot of pain—not just emotional, but physical pain, and mental pain, and that everything that his life had become since he was fifteen had been fundamentally shaped by Cooley killing Frank and, of course, Cooley killing their parents. I knew, too, that Cooley had become to James like what the great white whale was to Ahab in Herman Melville's *Moby Dick*—I knew from those that knew James best that he was obsessed with finding Cooley again, obsessed with getting even with Cooley for what Cooley had done to Frank and to their parents, and obsessed such a degree that, some say, James had become a madman. Some say that this madness was what kept James traveling and searching through most of Texas looking for Cooley without ever finding Cooley again—yes, there is no doubt that Cooley was James' great white whale and, just like Ahab, James spent most, if not all, of his adult life wanting to get even with Cooley, somehow and in some way.

Though I wasn't sure if James was familiar with Melville's story, the fact that James was never able to get whatever it was he wanted from Cooley is, in itself, something of a tragedy—similarly, it is quite apparent to me that what happens to Ahab is unmistakably a tragedy. Everyone I talked to about James told me the same thing—about James' obsession, about how James searched just about every town in northern and western Texas looking for places where Cooley was believed to be living, and about how this obsession wholly controlled James' life.

Some would tell me that James wasn't worth interviewing because he was, after all, just an old man now, and he had become, over time, an old man that wasn't connected to the real world anymore. Some would say, too, that James had become so violent that there would be no certainty that James would attack me at the mere mention of Cooley's name. Some would make sure that I knew how many men James killed during his travels through Texas as a younger man, whenever he believed someone looked like Cooley—and more men James is said to have killed when he traveled through certain parts of Oklahoma and Arizona. Essentially, some would say that James just starting killing people as a way to kill something in himself that couldn't be killed—or that, too, it was a way to kill in the same manner that Cooley killed, so that James could be sure that he would be the one doing the killing, and not the one doing the dying, like what happened to his little brother, Frank, and, of course, his parents.

With all of this in mind, dear reader, you can see how this was probably the most difficult interview I had to do, since James, even as such an old man, had become more like Cooley than James would have ever imagined—that would mean, then, because James was just as cold-blooded a killer as Cooley is said to have been, I had a feeling, beforehand, that James would be the closest I would get to getting face-to-face with Cooley himself.

What fascinated me, you see, was how anyone could live by the philosophy of making sure he was always the one doing the killing and everyone else was always the ones doing the dying—essentially, it was the philosophy of making sure you are always the one doing the living, or, quite frankly, all about self-preservation, always at the cost of what others must relinquish.

So, what I wondered, with respect to James, was if I would be making a terrible mistake, talking to him about something that remained a tragedy for him, about something that Cooley would forever be attached to, and about something that could very easily awaken something in James that had, some say, lay dormant in his old age.

Even so, when James agreed to meet with me—thanks to my having spread the word to those that I knew would know James—I knew that I couldn't meet with James without asking about how he and his brother Frank, as kids, tried to kill Cooley. Indeed, the story would be the centerpiece of my interview with James, given that so much is known about what happened and, at the same time, there is a lot that remains a part of lore—there was this broader mythology, I found, about Cooley killing Frank, and about why Cooley killed Frank's and James' parents in the first place, and about how James spent so much time in his twenties and thirties going from Texas to Oklahoma to Arizona killing anyone that Cooley knew, so James could send Cooley a message. As part of that broader mythology, some would say that what James was doing wasn't about getting even with Cooley at all—it was less about avenging what happened to Frank and his parents and more about James' madness. There was this sense that James wasn't really killing people that Cooley knew, or that it was somehow about killing people that were close to Cooley, or about the hope that all of James' killings would make Cooley want to get even with James. None of that was ever really true—that was the mythology of it all, which, in the end, never brought James any closer to Cooley than James had been at fifteen watching his little brother get killed and, presumedly, witnessing his parents get killed.

All of that went through my mind, dear reader, when I first arrived at the little farmhouse where James lived alone—seeing the dilapidated barn on the property, the nearby fields full of dead crops, all the overgrown grass around the main house, and the main house itself looking, from the outside, as if it hadn't been tended to—knowing that it was the same farmhouse that James had lived in since childhood, with his deceased brother Frank and his parents.

I pulled my carriage up to the front porch of James' house, tugging on the reins so that my horses would bring me to a stop near one of the house's curtain-drawn windows. Looking at the house, I saw how it looked so dilapidated that it looked uninhabited and abandoned, home—but, I knew James was supposed to be home, and that he was supposed to be waiting for my arrival.

As I retrieved my notebook out of my satchel, I looked at the dilapidated barn for a moment. It, too, looked horrible—it seemed as if it hadn't had a fresh coat of paint in many years and the sidings was cracked and noticeably peeling from many seasons of bad weather. The barn's front doors were hanging open, and barely remained on their hinges, with one of the doors looking as if it would fall away anytime. I remember how it could see inside and could see a carriage covered in the darkness. And there was grass grown high all around the barn, and unkempt in the fields just off to the side, with all those dead crops that had been probably dead for who knows how many seasons. Among all that high grass growth, I could just see what looked like make-shift tombstones situated in front of an overgrown oak—there were three of them, in fact.

I had heard from those that knew James well that he had buried his little brother Frank on the family property—the story was, based on what I have been able to put together, that James, at all of fifteen, had the carry his Frank's dead body back home. They say James slung Frank's dead body across Frank's horse, while James, riding his own horse, lead Frank's horse back home—for some reason, some say, James not only shot Frank's horse dead, but James shot his own horse dead, in some fit of anger over what Cooley did to Frank. Nobody knows, as far as I can tell, if that is true or not—all I know, dear reader, is that is part of the mythology around James.

Before Frank was killed though, they buried their parents here, too. With James all of fifteen and Frank all of thirteen, the story was that they carried their parents' dead bodies out to the fields just off from the barn. Their father had been in the barn when Cooley killed him—Frank carried that body out. Their mother had been killed in the house—James carried that body out. The brothers dug the two graves themselves and buried their parents' dead bodies coffin-less, and immediately packed up their things, climbed on their horses, and went looking for Cooley for revenge.

When all was said and done, dear reader, and Cooley killed Frank, and James had to bury his brother next to their buried parents, some say that James immediately tried to make a life for himself. At first, they say, it wasn't about wanting to get even with Cooley right away. In the years after Frank's killing, it was more about James just trying to find himself, and it was about being alone, and it was about looking for ways to make sense out of what happened to Frank and his parents, and it was also about making sense out of what was happening to him, and it was about being away from that house and the property that only reminded him of his family and the life that his father had worked hard to make for them, and it was about realizing that that house and property no longer meant what it once did, and it was about going out there and making sure that he was always the one doing the killing and everyone else was doing the dying. Eventually, some say, James realized that being the one doing the killing and making sure that others are always doing the dying only lasts so long—eventually, James found himself an old man with no more imaginary Cooleys to kill.

For a moment, I thought about that, as I looked out over James' property, which had once been his father's—the property that James' father had built up on his own for his wife and sons, but never knowing that his life would be cut short. I thought about how James, after his father's death, was unable to make anything out of his father's dreams— what I saw around me that day I went to visit with James was a representation, I thought, of what James' life had unfortunately become.

You see, dear reader, the moments I reflected on that, and I started thinking about what I was going to ask James, and I continued wondering if there was even a way to speak to him about Cooley without him taking any anger out on me, the front door to the house opened.

There was the sound of a knock, like wood on wood.

I caught sight of James' figure appearing in the doorway, quietly.

More importantly, I caught sight of his amputated right leg—from the right knee down, James had a peg, which reminded me, I remembered thinking at the time, of the peg leg that Melville describes Ahab having.

James' eyes peered at me from the darkness, "You the biographer man?"

I nodded that I was.

I asked him, "James, I presume?"

James laughed heartly at that, "Who the fuck else would I be?"

I flashed him a smile.

"Well," James said, looking me up and down. "Get on in here before I change my mind."

I thanked him for agreeing to meet with me. That is something I usually do, since I am always aware that nobody has to speak to me. Interviewing someone is always about courtesy—being thankful for their time and their accommodations, and for their willingness to speak about something that they, at times, probably don't want to talk about it.

"I appreciate your time," I told James.

He waved that off.

"Yeah, yeah, yeah."

He went inside and sat in a chair at the head of the table in the middle of what was cramped room. He motioned for me to sit in the other chair that was at the other end of the table.

I remember how badly it smelled in that house—I don't think I can even put into words, dear reader, what that smell was.

James watched me carefully, seemingly aware that I was aware of the smell.

Just as I caught sight of a rat scurrying by on the floor and disappearing under one of the many piles of trash all over the room, James laughed again, very robustly. "You ain't never seen a rat before?"

I assured him that I had, indeed, seen a rat before.

James laughed just the same.

"So, let's get on with it," he said, clapping his hands together. "What do you want to know?"

The moment I mentioned Cooley's name, the look on James' face changed.

"What about him?"

I told him, "I wanted you to give me an account of what happened the day you and your brother Frank went to kill Cooley."

"Account?"

"Yes," I said. "a narrative about it."

"Narrative?" He asked. "Look, I don't know any of these book words. I don't know what you're asking."

I explained that I wanted to know what happened and I wanted him to give me the details, so I could understand how it happened.

As James went about telling me what happened in greater detail than I expected, and eventually ended with, as I have explained to you already, saying how, in looking back after all these years, if he ever had the chance to run into Cooley again, ,he would make good on what he didn't do all those years ago.

James said, "I know I would, since me and him aren't even yet—and I want to get even."

I told him that I understood his point, even though Cooley had been dead for a long time now. I said, "I guess we can be assured that Cooley is where he deserves to be. Right? Somewhere in hell."

James looked at me, as if none of what I had said had made any sense to him.

"What do you mean? I'm still going to kill Cooley."

I saw something in his eyes that told me his mind was much more far-gone than I originally thought it was—and, to be sure, more far-gone than what some people already warned me about.

So, I nodded.

James asked me, "Do you know where he is?"

I told him, "No, I didn't."

James studied me, "Yeah, you do. You know where that bastard is. Don't you? Don't you? You know, right? You know where he is."

I tried to assure James that I didn't.

"And he sent you here, didn't he?" James asked. "To check on me. Right?"

I told him, "No, sir."

"What?"

"I said," I repeated. "No, sir.

Then, James jumped up from the table, limped shakily towards a corner of the room where there was trash stacked almost waist-high. He rummaged for something hurriedly.

"I think it is best, if I leave," I said. "I appreciate your help." I didn't know what else to do.

From behind that trash, James pulled out a shotgun, aiming it directly at me.

"You better tell me where he is, biographer man," James said. "Cuz I know you know where he is. Yeah, you do. Yeah, you know. You better tell me, or I'm going to blow your head off to kingdom come."

I showed James my hands, which I have found is the customary thing to do when someone is holding you at gunpoint. I did as best I could, while holding on to my notebook. I stood up and slowly backed away from the table and into what served as James' kitchen area. A table with a face bowl stopped me from backing back into the wall—that was when, you see, I realized that the wall was so close.

"Look," I told him. "I don't know what you're talking about."

"You don't know what I'm talking about, huh?"

No, I don't."

"Yeah, you do," he insisted. "You know. Yeah, you know. You know, cuz he sent you here, right? He wants to finish me off—kill me like he done my brother and my maw and paw. That's what it is, right? He sent you, right?"

I continued, as best as I could, telling James that I didn't know what he was talking about. I did my best to tell him that Cooley was dead, and that Cooley had been dead for a long time, and that he—James—should put the shotgun down. I continued, trying to reason with him—I began remembering those words from the Bible, in Proverbs, which tell us to not talk to fools because fools scorn the wisdom of your words, or something like that.

"Cooley is dead," I told him.

"No, he's not," James said, with his eyes rapidly blinking and his weight shifting from his good leg to the peg leg and back again. "He's not dead. Cooley's not dead. Cooley's alive. He's alive, and I'm going to kill him. You tell him that, okay. You hear me? You tell that summabitch that I'm going to find him and blow his fucking head off. You tell him that, biographer man. Okay? Tell Cooley I'm going to find him and kill him."

I nodded my head.

"I'll tell him, sir," I said, not knowing exactly how James would take it, and feeling how uncomfortable it was to go there. "If you let me go, I'll let him know, okay. I'll make sure he knows."

James' face remained blank and bland.

I remember, even now, how his eyes peered at me from behind the shotgun barrels, but his eyes seemed as if they were not really looking at me at all. It was as if he was seeing something that wasn't there. Maybe he was looking into the great beyond at Cooley. Perhaps, I was seeing something else—I don't know.

James told me, "Get the fuck outta here." He motioned towards his front door with his shotgun. "Go tell Cooley I am here and ready for that summabitch."

As I carefully made my way across the room to the front door, all while James shifted towards the side of the room where I had been standing, I told James I would tell Cooley—James' eyes never left mine, and they looked empty.

When I stepped out of James' house and quickly climbed into my carriage, I didn't bother putting my notebook away in my satchel, which I did customarily.

Instead, I just tightly grabbed hold of the reins, whipped them against the backs of my two horses, and rode away—the horses lurched forward, then we were off. I didn't bother looking back to see if James was watching me leave or if James still had his shotgun and, if so, if he was pointing it at me—I didn't want to.

22

At the time, Cooley was wiping out a shot glass behind the bar when he saw the stranger ride up on the flea-bitten horse.

At first, I think, Cooley was afraid of the guy—or, at least, that's what I thought. After all, Cooley was probably going on fifty or sixty at the time, and he was pretty feeble, and I know he had the shakes and rheumatism in his knees. But, if Cooley was really afraid of the stranger that rode up on the flea-bitten horse, dismounted, looked around for a moment, the stranger's eyes sparkling beneath the brim of his hat, Cooley never said a word. Not to anyone. Cooley just kept on wiping out the shot glass—his hands shaking, his eyes locked on the man who was coming in through the saloon doors.

When I first saw the stranger, I'd been playing a hand of blackjack with Smiley. My back was to the door, but I heard the saloon door swinging open just the same, then I looked up at Smiley.

Smiley's mouth had dropped open, and told me, "Hey, Mike, lookie thare."

That was when I heard his boots on the saloon's hardwood floors—the stranger's, I mean.

That sound, I'll never forget. I remember how it sounded like a heartbeat, and how the whole saloon went quiet suddenly. Anyone doing anything just dropped what they were doing. Alice the waitress stopped short of delivering drinks to this table sitting by the stairwell that went up to Cooley's real business, which was selling whores for twenty dollars a time. That was why, at least at first, I thought the stranger had come to Cooley's Bar in the first place—after all, nobody had ever seen the guy before, and it wasn't as if none of us had ever seen strange guys come around before, guys that were just looking to have a drink or two and buy themselves a respectable whore if they wanted one, if you're into that sort of thing. If it hadn't been for the two six shooters I saw in the stranger's belted holsters and that funny look on his dusty face, I would've thought so—I say, I would have thought he'd come to get himself a whore, maybe.

The stranger looked around the bar for what seemed like the longest, kept his hat on the whole time too, and went up to a vacant barstool right in front of old Cooley who was probably, by that point, wiping out that shot glass purely out of being scared instead of just wanting to get it clean for the next customer. Cooley wasn't the type of fellow that was overly-clean, if you know what I mean—he wasn't really into giving shot glasses any more than a couple second wipe down.

What got everybody quiet wasn't really because the stranger came in like he had or even because he had the two six-shooters, but because of how he kept looking around Cooley's joint. The whole time he was making his way up to the nearest barstool, he kept giving Alice a head to toe look. Then, he looked my way. Then, he finally took a seat.

He'd asked Cooley for some Bourbon.

I heard old Cooley tell the stranger that they were out of Bourbon, and that they had plenty of whiskey and rum and such, but they were plum out of Bourbon.

Well, that was when the stranger got angry.

It was then when the stranger reached over the bar, grabbed good old Cooley by the front of his shirt vest, and made Cooley let go of the handkerchief and shot glass he'd been wiping out. The shot glass shattering at Cooley's feet behind the bar. Everyone in the place holding their breaths. Alice choking back a scream and dropping the tray with the glasses of beer she was about to deliver to a table.

Cooley started to kind of plead to the stranger about not hurting him, about just keeping it cool, and relaxing, about how he—the stranger--didn't need to get in a huff over there not being any more Bourbon.

That made the stranger even angrier, I think, because all me and Smiley could do was look on when the stranger pulled out one of six-shooters—a Colt, I think it was, because of how the barrel looked and how big it was—and put the tip of the barrel up to Cooley's neck, right at his Adam's apple. Good old Cooley leaned his head back, kept begging and pleading until he started moaning and groaning, and having the shakes really badly—from the rheumatism I think it was or perhaps that bad heart he always said he had. Whatever the reason, Cooley didn't look all that well.

Smiley shouted at the stranger, "Let Cooley go. Cooley ain't nothing but an old man and having no Bourbon ain't a good enough reason to hurt no old man."

I agreed with that, you see.

That was when the stranger turned away from Cooley, and then turned the Colt away too. His fingers uncurled from around Cooley's collar and Cooley just kind of slinked away to the floor behind the bar gasping and coughing like a rattlesnake out of breath. The Colt pointed our way, and right away I don't think I've ever felt so scared. For once, I never wanted to be next to Smiley more in my life. And I'd known Smiley since we were kids skinny-dipping in Foster's Creek. If I had a choice, I would've left Smiley right there where he was and let him get filled up with Colt bullets—the thing was, as long as it wasn't me. We were good buddies, yes, but I wasn't going to die on account of him.

"Which one of yall sed that?" The stranger asked, his eyes two sparks pitted in black globes draped in the hat brim's shadow over half of his face. "Speak up. Fat man? Toothpick?"

I knew right away that I was the toothpick the stranger was talking about because if one of the two of us was the fat man it was Smiley—Smiley who could eat a cow under the table any time of the week, Smiley who had this big pot belly hanging over the waistline of his jeans like a bowl full of jelly I heard as a kid about Santa's stomach shook like.

I thought Smiley was man enough to admit it, to at least say that it was him that said it and not me. But, I suppose, I never really knew Smiley as well as I thought I did, and that maybe the guy I'd been friends with since we used to skinny-dip in Foster's Creek and used to go fishing with sometimes but mostly while playing hooky from our schoolhouse wasn't the same guy sitting across from me in Cooley's Bar. I thought that, because Smiley did something that angered and frightened and surprised me all at the same time.

He pointed at me—that's what, Smiley did.

And the stranger turned the Colt from aiming it at Smiley to aiming it at me.

All at once I could feel my bladder letting go in my lap as if it had been dammed up and the dam had burst open. It's not really because I'm any less than a man, I guess. It's just that when you've got a gun pointed at you and the guy that's pointing the gun at you is a stranger that you've never seen before it your life, a stranger that could very well be some outlaw with a chip on his shoulder ready to shoot at anything walking or crawling, you can get powerfully scared, you know.

If I ever had any hopes of my bladder holding, all those hopes went out the window when the stranger crossed from the bar through the two tables in front of ours and up to me and Smiley's table. It was then that the stranger pointed the Colt right at my nose—it was so close that I could smell the gunpowder, and smell the bullets in the chambers, and of course, smell the stranger's bad breath when he asked me if I'd ever seen the devil dance under the pale moonlight.

And, I told him I didn't know exactly what he meant.

The stranger cracked this kind of smile at me that I don't think I'll ever be able to forget as long as I live. His face was all rough and rugged and full of hair stubble and a haze of dust probably from the sandstorms that blow when you're heading into town off that trail from Big Valley. His eyes—I think that's what I'll never forget above that smile of his. Those eyes seemed as if they could look through your eyes to see your very soul inside.

"U scared, string bean?" was what he asked me, all calm and collected. That smile of his never faltered even a flinch. His eyes were studying mine, and, if they could see my soul, he could probably see my soul shaking in its boots. "U wanna see the devil?"

At first, I wanted to say naw—I wanted to say that, not to being scared, but to wanting to see the devil, because I already thought I was face-to-face with the devil. I'm not much of a believing man—what I mean is I don't go to church or read the Bible or pray to God. What I do believe, you see, is in the devil and hell. To me, the devil had incarnated himself in the body of a madman that looked as if he were about to shoot me over Cooley's Bar not having any more Bourbon.

There was a click just then, so soft and quick that the stranger barely had time to really react to it, at least not enough to do any more than an about-face and shoot his eyes in the direction the sound had come from, the stranger's eyes asking what was that.

But, me, I knew what that click was. And, Smiley did too. And, Alice the waitress, as dumb and ditzy as she can be sometimes, knew as well too. And, everybody in Cooley's knew also.

Just then, everybody made decisions. Either you were ducking under or behind a table or you were running out of the bar all together.

Me and Smiley ducked down, turned our table over on its side, and cowered behind it, because we knew that, even though Cooley was an old man, probably old enough to be dead already naturally, he had a Winchester behind the bar. More than that, we knew what we knew about Cooley, because, in a town like Sleepy Eye, we don't have a sheriff, at least not a real and elected one anyway. If anyone's the law in Sleepy Eye, I guess Cooley was it, and that Winchester is the law enforcer.

The stranger found that out right away. It was about how big and bad of a shotgun a Winchester is, but about how Cooley's as good a shot with that Winchester as any man half his age. That was the God's honest truth, you see.

Because, all I remember, was how the Winchester fired off, and how Alice screamed at the top of her lungs and dropped another tray with beer glasses on it onto the hardwood floor, and how Smiley squatted behind the overturned table next to me and squealed something about how he didn't want to die, and about how he still had a lot of life left to live, and how the stranger popped a quirky kind of round off into the ceiling bringing down some splinters from one of the overhead rafters and showering the splinters down in dust clouds, and how Cooley's Winchester exploded, and how a slug from Cooley's Winchester went into the stranger's chest and went clean through him and out his back like a flame-thrower through butter, the slug whizzing over my head like an asteroid, Smiley squealing even louder about not how he had a lot to live for but that he thought he'd been hit, how a chunk of wood blew out of the wall behind me just as the stranger fell backwards, dead, with his hat somehow still fixed on his head and what could've been—depending on if you ask me, or Smiley, or Cooley himself—a smile still cracked across his face.

Perhaps, actually smiling, because he'd had a death wish all along. Whatever the reason, none of us knew.

Cooley ran out from around the counter, told Alice to calm the hell down and everyone to go back to what they were doing, with the barrel of his Winchester still smoking. Cooley cocked the chamber again, just in case the stranger wasn't dead, even though the stranger was laying flat on his back, staring at the ceiling he'd shot at with the deadest eyes I'd ever seen.

It wasn't until then, when Cooley rushed up to where me and Smiley were squatted behind the table and slowing coming out from behind it and Smiley starting to realize that he hadn't been shot and that the slug had gone into the wall behind us and not him, when Cooley saw the stranger was dead and kicked the now-dead stranger's pistol out of the dead stranger's hand. That's when Cooley calmed down a little and squatted down by the dead man to go through the dead man's pockets.

I don't think any of us ever really figured out who the stranger was, because when me and Cooley and Smiley searched the dead guy laying on the floor for a billfold where the stranger would've kept his cash, all we found was this picture of some woman, perhaps around the stranger's age—she was pretty young, no older than twenty I don't think. And, there was this handwritten letter that started off with *Dear Joe, I'm leaving you…*

"S'pose she wrote the letter?" Smiley asked me, holding the picture of the woman we found in the stranger's billfold. He had this kind of grim look on his face, as if it was just starting to dawn on him that the stranger was dead and the three of us were basically going through a dead man's pockets.

I told Smiley that I thought so—I thought that the woman in the picture sure as hell wasn't the guy's mama or daughter or anything.

Maybe from the way my voice sounded when I'd answered Smiley's question, Smiley thought I was sore at him for what had just happened—I probably thought about how he nearly got me killed and all. Whatever it was, that's when he started telling me he was sorry about it, and that he'd just lost his head back there, and how he didn't know what he was thinking at the time, and that he was so scared he didn't know what he was saying or doing, and how he hoped I wasn't sore at him about it.

I just kind of looked at Smiley, maybe truly seeing him for the person he'd always been from the moment I'd met him in grade school and played hooky to go fishing and skinny-dipping in Foster's Creek was just the kind of guy you couldn't trust when the chips are down. That was a sad thing to realize, you see. To me, he had become the kind of yellow-bellied coward that would turn on you quicker than Benedict Arnold did the American revolutionaries.

All I could do was kind of shake my head at him. I said I was I wasn't sore at him. But, I was plenty sore, you know. I guess you could say that I'd had enough of his crap to last me a lifetime.

"Whaduya want us to do with the body, Cooley?" I asked.

I saw how Cooley had stood back up, turned away, and was headed back to the bar as if he'd seen enough of the stranger now laying dead on the floor of his place. Cooley had a kind of swagger in his walk that everybody in the place watched silently in a scared kind of fascination.

Once he reached the bar, Cooley turned back around, the Winchester down at his side, barrels to the floor, butt end under his arm, looking about as feeble in that brilliant and frightening moment as the stranger laying dead on the floor looked alive.

Cooley told me to drag the stranger's dead body out front and place it seated in one of the chairs—he was talking about those chairs where most of the guys that come to Cooley's Bar use to sit in and smoke their cigars.

"Out front?" I asked. "Why?" I was wondering what Cooley had in mind.

What Cooley had in mind, you see, I didn't find out until later.

Later—that was after me and Smiley dragged the stranger's dead body out on the porch out front and put it in one of the rocking chairs facing the main street running through town—that main street was just a dirt road that anybody passing through Sleepy Eye takes.

When Cooley came out through the saloon doors, looked at me and Smiley with a strange kind of smile on his face and something in his hands. He had some kind of sign he'd fashioned out of a big piece of tabletop—it was part of what the stranger had broken when he fell backwards after Cooley shot him in the chest.

"Put this on him," Cooley told me, handing me the sign that had some of Cooley's chicken scratch that passed for handwriting scribbled across it, reading THIS IS WHAT WE DO TO TROUBLEMAKERS AROUND HERE written in Cooley's horribly awful excuse for English.

Then, when Cooley turned back to go inside, giving the main street running through town an owner's glance, all I could think about, glancing at the sign and then at the dead stranger slumped forward in the rocking chair like someone taking a nap if it wasn't for the gunshot wound in the center of his chest, and then glancing at Smiley who swallowed a scared gulp of something down his throat and looked as scared as a pig in the slaughtering pen, was that Cooley had really gone too far this time. Cooley had crossed a line, you know. I don't know if it's about honor or simple decency—Cooley went too far. Putting the dead stranger's body out there in front of his bar like that was too much—maybe old man Cooley had finally lost his mind this time, and maybe it was a good idea to tell Cooley that what he was doing here wasn't really a good idea.

As much as I wanted to tell Cooley what I thought, I remember starting to realize how scared I was of Cooley just then. I don't know—maybe I was always scared of Cooley. Even if he was an old man, probably going on fifty, he still had a temper. That temper was legendary, you know. Not only that, but Cooley wasn't the kind of guy that liked being questioned or being told what to do—he didn't like being told he was doing something wrong or that he'd better rethink things.

More than that, if you crossed Cooley the wrong way, you'd end up staring down the barrel of his Winchester like the stranger had, and you wouldn't have to start any trouble over there not being any Bourbon.

23

This is only one of many accounts of Cooley putting a dead man—particularly, someone he killed himself—on display outside the bar. There are plenty other accounts about Cooley leaving a dead body for the town's undertaker, and plenty of instances when these incidents brought a lot of spectators from all corners of town, including whoever the town's mayor, however *de facto*, was at the time. There is even an account that Cooley killed a town sheriff once over a dispute—it was either an argument over a woman, as in who did the woman belong to, or a disagreement over authority, as in who controlled what happened in town. Whatever the reason, Cooley killed one of the town sheriffs and, as it seemed custom to Cooley, the sheriff's dead body was placed on display outside the bar, with a sign that Cooley made Billie, his main waitress, write, hanging around the dead sheriff's neck—the sheriff's dead body, some say, was propped up in a coffin that Cooley bought from the undertaker.

While it shouldn't be a surprise to you, dear reader, that Cooley would kill a stranger so easily and think that the dead body was meaningless enough to put on display—which is just what the account I have provided claims happened—it shouldn't be that much of surprise that Cooley would do the same thing whoever the town sheriff happened to be at the time.

As you know, if you have read my Silas Rondo book, towns like Cooley's routinely recycled town sheriffs. Sometimes, a town's sheriff would simply quit, if the job was too much to handle, or if the town was overrun with desperados. It wasn't out of the ordinary for a sheriff to simply walk away from the job, since the job is rather thankless and many of these men didn't see anything honorable or gallantly in being killed with a badge pinned in their chest. As I write in the Silas Rondo book, when Silas Rondo's gang—with Cooley included—overran a town, and began robbing and looting everything in sight, the town sheriff decided he would stand up to Silas Rondo's gang. Just this one town sheriff trying to protect his town against more than a dozen of Silas Rondo's men. As I write, this sheriff—whether you call him honorable or stupid—tried to challenge Silas Rondo's gang, as the desperados were in the process of looting the town's general store for food and supplies. The man that ran the general store had barricaded himself in a back room, and the sheriff, all alone, with just a shotgun, a badge, and a sense of authority, entered and told Silas Rondo's men to stop what they were doing and put their hands up—the sheriff threatened to kill each one of them if they didn't stop and leave town immediately. Some say that Silas Rondo laughed when he heard that ultimatum, and others say Silas Rondo told the sheriff to go to hell—whatever happened, Silas Rondo wasn't intimidated by the town sheriff, a man that was, it is believed, long in the tooth and well past his prime. Some say that Silas Rondo himself shot the sheriff instantly, directly in the face, and rolled the sheriff's dead body out of the general store and into the main street for everyone to see—all the townspeople had been watching from windows and doorways, hoping to stay alive by doing all they could individually to stay out of Silas Rondo's way. Though some say that Silas Rondo killed this sheriff, that remains a minority opinion, since Cooley, when he was part of the Silas Rondo gang, generally acted as an enforcer. There are many more stories of this incident that say that Cooley was the one that shot and killed this sheriff and, as I write in the Silas Rondo book, Cooley was the one that laughed, and shot the sheriff in the face, and went about rolling the sheriff's dead body out into the main street for all the townspeople to see. Silas Rondo was amused by this, laughing at the thought of a town sheriff, too old to do the job, would dare tell them what was fair in the buckwheat. Silas Rondo was also amused by Cooley shooting sheriff and rolling the dead body out into the main street— Silas Rondo, as I detail, thought that was funny, just as the rest of the gang. For Silas Rondo, what Cooley had done, as impulsive as it was, was something that Silas Rondo hoped would add to his own mythology at the time—for Silas Rondo, what Cooley did was only going to make Silas Rondo look all the better and more dangerous, and one of Silas Rondo's main concerns was making sure that his reputation went as far as possibly could.

In my view, just as I argue in the Silas Rondo book, this incident with Cooley killing the sheriff, as well as what Cooley did with the body, became a turning point in Cooley's involvement with the Silas Rondo gang and his relationship with Silas Rondo himself. At the time, Silas Rondo had simply thought that what Cooley had done was, again, funny, and that, as I say, it would advance the kind of mythology Silas Rondo wanted to have circulating about himself—but, for Cooley, it served as an opening for his own advancement.

The theory that I have advanced in my Silas Rondo book, dear reader, is that Cooley's killing of this sheriff was a turning point in the very state of the Silas Rondo gang. It was turning point for Silas Rondo's leadership of the group, and a turning point for what Silas Rondo meant to Cooley. It was turning point for the kind of business that Silas Rondo wanted his gang to conduct—until the killing of the sheriff, the Silas Rondo gang wasn't interested, as Silas Rondo dictated, in killing anyone. All that Silas Rondo wanted to do, I argue, is strike fear in people and threaten violence—there is no doubt in my mind, based on what has been said about Silas Rondo, by those that knew him well, that Silas Rondo would never have wanted to kill that sheriff and certainly not in the way Cooley had done it. In previous brushes with lawmen, Silas Rondo would use only the amount of force that was necessary—if he was shot at, Silas Rondo returned fire. When a lawman shot at Silas Rondo, Silas Rondo was only interested in wounding—there was plenty examples, as I outline in the Silas Rondo book, of Silas Rondo shooting lawmen in the leg, or in the arm, or in the foot, and always in a way that allowed Silas Rondo to escape, but never in a way that killed anyone. You could say that this was what made Silas Rondo something of a folk hero in those early days before Cooley joined the gang—once Cooley joined the gang, everything turned darker and more violent.

So, when Cooley shot and killed that sheriff, it was the beginning of the end for the Silas Rondo gang. I am sure that Silas Rondo didn't understand that reality for what it was, but I am sure that Cooley understood it quite well.

Some say that Cooley often bragged about killing that sheriff and bragged about how Silas Rondo being okay with it. The way that Cooley would tell it, Silas Rondo didn't have a choice but be okay with it, since Cooley felt like he was the one that was the real power behind Silas Rondo's power. Cooley saw himself as the heir apparent to a man—Silas Rondo—that would eventually find himself—Silas Rondo—without a kingdom.

Killing lawmen was a line that Silas Rondo didn't want to cross in those early days. It wasn't that Silas Rondo had any understanding of morality—it was all about cultivating the kind of mythology that Silas Rondo wanted to have define him. It was always about being the beloved outlaw, a kind of Robin Hood without the giving back anything to the poor—I say all of this, as you know, in the Silas Rondo book. The moment Silas Rondo allowed Cooley to join what was explicitly the Silas Rondo gang, that was the moment when the Silas Rondo gang devolved into something that Silas Rondo himself could no longer control. Cooley ate away at the edges, so to speak— introducing, then escalating violence to what the Silas Rondo gang was all about, dear reader, made the gang less about Silas Rondo and more about Cooley.

In the years that followed Cooley's killing of that sheriff, Cooley would kill other sheriffs across various territories—Arizona, Texas, Kansas—and, eventually, the mythology about Silas Rondo being a kind of Robin Hood and a folk hero changed into a mythology about Silas Rondo, the murderer of lawmen. Cooley was doing all the killing, but Silas Rondo, just as Cooley could see, was getting all the credit—given that the gang was called the Silas Rondo gang.

Some say, as I write in the Silas Rondo book, that this was what soured Cooley towards Silas Rondo and being part of the Silas Rondo gang—Cooley wanted credit and felt that Silas Rondo was holding him back from being all that Cooley believed he could be. It was then, dear reader, that Cooley decided he would be better off without Silas Rondo. For Cooley, it wasn't even an option to take over the Silas Rondo gang, since all the men that made up that gang were all of Silas Rondo's people and they were all loyal to Silas Rondo. For Cooley, even if it was possible to knock off Silas Rondo and take over the gang, I am sure that Cooley saw the gang as something that would just hold him back in the long run, and there was no guarantee, in Cooley's view, that the men that had been so loyal to Silas Rondo before Cooley joined the gang would be just as loyal to Cooley in the short run—for Cooley, there was always this suspicion that, in knocking off Silas Rondo and taking over the gang, someone in the gang would get the idea that Cooley, too, could be knocked off. That was why, as I write, Cooley decided that, if he was going to kill Silas Rondo, he—Cooley—would need to kill the rest of Silas Rondo's gang.

The killing of that sheriff was the beginning of how all these ideas grew in Cooley's mind—that he could overthrow Silas Rondo and become a better Silas Rondo than Silas Rondo could ever be. I think that was what inspired Cooley at first—the thought of outdoing what Silas Rondo was—and that was why, I would argue, Cooley figured it wouldn't be enough to just kill Silas Rondo, any more than it was enough to kill every member of the Silas Rondo gang.

That was when Cooley realized he needed to make an example out of Silas Rondo in the same manner Cooley had made an example out of that sheriff.

As I say in the Silas Rondo book, there is plenty of evidence that Cooley eventually killed Silas Rondo, as well as the rest of the Silas Rondo gang.

Yet, I do know that there is very little proof, if any, that suggests that Cooley had anything to do with Silas Rondo's dead body being put on display in front of the small jailhouse in Butchville, which was this very small town in northern Texas.

Some say that Silas Rondo was originally from this town and that Silas Rondo's dead body had been brought there to town, even though there is much to suggest that Silas Rondo was killed elsewhere. The idea is that whoever killed Silas Rondo went out of their way to bring the body back to Butchville—not to make sure Silas Rondo was buried properly, but to treat Silas Rondo's dead body as a prize, or an offering to the town. Though I don't go as far in the Silas Rondo book, there is no doubt in my mind that

Cooley put Silas Rondo's dead body on display in Butchville and the people of the town of Butchville let it happen.

24

If I had a nickel for every time I heard Cooley tell this story through the years, I'm sure I'd be richer than Andrew Carnegie.

But, I guess, some stories can be that way sometimes. They never—ever—get old. And, no matter how many times you hear them, you always find something fresh and new each time. That's, more than likely, the making of a hell of a good story, I think. And no story is as good as the one about Jake and Little Bob and the infamous card game.

Maybe, you've heard about it already—I don't know. Maybe, you were told about how the whole thing originally went down by someone else—I don't know. Or maybe this is your first time hearing anything about this. Anyway, the story is just too good a story not to tell over and over again.

Cooley always starts this particular story the same way, every time. He talks about how much Jake and Little Bob hated each other all because they'd liked the same woman. So, as you can probably imagine, there was a competition thing between these two guys—it was fierce, and below-the-belt, and as nasty as they come. Whether it was something as stupid as who could drink the most whiskey any given time, or who could throw some horseshoe the farthest, Jake and Little Bob were always betting on something—it was always about who could do what better than the other, you know. So, it certainly wasn't much of a surprise to anyone that knew about the hot and heated feud between them when Jake challenged Little Bob to a card game.

What was completely a surprise was that they'd bet, and that it wasn't your average bet, but that the winner of the bet would win Dana's hand in marriage.

Dana was the girl both the guys liked. And Cooley always compares her to a pot at the end of a rainbow that disappears once you actually get there at the end of the rainbow. All bells and whistles, and little else to show for it, as Cooley would say. And, in a weird way, he was right—I believed him, anyway. Dana wasn't much to look at, you see. Wasn't much of a prize, in any form or fashion. Though she wasn't particularly ugly, she wasn't the kind of girl two grown men should fight over. Not that any woman is ever really worth breaking up a friendship, Cooley would say.

And, they had been friends, once upon a time. And not that long ago. It was back when they were kids growing up in town. This was back when if you saw one you always saw the other. If you saw Jake, you saw Little Bob. They were as thick as thieves, in those days. They had the kind of friendship that seemed like it would last forever. But, when Dana and her family moved into town, that's when everything changed. Jake liked her immediately, and Little Bob liked her just as quickly. Neither of them really ever told the other about how much they liked the new girl in town, until they'd grown up into teenagers—I don't know why. Just like all teenagers, they wanted to go out on dates, and wanted everyone in town to know which girl they were going steady with—that was the things to do, in those days, you know. And, on the faithful day of the big school dance, when every boy in town wanted to go with the girl that was their dream girl, Jake and Little Bob had the same girl in mind—both of them thought of Dena. Jake didn't know about Little Bob's girl, and Little Bob didn't know about Jake's girl. They didn't know they were pursuing the same girl, until they happened to show up at Dana's family's home at the same time. Of course, Dana knew the both of them were friends, and that the both of them were pursuing her for the big dance, but she loved the attention. And who wouldn't? What young girl, as average-looking as she was, wouldn't like having two young studs chasing after them? Especially, two studs like Jake and Little Bob? So, when the both of them found out they were after the same girl, I guess you can imagine how sticky of a situation that was. And what do you think Dana did, while Jake and Little Bob argued about who had more of a right to take Dana to the big dance? She stood there and smiled—just cheesing, you know. Just smiled, and stood there, and enjoyed it all. All while she'd enjoyed them fighting over her, Jake and Little Bob continued to go at it over the years. Time and time again, they'd sometimes get into fistfights over her—it was always as if they were fighting over her honor as much as it was about fighting over who loved her the most. They fought so hard that they forgot that they had been friends—I guess figuring out why Dena walked around as if her shit smelled sweeter than any of the other girls mattered more than to them than being friends.

So, was their friendship worth breaking up all for an average-looking wallflower like Dana?

Well, Jake and Little Bob thought so. They both believed Dana was the only girl for them, and that them being friends didn't really matter in the long run. All that mattered was Dana, and how much both of them professed how much they loved her. They were both young and wet-behind-the-ears, so it's only logical, Cooley always supposed. Of course, there were other girls in town each of them could've had—girls that were a lot better looking than that Dana girl, I should say—but there was something about Dana that drew the both of them in. Something, I don't know what—something that made them want her, and only her. Damn being friends. All they knew was both of them wanted Dana, and only one could have her.

That was how all of the petty competitions began between them.

And Cooley would always say that Jake and Little Bob would always be looking for one another around town just to start up some new game—just to compete—and always making sure Dana was somewhere nearby to see what was going on.

Cooley would always compare them to two little brothers working to get attention from the same parent. In a way, that's just what they were like: working for the same attention from Dana. Hoping that they could impress Dana in some way she hadn't been impressed before. Maybe even impressing her enough to make her choose one of them, once and for all.

But, that would never happen.

Cooley would say how much Dana had liked the both of them fighting over her, and how she was such a wallflower with such a low self-esteem before either of the guys came along, and that she wouldn't stop them from doing what they were doing, because it always made her feel like she was playing God or something. In a way, Cooley would say, Dana was more to blame for what was happening than the two guys were. Dana could have put her foot down, and could have told them to stop fighting over her.

But, she didn't.

At least, she didn't the whole time, through all those years. She didn't put her foot down until that day in Cooley's bar when Jake challenged Little Bob to a card game for Dana's hand in marriage.

I've always heard different versions of what Dana actually said.

Some say she told them to stop right now, to not do this, and so on, and so forth. Something like that, anyway.

If you ask Cooley, he'll tell you that she told Jake and Little Bob that if they bet over her like that, she wouldn't care who won, because she wouldn't marry either of them.

I wasn't there, so I can't tell you anything for sure.

All I know is that, somehow, Dana didn't want to stay around long enough to see how the card game turned out. You see, she high-tailed it out of there, no sooner than Jake cut the card deck, and shuffled the cards out.

The whole time Jake and Little Bob went at it, head to head, man to man, in that card game that Cooley would say was for all the chips, neither of them knew that once Dana walked out the bar, they'd never see her again. They'd never know that until after the game, until Jake won over Little Bob with a full house and stood up over the table and gloated about how much of a jackass Little Bob was, and how he was going to marry Dana, once and for all, and there wasn't anything Little Bob could do about it, because that was the bet, and Jake had won fair and square. Little Bob couldn't say anything, because it was true.

Jake had won. And that was that.

And all Little Bob did was watch Jake go around the bar congratulating himself and tell everybody he was going to order them a round of drinks, on him. Cooley would always say that he'd never seen Jake so happy, as he was at that moment. Jake was on top of the world. But, being on top of the world like that didn't last for very long, because, when he'd left the bar to go to Dana's family's house, that's when he got the shock of his life, you see.

Dana's family—her mother and father—told him Dana had run off with a guy that happened to be Jake and Little Bob's friend growing up. To say Jake was devastated is such an understatement, and to say that his friendship with Little Bob was never really the same since is, as far as Cooley would say, even more of an understatement.

And, when Cooley would end this story, he would always say how Jake and Little Bob both ended up being losers in the whole thing. Sure, Jake had won the card game, and everything seemed settled and over with, but Jake ended up being just as much a loser as Little Bob was, in the end. And all on account of that average-looking girl Dana—the kind of girl that wasn't worth fighting over.

I guess you could say the whole thing ended up being funny. Maybe that's the reason why this story is such a good one, and maybe that's why nobody ever gets tired of hearing it, even if they've heard it enough times to practically know the story by heart, and, yes, even if, if you had a nickel for how many times you've heard this story, you'd be richer than Andrew Carnegie.

Cooley always says that, sometimes, good stories are like that.

Good stories never get old.

And, no matter what, you always find something new in a good story every time you hear it. Jake and Little Bob and the infamous card game is like that, I suppose. I don't know why—it just is, you see. Maybe it is, because of the way Cooley tells it—I don't know.

25

Dear reader, the story of Jake and Little Bob and the infamous card game is a story that probably didn't happen—that is to say, there is strong evidence to suggest that it is purely fictional. I would go so far to say that there is no Jake, no Little Bob, no Dana, and definitely no incident involving a card game. Frankly, the story is one of those narratives that are part of a larger mythology that Cooley created for himself, given that, each time I have heard the story myself, it is always recounted by someone that says Cooley told it to them.

I don't say such a thing lightly, dear reader. Similarly, I'm not interested in casting dispersions on anyone, or making judgments about whether or not those that recount the story about Jake, Little Bob, and the infamous card game actually know that it is a non-story. In other words, I doubt that anyone perpetuating the story does so for nefarious reasons—it seems to me, then, that the retelling of Jake, Little Bob, and the card game is as much as Cooley as it is about the one that tells the story.

Nonetheless, it seems to me that it is quite possible that all of these tellers of the story perpetuate the falsehoods of the tale unknowingly—that is why I would say that none of the people that retell the tale do so knowing the mythology behind it, or even that there would have been a strong likelihood that Cooley told the tale to them just to maintain that mythology, more for Cooley's own sake than any other reason. Clearly, though the story is about the relationship between Jake and Little Bob, the story does so much more for Cooley's stature in the end. I think it is fair to say that they were unaware of the broader implications of what they were doing and how retelling something that never happened was only contributing to the lie Cooley wanted to be told—and, more importantly, I think that none of them knew Cooley as well as they believed they did.

In each case, when retelling the story, I was always struck by how each individual, when pressed, never realized Cooley's sorted past. None of them had any understanding of how blatant a killer Cooley was—none of them knew how many lives Cooley had destroyed, and Cooley's philosophy, if you will, of always being the one doing the killing so that others can be the ones doing the dying. Even when I would bring some of that to the storyteller's attention, they tend to think that the Cooley they knew wasn't at all like that—what they would do is point to the story about Jake, Little Bob and the card game and proclaim that Cooley was just misunderstood.

If we consider the story about Jake, Little Bob, and the infamous card game served as a means for Cooley to develop a counter-narrative about himself, which would present him more positively, I certainly believe there is some credence to that. Given that, as I have made clear, there is no Jake, no Little Bob, no Dana, and no incident in which a card game was had between them, we know, as a result, that the story itself was manufactured—I have my doubts that there is anything about the story that can be traced to anything that actually happened, when taking into account the basic facts of the story and what little evidence I have been able to uncover that corroborates the story's content.

For the most part, and surprisingly, the narrative is generally the same, no matter who is telling it. There is very little difference between one person's telling of it and another—for that matter, having heard the story at least five times from five very different individuals, including the one I have provided for you, all hailing from different walks of life and having lived in different states, the only thing I can say with some relative degree of certainty is that Cooley wanted this story to be told, though I still wonder why.

Each time I have had the story recounted to me, in the end, I always ask, "Why do you think Cooley told you this story? What do you think it means?"

It shouldn't be a surprise to you that no one has been able to answer that question. Essentially, I tend to receive the same expression—it always as if I dumped a bucket of cold water of their heads.

There was always this idea, I think, for those that heard this story directly from Cooley that they were receiving some kind of insight into Cooley as a person. For each of them, the thought was that Cooley was sharing some piece of himself, which helped them feel—those that had first heard the story from Cooley—that Cooley had chosen to show them something that brought them closer to knowing Cooley on a deeper level than anyone else had.

In a way, dear reader, as important as the content of the story is, there is something just as important about the form of the story—when considering the relationship between form and content, the form of the story makes Cooley into a mediator. Apparently, Cooley acts as not only a mediator of sorts between Jake and Little Bob, but also as a mediator between the meaningfulness of the story and what is made meaningful to the person that hears the story.

If we can say, then, that the form and the content of the story comes to bear on the function of the story, and that the function of the story, as such, serves to mythologize Cooley in a meaningful way, it is certainly possible to view the story of Jake, Little Bob and the infamous card game as a significant piece of propaganda—it becomes, dear reader, as an advertisement for a version of Cooley that Cooley himself approved.

Unfortunately, it remains unknown what Cooley hoped this story would do and why he chose to tell the story in such a specific way—this is, of course, all about form and content. To suggest that it is just Cooley's own egoism would only be calculated guess. When it comes who heard the story, I can only assume that these individuals were carefully selected by Cooley himself, since, clearly, none of them have any connections with any of the people that actually occupied Cooley's life at given points in time—dear reader, I have come to conclusion that each time I have heard this story about Jake, Little Bob, and the infamous card game, each person that tells this story doesn't know who Cooley is and surely never knew who Cooley was.

To each person that told me the story of Jake, Little Bob, and the infamous card game, I would ask a question—it was always the same question. I would ask this particular question after each person shared what each of them felt was something about Cooley that I didn't know, which was always presented in such a way that each believed gave some additional insight into something about Cooley that each believed I didn't know, and only each of them had access to.

"What else can you tell me about the Cooley you experienced?" I would ask.

Each time, each would look confused at that question.

I knew the question was phrased in a way that, for me, made clear that each of them didn't know Cooley as well as each of them thought they did. I framed the question that way, you see, to make each of them think about the individual natures of their experiences and how those individual nature are, indeed, individual.

I would ask this as a follow-up, "How do you know the story is true?"

For example, one of them, in particular, said, "I'm not sure what you mean? I mean, are you saying it's not true? Why would it not be?"

"Well," I would begin. "did you know Jake or Little Bob?"

"Of course, I didn't," one of them would say. "I don't know anything about them, really. Just that Cooley mentioned them in the story."

"So," I would say. "How do you know that the two of them existed at all?"

There would be this expression of confusion.

"How do you know that it's all just a story?" I would ask. "How do you know that Cooley didn't make it up? Use you to pass it along?"

The expression of confusion would deepen, and broaden to the degree that it was impossible to respond with anything.

Once, the response I did receive was: "Why would Cooley make it up?"

Another time, someone asked me, "What reason would there be, you know, in making up something like that? I mean, seriously, what reason is there?"

I would always need to contextualize my questions, by making it clear about who Cooley really was, and about how the story Cooley told each of them was unlike anything else that is generally known about Cooley. I would tell them how many people that knew Cooley personally wouldn't agree with how the story about Jake, Little Bob, and the card game makes Cooley out to be. Then, I would tell them how many lives Cooley destroyed, either emotionally or by killing them—I would explain how the story that each of them has told, or always wanted to tell others, is only told by Cooley and by no one else—I would ask them, "Why do you think that is?"

All but one would shrug their shoulders—all but one had nothing to say.

Once, one of them said to me, "I don't know. I'm not sure what you mean. Hell, I guess Cooley had a reason?"

"Did you know him well?" I asked.

"Know him well?"

"Yes," I asked more carefully. "What did you know about Cooley beyond the story? Did you know him well?"

That was when this particular person—the very one whose account of the story had been provided to you, dear reader—admitted, "I never really knew Cooley. Not exactly. He asked me if I wanted to hear a story, and I said yes."

"So, he just asked you if you wanted to hear a story?"

"Yeah," this particular person said. "I was passing through this town—I don't remember the name of it—and went to the bar that was there. Needed a drink, before settling in the hotel. I asked the bartender for the hardest thing he had. So, he gave me something—I don't remember what it was—then, he asked me if I wanted to hear a story. So, he told me about Jake, Little Bob, and the infamous card game. That's what he called it, too. Those exact words. I listened as he told me, chugging the drink. I mean, it wasn't like I could do anything else. He talked, and I listened. Seemed to me, he just wanted someone to listen to him—I don't know. Then, when he was done—and I was done drinking—he told me his name. And that was that."

"So, you didn't know him?"

"I guess I didn't," this particular person said. "I didn't know anything about the man at the time. I don't even remember if he shook my hand or anything—no, I guess he didn't. There was just the story, and it just stuck with me, you see."

"Yes," I told him. "There is just the story."

Though, when speaking with this particular person, we were speaking about Cooley, I remember, at the time, thinking about myself and my own life. I do suppose that something like that is always part of the process, even when one spends so much of their time thinking about the subject and working through that subject's life in a biography. Indeed, for a biographer, there is always their own life that calibrates them towards what they are researching—this is no different for me. Though some would say that writing a biography means focusing exclusively on a given subject, the fact that there is always an author—the one who writes the damned thing—behind the project—the thing about someone else—remains unavoidable, when one is honest with oneself.

As much as I would like to say that I wholly separate myself from everything I write, that wouldn't be the truth—there is always, dear reader, some part of myself in what I write, no matter what subject I am researching.

So, when I reflected on what one of the people propagating the story about Jake, Little Bob, and the infamous card game said, it forced me to think about how I didn't know anything about my own father, other than stories told about him.

That was what crossed my mind, when I said, "There is just the story."

Like what Cooley meant to the particular person I was able to get to admit that all this particular person knew about Cooley was the story—that is, again, there was just the story—the same can be said about my own experiences with my father. When it came to him, when I gave it some thought, there was just the story, and it just stuck with me, too.

26

"Fuck, Cooley. That's all I have to say—fuck Cooley. Did you hear me?"

And I did hear him. I heard him quite well. But, I asked him: "Why?"

I watched him as he took a long chug from his drink, and slam his mug down on the bar. He looked pained for what seemed like a long moment. Perhaps, it was the fact that we had been drinking for a while—or it was because what had been a good conversation had shifted the very moment he saw Cooley walk in.

At last, he simply said, "Somebody oughta kill that guy."

"Huh?"

"Somebody oughta."

It was as if I wasn't sitting there with him anymore. It was as if the whole world went away until it was him and Cooley in it. It was as if he was saying *somebody oughta* to somebody else and not me—it was as if he was speaking it into the new world that had just been created.

"So, you're gonna do it?" I asked, laughing a little. "You're gonna kill him?"

Sure, the thought was funny to me. It was hilarious, in fact. I couldn't tell you the number of times I heard someone say they wanted to kill Cooley. Mostly, it was always when someone was mad enough and drunk enough to say it out loud—just like this guy was, being angry enough and blitzed enough could make a man think they can move mountains. And, in my experience, when someone says that they want to kill Cooley, they never really mean it. It's just something to say because it sounds good—something you say as a matter of fact, because you hope to make things right in the world, I guess.

So, yeah, it was funny to me—it was funny because it was highly unlikely.

Yet, he didn't think it was funny at all—his face told me he wasn't joking.

"You don't think I can do it?"

He had leaned in, with his face as dry as I have ever seen it. His eyes were watery, but they seemed steady.

I told him, "You wanna know how many times I have heard somebody say I'mma kill Cooley?"

His face was unchanged. His focus only heightened—his eyes were perching into mine, as if he wished to convince me that he was serious. His breathing steadied a bit, and his jaw clenched. He was a young guy and, having a young guy myself a very long time ago, I know that young guys don't think things through carefully. They cannot see the forest for the trees. They don't see the big picture. They view the world in black-and-white, refusing to understand that the world doesn't work that way. Not any world I have ever known. The real world is not so cut-and-dry and simple—you just don't go up to a man like Cooley and kill him, because I guy like Cooley isn't some typical guy that lets himself get killed, particularly not by some runny-nosed kid.

"Look, kid." I started, trying to speak as delicately as I could, before saying: "I don't know what Cooley's done to you that makes you want him dead. I don't care frankly."

And I didn't exactly care what the reasons were. It wasn't really my business, I guess. A man always has his own reasons, and who am I to say if someone's reasons are good reasons or bad ones? I hated Cooley too—and I had plenty reason to want him dead myself. But, I made peace with that a long time ago. And anyway, even if the kid had a reason as good as mine or anyone else's, the question is: is it worth it?

"Think about what you're saying," was what I told him, since I didn't really know what else to say. I mean, what else do you say to someone that has their mind made up and they are simply looking for you to validate what they already want to do.

"Somebody's gotta do it," he said, with a gleam in his eye that I didn't quite recognize. "You know it's been a long time coming."

"Sure," I said. "I know that. Hell, I don't think you could find a man within a thousand miles that didn't agree with you. But, is it worth it, kid?"

"Of course, it's worth it," the kid said. "It's long overdue, if you ask me."

I knew it was long overdue, too. But, I didn't want to say so. I didn't think it was my place to make the kid believe what he already seemed wholly into believing himself. In other words, I knew it wasn't my place to boost him up any more than he already was, since he had a mind to do whatever he had a mind to do.

"I ain't saying it ain't," I made clear to him. "All I'm saying is you gotta think about this more carefully. You think you're gonna just walk up on him and kill him?"

"Why not?"

He shook my head in disbelief. I had finished my beer and wished I hadn't. Talk like that deserved another cold one—I wanted to drink away what he had just said, so I could forget I had heard it.

The kid leaned in and softly said, "Cooley is just a man. Right? Just a man. He ain't a god or anything. He can be killed."

He had a point, you know. But, I wasn't sure what to make of it. Yes, Cooley was just a man. Sure, he wasn't god, but he certainly had a kind of divinity to him. I wasn't a church-going kind of guy, but I knew that there was something about Cooley that made him seem as if he wasn't of this world. I had come to realize that Cooley wasn't just a man after all. I had come to this over time in a way that the kid would never understand.

"Hey, I gotta idea," he said, with that gleam in his eye brightening and shining my way. "You can help me, huh."

I looked at him as if it was the first time I had ever seen him. In a way, it was the first time. He looked very different now. He looked like he had lost his mind—perhaps, he had lost it sometime after that third beer. I wasn't sure. What I was sure about, though, was that there was no way I would help him get himself killed.

"You kidding me?"

His eyes brightened even more, "All I'm asking is you help me get Cooley over here. That's all."

I was in disbelief. I couldn't believe him—I didn't want to believe him. I knew he had lost his mind. The kid was totally out of his depth and didn't realize what he was getting himself into. There was no way he did. This thing was getting out of hand and I didn't want to be a part of it. All I wanted to do was get another beer.

I motioned to the bartender for another beer.

"Just call Cooley over here, okay," the kid said. "Call him over here and I'll do the rest."

"Do the rest?" I laughed.

"I'm serious."

"I'm sure you are, kid."

"You don't think I can do it," the kid asked, in what seemed more like a statement. He leaned forward, grabbed my forearm, and squeezed. "You don't think I can kill him? I've killed a man before."

I pulled by forearm away, and said, "Sure, you have, kid."

"Well, I have," the kid said. "I have killed a man before. It was when I lived in Oklahoma. Shot him in the face. Right in the face. He had fucked my girl, so I walked right up to him in a bar kind of like this one and shot him right in the face."

I looked at the kid carefully and I could tell he was lying. I've already been good and being able to tell if someone was full of shit. I could tell the kid was—he was so full of shit that it was scary. The kid was delusional.

"That's what I'm gonna do to Cooley," the kid explained. "As soon as he comes over here, I'm gonna shoot him in the face. Right in the face. Might even shoot him twice, right between the eyes." The kid touched his holstered gun. "Right in the face. That's what I'm gonna do. I just need you to get him over here, so I can do it."

"Right in the face?"

"That's right," the kid said. "Up close and personal. I want the look right in the bastard's eyes and say, Cooley, look here, you're gonna meet your maker today."

I was trying not to laugh, but I couldn't help letting a chuckle out.

The kid's face had been stricken with such seriousness and concentration that my chuckle snapped him out of it. He was instantly offended by it.

"What so fucking funny?"

"Nothing."

The bartender brought my drink over. I took a drink immediately.

"Call him over here."

I didn't want to. I knew the kid knew that I didn't want to. I'm sure he could tell that I would much rather drink my beer and not be bothered. He could tell, I'm sure. Still, the kid wanted my help and, as far as I could tell, up to this point, I knew he couldn't take a "leave me the hell alone" for an answer.

"Then what?"

"So, I can kill him," the kid said. "That's what. What do you mean *then what*?"

"I mean, then what," I said. "As, then what? You get killed, that's what."

The kid didn't believe me. As far as the kid thought, killing Cooley would be as easy as—I don't know—putting on a boot. But, I knew better. The problem was that the kid didn't know any better—the kid believed killing Cooley would be as simple as calling Cooley over to where the two of us were seated at the bar, as simple as having Cooley just stand here and let you shoot Cooley in the face.

"He ain't killing me," the kid said. "That's bullshit. You don't know shit."

"I don't, huh."

"Yeah, that's right," the kid said. He was mad now. He leaned towards me and, for the first time, I wondered if I had ticked him off enough for him to want to kill me. Perhaps, he would shoot me right in the face. But, looking in his eyes, I knew he didn't have the balls to do that—the kid was just a kid and, as a kid, his balls probably hadn't dropped yet. Then, he said, "You're really starting to piss me off."

I told him to take it easy, to calm down, and to cool it.

"You don't know nothing about me," the kid said. "Like I said, I killed a man once. I don't give a fuck about killing again. You don't know nothing about me."

"Look, kid," I said. "I ain't saying nothing about nothing. I don't know nothing about you. What I do know is that Cooley ain't just some guy you can just go up and shoot dead. That's not the kind of guy he is."

"That old ass motherfucker?"

I decided not to say anything to that. Obviously, the kid did not know Cooley as well as I did, and I didn't feel like it was my place to inform him. Sometimes, particularly kids like this one, a man has to find out some cold hard truths on their own.

"You know what?" The kid was mad again. "I don't need your help. I'll just call him over here myself."

"If you say so," was all I was able to say. I figured it would be one of the last things the kid would ever hear anyone say to him.

That was when he shot up from his stool, directed his attention to the other side of the tavern, and shouted at Cooley. The kid said, "Cooley, come over here."

Cooley was in the middle of a conversation with two young women—one woman on one side, the other on the other side. In the middle, Cooley had been saying something to the two women that had them laughing. Knowing Cooley, he was probably flirting with the women, telling them what he would do to them when he got them alone in his bedroom. That was the way Cooley was with the ladies, I knew. So, to have something like that interrupted, you could tell Cooley was instantly pissed off—yet, when Cooley looked our direction, that instant anger turned into something else: the very thing that made Cooley who he was, the thing that allowed Cooley to live as long as he had and manage to cheat death more times than I could count.

The two women to either side of Cooley had stopped laughing.

The whole tavern went quiet right away.

"I said," the kid shouted. "Come over here. Now!"

Card-playing stopped, drinking stopped, and everything in the tavern stopped. The bartender had been filling up a glass for another customer and the tap started running over, surprising the poor bartender. Two old men seated at a table near the entrance decided to get up slowly and leave while the leaving was good.

I thought about leaving myself, but I guess I wanted to see what would happen. I guess—well, I know I wanted to see what would happen to the kid.

Cooley stood up slowly and motioned to the two women to leave—the two women ushered themselves out of the way quickly, navigating themselves to the piano side of the tavern. On that side, the piano player had already stopped playing and was hiding behind the stand-up piano for protection. The two women joined him.

I kept himself facing forward in my barstool, looking at Cooley in the reflection in the long mirror behind the bar. I tried to keep as a still as possible—others in the bar that decided to stay kept still as well. It was so quiet you could hear the spurs on the kid's boots jingle as he took a step forward.

"Come over here," the kid said again, making sure Cooley saw the kid was armed.

I could see that Cooley wasn't armed. But also, I could see that Cooley wasn't concerned about the kid being armed either.

"Kid," I tried to get his attention, you know. "You're gonna get yourself killed, you know."

Either the kid didn't hear me or he simply ignored me. Either way, the kid never looked my way and kept his eyes trained on Cooley.

"I said, come here," the kid shouted at Cooley. "Come over here!"

Cooley didn't move.

I thought about not moving either, but, instead, I took another drink.

"Did you hear what I said, old man?" The kid raised his voice. It squeaked just a little with a frog in his throat. "I said come here."

Cooley still didn't move. Just a trace of a smile appeared on his face—it was a subtle smile, or smirk of some sort. I had seen it before. To me, it looked like Cooley found the kid humorous and wanted to fuck with him a bit.

It was then that the kid pulled his gun out of the holster and pointed it at Cooley. The hammer of the revolver clicked back. The kid's arm was mostly steady, but you could tell that the kid was getting nervous. There was a small shake, and the tip of the revolver shook just a bit too. The kid's arm shook a bit as the kid widened his stance—his spurs chimed once and then twice.

At this point, I knew the kid was done for. There was no going back, you see. The kid had crossed whatever line between making it out of here alive and finding himself dead on the tavern floor. I knew full well what that line looked like—with guys like Cooley, guys that are killers through and through, that line is as clear as day. I'm not saying I'm a killer, but I know what that line is. I've been on both side of a gun enough times to know when someone is practically sealing their fate—the kid had sealed his fate, but he didn't know it yet. But, how would he? As far as the kid was concerned, he had Cooley right where he wanted Cooley: at gunpoint and a trigger's pull away.

With his left hand, Cooley slowly reached around his waist to his lower back for something.

"Don't you make a move, fucker," the kid shouted, taking another step forward, with his gun still pointed at Cooley. "Make another move—I'll put a bullet in your head."

Cooley didn't heed the kid's commands and reached for something that was holstered behind him. Cooley's eyes never left from the kid's eyes. Cooley kept that hand behind his back, and his other hand flipped the kid off.

"I said, stop," the kid commanded. "Show me both of your hands, fucker."

Not only did Cooley not show the kid both of his hands, but Cooley also kept that finger up flipping the kid off. A smile slowly appeared on Cooley's face. A gleam began to glow in Cooley's eyes. That smile and those eyes recognized something relished whatever it was.

"I said—"

The kid wouldn't get a chance to finish that. Whatever he was making sure Cooley understood didn't make its way out of the kid's mouth.

In a blink of the eye, Cooley pulled what was surely a six-inch knife out of that holster at the small of his back and chunked it under-handedly towards the kid. About half of the blade of that knife caught the kid in his lower throat. The kid gurgled, lurched backward a step, and blood shot out from the wound.

The kid dropped his revolver on the floor and pawed at the handle of the knife.

The kid's widening eyes found mine—the kid's eyes had this shock in them that seemed to ask what happened, but also seemed to question everything in the whole wide world right now. Everything the kid thought he knew about anything seemed to wash all over his face, as he looked at me in disbelief, in fear, and in what was certainly the realization that he was about to die in what had to be the most painful way possible.

I looked away from the kid's eyes, and I took another drink.

The kid backed into the bar, backed into the stool he had been seated in, knocked it over to the floor just as the kid slipped to the floor, still pawing at the knife's handle. The kid gurgled and choked on his own blood, as blood bubbled out of his mouth—his legs shook violently, as the whole body convulsed.

I took another drink, finding myself not wanting to watch the kid die.

In the reflection in the mirror behind the bar, I could see Cooley slowly walking over. He walked so casually you would think that he didn't just hurl at knife into a guy's neck. It was as casual and as calm as I had ever seen him.

After another shake or two of the leg and another gurgling cough or two, the kid went silent—I took a glance downward at him, but I kept my eyes on Cooley.

Cooley walked to where the kid had dropped his revolver, picked it up, looked at it, and brought it to the bar. Cooley stepped over the kid's dead body, handed the bartender the kid's revolver, and told the bartender, "Put this behind the bar, will ya."

I looked straight ahead as Cooley pulled up the barstool next to me. I took another drink, and I watched everyone else in the tavern slowly find their normal again— Cooley's girls emerged from behind the piano while the piano player settled back into his bench, limbering his fingers and beginning to pick up where he left off.

"Oh, and Eddie," Cooley told the bartender. "Get that undertaker fella over here to get this shit off the floor, okay."

The bartender nodded and left.

It just so happened that the undertaker's shop was right across the street. That was, I always thought, a very wise location for the undertaker, given that there was always someone coming to the tavern to kill Cooley and Cooley always managed to make sure that whoever came to kill him were killed themselves. The kid was really nothing new.

"I guess I should get my knife back," Cooley said, seemingly in my direction, but not exactly looking at me. Maybe he was just talking to himself. Then, he turned to me, after glancing down at the dead body, "Seems like they're getting younger and younger, too. Just kids now."

I nodded.

"What did he say?" Cooley asked me. "What did this kid say?"

"He said he wanted to kill you."

"Shit, I know that. But what else?"

I shrugged and told him that there wasn't really anything more than that. Sure, I figured it had to be more to it than what the kid had told me. I mean, there had to be more to it, when it comes to Cooley. But, the kid's actual words were few.

Cooley stooped down to pull the knife out of the kid's dead body. Just then, the undertaker came in and tended to the dead body—as always, the undertaker, a small and slight fellow with clothes just a bit too large in size for his skinny frame, seemed excited. Cooley stepped aside and watched the undertaker do his business.

"What is the deceased's name?" The undertaker asked, seemingly asking Cooley, though he looked in my direction too.

I didn't know the kid's name.

For a moment, I wondered if Cooley knew himself, since Cooley didn't respond right away. And yet, though he didn't speak up as quickly as I thought he would, I figured that there was no way Cooley didn't know who the kid was. Cooley always knew. When it came to somebody coming to kill him—going to the trouble of locating what town he was in and coming armed—Cooley always knew who was coming for him. Maybe Cooley didn't always know the reasons, but he knew the person. I had been around long enough to know that Cooley always knew. And, this case was no different. What was different, though, was that Cooley seemed pained at responding.

"I'll need a name," the undertaker said, always following with what became his slogan, it seemed: "Respect for the dead."

"Put 'Junior' on the tombstone," Cooley said, at last. He turned his back to the undertaker and to me.

"Junior?" The undertaker asked.

"Yep, just that," Cooley said, walking away. "I'll pay for the burial."

As the undertaker shrugged and jotted down the name on a small slip of paper—perhaps, even noting that Cooley was paying, since the undertaker, as a businessman, was always concerned with who was paying—I watched Cooley disappear into a back room. I looked down at the dead kid's face, and I wondered. The age was about right. But, I wasn't all-together sure. But, I knew the age was about right, if my instincts were holding true. The name "Junior" didn't really ring a bell, but I found myself wondering if the dead kid was who I was slowly beginning to think it was. I can't be completely sure, you know—I just wonder.

27

Dear reader, you do not know this, but, technically, I am a "Junior" too, since I am named after my father. I should say, though, I have the misfortunate of being named after him, since he is someone that I share practically nothing else with—for that matter, given that my father was mostly an unknowable man, it is rather ironic or perhaps distinctly tragic to be named after him, which stands to reason why I don't use "Junior" on my books, nor in my daily life.

That isn't the main reason I don't use "Junior"—not just on my books, but in my daily life—but rather, it is because I have made a concerted effort to not give him any undue credit, when he doesn't deserve any. He was a bitter man—warped and frustrated, cynical and cruel, egotistical and small-minded, cared about nothing and worried about everything, and deeply invested in his own grandiose opinions of his self-importance, which is why I haven't had a relationship with him for long time. Frankly, I can't even remember the last time I saw him—all I know, with any degree of certainty, is that I left him in New York City, just as bitter as ever, just as warped and frustrated as he had ever been, and just as deeply invested in his own grandiose opinions of his self-importance as he liked to be. I was happy to leave him there once my mother passed away, indeed—and even happier, dare I say, when I received word by telegraph of his passing some years ago.

With all that said, it shouldn't be a surprise to you, dear reader, that I didn't attend his funeral—I returned word by telegraph that I was unavoidably detained and unable to attend. I eventually made my way back to New York a year or so after the funeral to visit his grave, if for no other reason than to make sure he was really dead and buried. I wish I could say it saddened me to know he had passed or, somehow, it filled me up with regret at the sight of his gravestone. I wish I could say either of those things, but neither crossed my mind—all I felt, you see, was an unmistakable relief at the thought that he was gone forever.

Typically, I don't speak about things like this, since this is the kind of matter that no reader would be interested in knowing. I say that to acknowledge—or reaffirm—that this book is about Cooley and not about me, insofar as this book is about telling Cooley's story and not about telling my own. I am fully aware that this is a biography and not meant to be a memoir—I am a decidedly writer of biographies, not a writer of memoirs.

But, yet, here I am, dear reader, sharing something about myself with you, when this should only be about Cooley—though I know it is Cooley that brings you to a work like this, I do know that authors play an important role in that process. This is certainly not lost on me, even after having written as many books as I have over the years, and after having selling as many copies as I have, I have no illusions that there is a certain amount of celebrity that accompanies my name and the extent that my name offers a promissory note to the reader. Neither can be helped, I know—still, I am fully aware that you may wonder why my personal life has infiltrated a book on what should be an uncovering of Cooley's life.

. When thinking about the broader implications that a story on Cooley serves and the possibility that, despite my efforts, Cooley could still remain unknowable, it brings me to consider—just as I have done over the years—what any of us can actually know about someone else. In other words, given all the gaps in Cooley's life, I know it is unlikely that a true biography on Cooley could do Cooley's life the kind of justice it deserves. The blind-spots, you see, defy illumination, no matter how many people I interview, how many threads of stories I weave together, and how many connections I try to make—Cooley remains predominantly unknowable, in many ways.

I say that, realizing that my own father, again, was unknowable—like I have tried to do for Cooley's story, I have tried to piece together what I knew about my father in order to make connections that, on the whole, tell a story of some sort. I remember asking family members about my father, or even approaching former friends of his, and the only thing that remained clear to me is that everyone that has ever crossed paths with my father recognized how unknowable he was—each of them had come to terms, in their own ways, that they would never know him in any realistic way. There were always blind-spots—this made distance insurmountable. Essentially, I had to come to the same conclusions—what remained unknowable looms too large, and the gaps are too vast, and the connections are fewer in between.

In the end, all there is, dear reader, is my father's tombstone, which is as sparse and bland as the man himself was—the name etched on the tombstone with the year he was born and the year he died are the only meaningful facts I will ever have. The same can be said about Cooley, though, for Cooley, there is more than one tombstone marking where Cooley is buried.

I know that sounds strange—for someone to have more than one tombstone marking more than one grave. Indeed, it is an odd thing to uncover—and what is even stranger, for that matter, is that these different graves are in different states.

Some say there is the tombstone in Kansas, just outside of Wichita, marking Cooley's real grave, while others say Cooley is really buried in Arizona, just outside Tucson. Still, there are others claiming that there is a grave near Lexington, Kentucky with Cooley's remains in it. And, even more insisting that Cooley was buried in the vicinity of Independence, Missouri. These are just four, but, dear reader, there are many other unmarked graves that have, over time, become part of a mythology surrounding Cooley's death.

I am confident that none of the unmarked graves hold Cooley's remains. Each that I have investigated, which are seven in total, in five separate locations, can be explained one way or another, through careful interviews with each undertaker responsible for each burial—though three of the undertakers kept fairly good records that were extremely helpful for me, the two that didn't keep records of who they buried and when were still able to tell me whom specific graves belonged to. In each of these cases, there were different reasons why the gravesites were unmarked—sometimes the family of the deceased didn't have the money, and sometimes the deceased person's identity was unknown. Nonetheless, it was clear to me that, in the cases where the family didn't have the money for tombstones, none of the deceased was Cooley—similarly, even in the cases when the deceased person was unknown, judging from the physical descriptions of the deceased, none of them were Cooley either. So, in the end, in ruling out all of the unmarked graves, and refuting whatever mythology circulated around Cooley possibly being in any of them, I was certain that Cooley wasn't buried in an unmarked grave, even though several people I interviewed made a variety of different claims about how Cooley died, all of which merely contributes to a mythologizing of Cooley's life.

In this mythology, there are a wide range of stories about where Cooley is believed to have died—some say Cooley simply died of natural causes, others say that he passed away in his sleep, one claimed Cooley died after a drinking binge, two claimed Cooley died in the throes of passion with one of his whores, and some believe Cooley was killed by someone that wanted to get even with him.

It is still unclear to me which of these explains Cooley's death. I wish I could tell you that one of these can be completely ruled out, such as the possibility that Cooley died giving good to one of his whores. Or, that someone as advanced in age as Cooley ended up being would have drank himself to death, after a lifetime of drinking. I just don't believe either of them, since, if we can say that both contributes one way or another to the mythology around Cooley, neither seems grounded in the reality of Cooley's life, as I have come to know it.

When I think about the three possibilities of Cooley's dying of natural causes, or passing away in his sleep, or being killed by someone, I can't say with any degree of certainty that any of them can be ruled out. As much as I seriously doubt anyone would have been able to kill Cooley, I can't help wondering if Cooley's belief in always being the one doing the killing and others doing the dying was a belief that ran its course at some point in time. In the same way, when I think about Cooley possibly dying of natural causes or, more specially, dying in his sleep, both sound possible, given that Cooley is said to have died somewhere around the age of seventy-five—some say Cooley could have made it to eighty, and others estimate that Cooley was just about seventy. However, based on what little documentation I could locate on Cooley, there is strong evidence to suggest he lived at least until seventy-five.

Whether or not my estimation holds true, I was unable to cross-reference this with any of the documents maintained by undertakers handling the burials in Kansas, Arizona, Kentucky, and Missouri. Each birth date that each of the undertakers had in their records for a Cooley that died in their state was different—and, of course, all the death dates differed too.

Frankly, one of the many unknowable things about Cooley is exactly how old he was when he died—that is made problematic not just because of his unknown birth date, but also because of his unknown death date. Where Cooley died remains unknowable, too—I can't commit to even affirming if any of the four states I have mentioned is the accurate one. For that matter, you will be surprised to know, I'm not completely sure that Cooley's name was actually Cooley—I don't know if it was simply a nickname or if it was merely an alias of some sort, but one of the pieces to the mythology around Cooley is that he wanted to be unknowable.

The easiest way to make oneself unknowable, dear reader, is to deny others the access to your name. If you think about it, what we call each other is the means by which we know one another—we gain access into each other's worlds by way of the names we call one another. That is also so, I believe, when it comes to the way the world works, and how everything in the world has a name—when one doesn't know the name of something, that something remains a something and it becomes impossible to know what that something is.

I think this says a lot about the incident that I have provided for you, with respect to a young man that came to kill Cooley, only to find himself killed by Cooley. If you recall, once Cooley killed this young man and the undertaker was due to collect the dead body, the undertaker needed a name—if you recall, Cooley provided the undertaker with the name "Junior."

Though this says a lot of about the dead young man, I think it says even more about Cooley himself. For Cooley, it was about making sure the young man was knowable, when the young man had been, at least up to his death at Cooley's hands, unknowable. But, even with Cooley providing the name "Junior," the problem remains: the young man is still unknowable, since it remains difficult to say if the young man Cooley killed that day was actually Cooley's son—there is no doubt in my mind that Cooley had children numbering more than a dozen and, among those children, Cooley had at least seven sons, that I know of.

Evidence suggests that there is a strong likelihood that the young man that Cooley killed and named "Junior" was one of Cooley's sons. The records maintained by the undertaker that handled the burial of this young man—a burial that Cooley, true to his word, paid for—lists the mother as unknown and lists the father as Cooley. For the undertaker to list this information, the undertaker would have received that information from Cooley himself—in fact, when interviewing this undertaker, he confirmed that Cooley wanted his name listed on the young man's death records, so it would be clear that Cooley was the young man's father.

I can only imagine why the young man wanted to kill Cooley, though we know, of course, why Cooley killed the young man—for Cooley, there was always the belief that he had to be the one doing the killing and others were always the ones doing the dying. Some say that Cooley called saw that belief as the balance of life—either you were doing the killing or the dying, and nothing else mattered.

For me, dear reader, I think something else mattered for Cooley too—it was that his name meant so much to everyone else, though it didn't mean all that much to him. Cooley's name was just a way to carry out the balance of life—perhaps, you could say that this was just another way for Cooley to always be the one doing the living, while others were always the ones doing the dying. Maybe, too, it was easier for Cooley to do the killing, when, to those that he killed, Cooley would always be unknowable. Undoubtedly, whenever Cooley was the one doing the killing, being unknowable to those that he killed was part of the process—that doesn't just go for any random cowpoke that crossed paths with Cooley, but also the occasional young man that had the misfortune of having Cooley as a father.

Like Cooley, my father was someone that enjoyed being totally unknowable. There was something about it that made him—my father—believe he had power over others, so that he would always be the sole arbiter of reality. For a man like a father—someone I know remained unknowable to me—being unknowable was a way to always be the one doing the living, while others were doing the dying.

To be unknowable like that, you see, is a kind of killing, whenever it's committed purposefully to others—it's about making sure, by being unknowable, that you are the one doing the killing.

28

The last time I saw Cooley, you see, it was the best day of my life. I say that, because I knew I wouldn't see him again—and, you know, that was just fine with me. After all the time I spent trying to love that man, and all the effort I put into making something work with him, I was more than happy that things were over. You see, when you love a man like Cooley, that love is bigger for you than it is for him—for Cooley, there is no such thing as love, or being in love, or even saying I love you. For Cooley, love was always about taking, and always taking as much as he could. And, let me tell you, he took a lot from me the whole time we were together—you could say that he took the very best parts of me, and that took me away from all the people in my life that really loved me, and that he took me out of what was real, and that he took me to a place where everything I knew had him at the center.

That's not love, you know. I can say, you see, that Cooley didn't love me, and that the love I had for him was the kind of love I deserved from him. I know that, now—but,

I'm sorry to say that it took me a long time to figure that out—when I did, though, I knew there would be no turning back.

When I think back on the very last time I saw him, we were laying in bed. Funny—we had just finished making love, and Cooley had just climbed off of me and had rolled over to his side of the bed.

"Well," Cooley said, sighing. "I guess I'll be on my way now."

"On your way?" I asked.

"Yeah," he said, looking up at the ceiling. "I think it's best that I keep moving along."

I looked at him and saw that he couldn't look back at me. You could say, you know, that I knew what he meant. He had told me that the time would come. I guess I wasn't surprised exactly—it was more like being numbed. The whole thing had me numbed.

I asked him, "Where are you going?"

"I don't rightly know," he had said. His eyes rolled down towards the length of my body, but he looked like he was looking at something else just beyond the foot of the bed. "All I know is it's time."

"Time?"

I didn't know what else to say.

For a moment, Cooley seemed as if he didn't know what to say, either. But, I knew he was just trying to make it easier for him than for me—you see, it was always about what he needed to feel better about himself than it was ever about me.

Cooley nodded.

"Was that why you wanted some?"

"Maybe," he said.

"Is that why you didn't leave last night?"

"What makes you think I wanted to leave last night?"

"I could tell," I told him. "I know you as well as any woman can know a man, you know. That's how."

That made Cooley laugh. I don't know if he was laughing at the thought of a woman knowing a man, or if it was the idea that I had said it and he didn't believe it. Maybe, he had laughed because it was all just silly nonsense to him—maybe, to him, I was just some stupid woman that was nothing more than something a man could climb on top of, and nothing more than something a man could stick their junk in whenever they wanted, and nothing more than something a man could get off on like all those whores Cooley employed.

"You could tell, huh?"

I told him, yeah, I could tell. I told him that I could tell because I knew he was getting weary and tired of me. I knew because he wasn't coming home every night, and that each time he had come home in the past three months he had been drunk. I told him I knew because he wasn't beating me as much, and all he was wanting, it seems, was to climb on top of me.

"You don't know anything, woman," Cooley laughed. "What do you know about anything?"

He had asked me something like that before, Cooley was always telling me I didn't know anything and that I was just a woman. He would always tell me and put me down. You know, it was as if he had more hatred for me than love—or, maybe, it was because he hated all women.

"You are nothing without me," he said. "And you will never be nothing. You ain't nothing without what I made you to be."

He had said those things before, too. He always told me I wasn't nothing without him, and that he made a life for me in a way that I couldn't make for myself, and that everything I would ever be would be through what he was to me.

You know, I always figured that Cooley climbed on top of me to do me a favor. It wasn't love making to him—it was always a favor. That was why he wanted me to just lay there and take it. I'm not talking just about the love making, but also the times he beat me—I was always supposed to just take it, because I was lucky to be with him. Whether it was love making or beating, I was always the one that was lucky to get whatever I was getting from him.

When he told me for the umpteenth time that I was nothing without him, I rolled my eyes towards him and looked at the side of his face.

Cooley still couldn't look at me—he wouldn't look at me.

I remember seeing something in him that I had always seen. I saw what I had seen the very first moment we met—there was that disgust and hatred, and there was this certainty and meanness. It was all there just then, just as it had always been. I saw that he didn't love me just then any more than he ever had.

I don't know. Maybe, I thought, over time, he would love me. Maybe, I thought that, somehow, I would be different and that Cooley would do right by me—at least, at some point time while we were together. I thought that, eventually, something would change him for the better. Maybe, after all the times I let him climb on top of me, and all the times I let him beat me, and all the times I let him come home drunk, and all times I didn't question anything he did or said, and all the times I lay there in bed at night hating him, and all the times I cooked for him knowing that he didn't appreciate it, and all the times I sat across the table from him wishing I didn't have to share a meal with him, I figured that Cooley deserved me as much as deserved him.

With the way I grew up before Cooley came along, I believed that I deserved as asshole husband like Cooley.

I thought about all of that on that last morning—which was the last morning I would ever wake up as Cooley's wife. I thought about it, and didn't care anymore. I knew there wasn't anything else I could say, or anything else I could do—I had said and done more than any wife could hope to for a husband like Cooley. All the saying and doing was over.

I was lying there naked, and he was lying there naked. The room smelled like love-making. For once, I felt more naked than on the inside, you know. It's one thing to be naked physically, and another to be naked mentally. That's why, I think, my body was so numb to the love-making—being naked mentally always gave me the sense that I was simply going through motions, you know. Cooley would give me that look, which told me he was ready. Even when I wasn't ready—or even cared—I would let him climb on top of me. I guess I just wanted to get the whole thing over with as soon as possible. When I look back on it, I think I always felt that way. I figured, you see, that it was simply what I was supposed to do: to let him climb on top of me whenever he wanted—I always felt like what I wanted didn't matter and wasn't supposed to matter.

So, when he told me that I was nothing without what he made me to be, I believed he was right. Everything I was, you see, was because of Cooley—and I knew, at the time, that that was the God-honest truth.

So, I didn't know what to say, when he said that. I didn't have the words.

Cooley laughed.

He sat himself up on his side of the bed, turned his back to me, and there was no doubt in my mind that he thought I was stupidest woman in the whole wide world. He thought, I knew, that I wouldn't be anything without him, and that, because I loved him, that was what made me dependent on him.

When he stood up and faced me, he had a smile on his face.

I had been with Cooley long enough to see him smile, but this smile was different from anything else I had ever seen. I don't know if I know how to describe it. There was something funny about it. I don't mean funny as in humorous—I mean funny as in peculiar, or strange. I couldn't put my finger on it at the time, and I certainly can't understand it now, even after all these years. All I can say was it was a smile that spoke differently to me. There was something judging me in that smile. There was something in it that made me feel uncomfortable, and something that made me draw the sheets over my naked body in shame—something like how Adam and Eve felt when they realized they were naked, you know. That's how I felt—for once, I felt my nakedness.

The funny thing—the strange thing, I mean—was that I had been naked in front of Cooley who knows how many times over the course of our marriage. But, then, at that moment, as he smiled at me, and looked at me as if my body was disgusting to him, I felt truly embarrassed.

"You think your shit is so sweet, don't' you?" Cooley said, with that smile weighing down on me. "Those saggy tits and that pitiful pussy. I got whores that have worked for thirty years with better shit than yours."

I didn't know what to say that—I didn't know if there was anything I could say to that, or if anything I could say would matter all that much.

I don't know if he expected me to say anything. Maybe, he didn't. Maybe, it was just a way to hurt me—which he did a lot. Maybe, it was just a way to make me hate him and fall out of love with him—that had already happened, mostly. Or, maybe, he just wanted to place more distance between us, so he could feel better about himself and what he was doing.

That was why I didn't say anything. It wasn't that I didn't have plenty to say, but it was that I had said all I could say—I didn't have any more words.

Cooley began to get his clothes on and gather his things. He would look at me here and there to see what kind of expression I had on my face, or if I was about to cry, or if I was crying already. But, I wasn't crying. I was sure he could tell that I didn't have any tears in my eyes, or that I didn't look heartbroken, and that whatever rise he wanted to get out of me wasn't happening the way he wanted it to—he gathered his things up from the floor, from his nightstand, from the dresser, and from the straight-back chair in the corner of the room, until he stood there at the foot of the bed for a moment.

I knew, in what was a long pause, that things were coming to an end.

"Goodbye," I told him.

"That's all you have to say."

I asked, "What do you want me to say?"

Cooley said, "Something more than just goodbye."

"Just go," I told him. "Just go."

Cooley laughed.

"Just go," I repeated—it was the only thing I had left to say, and it was the only thing I could get out into words. "Just go."

"I'm going," he said. "I'm going."

But, he wasn't going right away. He just stood there watching me. It was clear to me that he knew, too, that it would be the last time we saw each other. It was if he wanted to take it all in one last time—or that he wanted to say one last thing to me, which he felt would bring closure. You see, I don't know if it was about giving me closure, or about finding closure for himself—whatever it was, you know, I could tell he wanted the last word. Cooley always wanted to last word.

"Just go," I said, again. "Go to hell, Cooley."

Cooley laughed heartily at that.

He said, "I can't go to hell, if I'm already there, honey."

Then, he turned and walked out.

Eventually, I heard his footsteps clubbing across the sitting room. He paused for a moment, then continued out of the front door, slamming the door behind him.

I don't know why, but I jumped out of the bed. I wrapped the sheets around me and walked to the bedroom window, which looked out on the front of the house. I don't know what I expected to see, or what I hoped would be out there—but I stood there, watching Cooley stow his things in the knapsacks on the saddle of his horse. His back was to me—he never turned to look back.

Whether he knew I was watching or not, I can't say.

You know, I'd like to think that he could feel me watching. Maybe, that was why he didn't want to look my way.

But, I watched him, you see, climb up on his horse, grab the reins, and swing the horse around so that Cooley was facing me.

I remember how his eyes locked in with mine. There was an emptiness in his eyes then, as if he didn't know what he was looking at, or if I was on the other side of the world from where he was. We were on two sides of the world, you know. It had been that way from the very beginning, but I couldn't see it for what it was—you see, there was always this distance between us.

I guess that distance was part of what makes Cooley who he was—you know, there was always a distance between the present and the past, between right and wrong, between the love I had hoped to have from him and the love he decided to show me, and between him and God. I guess you say that the fogged window I watched him through just then, and what he could see me through, summed up everything for us and the years I was with him—I was on the inside, and he was the outside. I couldn't see him clearly and he couldn't see me clearly. I wanted to make a home, and he was always going.

What I remember most, you see, was how he looked more like a stranger to me than anything else—and I'm sure I looked the same way to him.

Looking at him then, I knew it would be the last time I would ever see him. I could feel it, you see. I wasn't sure what it meant or why that thought came into my head, but I was certain of it just the same. My thought, you see, was that, maybe, the next time I would see him he would be in a pine box—I was sure that I would never see him again.

I can't say if he thought the same thing. I'd like to think that Cooley thought about all the things he had done to me over the years and how I didn't deserve any of it. I'd like to think that he was remorseful, you know, for leaving the way that he was, or that he felt ashamed that he didn't give me any kids, when he knew how much I wanted some—and the fact that he had promised me a bunch of kids when we got together, but he knew, deep down, that he never wanted any. I'd like to believe that Cooley had second thoughts about leaving, or that he wondered if he could, somehow, make things work with me after all. I'd like to think those things, you see, but I know Cooley well enough to know that none of things would have gone through his mind then.

I remember how long he looked at me from that horse, and how I watched him reach for his pistol, and pull it out of its holster smoothly, and point it in my direction.

Cooley was aiming it very carefully—his hand was steady and calm.

I remember wondering, at that time, if he was going to shoot me through the window, and I remember being scared at the thought that he would—and, at the time, I remember thinking about all the times we were together when he would tell me he would kill me for this or kill me for that. I had always known, you see, that Cooley meant it. There was no doubt in my mind, when he said he would kill me, he would. These weren't just threats, you know. Cooley was capable of anything.

So, when he pointed that pistol at me, I wondered if he would finally follow through with what he said he wanted to do. I don't know if I was exactly scared—I think I was more confused, because shooting me that way didn't make a lot of sense to me. I kept wondering why he didn't just shoot me inside the house, if that was what he wanted to do. Shooting me from twenty yards away through a window just didn't seem like something Cooley would have wanted to do—it didn't seem Cooley enough, you know.

When all this went through my mind, I watched Cooley lower his aim to a spot just below the bedroom window. Then, he started shooting the ground.

I remember screaming.

I ran away from the window, then out of the bedroom, with those bed sheets still wrapped around me, and then out the door. By that time, Cooley had stopped shooting and was galloping away—this huge cloud of dust and dirt filled the air behind him, as if he disappeared into it.

I looked at the spot where Cooley was shooting—that spot just below the bedroom window. It was a spot where I had planted a lot of flowers over the years. I had taken a lot of time on those flowers—watering them, and caring for them, and watching them bloom such wonderful colors, and treating them like the children Cooley would never have with me. To see that Cooley had shot up those flowers really broke my heart, you know—mainly because I knew he had done it to hurt me, and that it was something he didn't have to do.

29

This particular incident, as I have provided to you, is an important part of the mythology of Cooley's life, especially with respect to the legendary way that Cooley is said to have treated women. From this kind of incident, as well as others that I am happy to present to you in brief, it is clear that Cooley was, at best, very misogynistic towards women and mistreated various women in his life on the basis of a very staunch view of a woman's place in what Cooley believed was a man's world—at worst, and probably more accurately, Cooley had a great deal of hatred towards women, which, frankly, isn't talked about as much as it should be.

Generally, many of the men I have managed to interview who had experiences with Cooley would laugh at—and laugh off—the stories about what Cooley is said to have done to certain women. It would seem to me that, by simply discounting Cooley's exploits against women as humorous—or, at times, simply about Cooley making sure some woman was put in her place—was part of a larger misogyny, which, for sure, was a predominant mode among men of Cooley's era.

I'm speaking about men that mistreat women for sport. Indeed, Cooley was one of these kind of men—Cooley's cruelty towards women was always different from the general cruelty he dished out at men. Yet, while Cooley's belief about always being the one doing the killing so that others can be the ones doing the dying was reserved for men, when it came to women, Cooley seemed to live by the general rule that women needed to suffer—for Cooley, with respect to women, to be the one doing the killing didn't mean that women would be the ones doing the dying. Instead, for Cooley, for women to be the ones doing the suffering, women had the ones doing the living, so that the whole idea of killing was about killing a woman's peace of mind, killing her confidence in herself, killing her sense of the goodness in others and, hopefully, in due time, killing whatever belief in God she had. Cooley's cruelty, then, was ultimately inflicted upon the women in his life so that they would be worse off after him than they had been before he came along.

Somehow, for most of the men I interviewed about Cooley, there remains a mythology around Cooley's mistreatment of women—in fact, in the memories of those that know best, there was something both legendary about Cooley's use and misuse of women that, oddly enough, seemed to be admired and held as some strange standard about what it means to be a man.

One individual—I need not name—told me that he witnessed Cooley slapping one of his whores one day. Apparently, Cooley didn't like something that the whore did or didn't do, and wanted to make an example out of her.

"Yeah," this man told me. "Cooley just kept slapping and slapping and slapping this bitch. Must have been—I don't know many times. He just kept slapping her, you see, until she was slapping off her feet to the floor."

"Why didn't anyone stop him?" I asked.

"Stop him?"

"Yes," I said. "Why didn't anyone stop Cooley from brutalizing this poor woman?"

The man laughed, "Poor woman? I don't know what brutalizing means. But, no, nobody stopped Cooley. I mean, a man has got a right to do whatever he wants to his bitch."

"So," I asked him. "You didn't see anything wrong with that?"

The man shook his head and shrugged. "I don't know. Seemed rightful to me. She probably had it coming, you know."

This individual's words didn't necessary shock me as much as it left me unhappy. To hear men speaking of women this way mostly made me angered, since, in my view, when men think of women as nothing more than things that do not deserve humanity, it still makes me wonder what sort of experiences they have had with women in the past that would bring them to such a belief.

Another man—who need not be named, either—told me that he watched Cooley choke a woman once, until she passed out. Apparently, this happened to a woman Cooley was involved with at the time—she said something Cooley didn't approve of and said whatever it was in front of too many listening men, and Cooley lost it. This other man said, "Yeah, so he was just choking her. Just really choking her. We didn't know what was going to happen, but none of us wanted to get involved. You see, this was Cooley's girl and, if she did something he didn't like, well, then, she deserved what she got."

"Did Cooley ever stop choking her?" I asked.

"Stop?"

"Yes," I asked. "Did he stop choking her at some point?"

"Naw," this other man said. "Not really. He didn't really stop all that much. The girl passed out. That's what stopped Cooley—she passed out. I think he would have killed that girl if he hadn't passed out."

I asked, "What happened thereafter?"

"Thereafter?" He asked. "I don't know what you mean. I don't know that word, mister man."

I tried to rephrase what I was asking, by asking, "What happened after the young lady passed out?"

The other man laughed, "Cooley just left the bitch on the floor. She was passed out after all. And oh yeah, Cooley spat on her, too. And he called her a bitch, and kicked her right in her fucking face, too."

The way this other man casually spoke about Cooley spitting on this unconscious woman and kicking her in the face was disturbing to me. It demonstrated that this other man, like the other individual I interviewed, lacked any respect for women. It was curious to me—I wondered what would make a man dislike a woman so much that he would physically abuse in such a way and spit on her and kick her in the face. It was also curious, for those that witnessed it happening, what would bring a man to think that this sort of mistreatment is okay.

I thought about, too, dear reader, how my father treated—or mistreated—my mother, and how that greatly curtailed my mother's chance at happiness, and how my father seemed to abuse my mother's into an irreversible madness. To be clear, my father never physically abused my mother in any way—all there was, in fact, was the kind of abuse that shaped her view of reality. For my mother, my father's abuse was what made her believe that there was no life without him and that, in the end, there was no such thing as living without suffering—my mother would always say that it was better to suffer wrong than to do wrong.

In the end, while my mother was always the one doing the suffering, my father was always the one doing the wrong.

Though I know, in death, my mother will no longer be suffering and will be free to be the one doing the living in heaven, I can only hope—and pray, of course—that, in death, my father will be the one doing the suffering for eternity.

30

Let me tell you: when Cooley first found out we were expecting a baby, he wasn't happy about it at all. I mean that—he wasn't happy at all. That surprised me, you know. In the two years we had been together by that time, I thought I knew him pretty well—I thought Cooley would be pleased with the news. What I found out, you see, very quickly, was that Cooley didn't want to have any children.

When I think back on it, I don't remember me and Cooley ever talking about having children. The subject never came up, I guess. In a way, I figured, since he had a little girl already, he would want another child—I thought Cooley would want a son. That made sense to me, anyway. It was something I thought all men would want—I thought that having son was something Cooley would be excited about. For that matter, I thought he would want us to have children together, since his daughter was by his previous marriage. I thought this, you see—I didn't think we had to have a talk about it, since I thought Cooley would want children, especially since we hadn't had any together.

In those two years before we found out, Cooley never said much about his daughter. She was, I think, five or so, when we got married—his daughter lived with Cooley's first wife and the two of them lived on the east coast.

Cooley would always tell me that it wasn't safe for his daughter to live with him, since life in the territories was dangerous—I always said it was best for her to live with her mother back east. I never questioned that—I knew life in the territories was dangerous, indeed, and that so many bad things can happen. At that time, Oklahoma had problems with random desperados passing through, looking to rob and kill—I knew this full well, ever since my daddy was gunned down on our farm when I was a little girl, and my mom had to learn to shoot a shotgun to protect us and the land. So, I knew about how dangerous things could be. I guess that was why I learned long ago how to shoot a shotgun myself. The last thing I ever wanted to be was a helpless female, needing a man for protection—I know I got that from my mom during those years after daddy was killed, but I also told myself that I didn't need to depend on a man for anything and that, you see, I could get by on my own without one.

Then, Cooley came along—and fell in love with him.

I knew Cooley wouldn't be good for me, you know. I knew my daddy, if he had lived, would have never approved of Cooley. I was sure my momma didn't either—though she didn't say anything me upfront, I could definitely tell. The rest of my family was the same way—my older sister and my brothers, all couldn't stand Cooley.

Some say that Cooley had a way about him—a certain way he walked, a certain way he looked at you, and a certain way he talked. It was something about him that made people generally not like him. I don't know what it was. My family saw it all right away—of course, I didn't. I don't know what it was for me—he was always sweet to me, and always kind, and always told me about the kind of life we would have together. It always sounded good to me, since my whole life was wrapped up in my family—Cooley, I think, provided a way out.

I don't mean to say that my life wasn't any good. It wasn't terrible, you know. What I wanted was something more—I wanted to have a family of my own and I knew I would never have that if I never left my family.

You see, I think I was always the one that my parents wanted more for. My sister and my brothers had only gone so far in their lives, so I think both my parents—even my daddy when he was alive—figured I would make something of myself. I guess you could say that they wanted to live through me—to do that, you see, that meant I couldn't be married. They didn't want me to be, anyway. They never came out and said it—but I knew. I always knew that that was why they protected me so much, even when I was a child. They believed—my parents—that marriage would just get in the way, and that having a husband was something that God wanted for me.

As much as I prayed to God about it, I always thought that there was some truth to it—to the idea that God wanted something else for me. I prayed, you see, to have children of my own, but I knew that there was no way that could happen without a husband. So, I accepted it—I didn't have a reason, you know, to think my family didn't want the best for me.

I thought I had everything figured out—then, Cooley came along.

I don't know what it was about Cooley when I first met him—there was something about him that made me fall in love with him, you see. I know that. There was something that made me think that he was the one for me—there was something that told me, yeah, it's going to be okay.

My family wasn't happy with it, but Cooley told me that they were all just jealous of me. All of them—my momma, my sister, and my brothers. Cooley told me they were all jealous of what we had together and all of them couldn't be happy for me, for that reason. Cooley made me believe that my family wasn't good for me, and that they were the ones that were bringing me down—Cooley made me believe, you see, that he was right for me and that God wanted us to be together.

I remember wondering, at the time, how God revealed that to Cooley and not to me. I prayed, and prayed, and prayed, and God never revealed anything about Cooley to me—that should have been when I knew enough to not to turn my back on my family just to be with Cooley. I knew that I shouldn't have to choose between the two—the fact that Cooley was making me choose should have told me something about him.

But, none of that mattered, I suppose. You see, my mind was focused on wanting kids—and I knew that Cooley, as my husband, was the way to make that dream come true.

I don't know—I guess I thought that Cooley wanted what I wanted, and that if I wanted to have kids, he would want the same. I guess I didn't think I needed to ask him, or that we needed to have a talk about it—I just thought he would want kids just as much as I did.

So, like I said, we never talked about having kids—it never came up in the beginning. Once I realized I was expecting, it never crossed my mind that telling Cooley would be a bad idea, or that telling him would tell me something about him that I didn't know at the time, or that the news wouldn't make him as happy as it had made me. None of that crossed my mind, you know.

So, the day I told him, I waited for him to come home—he came home that day the same way he had any other day: happy to see me, and happy to be home.

I told him, "I've got some good news for you."

"What?"

"You remember how sickly I've been lately."

Cooley nodded, yes—he was washing his face in the bowl we keep in the kitchen. "So, you went into town to see Doc Baker."

I told him, yes—"Yeah, I saw him."

"So," Cooley said, turning to look at me. "What did Baker say?"

I couldn't wait to come out with it. I had thought the words through in my head, you see, a thousand times after I left Doc Baker's house. I imagined how happy Cooley would be the whole time I made my way home—I kept thinking about how our lives would be so blessed with a little one, and that this little one would be one of many little ones for me and Cooley. The whole day, I thought about what it would be like to have little ones running around the house and playing outside by the barn—I thought about how Cooley would need to build a little bed for the new baby, since all we had was the one bed that the two of us slept in, which Cooley had built himself.

I just came out with it, "I'm expecting."

Cooley's smile slipped away—his face went blank.

"Doc Baker said," I went on happily. "We are going to have a little one."

Cooley's face was still blank, but I didn't think anything of it, right away. I just thought, I guess, that he was surprised—I thought he was so happy and surprised that he didn't know what to say or do.

I said, "Isn't that exciting?"

Cooley's face never changed. He made his way to our table and sat in a chair. "Exciting," he had said.

"You know what that means?"

Cooley just looked at me, but he didn't respond.

"It means," I went on, sitting down in the chair next him. "that when the baby comes, I'll have to give it all my attention, you know."

I was beaming—I was smiling so much I could feel how sore my cheeks were. I looked to Cooley and grabbed his hands, but he threw my hands off.

"No," he had said. "you'll keep giving me all your attention, see, and don't you change that, see, because you're supposed to serve me—not the baby."

Cooley leaned into me, just then, and grabbed me by the shoulders—he shook me as if he wanted to pound what he had said into my head. His eyes were wide and wild—for the first time, I saw something in his face that I hadn't seen before. It scared me, you know—but, once I saw what I saw, it showed me something about him.

Sure, you can say how terrible it is for a man to say that to a woman, and how horrible it is for expecting father to say that to an expecting mother. I know all of that, you know. I thought the same thing myself—and I though the same thing a thousand times in my head since. I thought about how little I knew Cooley—and I thought about how wrong I had been about him. That scared me too, you know. It was powerfully scary it was to see the one you love becoming something you never knew they would ever be. That was a powerful thing—to have that idea come to you.

You don't have to tell me—I know that men aren't supposed to say those kinds of things to their wives. I knew that then, too. But, at the time, the only that kept running through my mind was how much I loved Cooley and how much I figured he loved me—something wanted me to think he was just joking, even if I knew how serious he was, and something wanted me to think he would change his mind, even if I knew that was impossible.

I knew I should've left Cooley the moment he said what he said to me—I know that now, you know. But, at the time, I didn't see it through.

The whole time I was expecting, Cooley was cold and distant. He would look at me as if I was the most disgusting thing he ever saw in all his born days—he would leave earlier in the morning than normal and come home later than normal. He would sleep out in the barn—he would always say he did that so I could get some sleep, but I knew that wasn't the reason. He stopped kissing me, and stopped telling me he loved me, and stopped wanting to be around me all together—by the time I went into labor and Doc Baker came by to help with the delivery, Cooley stayed out on the barn. You see, he didn't want to be involved. Doc Baker had to go to Cooley to tell him when the baby came, before Doc Baker had to leave for another house call—I laid there with our son in my arms, waiting for Cooley to come inside and meet his son. He never came—hours went by, and he never came. I remember getting up with the baby, going to the window, knowing I could barely walk, and looking for him outside—I remember how Cooley sat out in the barn in the darkness, with just the lighted end of his cigar glowing through the opened barn doors.

Cooley spent a lot of time out in the barn after that. I would stay out there, sometimes, most of the night—I knew it was on account of wanting to get away.

I often wondered, you know, why he didn't just leave me and our son. It always seemed like that was what he wanted to do—he didn't want to have anything to do with our son, or with me, or with anything that had anything to do our family. That would have made better sense, you know: if he had just left. I know now, just as much as I knew then, that we all would have been better off if he had just left—he had done it before to other women, so it made sense, you see.

But, for some reason, he didn't—I don't know if he wouldn't or if he couldn't, since those are two different things. It wasn't that he cared about being a good husband or even a good father—neither of those things mattered to him—or about just keeping our family together in a way that would have been the right thing to do. All that is what I call the wouldn't of it all. And it wasn't that he found himself unable to leave—he had his horse out there in barn and a thousand of places to go. All of that is what I call the couldn't of it all. So, I don't why he either wouldn't or couldn't leave, when that seemed to be what would have made him happy. Being at home with me and our son didn't do that—Cooley always looked terribly unhappy.

I was unhappy, too, you know. I don't ever remember a time, once our son was born, that I didn't feel unhappy. I was always unhappy, until that was just a way of life.

That unhappiness, you know, was something that I had to come to terms with, as if it was something that God himself had destined for me—I didn't have any other explanation, you see, and, even though I prayed everyday for Cooley to be different, not just to me but to our son, the fact that none of those prayers came true made me believe that God wanted all of this for me.

So, yes, Cooley stayed with me and our son—he stayed with me longer than any other woman he had ever been with. He stayed—but things would have been better, you see, if he had just left.

I guess, when I think back on it, our son would have been better off, too. I know I have just talked about myself, and what Cooley's leaving would have meant to me—but, when I think about our son, and I think about how I had to be both ma and pa for him, and when I think about our son growing up and seeing Cooley there everyday, but knowing that Cooley was never really having anything to do with him, I know my son would eventually have to deal with what all of that meant. I didn't want my son to have to see me the way I was, and the way Cooley was, and how all of that wasn't the way husbands treated their wives, and how that wasn't how father should be—I knew my son would have to make sense of all that.

And I knew, you see, that I didn't have what it took to explain any of that to my son whenever he needed it most—I just didn't have the words, and I couldn't get my head around it all. I guess, I was just doing the best I could—partly, I guess, I didn't want to end up like Billie, going insane.

But, the biggest part of it, I know, was that I didn't want to think about what life with Cooley stood for, what life without him could hold, and how I should have left him long ago, and that I shouldn't have put myself through all the stuff he put me through. I blamed myself, you see. I knew I didn't have to suffer the way I did—but I just went along with it, because I always believed that God had something better for me eventually. Like my mother used to say: it's better to suffer wrong than to do wrong—I figured that the more I suffered by Cooley the greater reward I would have in heaven with God.

Sure, I know you may think that that doesn't make any sense.

My son always thought the same thing, whenever we talked about Cooley and whenever my son remembered all the things Cooley had put him through, too. My son always worried about me thinking that way—thinking that I was suffering when I didn't have to. For my son, it didn't make any sense. Somehow, it made sense to me, you see—the thought that something better waited for me in the afterlife was what I used to keep myself thinking about, so I wouldn't go crazy.

So, yes, I felt sorry for Billie. I felt sorry for how she lost her mind—and I knew, you see, that Cooley was what Billie lost her mind over.

As much as my son would warn me that I would end up like Billie, and that, some day, no matter how strong I was, something would let go. We would talk a lot about that, you know. But, I kept telling him—my son—that God was on my side, and God wouldn't let me lose my mind, and God would never forsake me, and God was looking over me.

You may think all of that is crazy. I don't know if you believe in God, but you may think that none of what I am saying makes any sense—you may think that I'm already crazy and just don't know it.

I don't know anymore—I just don't know anymore.

31

Dear reader, please know that interviewing the woman that Cooley was married to the longest—Ann, is her name—was extremely difficult for me. It wasn't that I had problems getting her to talk to me—which is sometimes the case—or that there were certain questions she wouldn't answer—which is also the case at times—but it was because she was already in a mental hospital. It just so happened, if you must know, that Ann was committed to the same asylum that Billie lived out the rest of her committed to.

The irony of that wasn't lost on me. It should be no surprise to you that, some say, Cooley drove Ann crazy just as he had Billie—the difference, though, was that Billie's family committed her, while Cooley committed Ann.

I did the best I could to find out what sort of medical condition Ann had at the time of her committal. I suppose there are some things that even a biographer is not privy to knowing—even as someone as myself, who is, for the most part, capable of finding anything out from anyone. But, in this instance, I'm afraid I ran into trouble—and what I have always believed to be an ability to convince anyone from telling me what I needed to know didn't work for me. Suffice it to say, no one at the Lunatic Asylum at Utica would provide me with any information. The only thing I could gather, by simply asking the right questions and reading between the lines, was that Ann had had a nervous breakdown of some sort. I have seen what that sort of thing looks like, particularly judging from the kind of room Ann was in, the kind of medication she was being given, and the kind of care she had—I could tell, too, that, when I first interviewed Ann, she had probably been at Utica for no more than a couple of months, judging from the small amount of paperwork I managed to get a look at, thanks to trading this information for autographing one of my books.

You could say, dear reader, that my celebrity—yes, as a writer—has some kind of currency in a place like Utica. That is, even if it is with just the nurses and orderlies. That celebrity, I must say, allowed me to visit Utica without previous notice and find out what room Ann was in, even though, generally speaking, only the family members get that kind of access.

I will never forget the first day I went to visit Ann at Utica.

I had never been to Utica before, if you must know. Sure, I had certainly been to other mental hospitals in the past, particularly when I was researching my previous book—I need not remind you about that book. In this case, my interests were not so much on why individuals are committed to asylums nor how they are treated once they are under the care of such facilities and doctors—in this case, my interests were in speaking with Ann, so I could find out what she could tell me about Cooley. There was no doubt in my mind, dear reader, that Ann could shed some light on certain aspects of Cooley's life—she had lived with Cooley the longest and, in my estimation, she had suffered the most from having done so.

Billie, of course, suffered a lot, too. That is, I admit, without question—what happened to Billie is nothing short of a tragedy, if you ask me. How some say she lost her mind and had to be wrestled to the ground buck-naked as she ran around Sleepy Eye seems almost too fantastical to be true—I have no doubt that it actually happened, given all of the people I interviewed that say that saw it happen.

Yet, what largely remains a mystery to me is what Cooley was thinking when it happened. I can only assume that Cooley didn't care about what happened to Billie—Billie's family told me that much. The nurses and orderlies that cared for Billie seemed to think so too.

What happened to Billie had been my mind the day I went to visit Ann for the first time. It couldn't be avoided, I suppose—both women were connected to Cooley, one spent the rest of her life at Utica, and the other had been recently committed, and there remained the sentiment that Cooley was the reason both women lost their minds. The thing with Billie, though, seemed to speak to Ann's situation in a way that everyone I interviewed agreed. It was this idea, dear reader, that Billie was becoming forgotten in many ways because of what had more recently happened to Ann—essentially, Ann had become the new and more tragic Billie. It seems to me, then, that, though what happened to Billie was just as much of a tragedy as what happened to Ann, what made Ann's situation more mournful was that she knew about Billie, and Cooley's culpability in it, but chose to proceed down a path that, even in Ann's mind, could never end well.

Perhaps, it is possible to say that Billie didn't have any hindsight to what would happen to her. Yes, her family had warned her, I suppose, and Billie had been around Cooley enough over the years to know what Cooley was all about. You must remember, dear reader, that Billie had had a very long plutonic relationship with Cooley long before anything romantic developed—in all that time, Billie should have known what kind of man Cooley was and that, based on that, it shouldn't have been much of a surprise when Cooley finally left her.

Some say that Billie had had previous mental issues, long before Cooley came into her life—that is, much earlier than when she first went to work for Cooley at the bar as Cooley's main waitress. We are talking, dear reader, about things that are supposed to have happened to Billie in her childhood, between her and her father. I don't know if it is worth mentioning what are, essentially, rumors.

Since I deal with facts, rumors are things I can't substantiate—no matter how many times I have heard about what Billie went through at the hands of her father when she was a little girl, I can't corroborate any of the things I have heard into anything coherent—so, perhaps, it is best that I leave that there.

What can be corroborated, nonetheless, is that Billie certainly experienced trauma during her time working for Cooley—Cooley's verbal abuse, witnessing the occasional altercation that generally ended with Cooley shooting someone dead, all the come-ons from all the male customers, and the instances when Cooley would make Billie turn a trick sometimes with the rest of the whores that turned tricks for a living. All of that, I believe, had a cumulative impact on Billie's psyche—of course, dear reader, though you know I'm not the kind of doctor you will find at Utica, but I do feel I know enough about history to know that events add up and the narrative that always, eventually, develops in the end stands for something.

What it stands for, dear reader, came to me when I visited Utica to learn more about Ann. It was then, when I was being led to Ann's room, when I found out where Billie's room was located—the room Billie died in. It occurred to me, at the time, that Billie's room was on the same floor and in the same hallway as Ann's, and the orderly that took me to Ann's room validated that for me.

On the way down the dark hallway, the orderly stopped me in front of the outside of Ann's room. He told me to wait there—so I waited.

As the orderly went inside Ann's room—I presume to check on things before I entered—I looked down both ends of the hallway. It surprised as to how quiet it was there. You imagine that there would be the sound of screaming or shouting from patients, or perhaps the sounds of patients banging around in their rooms. That wasn't the case at Utica—based on my research, Utica was one of the better run facilities and the patients committed there are under the kind of care that is among the best on the east coast. Even so, that is not to say that patients don't die while they are committed—no matter how good the care, you can't do anything about death from natural causes.

The thing about Billie's death, though, always seemed to me to be something other than natural causes. That was always my hunch, anyway. Sure, the Utica staff never documented Billie's death as anything other than natural causes, but I knew that her family certainly thought otherwise—there was this rumor that Cooley had something to do with Billie's death.

For a long time, I thought that it wasn't possible for Cooley to have anything to do with Billie's death. Mostly, dear reader, that was because there is no evidence to suggest that Cooley ever visited Utica while Billie was committed there—there were visitor logs and Cooley's name does not appear in any of them across the duration of Billie's time at Utica.

Some might say that what the visitor logs provide is plenty evidence that Cooley was never there—this would be based on the idea that no visitor would gain admittance to Utica without signing in.

Even if it hadn't been for the visitor logs—let's say we remove this fact from the table—the idea was that Cooley didn't have a reason to do anything to Billie. Those that say this, dear reader, believe that there wasn't anything more that Cooley could have done to Billie beyond forcing her into losing her mind. From this, the implication is that Cooley didn't have a reason to want Billie dead and, for that matter, Cooley wouldn't need to go to the trouble of visiting her at Utica, once she was committed, to do this. And, of course, it would have been going to the trouble to do so, you see—Utica was at least a couple of days travel from Cooley's last known address—to go to Utica to simply kill someone seems, at least to some, a bit too far-fetched.

Yet, Billie's family certainly didn't think so—they didn't think there was anything far-fetched about it. They believed that, if Cooley wanted Billie dead, there would be nothing that keep Cooley from seeing that through.

The bottom line here is this: what reason would move Cooley to want Billie dead? I am sure you, dear reader, are asking yourself that very question. I also wondered the same thing. Then, it came to me, when I stood there in that dark hallway in front of Ann's room, while I looked in the direction of the room where I believed Billie once lived until her death: keeping Billie alive would have interfered with Cooley moving on, if the idea, then, is that Cooley wished to begin a new relationship with Ann—for Cooley, Billie's death would have cleared the way for Cooley to be with Ann.

That was the theory Billie's family had, anyway. I must say, I didn't know what to make of that. For me, as a historian and biographer, I wasn't interested in being a detective. Being a detective is an entirely different thing from what I do. Sure, you may say that historians, biographers, and detectives all search for facts and accumulate what they find into something that they can use for a specific purpose—while historians and biographers do so, in order to write a book, a detective is doing so, in order to solve a case. Indeed, there probably isn't a lot of daylight between what I do and what a detective does—in a way, you could say that my search for Cooley is the building of a case against Cooley.

So, in a way, I am happy to concede that what I do and what a detective does is not all that different—just like I let the facts lead me where they lead me, there is no doubt in my mind that a detective does the same.

Standing there in that hallway, waiting on the orderly to let me know when I could go in and visit with Ann, I took another look down the long hallway—particularly, I looked towards the end of the hallway where there was a large window looking outside rear grounds, where patients would be allowed to get fresh air at scheduled times of the day. At that end of the hallway, the last door on the right was the room Billie had lived in—it was Room 16.

I recognized, even at a distance, that it had been Billie's room, since Billie's family told me details about the painting that hung on the wall nearby—I carefully made my way down the hall in that direction, so I could double-check that the same painting was still there. And it was, indeed—to me, it was just a painting of mountains, cliffs, valleys, and trees in an array of browns, greens, and blacks.

I stepped back from the painting just a bit and looked down the other end of the hallway towards Billie's room—the door was still closed, the orderly was still inside, and I was still supposed to be waiting.

Looking back at Room 16 and at the painting hanging on the wall to the right of the doorway, I thought about what Billie's family told me—about how they knew Cooley had something to do with Billie's death and that Billie hadn't died of natural causes. I moved closer to the painting, thinking about what Billie's family believed Cooley had left behind as a marker, which they believed proved Cooley had been there at Utica—and proved that Cooley wanted them to know he had been there.

Dear reader, I wanted to believe that Billie's family had simply had a vibrant imagination. The idea that Cooley had been there, somehow, still seemed to me to be nothing but a fairy-tale—I wanted to believe that they had had wishful thinking, and that Cooley was the answer to a question that wasn't worth asking. I wanted to believe, dear reader, that Billie's family was just blowing Billie's death out of proportion—and that they were making it all into something more overblown and more fanciful than it needed to be. I wanted to believe that Billie had just died of natural causes—and that that, as they say, was all she wrote.

"Look in the lower left corner of the painting," Billie's older sister had told me. "That's where you will see it."

"Yes," the other sister—the one in the middle—said, "It's in the lower left corner. We saw it there."

The older one said, "We're sure of it."

"Really?" I asked them.

Both sisters had nodded—both were serious and sure.

"Just go there," the older one told me. "And see for yourself."

"You can't miss it," the other sister said.

"Remember," the older sister said. "It's in the lower left corner."

"He carved it there."

"We know it," the older sister said. "It's his marker, you know."

"Marker?" I asked.

"You know about his marker, don't you?"

I told the both of them that I wasn't sure what they were talking about. I hated saying that, but I realized I couldn't fake it—I had to set my ego aside. Indeed, as much research as I had done on Cooley up to that point, whatever they were talking about was news to me.

"What he leaves behind."

"Yeah, it's what he leaves behind."

"Like a signature, I guess."

"Yes," the older sister said. "It's like a signature. Like signing a document to make things legal or official, you know."

The sisters nodded in agreement.

"Like what he cut into the chest of that guy he killed in Missouri," the other sister told me. "Do you know about that man?"

I said, "Yes, I know about the man in Missouri. Cooley is said to have killed the guy over a woman."

The sisters glanced at each other, as if what I had said was humorous.

"That's what they say," the older sister said.

"That is, indeed, what they say," the other sister said. "They say a lot of things about what Cooley did or didn't do, you know."

"Ah yes, they certainly do."

"What do you think?" I asked them.

"About if he killed that man?"

"No," I said. "The reasons for it. Was it really over a woman?"

"Well, who knows if it was over a woman or not."

"Nobody knows for sure."

"We have already believed that it was."

"Yes, it was over a woman."

"It had to be."

"That's what we heard, anyway."

I asked them, "Who did you hear this from?" I wanted to make a note of it, as a way of nailing down some of the facts regarding the story.

"Billie."

I was surprised to hear this, but I tried to not let my surprise show too obviously. I don't know if I did a good job of that, though.

"Didn't know that, did you?"

I kept as straight a face as I could.

"How could he know?" the older sister said. "I don't think anybody else would know."

"That's right. That's right."

I started wondering how Billie knew about the man Cooley is said to have killed in Missouri. The moment I started wondering, the more I realized how Billie would have known—if the incident happened due to the conflict between Cooley and another man over a woman, I had to wonder if that woman was Billie.

"Billie was there."

"Ah, yes, she was there."

"She told us about it."

"About what Cooley did?" I asked.

"Yes," the older sister said. "She told us all about it."

"There were only three people there at the time, you know," the other sister said. "Cooley, Billie, and the man. What was his name?"

"I don't remember."

"I guess, it's not important."

"No, not important."

"He was just some guy that Billie had a fling with."

"And Cooley didn't like that."

"No, he didn't."

"He was hopping mad."

"Ah, yes, he was hopping mad."

"So mad he wanted to kill that man."

"But, he didn't have to kill him, you know. Cooley didn't have to do that."

"Still," the other sister said. "Cooley killed that man, just the same. And when he did, he cut something into the dead man's chest."

It was then that I pulled out the little pad I used to take notes—I wanted to memorialize exactly what the two sisters were saying, so I could cross-reference with some other things I had written down in notes I didn't have with me at the time. I started scribbling away in my little pad—I'm sure I looked odd to them.

The two sisters were watching me.

"It was an O and an X."

The older sister said, "That's right. The O was like a skull and the X was beneath it like crossbones."

"A skull and crossbones, you said?" I asked.

I flipped over the page I was writing on to a clean page—they didn't need to see my notes—then sketched it out: a skull, with two small dots for eyes and a set of crossbones beneath it. I showed my sketch to them.

The older sister looked at that crude sketch, "That looks right."

"Yes," the other sister said, looking my sketch, too. "That's what it was."

"Cooley cut it right into the dead man's chest."

"Right into his chest," the other sister echoed.

I asked them, "How do you know this?"

I asked them that, because that little tidbit of information they had given me was something I had never heard about. I think of myself, dear reader, as the kind of guy that can find out everything—I think you have to be thorough as a historian and a biographer, if you ever want to be any good at such occupations. I like to think that I make sure no stone is left unturned, as they say—being detailed that way, I think, is the difference between a subpar historian and a great one, a mediocre biographer and an excellent one.

Sure, I knew about as much as I could about the man Cooley is said to have killed in Missouri. I talked to some of the witnesses that saw the incident happen—two of the four witnesses told me that Cooley and this unknown man were fighting over a woman. Though the other two couldn't say for sure if it was, indeed, about a woman, when posed with that possibility, the other two though it was a likely reason. So, it is safe to say that was over a woman, though it may not be important as to who that woman was. Though I didn't pursue that fact, I felt embarrassed that I didn't know about the carving of a skull and a set of crossbones into the dead man's chest. That thought—that fact, as it were—was something I was surprised I hadn't found out about already, though there was plenty to be surprised about in the connection of the whole thing to Billie at the time of the killing of the unknown man and to Billie at Utica.

"Billie told us."

"That's right," the older sister said. "Billie told us."

"That's why he did the same thing to her."

The older sister said, "Not exactly the same thing, though."

"No," the other sister said. "Not exactly. If you mean carving the skull and crossbones into her, then, no."

"But, still something like it."

"That's what I meant. Something like it."

"But, scratched into the painting outside of Billie's room at Utica."

"Yes, scratched there."

"Still Cooley's signature, you know."

"Ah, yes, still Cooley's signature."

"Remember this, when you visit Utica," both sisters said to me almost simultaneously.

"I'll remember," I told them.

And I remembered, dear reader. I couldn't forget, even if I had tried—I remembered what they had described, and I had had that description in my head so concretely that I felt as if my eyes were drawn to the lower left corner of the painting. It was, then, dear reader, when I saw what the sisters had described—it was, indeed, as plain as day right where they said it would be. There was no doubt about it—it was there just as concretely as I had imagined it:

The crude skull and crossbones had been cut into the surface of the painting at the lower left corner—at just the right angle with the right amount of light, you could see it.

The crude etching didn't belong there, gouged heavily into the surface of the canvas, displacing the oil medium—that is, to say, it wasn't something that the painter intended. It looked like it had been cut into the surface with a pocketknife—and cut in such a way that it wouldn't be obvious, and you had to know what you were looking for to even see it all.

I knew exactly what it meant, and when that realization came to me, I immediately realized that it was proof that Cooley had been there at Utica. For a moment, my mind swirled around how that was possible. How could Cooley have been inside Utica without signing in and without anyone—at least the people I was able to talk to—seeing anyone come to visit Billie other than Billie's two sisters.

I just didn't make sense to me, dear reader. Yet, given that Utica wasn't exactly a high security facility, something told me that Cooley had taken advantage of that, somehow.

I began reflecting on the last time I saw Billie. Dear reader, this was long before she had been committed to Utica—this had been when she was, for the most part, still sane. I remembered how she felt that Cooley probably wanted her dead—I remember, at the time, asking her why she thought that, and how she told me she didn't know how to explain it, and how it was something she could feel, and how she knew that Cooley probably wanted to shoot her the day he left, and that, though Cooley had shot up her flowers, Cooley probably wished he was shooting her up, and how she always lay awake at night wondering when Cooley would come, and how she had had nightmares dreaming about Cooley gunning her down the way he had gunned down those flowers the day he left, and how, by the time she was committed to Utica, she continued having nightmares about Cooley, and how, as she descended further into insanity, she kept believing she saw Cooley standing in her Utica room in the middle of the night, and how she would tell nurses and orderlies that she saw Cooley hiding behind a tree or some bushes when she was outside for recreation on Utica's grounds, and how she kept telling her sisters that, if something happened to her, if she died somehow, Cooley would be the one to blame.

At last, when the orderly told me I could see Ann now, I kept what I knew had happened to Billie in the back of my mind, when I made my way inside Ann's room to speak with her about Cooley. I wasn't sure, at the time, if Ann would know anything about what had happened to Billie—the idea that Billie didn't die of natural causes—but I was sure Ann could fill in some gaps.

32

To be honest, I never really knew Cooley. Even if he was, frankly, my father. Even if we do, technically, share the same name, I never really knew the man at all—that's the truth of it all

That's probably something you don't want to hear. I'm sure you were hoping I could shed some light on him and his life—you would think that his only living son would be a great source of information. I understand that. I do truly understand why anyone would think such a thing, especially someone writing a biography about Cooley. But, again, I am afraid I will disappoint you—I don't know Cooley, and I know, now, that I never really did.

In a certain sense, he is—and will always be—a stranger to me, you see. Sure, anyone looking at the thing from the outside would wonder: how could a son see his father as a stranger? You may be asking yourself that question, too. I know you have asked a lot of people about Cooley, and I'm sure you have gotten a lot of stories about what he did here and what he did there. I know there are a lot of stories out there about his past—what he supposed to have done in Kansas, or what he is supposed to have done in Oklahoma—but, for me, I can't make any sense of any of those stories. I don't mean that they aren't true. I am certainly not one to say that anything is true or not true—I simply don't know, you know. All I can say, you see, is there is a lot of things out there about Cooley, which make him larger than life. To me, these stories don't tell me anything more about him, or even fill in any gaps in the things I believe I can say I know about him—they are just stories, you know.

I know you are a biographer, and I know you want to get to the heart of the story about Cooley. I know that—I know you want to make sense of his life, so you can make up—what do they call it—a narrative.

Yes, I know your work. I know the kind of books you have written. I know what a biographer is supposed to do—I know all that, you see. Though I know your work, I don't own any of your books—I'm not much of a reader. I have lived the kind of life that people read about, I suppose. And, anyway, I never found the need to read anything, since I always thought it was just a waste of time—all that book learning stuff doesn't put food on the table, or a roof over your head, or keep the cattle tended to. You see the way I live—here on this farm, with all the things I have to do, I never believed reading was ever worth it.

Don't get me wrong. I know what I know, and I know what I know on account of learning things along the way. Being a man, I believe, is about learning what you can and putting it to good use. And, I always believed that an important part of learning is about how you treat others—that is the kind of legacy I want to leave behind, you know. I want to be the kind of guy that others will be glad they knew, and that others will think of fondly.

Cooley is not that kind of guy. You have probably figured that out already. You have probably figured out that Cooley has burned bridges—as they say—all over the place with all sorts of people from all walks of life.

You can ask anyone—they will tell you how much of an asshole Cooley was, and how selfish he was, and how he always strutted around with his chest out, and how he looked down on others, and how he treated his wives like shit when he was married. I don't think Cooley had any real friends. Sure, you may hear some stories here and there by people that say they were Cooley's friends, but I don't think Cooley was ever capable of having friends. You see, to have friends, you have to be a real person with people. I don't know how to say it—you have to deal in facts and not be full of yourself. To have friends, you see, you have to show something likeable about yourself—you have to meet people where they are. Cooley never had that quality. Cooley was always floating about everything and everyone, in a way that made it impossible to know the man—if you never let anyone really know who you are, it's impossible to actually have friends or be friends with anyone.

In the same way, Cooley wasn't the kind of guy that was capable of being a father.

It just wasn't in him, you know. I'm sure you hear things out there about some son somewhere coming to kill Cooley, or some guy that nobody had ever seen before coming into the bar to kill Cooley and everyone finding out the guy was Cooley's son. Sure, I've heard those stories too—I can't say if they are true.

I don't want to say that what you have heard was a lie—particularly about a son or two coming to kill to Cooley, and failing to do it, and Cooley ending up killing them. I don't know. Who I am to say what someone heard, or believe they know? Who I am to say that anyone that told you such things are flat out lying?

As far as I can tell, Cooley had only one son—and that is me.

At the same time, I can't say for sure that Cooley didn't have any other kids somewhere out there. I think anything is possible, when it comes to Cooley's past. Nothing would surprise me, you see—there is no doubt in my mind that Cooley hid a lot about himself. There was a lot about his life that remained a mystery to me and my ma, so who's to say he didn't have a son or two out there?

For that matter, I can't say anything about any woman you might find that says she was married to Cooley at some point in time or another. Who knows how many of those there are? I can't speak to what experiences they say they had with Cooley—like the woman I know you talked to that Cooley left her and shot up her flowers on the way out, or the other woman that told you that Cooley left her the moment he found out she was expecting. Like I said, Cooley burned a lot of bridges everywhere—even Billie, you know, the waitress that Cooley was married to for a while, got the raw end of the deal from Cooley eventually.

You know about Billie, right?

Billie loved Cooley, you know. I don't know why, but she did. It was something about Cooley that she couldn't shake, no matter how hard to tried. There was something about Cooley that made her believe she could have a home with him and a family— something that helped her see the good in him when nobody else did. Like any other woman in Cooley's life, he treated Billie like shit—he talked down to her and didn't do anything around the house. I know Billie wanted to leave Cooley, but she couldn't bring herself to do it, somehow—I don't know why. Eventually, you know, Cooley left Billie—some say that that was what sent Billie over the edge, and that was what made something in Billie snap mentally, and that was what caused her family to send her to New York to be committed to the Lunatic Asylum at Utica.

I always thought it was such a shame what happened to Billie. After all those years working in Cooley's bar, and dealing with all of Cooley's shit over the years, and deciding to let him marry her, it was just such a shame where she ended up. I'm not saying that Billie didn't deserve being committed at Utica—I think it was for her own good, you know. I know you heard about how she tried to kill herself. But, did you know how many times she had tried? I think it was something like five times—thankfully, on account of her family, she was never successful. When Cooley left her, Billie's two sisters knew Billie wouldn't be able to make it on her own and took her in—all those times she tried to commit to suicide, Billie had been at her sisters' place and, each of those times, her sisters managed to stop Billie from following through with it. But, you know, that alone wasn't what forced her family to commit Billie to Utica—they kept those suicide attempts among themselves, you see. They didn't want it to get out about how bad of a shape Billie was in mentally. What made her sisters realize that Billie needed to be sent to an asylum was when Billie sneaked out of the house, made her way to Sleepy Eye—about a two mile walk away—and ended up wandering up and down the center of town. She was naked, foaming at the mouth, and babbling nonsense. And let me tell you how much of a shock that was for everyone in town—I remember hearing that Cooley had been in the bar at the time, and didn't care about Billie, one way or another.

I can't say what he thought at the time, if that is what you are asking me.

I don't think anyone can really ever know what went through Cooley's mind when he watched Billie wander through the streets, gone mad. Sure, you may want to think that Cooley felt sorry for Billie, but I don't think he did—I may not know what goes through the mind of a guy like Cooley, but I am sure, you know, that remorse is not one of those things.

Some people have told me that Cooley laughed when he saw Billie like that. You may have heard that yourself. But, others say that Cooley didn't pay it much attention—they say that Cooley just minded his business as if none of it was happening outside, and as if nobody had gathered in the doorways of every business on the main street just to watch what had become of Billie.

I don't think we will ever know what Cooley did at the time—there may be a little bit of truth in both stories. If you ask me, I think the bottom line is that Cooley didn't care about what he had done to Billie—she didn't matter to him anymore. You see, nobody mattered to Cooley—the only person that mattered to him was himself. And that's just the truth of it. Sure, you may find people out there that will tell you stories about something nice Cooley had done for them, or that he was a good friend of theirs, or that Cooley wasn't as bad as some say he was—you can find anyone out there that will tell you those things. What you have to remember, you know, is that Cooley had a way of being whatever he wanted to be to anyone—yes, he could nice, and charming, and generous, but all those things always had something attached to it. You see, Cooley never did anything for anyone unless he was sure he was going to get something back in return—any of those people you may have talked to that have nice stories about Cooley, if pressed, will tell you that whatever Cooley did for them had a price attached to it. If he gave you a free drink at the bar, you would pay him back in some other way. If he did some nice turn for you—like when he took in old woman Henderson's clothes from the line when she was sick—you always had to pay him back. In some way, you always had to. In the old woman Henderson's case, she let Cooley have one of her extra cows.

So, when it came to doing anything for the sake of doing anything, Cooley didn't work that way. That was why he didn't care much about Billie once she had gone mad—Billie had already run out her usefulness, you know.

And anyway, when Billie wandered through the street until she had to be wrestled under control, Cooley had already moved on to the next woman—that next woman was my mom.

My mom was the schoolteacher in town at the time—she taught kids in the little chapel just off the main street to town. The reverend let her do it, you know, since he only needed to chapel on Sundays. It worked really good—at the most, she taught about fifteen kids. All the parents like her. Everyone in town knew her, and she was given standing credit at the drug store—the couple that owned the drug store had two kids in my mom's class, and they were more than happy to let her have anything she wanted for free.

So, it was on one of her trips to the drug store to get her odds and ends when she heard the commotion about Billie in the street. Like everyone else watching, my mom was watching from the drug store—at the time, she was leaving the drug store and was on her way to the barber who had a shop right across the street from Cooley's. As everyone gawked at what Billie had become—I can only imagine how scary and interesting the whole thing was, especially to all those people that knew Billie—my mom was making her way to the barber to tell him that his kid needed a lot of help with his arithmetic.

My mom, at the time, didn't know Billie. I'm very sure of that.

That was because my mom had been new to town, you see—at the time, all she cared about, I think, was getting the schoolhouse setup and running. The schoolhouse had been abandoned for years, ever since, as my mom would tell it, the town's last teacher decided she would get married and move to Virginia. That was the reason why the town needed a new teacher in the first place, and, for that matter, that was why the town agreed to let my mom reopen the school—the idea was that she would be more dedicated to schooling the town's children and would focus only on that. The small group of men that ran the town believed that only an unmarried woman would do well as a teacher. I can't say if my mom agreed with that or knew anything about it before coming into town—all I know is that the last thing on her mind at the time, once she moved to town, was about getting married.

After being in town for a couple of months, the only thing that mattered to her was being the best teacher she could be—she cared about her students, you know, which was why she was going to the barber to tell him about his kid, in the first place. Women didn't go to the barber's shop, you know—in those days, women had no business there, you know. In those days, women always knew their place. The barber's shop was a place where women just didn't belong—it was a place where only the menfolk gathered and talked about what they always called man's business, whatever that was.

So, for my mom to just walk right into the barber's shop one day to tell the barber that his kid needed help with his arithmetic was something that everyone took notice to— I'd like to think that whoever was there realized that my mom wasn't like the last teacher and that she wasn't a typical female. These two things traveled like tumbleweed, and all on account of the fact that none of the men at the barber's shop that day had ever seen a woman like her talk to the barber like that—some would call that being onery, and some would say that she needed to be put in her place by someone, and some would believe that she was an example of what was wrong with a woman being unmarried.

You see, this was how Cooley first saw my mom: when she left the barber's shop that day, with all the men that were there disbelieving that they had just heard a woman talk to a man that way, even if the barber was the kind of guy that generally didn't get much respect anyway.

The way Cooley would tell it, Cooley had caught sight of her from across the way at his bar as she left the barber's shop—the story is, you know, that Cooley asked someone about her. Who Cooley asked is always the same—it was a guy named Charlie, who owned the building where school was held during the week and where the town preacher held Sunday services.

According to Cooley, Charlie had been seated at the bar, when Cooley asked him about the woman coming out of the barber's shop.

Charlie told Cooley who the woman was—and from that very moment, Cooley knew that the new teacher that was new to town was someone he wanted to get to know better. I don't know if it was that same day, or perhaps the next day, but Cooley made a point, you know, to stop by the school building while school was in session—as my mom would tell it, Cooley would slip in while she was in the middle of a lesson, ease into a back pew, and listen. My mom knew right away—she would tell me—that the man wasn't there because he was interested in how she was teaching the times tables. My mom always told me, you see, that she knew Cooley was interested in her, even if Cooley made it point, you see, to say that he was there to check on a couple of boys he claimed to be mentoring—I say claimed, since, to this day, I sincerely doubt Cooley was mentoring anyone. You see, my mom knew it wasn't about mentoring—for her, she would never go so far as to believe that Cooley's mentoring story was a lie. For my mom, she always took Cooley's mentoring story at face value. I don't know if it was some kind of naivety about what Cooley's real intentions were—whatever the reason, my mom always took Cooley at his word and didn't think otherwise.

I remember how she told me that, when Cooley shifted their first conversation from talking about mentoring those boys and what kind of help the boys needed to do better in arithmetic to asking her to dinner, she realized that Cooley was more interested in her—she knew, on some level, I think, that it really wasn't about the boys doing better in arithmetic. Before long, as the story goes, Cooley would woo my mom—the rest, as they say, is history.

Now, I am the one left to tell the story, since my mom can't speak for herself and Cooley, if he could speak, would tell you nothing but lies. I am the only one that can tell the story the way it needs to be told.

I can't tell you how many times I have heard the story—about how Cooley saw my mom for the first time, and about how he courted her, and about how they married only six months later. Cooley liked to tell it himself. He always told it the same way, too. It was always about how he saw her, and about how he asked someone about her, and about how he decided that he needed to meet her. It was always told as if the story was more about him than about her. There was always this idea that my mom was living an uneventful life, which wasn't a life worth living. And, there was always this way he told the story that made you wonder if it was true or not—there was this creepiness to it, you know. There was always something about it, you know, that always made it seem as if Cooley had come into my mom's life and saved her—this idea, you see, that it wasn't enough just being the one doing the living. As he saw it, he was her savior, I guess—it was like my mom didn't start living until Cooley walked into her life, and then, of course, she became the one doing the dying.

What happened to my mom—how she went from the one doing the living to the one doing the dying, and how she went from teaching in a classroom to wasting away in an asylum—is an important part of Cooley's story, you know. If you really want to know who Cooley is—I mean, what kind of man he really is—you have to start with what happened to my mom.

I know you are a biographer, and I'm not trying to tell you how to write. And, I know you know what happened to Billie, and how people say Cooley killed more people than can be accounted for, and how Cooley is supposed to have dozens of children by dozens of women—and I know you have tried to interview as many people as you can, so you can get an understanding about what makes Cooley who he is. After all, that's why you asked to speak to me—and I know, in asking to speak to me, you would think that I would be able to tell you something about Cooley that you could use. I know I am who I am—and I can't change that—and that who I am should mean something, when Cooley is, frankly, my father.

But, like I told you, I never really knew Cooley—and that's the God's honest truth. That might sound like a strange thing to say—no matter how many times I say it, I'm sure it still sounds strange to you. I don't know where you stand on this—but, in my experience, it is possible to never know someone, if that certain someone is your father. It is possible that a man can make himself into a stranger to his own children—just because a son should mean something to his father, none of that means anything to someone that spent his life always being the one doing the killing.

That's why Cooley is more a stranger to me than a father—and, for me, I always find it troublesome to even call him a father at all.

When you think about each of the young men, claiming to be one of Cooley's sons, coming to kill Cooley, that should tell you something. Sure, I know it says a lot about each of the young men, and how far they were willing to travel, and what they were willing to die for, but I think it says even more about Cooley himself. Sure, I don't know any of these young men, but I can imagine that each of them felt the same way about Cooley—I can imagine that each of them didn't know Cooley all that well, but knew, just the same, that killing Cooley would help them learn something about themselves. Each of them wanted to be the one doing the killing, since being the ones doing the living often means also doing the dying. To hold so much hatred for Cooley—and I'm sure it was a whole lot of hatred, too—only turns you into someone doing the dying. So, in the end, if I can speak for what possibly went through the minds of each of those young men that tried to kill Cooley, if you're already doing the dying, you might as well try to be the one doing the killing.

I know you have probably drawn your own conclusions about each of the young men that tried to kill Cooley, and you have probably made sense out of what each of their deaths mean—and I'm sure nothing I say will add anything to what you already know, or what you can figure out of your own.

All I know is, when I think about how all those young men got killed by Cooley, and what Cooley certainly did to so many other women along the way, and what Cooley did to my mom, I know what it's like to be someone doing the dying—and what it means to be the one doing the dying until you want to be the one doing the killing, for a change. I know what that's like, you know. I know what it's like, you see, to think that being the one doing the killing can, in the end, make you become the one doing the living.

That's why I did what I did, you see—I didn't want to be the one doing the dying anymore. I wanted to be the one doing the living. And, for me, the only way to do that was to be the one doing the killing—the only way to see something like that all the way through was to do what I did: kill Cooley.

33

Dear reader, in interviewing the man that killed Cooley, you must know that there remains some uncertainty as to whether he actually killed Cooley, even if the man currently sits in a state sanitarium.

To be clear, there is little doubt that Cooley was killed somewhere and by someone—that can be corroborated by a trail of plenty of documentation—but there are plenty people that question whether the man I interviewed was actually the person that killed Cooley. Some say that whoever killed Cooley was himself killed by someone else, and that whoever killed Cooley was a hired gun, who, coincidently, was killed by another hired gun. That's only part of the story, dear reader—so bear with me a moment, since the story about Cooley's hired gun is worth parsing a bit further. Those that believe this story about Cooley's death also believe the larger narrative about Cooley having faked his death altogether, under the notion that Cooley himself paid a hired gun to take the blame and Cooley, sometime shortly thereafter, double-crossed and killed this hired gun, so the hired gun wouldn't divulge Cooley's secret. Some even claim to know the hired gun's name—but that is not important. Some even claim to know the name of the man that Cooley killed, in order to be dead body that would be identified as Cooley himself—but that is not important either.

What remains important, however, is what role the man that currently stays in a sanitarium in Arizona plays in the story of Cooley's death. Here, dear reader, I'm not speaking about what the man is believed to have done—that is, what he is in prison for—but about want the man represents more broadly.

Some would say that he isn't one of Cooley's sons at all, but Cooley's hired gun. On the other hand, others would say that he isn't Cooley's hired gun, but someone that simply took the fall for Cooley's death—someone that didn't have anything to do with Cooley's death whatsoever. Still, there are others believe that don't believe either of these things—that don't believe he's Cooley's hired gun nor some random man taking the blame for something he didn't do—and, instead, choose to believe that the man is actually Cooley himself.

Interestingly, the consensus is that the man isn't who he claims to be. Just about everyone I have talked to, with maybe only one or two outliers, believes that the man isn't Cooley's son—even if the man's official name in every document I have been able to find shows he is named after Cooley, with the generational suffix of "junior." It's difficult to say, though, if this disbelief is rooted in a disbelief in the man's story, or if it's a disbelief in the idea that one of Cooley's sons would actually kill Cooley, even if it is widely known that there have been plenty of young men, each claiming to be Cooley's son, that have tried to kill Cooley—or, if it's a disbelief that someone like Cooley, larger than life, could be killed in such an easily explainable way. For most, there's this expectation that there is much more to the story—for most, dear reader, the whole thing seemed too simple to be true.

"So, what do you think?"

The man named after Cooley asked me—the man that, in some corners of mythology about Cooley, some disbelieve that he is actually Cooley's son. He—the man that called himself Cooley's son—was seated across the table from me. His face pale and gaunt from the consumption, coughing frequently.

"What do you mean?"

He coughed, "Do you think I'm not who I say I am?"

I told him that it wasn't my place to make judgments. I told him that I was concerned with was the facts, and that those facts could be pieced together into something that made sense.

"Sure," he said—his eyes looked at me disbelievingly. "You don't make any judgments, huh. Just the facts, right?"

I told him that was right.

"Then," he said. "why are you here?"

I didn't follow what he was trying to say.

"The facts are," he began. "that Cooley wasn't killed, right? Those are the facts—at least, those that want to believe that Cooley couldn't have been killed. A lot of people say that, right?"

"Yes, they do."

"And those are facts for some people, right?"

"I suppose so," I told him. "That's what some people believe."

"Do you believe it?"

I told him, "I'm not here to make judgments." I said that again, but, this time, I realized I had a smile on my face. It couldn't be helped.

"Sure," he laughed, and coughed. "you're not here to make judgments."

Again, I told him I wasn't here to make judgments—I told him that in as clear a way as I could, even though I could tell that there was something about those words that he didn't believe.

"Then," he said. "I ask you again: why are you here?"

"Because I want your side of the story."

"My side of the story?"

"Yes," I told him. "I want to know what you know."

"What I know," he laughed .

"Yes," I said. "What you know."

"What could I possibly know," he asked, looking at his hands.

I told him, "I think what you know is important."

"Important?" He laughed.

"Yes, important."

"So," he laughed and coughed. "You are here to make judgments, huh? If you think what I know is important, you have made a judgment on that, right?"

I didn't know what to say.

"And you want my side of the story, right?" He asked. "You want to know what I know? You think what I know is important—so you can write your book. So, you can write whatever it is you are going to write about Cooley, huh? You don't want my side of the story—there is no side of the story. There is no such thing as what I know, or what anybody else knows. What do any of us know, you know? I don't know anything, you see. I told you that I never really knew Cooley. Didn't I? I said that, right? From the very beginning, I said that, right?"

I told him, yes—yes, he told me that from the very beginning. But, if he is Cooley's son, as he has claimed he is, I said, "Then you know quite a lot."

He laughed at that—it made him have a coughing for a moment, until he placed a handkerchief over his mouth and coughed deeply and heavily into it. He took a deep breath after the coughing, looked at me, and tried to roll up the handkerchief so I couldn't see that it had blood in it—he had coughed up blood.

I laughed, "And you say you aren't here to make any judgments."

"I'm not."

"You never answered my question, mister biographer man," he said. "If you're not here to make any judgments, why won't you answer my question?"

"What question was that?"

Though I said that, I knew what question I purposefully left unanswered. I knew that just as well as I knew he did—it was a question that led me to him, and a question that was at the very center of the mythology surrounding Cooley. It was a question that I had, dear reader, asked myself and found it resoundingly answered the very moment I found out that there was a man named after Cooley and that that man was believed to be Cooley's only surviving son—it was a question, once answered, that made it easy to refute all the nonsense about Cooley finding a hired gun to fake his death, and see through all the mythology that continues to make it difficult to ascertain who the real Cooley was. It was a question, once answered, that allowed me, as a biographer, to separate the mythologized Cooley from the real one—separating the Cooley that has been doing the living in so many people's stories about Cooley from the Cooley that, at some point in time, was the one doing the dying after someone else was the one doing the killing, for a change. It was a question, once answered, which placed me, even as a biographer, in the middle of the biographical narrative I wish to make—which, I admit to you, dear reader, was a new experience for me.

With all that in mind, dear reader, the man named after Cooley—the man who, based on what was relayed to me by his doctor, wasn't expected to live very long with tuberculosis—asked me, "Do you think I'm not who I say I am?"

I looked him in his eyes, and I saw something looking back at me that seemed all too familiar—it was as if I was looking at my own eyes in the mirror, dear reader. I can't explain what that was, or even why that was, but I do know what I saw—something. Whatever it was—if it was pain, or if it was sadness, or if it was numbness, or a combination of all three--

Before I could say anything, the man named after Cooley stopped me with a wave of the hand—he let out a series of hard coughs so deep it seemed as if he would choke on those coughs.

He muffled the coughs with his handkerchief—again, I saw blood.

"Look," I told me. "I don't have a lot of time. I'm dying."

I told him that I wasn't sure what he was saying. And, of course, I wasn't sure what he was saying—sure, I knew, based on what his doctor told me, and based on what I already knew about people admitted to sanitariums, there was only a matter of time. There was no doubt in my mind that such convalescence only lasts so long, and, when one is admitted to a sanitarium, it is only a matter of making sure those that are admitted are living out the rest of their days as comfortably as possible—so, I knew, generally speaking, that the man named after Cooley didn't have a lot of time. For me, dear reader, that was why I sought him out to interview—I knew he didn't have a lot of time.

What I didn't know, though, was that his not having a lot of time was only part of a bigger picture—and, again, rather than keep myself as objective and as distanced as I preferred being when researching and writing about the subject of a biographical narrative, I would find myself put firmly in the center of this biographical narrative, nonetheless.

"I know you know I'm dying," he said. "That's why I'm here, you know."

I listened.

"So," he told me. "I don't have a lot of time. I want to make sure you hear something important—very important. Only I know it—nobody else. If you want to write about Cooley, you'll need to know this—and I need to get it off my chest, you know. I can't take this shit with me—and I won't, you know. This will do you some good, too, I think—maybe it'll help you somehow."

He began to cough violently, convulsing with each cough. He tried to muffle the coughs with his handkerchief—each time he did, I could see more blood and bloody spittle left behind.

I waited for him to tell me what it was he wanted me to know. He piqued my interest with saying that whatever it was he wanted to tell me would do me some good.

Though I didn't know what he meant, I had a strange feeling about it.

"Do me some good?" I asked. "What do you mean?"

"Cooley's grave," he said, rather flatly, watching my eyes to determine what kind of reaction I was showing.

I'm not sure if I had much of a reaction to what he had said. After all, I knew very well about Cooley's grave, or that there is a lot of mythology around where Cooley is said to be buried—as best as I could tell, there is no consensus on where Cooley's grave is located, even if there seems to be some larger agreement that Cooley is, in fact, buried somewhere.

So, I asked him, "What about it?"

"So, you know that nobody knows where it is, right? I'm sure you know that, right?"

I told him that I did know that.

"What if I were to tell you—" he began, pausing to cough up more blood into his handkerchief. "that I know where it is—Cooley's grave?"

It was easy for me to not believe him. There were many theories about Cooley's grave that it was easy to think that he was going to provide me with yet another theory. To be honest, dear reader, the last thing that I wanted to hear was another theory about where Cooley's grave was, since I had, at that time, followed up with every theory, which sent me to various states, and eventually brought me to the conclusion that it was probably unlikely that Cooley's grave would ever be found—that is, of course, if we are to assume that Cooley was, in fact, buried somewhere. I wasn't completely convinced of that.

I let him know that I followed up on every theory about it.

"Theory?"

"Yes," I said. "Where people believe his grave is. I checked on them all. From Kansas to Arizona, from Kentucky to Missouri. I know about them all, and none of the graves I found there are believably Cooley's."

The man named after Cooley laughed heartily at me.

I wasn't sure what it was that I had said that was so funny.

He laughed so heartily that he started coughing again. This time, he didn't cough up blood.

He asked me, "You say you've been to Arizona?"

"Yes," I told him. "To the grave outside Tucson. I've been there. Cooley's name is on the grave, sure, but I know for a fact that Cooley is not buried there."

"Of course, he's not," he said. "I know the grave you're talking about—of course, he's not buried there. I know that, too. I know, because I put that grave there myself."

Dear reader, that stopped me in my tracks—it would be an understatement to say he surprised me. What he said hit me so hard and so fast that I didn't know what to say right away. I was speechless for a moment. That was certainly unusual for me, since I am rarely surprised and, for that matter, I am not used to finding myself without words. In this instance, I wasn't only surprised and without words, but I also realized that what the man named after Cooley had said was something I missed in research—though I talked to an undertaker in Arizona, who was able to tell me from his records that Cooley wasn't the body buried in that grave outside Tucson, it didn't occur to me to ask more about the background of the grave itself.

"You put that grave there?"

The man named after Cooley smiled broadly.

I told him to wait just a minute—to just wait just one minute. I wanted to make sure that what he said wasn't just something he had made up—something that he was using the play games with me.

"You talked to the undertaker there in Arizona, right?"

I told him I had.

"Jebediah?"

I told him, "Yes, that's him. How do you—?" I stopped myself there, since I realized I always knew the answer.

"Yep, I know Jebediah," he told me. "Just like I remember when you came to— what's the word you use—interview—yeah, that's it. I remember when you came to interview Jeb, because I told Jeb what to tell you."

I still had a difficult time believing what I was being told. I thought back to my interview with Jebediah, and I thought about how helpful he had been, and about how, as an undertaker, Jebediah kept very detailed records of every single person that had died and been buried since Jebediah had been undertaker—I also remembered how Jebediah maintained his father's records, given that Jebediah's father had been the town's undertaker before that. I thought about how Jebediah could tell me the name of the person buried in that grave with Cooley's name on the tombstone, and how he had told me that someone from the dead man's family paid for the tombstone to have Cooley's name on it, and how, according to Jebediah, the dead man buried under that tombstone had "Cooley" as a nickname.

"Yeah, sure," the man named after Cooley said. "I can tell you remember. All that about the dead man's nickname being 'Cooley"? Yep, I had Jeb tell you that, so you wouldn't think otherwise."

I didn't know what to say.

"That's one of the things you need to know," he said.

"So, who was the dead man in the grave?" I asked.

"Does it matter?"

I told him, yes, it did matter.

He laughed and coughed, "Somebody Cooley killed. That's all I know."

"Somebody Cooley killed?"

"Yep," he said. He looked at me, shrugging his shoulders.

"But why would Cooley put his name on the tombstone?" I asked. "Why not leave it blank, or leave the grave unmarked altogether?"

He said, "Cooley wanted it that way. He wanted people—like you, I suppose—to think he was dead and that was his grave, you know."

I started thinking, again, about what the undertaker told me. I remembered how the undertaker never actually said anything about how the dead body in the grave marked with Cooley's name became dead, in the first place. All he had told me, I remembered, was that someone paid for the tombstone to have Cooley's name on it—I remembered how carefully he had said that. He didn't say that the name on the tombstone and the dead body went together—what he had said the dead man went by "Cooley," but that this nickname was provided by someone that paid for the tombstone. The undertaker—Jebediah—had been very careful, so that I would think, I began realizing, that the tombstone with Cooley's name on it had nothing to do with Cooley at all. Jebediah had made it clear, I remembered, that there was absolutely no connection between Cooley and the dead body in the grave, and Jebediah made it a point to show me the records he had, showing that someone from the dead man's family—with the dead man's name still unknown—paid for the burial, and even paid to have the tombstone say what it said. I remembered Jebediah telling me that a young woman paid for it—she was presumedly, according to Jebediah, the dead man's widow, so I brought this up with the man named after Cooley.

He laughed, "I told Jeb to tell you that, too."

To be honest, dear reader, I was upset—but, at the time, I was so confused that it was difficult to be as upset as I should have been.

"I suppose I shouldn't ask who the young woman was?"

"Sure," he told me. "you can ask. In fact, she's someone you've heard of."

I wasn't sure what to say.

"Billie," he said. "You know Billie, right? Ah, sure you do. You know all about how she went crazy, right? How Cooley was the reason for that? Sure, sure, you know all about it—I heard you went to see her at Utica, too."

I couldn't help asking, "How do you know that?"

He laughed, "I just know—that's all I'm going to say. I know things."

I watched his face carefully, and I couldn't help feeling strange about his bragging. There was something to do it that made me feel uneasy. I can't say what it was—but it was an unmistakable feeling that was unlike anything I had ever felt before. It was a first for me, you see—feeling as if someone was in more control than I was. I had spent so much of my career as a biographer calling the shots, asking questions to those that I felt had the answers, and being able to construct the kind of narratives I wanted to. Now, not only was I finding myself a part of a narrative that I didn't want to be a part of, but I was also realizing that the narrative was beyond my control—the man named after Cooley was ensuring that.

"Just like I know you visited my mother, too," he said. "Didn't think I knew about that, did you? When you were at Utica."

All I could say was, "I don't follow."

The man named after Cooley seemed to grow agitated that—it was more of a question than a statement, I suppose, since I wasn't sure who he was talking about. I wasn't sure how he had known I visited Billie and Ann at Utica.

"Sure," he said. "You follow. I know you do. I know you understand me—and we understand each other. Right? We understand each other?"

I nodded my head, since that was all I could do—I wasn't sure what was understood between us, and I certainly wasn't sure how. For that matter, I wasn't sure why anything needed to be understood between us. I was the one writing the biography on Cooley, and he was just someone I wanted to interview, in order to collect the information that I needed for the book.

"Look," he said, letting out of couple of small coughs. "I know what my mother, Ann, told you, and know what you have been trying to find."

I looked confused, I'm sure. It wasn't because I was genuinely confused, but because I had a sinking feeling that he did, indeed, know what I was trying to find: Cooley's grave. Finding Cooley's grave, dear reader, was immensely important to me— when it comes to any subject of any biography I have ever written, I have always located where my subject is buried, as a means of tying together the subject's life and the subject's death. Finding someone's grave tells you a lot about the person—when it came to Cooley, the fact that there was no agreement on where he was buried, this told me a lot about him. It's not just that it tells you about their death—which it does quite explicitly— but it tells you about their life. A grave always points to a life, dear reader—we are born, and we live, and then we die. These are the benchmarks for a biographer, and they are the benchmarks which have always guided me as a writer—each and every subject I have ever written a biographical narrative about, dear reader, has required a visit to where they are buried. I have found that a grave speaks to you, somehow—and there hasn't been a single grave I have ever needed to visit, for the sake of writing a biographical narrative about someone, that hasn't spoken to me in some way.

Without a grave, I felt as if Cooley would be perpetually at arm's reach from me—he would be impossible to know. Indeed, there are plenty of stories that provide wonderful anecdotes about Cooley, but most of those anecdotes—what people say about Cooley, or what rumor mythologizes—aren't enough for a biographer. Without a grave to locate and visit, Cooley's mythology, dear reader, is only enlarged and emboldened, until the real Cooley—whoever he was and whatever can be said about him—remains unknowable.

"That's what I want to tell you," the man named after Cooley said. "I want you to know, since we don't have a lot of time—I don't have a lot of time."

I listened carefully.

He reminded me about the grave outside Tucson, Arizona with the tombstone that has Cooley's name etched in it—the one that Jebediah, the undertaker told me about. He reminded me about the man buried in the grave isn't Cooley, but just some guy Cooley killed once upon a time. He reminded me about how the grave sat in the middle of a large patch of land—and how, on that patch of land, the grave sat in the open without nothing around it for hundred yards in every direction. He reminded me, too, that the grave was positioned in that large field, the way that I was, for a reason—it was so, so that whoever was looking for Cooley could easily locate the grave, and any reading of the tombstone would be obvious. He reminded me that there were plenty of people looking to kill Cooley—so many that Cooley grew tired of it.

"As he got older," he told me. "with each bastard that came along wanting to kill Cooley for one reason or another, Cooley got mighty tired of it. You know what I mean? Waking up everyday wondering who was going to track you down, wondering how many there were at any given time, and wondering if you had enough to hold them off. That's how it was for Cooley, you know. The older he got, the harder it was—the harder it was to keep being Cooley."

He coughed heartily again, spitting up blood in his handkerchief.

"But," he said. "don't get me wrong, though. As old as he got, he was still able to shoot the best of them—and he was always ready, you know. No matter who was coming or when they came for him, Cooley was ready. All the way up to the day he died."

"The day he died?"

"Yep," he said. "even on the day he died, he was ready—I just don't think he was ready for someone like me."

I asked him, "What do you mean?"

"I didn't barge in, announcing I wanted to kill him," he told me. "That was the difference—to him, it didn't look like I wanted to kill him. That's what I wanted to do though, from the very beginning. Yep, from the very beginning—I wanted to kill that sonmabitch. I just didn't let that be too obvious, you know."

"So," I asked him. "you wanted to kill Cooley all along?"

He laughed, "Well, of course. I hated that sonmabitch—for what he did to my mother, and to me. Of course, I wanted him to pay for that shit. I was no different from anybody else in that way, I guess—I wanted to blow him to kingdom come for reason. What I knew, you see, was that if I wanted to kill him, and not end up getting killed myself—which, you know, happened to many a man along the way—I had to do things differently."

He began to tell me how he tracked Cooley down for a few years, until he found out where Cooley's bar was located. He told me how watched Cooley for about a week— never once entering the bar. In that week, he knew that Cooley slept in one of the upper rooms that one of the whores used for their tricks. He watched until he figured out when Cooley would shut down the bar—there wasn't a set time of the day, which was probably a way to Cooley to prevent anyone from determining if there was any routine to it all. Yet, he told me, without a routine for closing time and opening time, he was able to get a good idea about Cooley's daily routines—just like how he knew about the shotgun

Cooley kept behind the bar, and how there was another shotgun in Cooley's back room, and how Cooley slept with rifles and pistols in that upper room that overlooked the road coming through town, and how, from the window of that upper room, Cooley could see whoever was coming into town from either end of that road, and how Cooley slept propped up with the bed pushed against a wall, with the door to the room wide open, so Cooley could hear any steps coming his way on the squeaky floorboards and the stairsteps, and how Cooley would keep a lantern glowing downstairs in that back room as a decoy for whoever tried to come into the bar at night, while Cooley made sure that the upstairs room, where he slept, was kept in pitch darkness throughout the night.

"But," he said. "Cooley didn't sleep much. I don't think Cooley slept any more than a couple hours a night."

He told me about how, during that week he watched Cooley from different vantage points across from the bar, he watched two men come to kill Cooley, when they both thought Cooley was asleep and vulnerable. One man had been watching Cooley for a day or two, and waited until Cooley shut the bar down for the night, and tried to sneak in through the front door—Cooley shot him and threw the man's body outside. The other man came at a different time, watched Cooley for about a day or so, too, went inside during serving hours for a drink, waited until the bar closed down for the night, and tried to sneak into the upstairs room Cooley slept in overnight—Cooley shot this man somewhere inside the upstairs room, opened the upstairs window, and tossed this other man's dead body out onto the street.

"I remember seeing," he told me. "how Cooley threw that man's body out of the window and how the body landed plum in the horse trough below."

"And you saw this from across the street?"

I was trying to imagine the layout of the buildings in that section of town, based on what I already knew. Indeed, the town had one long main road that ran through the middle of it. Cooley's bar was across the road from the barber's shop.

"Yep," he said. "I was standing up against the side of the barber's shop. There was this alley between the barber's shop and the general store—from there, you could see the whole front of Cooley's bar. And even the upstairs window to the room Cooley liked to stay in overnight. Yep, I kept myself put right there that whole week, you see."

"Sound like you didn't get much sleep either," I said. It wasn't really a question, but more of a statement.

However he heard what I said, I could tell that he didn't appreciate it very much. His eyes peered closely into mine, his face dropped just a bit, and he leaned forward in his seat.

"Sleeping will get a man killed, you know," he said.

I just looked at him, since I didn't know what to say.

"How many men have you killed, mister biographer man?"

"None," I told him.

He laughed.

"I'm just a writer," I added.

He laughed, "Just a writer? Yep, just a writer. So, what do you know about anything? What do you know about killing a man? What do you know about what it takes? To not get yourself killed? To be the one that keeps on living, and making sure the other guy is the one getting killed? What do you know about any of that, mister biographer man? With your books and your stories and your fancy words? What do you know about any of that?"

I told him, plainly, "I don't know anything about killing a man."

He continued laughing, until he began coughing.

"That's why I'm here talking to you," I said. "Because people say that you know what it means to kill a man—especially Cooley."

He looked at me for a long time—or, at least, what seemed like a long time.

He asked, "Do you believe what people say?"

I told him that it didn't matter whether I believed or not. And that was the truth, dear reader. I told him, just as I would tell you, I was there to only trace facts, whether those facts went, and include as many of those facts in what I was writing about Cooley as I possibly could.

"Facts," he laughed, and coughed. "You love that word, don't you?"

"I am a biographer," I told him. "Facts are my business."

He laughed again at that—and coughed while he laughed.

"I'll give you some facts, mister biographer man," he said. "You want facts? Here's some facts—Cooley's dead body, Cooley's grave, and where it is. Are those facts for you?"

I nodded.

"That grave with the tombstone," he said. "You, me, and Jebediah are the only ones that know Cooley's not really buried there. Everybody else thinks so, but not us. Right?"

I nodded.

"Okay."

He thought for a moment.

"But, there's another grave," he said. "About a hundred yards away, I'd say. But, unmarked, beneath a tree, at the edge of the property—do you remember seeing that tree?"

I did, indeed, remembering seeing a large tree at the outer perimeter of the property on which Cooley's grave was—the one with the obvious tombstone. I remembered seeing that tree—I couldn't remember if it was about a hundred yards away, but it likely was. I remembered the tree, not so much for its size, but because this tree was the only tree planted there on that property. The tree had a broad trunk and a lot of thick green foliage for its head—it was something that stood out, indeed. So, I nodded that I remembered.

He stopped and thought for another moment, then said, motioning with his hands, "Well, this other grave is unmarked—but still marked with a rock, about this size, with a black X drawn into it."

I listened, not knowing exactly what his point was—yet, I could feel where the conversation was going.

"Look," he told me. "if you want to find a fact for your book, that other grave is the biggest fucking fact of all, mister. I oughta know—I digged that grave too. And I put Cooley—the real Cooley—in it."

I didn't know what to say.

"If you go there," he said. "and look under that rock with the X on it, you'll find Cooley's body. The skull first—I think you'll find the skull first. That skull—Cooley's skull—is what you want to find."

"How do I know it's Cooley?"

He looked at me, "You don't know?"

I didn't know, and I told him so. I wasn't sure what it was that would tell me the skull and the remains were Cooley's, when the dead body could be anyone's. It wasn't that I didn't believe him—again, I wasn't in the position to say I believed or disbelieved anyone or anything—I was only looking for facts. Without anything factual telling me—or making it explicit—that the remains were Cooley's, I didn't know if any effort on my part to exhume would be worth it. I wasn't in the business to dig up dead bodies, you know, dear reader. The only thing that interested me were tombstones and documentation—all the things that are factual. If there is on tombstone and no documentation, I felt uneasy pursuing anything.

"You know," he said. "There's a sure-fire way to make sure you know it's Cooley. Look, I get it—you're not sure. But, if you want to be sure—"

"I want facts," I told him.

He laughed, "You want facts. Right? So, if you want facts, mister biographer man, you will want to check the skull's teeth. You know what I mean? You know what it is about Cooley's teeth—do you know about this fact?"

I thought for a moment.

"Cooley's teeth," he said. "That'll show you. That's a helluva fact."

I began remembering something several people said about Cooley's appearance. Some told me that Cooley's wore a set of upper and lower dentures, and that Cooley's dentures were made up of other men's teeth—the story is, dear reader, that Cooley would take the teeth out of the mouths of people he killed here and there. All different shapes and sizes. Of the thirty or so teeth Cooley is believed to have had in his mouth, just about all of them were taken from other people—some say Cooley always bragged about how being the one doing the killing, while others are the ones doing the dying, means taking something away from others, so you can be the one doing the living. In a certain sense, the impression I gathered from that, based on what Cooley is believed to have said, is that taking the teeth out of dead bodies was part of Cooley's process when he was the one doing the killing.

34

Dear reader, the moment I left the man named after Cooley at the Oregon State Tuberculosis Hospital in Salem, Oregon, I booked the next train for Arizona—it took about two days by Southern Pacific. During the trip, I thought about how likely it was that I wouldn't see the man named after Cooley again—I remember how palpable that idea was, when we bid each other farewell. Judging by how much he continued to cough, how much blood always appeared in his handkerchief, and how his physician seemed to believe, as did the man himself, that he didn't have long to live—based on his deteriorating condition, the thought was that the man named after Cooley had about month, but no more than that.

Even so, there was in doubt in my mind that I could make a trip to Arizona and return to Oregon, just to follow-up with the man named after Cooley. I figured I would need only a day or two in Arizona, then, with another two-day trip, I could be back to Oregon—so, I thought I had plenty of time, even though the man named after Cooley only had a short time to live. Essentially, after relocating the unmarked grave and following up with Jebediah, I believed I could always return and interview the man named after Cooley—there remained a lot of unanswered questions that I believed only he could answer, particularly if he was really named after Cooley.

But, I knew I had to think about it further—something was telling me that the answers I was looking for wouldn't be in that unmarked grave he was telling me about. Something about it seemed too foreign and too suspicious—then, of course, dear reader, there was the fact that Jebediah, the undertaker, never mentioned anything about another grave on that property with the marked grave Cooley was believed to be buried in—that confused me, and it made me question what I thought I already knew. In one sense, it confused me, since I hadn't believed that Jebediah had withheld anything from me, and, simultaneously, it made me question whether what Jebediah told me was all there was to know.

Once disembarking the train at the station, I made my way to the Western Union office to send word to my publisher about my detour—a return trip to Arizona would need to be approved, just as any return trip Oregon would need to be. It wasn't that there was a possibility that my publisher wouldn't want me to return to places I have already been—being the kind of author that I am, and the kind of reputation that I had built up for myself over the years, my publisher grants me a lot of leeway. For me, dear reader, it was just a common courtesy on my part, so that my publisher would always know my whereabouts if something ever happened to me—so many things can go wrong for writers traveling the western territories, even when you make sure you are armed, as I always was.

At the Western Union window, I told the clerk my name and provided the information I wanted to send back east to New York.

The clerk recognized my name—which was usual for me—and told me he was familiar with my previous books, which was also usual for me. Then, he told me how much he loved my books about the West—all of them—and how all that I had written about various gunslingers, lawless towns, and loose women were things that inspired him to move to Arizona, after spending most of his life in Boston with his parents.

He said, "I guess I was looking for adventure, you know. I wanted to come out here for adventure. The kind of stuff you write about. You know what I mean?"

I nodded.

As I expected, he asked for my autograph, and prefaced that request with: "I hope you don't mind."

Generally, I didn't mind. But, at the time, I felt compelled to decline the request, since I was in a rush and needed to take the next available stagecoach into town—I noticed a free coach nearby and I knew it wouldn't be free for long. Yet, I was without words in a way I had never been without words before—I paused for so long, I think, that it gave an affirmative impression.

"Let me get it," the clerk said, shuffling through stuff on the counter on his side of the service window. "Ah, yes. Here it is. Right here will be fine."

Instead of a scrap of paper, he had a book, and he opened it to the title page, gesturing for me to autograph there.

I didn't recognize the book right away, until I saw the title page. That was when I realized that he had presented me with his copy of my book on Silas Rondo, which was published some three years ago. I'm sure you are familiar with this book, dear reader—it was a bestseller and, due to the success of that book, my publisher provided me with the largest advance I have ever received for this current book on Cooley. It was the Silas Rondo book, you see, that gave me the idea about writing about Cooley in the first place. Though Silas was considered one of the most despised men in his time and, because of that, he died a very violent death, in researching about Silas's life, I came across Cooley's story—those that knew and hated Silas always told me that Cooley was much worse. When I wrote about Silas's life—about a desperado that robbed trains, killed sheriffs in many counties, and raped a number of women—I never lost sight of how much bigger a book on Cooley would be, primarily because Cooley's life was constructed around so much mythology. That's not to say, though, that Silas's own life didn't revolve around a certain amount of mythology—the difference was that, for Cooley, there was so much more that remained unknown, such as how Cooley died and where Cooley was buried. At least for Silas, as I mention in that book, there was no doubt that Silas died the way he had—in a gun battle with a posse of lawmen—and that he had been buried, after his dead body had been paraded from state to state, and county to county, and town to town.

"This was my favorite of yours," the clerk told me. "Silas was such a bastard, you know. The way you write about him—it really makes him come alive on the page, you know. Such a bastard, he was! And killed so many people. And robbed so many. Such a great book—my father loved this book too."

I nodded and smiled.

"I'm glad you enjoyed it," I told him.

This was something I tended to say—as a habit—whenever someone droned on about how much they loved one of my books. It's not that I didn't care, dear reader, or that I didn't appreciate their appreciation, it was that, once a book was written and published, it doesn't feel like mine anymore—when I look at the finished product, such as the binding, the cover with the title and my name, the inside title page with the title and my name, the whole thing seemed more otherworldly than of this world. I can flip through to the first page and read the first few sentences, wishing—rather instantly—that I had written those first few sentences differently. So, there's always the craft of it all— the idea that something is never really finished artistically, and that something is always left unsaid.

"I have a foundation pen here," he told me, fumbling for a moment for one on the other side of the window counter.

He handed the foundation pen to me, and I took it—I autographed the book's title page.

"Father won't believe this," he said, mostly to himself. Then, to me, "My father, you see, he has all your books. He has a copy of the Silas Rondo book, too. He went to a book reading—or a lecture, or talk, or whatever it was called—you had back in Boston last year. He said it was amazing. He got me into Silas Rondo after that—I read his copy, then saved up to buy my own. That's this one—the first book I ever read cover to cover. Boy, that Silas Rondo was a bastard."

I nodded and smiled.

"Anyway," the clerk went on. "once I read about Silas Rondo, that's when I got the idea—about coming West. That's why I came here, you know. To go to the very spot where they gunned him down. That Silas Rondo—what a book. Changed my life, you know."

I did, indeed, know, since it was in a little town outside of Tucson where Silas

Rondo was finally gunned down.

I handed the book—now autographed—back to him, and said, "Thank you."

He took the book, looked at my autograph inside, closed it, and cradled the book to his chest. He said to himself, "Father just won't believe this—I should send him a telegram, Western Union."

I said, rather smartly, "Well, you're in the right place to do that."

The clerk laughed heartily. "Father is a telegraph operator just like I am."

"Sounds like telegrams are the family business," I said.

He laughed so hard he snorted a little.

I smiled.

I paused a moment, beginning to thank him again for sending my telegram and for being such a great reader. I was just about to tell him to give his father my best and to wish him—the clerk—well, when the clerk stopped me.

"Wait a minute," he said, then to himself, "Wait a minute. Ah, yes."

I watched him fumble through a small stack of what looked like telegrams that had just arrived. He thumbed carefully through them.

"There was a telegram for you," he told me. "Ah, yes. Here it is."

He handed me the note and I read it to myself—the note had come from the Oregon State Tuberculosis Hospital in Salem, Oregon, from the physician I spoke to, who was caring for the man named after Cooley. In the note, the physician informed me, in this formal language, that the man named after Cooley had died overnight, choking on his coughs.

I'm sure the expression on my face gave the clerk the idea that the telegram I received wasn't good news. Still, I was sure he had already read it himself.

"Bad news?" He asked.

I told him, "Something like that."

I folded the telegram and shoved it into my knapsack. I proceeded to wish the clerk well again, and thank him for being such a great reader, and to give my best to his father—then I turned to leave.

He stopped me again, "I hope you don't mind me asking."

I stopped and turned back.

"I don't know how to ask this," he said. "I mean, who am I to ask you, right? But, I was just wondering if you were working on another book now—like the Silas Rondo book—and what it's about, if you don't mind. I just love your work, you know. Hey, wait—is that why you're here in Arizona?"

I smiled and nodded.

"I knew it," he said. "I knew it, I knew it."

I told him I was working on another biography and, yes, it would be something like the Silas Rondo book. I said, "This one, though, he is much worse a guy than Silas Rondo ever was."

"Much worse?" He asked. "Worse than Silas Rondo?"

I told him, yes.

"Is it anyone I've heard of?" He asked.

I mentioned Cooley's name.

"Cooley?" He said, sounding like a question, though it was much more of a statement. "Cooley—yes. Yes, I've heard of him. Oh, yes—he was a cold-blooded killer, right? Silas killed people, but Cooley really killed people, you know. I heard he killed a whole family once—something like six of them, I think. Shot all the poor children right in the head, I heard. And killed the wife—she was pregnant, they say. And they say he killed a lot of people, too. No one knows how many, but he's supposed to have killed a lot of people. People say so many things about him."

I nodded, "They do, indeed."

"A book on Cooley," he said to himself. "I can't wait to read it."

I smiled.

"Do you know when it will be published?" He asked.

I told him I didn't know—I could have said a bit more, but I didn't want to say anything more than I already had. It didn't completely have to do with the fact that I needed to leave—even if I had more time to chat, I still wouldn't have said much more.

"I have to tell father about this," he said to himself. "A book on Cooley—oh, father will be pleased to hear about that." Then, directed at me, he said, "He's a big fan of your work, too. Did I tell you that already? He's just as big a fan as I am."

I nodded.

Then, I told him, in as polite a way as I could, that I had to be moving along. I didn't want to be rude about it, but I did need to leave. You understand that, dear reader. As much as it buoys my spirits to hear someone speak about how much they appreciate my work—and I do, in fact, greatly appreciate such words—I made it clear to the clerk that I must be on my way.

"Oh—that's right," he said. "I understand. Not a problem. It's such an honor to meet you—I can't wait to let father know. Father won't believe this—he just won't believe this."

I bid him farewell and turned to walk away.

He said, "Best of luck on the new book." He waved at me enthusiastically.

I stopped and looked back at the clerk for a moment—I could see he had stepped away from the service window, and I could only see the mound of his back as he hunched over the counter behind the window. Immediately, I could hear the unmistakable clicking sound of the telegraph in-use—those short and long keypresses of a message being sent from one telegraph operator to another, from one machine to another machine. I knew, dear reader, that the clerk was doing exactly what he said he wanted to do—he was sending a telegram to his father. I knew, too, that, if his father was also a telegraph operator, he was probably sending the telegram directly to his father's telegraph office—it was quite easy for me to imagine that happening.

35

When the stagecoach took me and a couple of other passengers—an elderly woman and a younger woman, who appeared to be related to one another, but I didn't care to ask, and did my best to not make eye contact—from the station into town, the reinsman pulled the team to a stop in front of the general store. The reinsman hopped down from the box and helped the women down and out of the wagon, so they wouldn't trip on or be snaggled by their flowy dresses, while the conductor fellow gathered the two women's luggage from the boot—the two of them had about six huge pieces collectively, not to mention to a large duffel bag in the younger woman's lap.

The elderly woman stepped out first, and the younger woman passed down the large duffel to the reinsman. Before the younger stepped out, she paused to look at me— it was if she was seeing me for the first time, even though she had gazed at me the whole trip from the station into town.

"You're that author, aren't you?" She asked me.

I smiled—being recognized, especially in situations like these, I tended to find that the best response was to make as simple a response as possible. For me, in my experience, a smile always sufficed. If I had a hat on—and in this case, I did—I would tip the brim.

"Mother," she called to the elderly woman. "You were right—it is him."

The elderly woman looked up at me from outside the coach. She located some spectacles and fixed them on her face—her two eyes peered carefully.

"Lamb's sake," the elderly woman said. "I thought so—yes, I did."

The younger woman asked, "You wrote that book—what's it called. Aw, shoot. What's the name of it, mother?"

The elderly woman said, straightaway, "Silas Rondo, dear."

"Ah," the younger man said. "that's right. Silas Rondo—that's right."

The elderly woman smiled at the younger woman—her daughter, which became increasingly obvious to me, given their striking resemblance to one another—then smiled at me.

"We just love that book," the younger woman said. "My mother and I both. Right, mother?"

The elderly woman nodded and smiled, mostly at me. It was then, dear reader, when I noticed that the elderly woman was looking at me very carefully, in much the same way when they find what they are looking at aesthetically pleasing. Men look at attractive women that way—and women look at attractive men that way. The elderly woman looked at me that way—I don't mean to say that to say anything specific about me. I just know the look—and the younger woman had the same look, gazing into my eyes very carefully.

"Didn't we read that book twice, mother?" The younger woman asked.

"That we did," the elderly woman confirmed, still smiling.

The conductor fellow had stacked the two women's luggage behind them on the walkway in front of the general store. A fellow from the hotel, next door to the general store, hurried out to gather up the two women's luggage—the elderly woman barely noticed and, instead, kept her attention on me.

"We did indeed," the younger woman said to me. "Like I said, we loved that book. You write about Silas Rondo so honestly. He's such a—what did you call him, mother? What did you say Silas Rondo was?"

"A desperado," the elderly woman said.

"That's right," the younger woman said. "A desperado—such a desperado. Such a very bad man. Such a horrible man. Such a wonderful book."

The elderly woman said, "Just wonderful, yes."

I smiled and nodded. I didn't know what else to do, since, as you know, dear reader, I find it difficult hearing how much a reader enjoys my work. No matter how many books I published, situations such as these always seems foreign to me.

"Well," I said. "I'm glad you enjoyed it. And I appreciate your readership—both of you."

The younger woman noticeably blushed, and the elderly woman broadly grinned. The two of them, so transfixed on me, seemed to forget that the reinsman and the conductor, not to mention the fellow from the hotel, were waiting on them.

"Madams," the reinsman called. "We gotta schedule to keep, you know."

"Yep, gotta keep our schedule," the conductor chimed in—he had already climbed back up into the box.

The two women were profusely apologetic. While the elderly woman turned, began to tend to their luggage, and interacted with the fellow from the hotel, the younger woman gave me a smile, stepped out of the coach, with the gentlemanly helping hand of the reinsman—a gulf of wind puffed through blowing her dress so that you could see her petticoat peek out from underneath, as she kept a gloved hand on her hat and the other on her parasol.

I stepped down myself and gave the reinsman two silver dollars for a tip.

The reinsman tipped his hat to him in thanks, secured the coach door with a turn of the latch, and disappeared around the back of the coach. Quickly, he climbed back up into the box next to the conductor—the reinsman took the control of the team and told the conductor about the tip.

"One for you," the reinsman said. "and one for me."

"Thanks, father," the conductor said.

It was then that I realized that the two men—the bearded reinsman obviously older than the smooth-faced conductor—shared a resemblance, in fact. I could tell, then, that there were, indeed, father and son.

"I hope you don't my asking, sir," the younger woman said, grabbing my attention. "But, how long will you be in town?"

I told her I wouldn't be there longer than a day, or perhaps two at the most.

"Well," the younger woman said. "Mother and I will be staying here for—"

The elderly woman jumped in, "Two weeks."

"Yes, two weeks," the younger woman told me. "So, I—or we would love to have you come by sometime. Anytime. Or, at least before you leave town. We could have drinks, you know—the three of us, you know."

I glanced at the elderly woman, and it was clear to me that she didn't look like the kind of person that had drinks with anyone. Perhaps, I figured, that was something she had done long ago—maybe, before her daughter was born—but it certainly wasn't something she was inclined to do these days. I was certain I was reading her feebleness well—as a writer, dear reader, one of the things one must be competent in is characterization, and I had no doubt in my mind, when falling on all the people I had written about over the years in so many different books, that the elderly woman had a saintly appearance. In fact, she seemed so saintly that she reminded me of my own mother.

The elderly woman asked me, "You like whiskey?"

I nodded, "Sure, ma'am."

The elderly woman smiled broadly, "Great—then we will all get some shots before you leave. Okay?"

I nodded, still surprised at the way she was speaking.

"And, by the way," the elderly woman said. "Don't call me ma'am. I ain't that old. Ma'am is what you call an old person—someone just about in the grave, if you ask me. So, do me a favor, don't call me ma'am—just drives me crazy."

I told her I wouldn't call her that.

"So," the younger woman said. "we'll see you later. Maybe tonight. Is that okay? Drinks tonight—all three of us. What do you say?"

"Yes," the elderly woman said. "What do you say?"

The thought of having drinks with the two of them was the last thing I wanted to do. It wasn't that anything was wrong with the two of them, or that I wasn't the kind of person that liked having a good drink here and there. What it was, dear reader, was that I was in Tucson for a specific reason—and seeing that reason all the way through required keeping as clear a head as possible.

"As lovely as it sounds," I told them. "I'm afraid I can't do it tonight. I—"

"Ah," the elderly woman said to the younger woman. "don't you see?"

The younger woman's face had a glint of recognition, even though she was obviously disappointed.

The elderly woman said, "Of course! He's probably busy—is that it?"

The younger woman stared into my eyes.

The elderly woman went on, "Busy with your next book? Is that it? Sure, I'm sure that's what it is—yes. The next one—is that why you're here? Sure, that's what it is. That's it, indeed."

I nodded.

The younger woman continued staring into my eyes until it had become uncomfortable for me. Still, for her, nothing was uncomfortable—for her, there was no crossing a line where staring at someone so long became this violent act.

"Darling," the elderly woman said to the younger woman. "you see, don't you? He's working on his next one."

The younger woman asked, "The next one?" The question wasn't just directed to the elderly woman, but also to me, somehow.

"Are you working on the next one?" The elderly woman asked me.

I told her that I was, indeed.

"Oh, for joy," the elderly woman said. "That's wonderful! Glory be." She grasped her hands together, as if I, somehow, had become an altar to be prayed to.

The younger woman asked, "Is it another one on Silas Rondo?"

"I do hope so," the elderly woman said. "Another Silas Rondo book would be a blessing. We just loved that book—you know. I know the book ends the way it does—with Silas getting shot up—but I still keep wondering about all the money Silas stole in that last job. Whatever happened to it? That would make a good story, you know. And, talking about the surviving members of Silas's gang—Butch, Huey, and that other guy. What's his name?"

The younger woman said, "Cooley, mother."

"Ah yes," the elderly woman said. "Cooley—that's his name. The one that helped Silas kill that family. Right?"

The younger woman nodded, but her eyes never left mine.

"Yes—that Cooley fellow, whatever happened to him?"

I told the elderly woman that Cooley was, in fact, the subject of the book I was currently at work on.

"Oh, glory be," the elderly woman exclaimed, grasping her hands together again. "That's just wonderful—a book on Cooley. That's fantastic. He was my favorite character from the Silas Rondo book—of course, other than Silas himself, I mean."

"Mine too," the younger woman said. "What a horrible man!"

"Yes," the elderly woman said. "Just horrible."

A man that looked like the hotel's proprietor came out of the hotel and stood beside the other man that was gathering together the two women's luggage.

"Your room is ready," he said, perhaps to both the elderly woman and the younger woman, though it seemed as if he was directing most of what he was saying to the elderly woman in particular. "May I get you checked in?"

"Ah, sure," the elderly woman said, turning towards the proprietor, with her hands now clasped as if he, now, was an altar to be prayed to. "Please do, my good man, yes."

The proprietor nodded in satisfaction and directed the man gathering the women's bags to take them inside the hotel. The proprietor headed inside the hotel with the baggage handler person leading the way—somehow, the baggage handler managed to gather all of the two women's luggage under either arm and in either hand, until he was sure to have it all in one trip, however exasperated he looked in accomplishing this.

The elderly woman turned to me, with her gloved hand reaching, with the palm down, "It was so nice to have made your acquaintance."

I took her hand and kissed the back of it in a gentlemanly way—the younger woman took a step to the side and watched me. I bowed to the elderly woman sightly— there was just something regal about the elderly woman that required strict adherence to one's etiquette, even if, for me, I tended to believe that chivalric etiquette like that was outdated in a world where men like Cooley could kill innocent, pregnant women. So, it was something of a breath of fresh air—the elderly woman reminded me of my mother's antebellum Southern belle charm, before the war changed all of that. It reminded me, too, about how my mother referred to the war as the War of Northern Aggression, which always seemed so historically revisionist to me.

She went on, "Do stop by before you leave town—we would love to hear more about your book in-progress—about that horrible Cooley. Right, darling?"

As the elderly woman stepped aside, the younger woman reached her gloved hand to me as well, with the palm facing down. Her eyes peered into mine, as if she could read my soul. She said, "Right, mother. We would love—just love that."

When I kissed the back of the younger woman's hand, I noted how much emphasis she had placed on the word love—she had mouthed it in a way that seemed, quite clearly, intent on seducing me in some way. It reminded me of another kind of Southern belle charm, in which women engaged in a kind of Southern aggression.

"Come, darling," the elderly woman said. "We must let him be on his way now. We have held him up long enough, you know."

"Yes, we have—" the younger woman said, squeezing my hand just as I had tried to let go. "We have held him up—" In a whisper that only I could hear, "We can hold each other up—you can hold me up anytime."

I bowed my head to her.

"Anytime," the younger woman repeated, gripping my hand, but finally letting it go. She turned and said, "Yes, mother, we must let him be on his way."

She turned back to me and bowed her head.

When she turned to walk away, I could smell her perfume—it was sweet and luxurious in the still air. The long blonde locks of her hair had a golden gloss in the sunlight—the soft curls were put up and wrapped tightly under her hat. Once she turned, from behind, I noticed how slim her waist was, and how, when she walked, she bounced and seemed to float with each stride, and how she carried herself with a high level of confidence but also grace.

Instantly, dear reader, there was no doubt in my mind that she reminded me of my wife—my estranged wife, to be more exact—and how that wasn't a good thing for me. She reminded me about that other world that I have tried to not think about for a long time—that other world where it doesn't matter how many books I write and publish, or how many fans love my work, or what wonderful things Theodore Roosevelt said about my last book, or how many copies my Silas Rondo book sold. She reminded me of a simpler time—she reminded me of all things I gave up just to write the Silas Rondo book, and how much I was still giving up just to write a book on Cooley.

Just before the younger woman disappeared in the hotel behind the elderly woman, she turned over a shoulder, smiled and winked at me. I don't need to tell you, dear reader, what that meant, any more than I need to tell what all of my interactions with her meant—none of it was lost on me.

Still, I knew that that would probably be the last time I would ever see the younger woman—in knew this, dear reader, in the same way I knew it would be the last time I would ever see my wife. The difference between the last time I saw the younger woman and the last time I saw my wife was that my wife didn't smile nor wink at me—she looked at me with disdain, with hatred, and told to me to go to hell and that I wouldn't see my little son ever again.

That was three years ago—just before my book on Silas Rondo was published, and I told my wife I needed to go on tour to market the book and research the follow-up book on Cooley, and she told me that she was tired of my being away from home so much, and how my work was always more important than her and my son, and how I wasn't being much of a husband and that I was being a horrible father, and I told her she was overreacting, and she told me that I could just go to hell—and whatever life I was living, while researching Cooley and realizing how increasingly unknowable Cooley was becoming, was also becoming a kind of hell that was only consuming me, even if it was a lonely kind of hell of my own making.

36

Jebediah's place was just a five-minute walk off the main street, just beyond the town mill and the building where townspeople worshipped God. Next door to Jebediah's place—which had his undertaker services in the front parlor and, in back, had a small room where Jebediah lived—was a little shack where the town doctor practiced. It was no coincidence, of course, that the town doctor and the town undertaker had buildings so close to one another—there was no doubt in my mind, dear reader, that having the town doctor next door was good for Jebediah's business, which was exactly what Jebediah admitted to me.

Jebediah's carriage and team were hitched at the post in front of Jebediah's place—that told me he was there, and not out on calls looking for business.

As I made my way up to Jebediah's front door, I could tell that the town doctor wasn't in, since there was a sign indicating this in the town doctor's front window. Out front, lying on the ground between the two buildings, were three new wooden coffins, all topless. Nothing was inside any of them. But, I knew, based on what Jebediah once told me, that, if empty coffins were sitting out there in the open, that meant that some dead bodies would be filling them very soon.

Just as I stepped on Jebediah's front porch, but before I could knock on the door, the door opened and a young man I had never seen before, dressed in a poorly-fitted black suit, stepped out.

"Howdy," he said.

I had the impression that the young man had watched me walk up and figured that I was a customer that needed undertaker services.

"What's the name of the deceased?" The young man immediately asked me. His eager eyes looked at me and he was rubbing his hands together. "I can get another coffin ready in a couple of hours—I just need the measurements."

I told him that that wasn't why I was there—I wasn't there to bury anyone.

"Oh," the young man said, disappointedly. He pointed to the town doctor's building next door and said, "Doc Baker will be back afterwhile. The Hansens went into labor—Mrs. Hansen did, I mean. So, he should be back afterwhile—I don't know when, exactly."

I told him, "I'm not here to see the doctor."

The young man looked confused. For him, if I wasn't there for undertaker services and I wasn't there for the doctor, he couldn't wrap his mind around what other possibility there could have been. He was so confused he didn't know what to say—not knowing what to say placed the young man so much at unease that, I think, he thought I was there to kill him, perhaps.

So, I reached inside my bag for something that would place the young man at ease and explain why I was there.

"Look," he said, showing me his hands. "I don't want no trouble, mister."

I scoffed at that, and retrieved a letter—though folded neatly, it was clear to the young man that I didn't have a gun, which would have required his showing me his hands the way that he was. Indeed, a letter wasn't a gun.

"You don't understand," I said.

He lowered his hands slowly. He didn't seem to understand, but wasn't sure about where his hands needed to be, even with not understanding what was happening, or what was about to happen.

I brandished the letter, so he could see very clearly that the paper had writing on it, even if I was sure he wouldn't be able to actually read it.

"I'm looking for Jebediah," I said.

"You're looking at him," he said.

I was confused, because this young man wasn't Jebediah. I knew who Jebediah was—I had met him. "You're not Jebediah—I know Jebediah—the undertaker here. This is a letter he sent me a couple months ago—he's expecting me. Jebediah is—he's expecting me."

The young man looked at me closely.

"Like I told you—" the young man said. "I'm Jebediah—that's my name."

I was now looking at him closely. I wasn't sure what to make out of what he was saying. There was still something, for me, that wasn't adding up.

"You're looking for my pa," the young man said. "He's the senior, and I'm the junior. I'm named after him."

It was slow to dawn on me that the young man that I was talking to was Jebediah's son. In fact, dear reader, I didn't know Jebediah had a son. Meeting him all those months ago, before he began exchanging letters here and there, I always had the impression that Jebediah didn't have a family—that he didn't have a wife, and hadn't ever been married, and that he certainly didn't have any children. Indeed, if he had any children—a son, in fact—he would have mentioned it. In my experiences, both professional and personal, I had never known a man that didn't mention their children—and there is always a certain amount of pride for men who have sons, I would say, and still more pride when sons carry their father's name.

"His son?" I asked—I had said that out loud, though it was more about saying it to myself.

He nodded.

"Where's Jebediah—your father?" I asked, peering towards the building behind the young man and hoping that the Jebediah that I had come there to see would come out the same door the young man had. "Is he around? You see—he's expecting me."

The young man said, "I understand that, mister. But, my pa isn't around. I mean, he's passed on."

What he had said didn't register right away.

"He passed away last month," the young man said. "I guess you didn't know. Yeah, he passed away last month—died right back there in the back of the building. In that little room. In his sleep, he did—Doc Baker said he died in his sleep. Just like that, I guess. Don't know why, or what caused it—but, it was just like that. The way he died, I mean—in his sleep."

I looked carefully into the young man's face and increasingly recognized that the young man and the Jebediah I knew shared a striking resemblance.

The young man went on, "Doc Baker says my pa probably didn't suffer none—when you die in your sleep, there's no suffering, Doc Baker says. But, it happened pretty suddenly. Nobody told you—I'm sorry you came all this way. You said he was expecting you—that he wrote you a letter?"

I showed the young man the last piece of correspondence I received from Jebediah. The young man took the letter, held it with both hands, and skimmed the writing—Jebediah's sweeping letters with the ink from the fountain pen he had used soaking through the paper.

"Wait a minute," the young man said. "You're the one writing that book on Cooley, right?"

I nodded.

"Ah, yes," the young man said. "There's something in here—something my pa wrote about you, or about Cooley, or something like that. It's in here."

He turned and went inside, and I followed.

"After he passed, I took over pa's business," the young man said. "I never had much of a relationship with him, you see—he left my ma when I was, they say, knee high to a June bug. My ma and I lived in Virginia. She's still there now—in Virginia. But, I came here once I heard about pa's passing—I came here and took over things. My ma thought it was crazy—to come all the way here to run a business I don't know nothing about and for someone that never cared about me. Never cared about me or my ma. But, here I am—I came anyway. I guess it was a way to learn who he was—and who I am, too. You probably don't want to hear all of that—you're here for the Cooley stuff."

"I don't mind at all," I told him. And, I didn't mind, since I remained curious about who the young man was, and even more curious about his history.

We passed through the large front area of the building, where Jebediah prepared dead bodies for burials and constructed the pine boxes for coffins. All of his tools—now the young man's, the younger Jebediah's—gathered nearly on a desk in a corner. All of Jebediah's records, bound in ledger books, stacked on the floor, up against a wall—it was among them, dear reader, where Jebediah pointed out his records of Cooley's burial and the location of Cooley's grave.

He stepped into the back room where Jebediah slept in a little, narrow bed, a tub, a stove, and a little safe.

Though I stopped in the doorway between that back room and the front parlor, he beckoned me to follow him—he motioned for me to sit in a rose-colored armchair in the corner of the back room, near the foot of the bed.

"There was something," he said, sifting through another stack of bound ledger books stacked on top of the safe. "that he wanted you to know about—it was something that Doc Baker told me about. Something about a grave you'd be interested in—pa drew it on a map for you, I guess. Here, take a look."

He handed me a piece of paper that had been wedged in one of the bound ledger books. It was clear to me that the young man wasn't sure what it was that he was giving me—the piece of paper may as well have contained nothing but a foreign language. On it, there was a crudely drawn map—no doubt, in Jebediah's handwriting—that noted the area where the grave marked as Cooley's grave was located and another area near a tree where there was another grave.

"Do you know what it is?" The young man asked me. "I know it's a map, but do you know what it means?"

I looked up at him and nodded.

"Doc Baker wouldn't tell me anything," the young man said. "I'm sure he knows, but he won't say. All I know is that pa left this for you—that's what Doc Baker told me, you know."

I studied the map carefully, being reminded about what the man named after Cooley had told me. On the reverse side of the piece of paper, Jebediah wrote the word "teeth." Nothing else—just that one word. I knew, then, if I hadn't completely known already, that what the man named after Cooley had told me was the truth and, for that matter, that Jebediah, from the afterlife, was pointing me in the direction I needed to go, even if he had lied to me in the here and now.

The young man went on, "That one mark, there, is where Cooley was buried—I don't know what that other mark, there, is. I know it's another grave, but not whose grave it is."

I thought about filling him in, but I decided against it. I wasn't sure if it was something that Jebediah wanted his son to know about fully.

There was the sound of a horse-drawn carriage approaching until the sound made it clear that someone had arrived outside. I turned to look out through the doorway to the front parlor and out through the front door to the front of the building, seeing the dirt dust settling, hearing the grunting of horses, and the soft murmuring of someone taking to their horses.

"Looks like Doc Baker is back," the young man told me. "I guess he must've finished delivering the Hansens' baby."

The footfalls of boots reached the outside of the front door and stopped.

"I heard you were in town," the man—Doc Baker—standing in the doorway said to me. "And, I take it, Jeb has given you the map, too?"

"That I am," I said. "And, yes."

The young man jumped in, "I surely did."

Doc Baker was an older man, very slim, with horn-brim glasses. His hair was thinning on top and he had whiskers contouring his jawline, but no mustache. To me, dear reader, he resembled Abraham Lincoln, if Lincoln had been about twenty years older and a country doctor.

"Did the Hansens have their baby?" The young man asked.

Doc Baker stepped inside the doorway, sat on a stool just inside, and placed his medical bag on the floor at his feet. It was clear that he was tired—he had sweat stains in the armpits of his white dress shirt, with a thin layer of dust covered his black vest, black pants, and black boots.

"They did, indeed," Doc Baker told the young man, even though Doc Baker's eyes remained on me. "A boy—healthy. The mother is resting now—she's fine. Mister Hansen is naming the newborn after his father—he's the one that—well, the one that Cooley killed."

"That's right," the young man said, mostly to himself. "I heard about that."

"And you want to write a book about Cooley?" Doc Baker asked me, peering into my eyes carefully. "About a cold-blooded killer? A man that turned this town upside down? Killing women, killing children, killing old men, killing horses even—nearly killed me, too. A book about Cooley? Anything for a buck, huh? It's not enough that you have to write a book about that Silas Rondo fellow—that killer? Now, a book about Cooley of all people? Good God almighty!"

I didn't know what to say to him. It was clear to me that he wasn't interested in anything that had to do with Cooley. Certainly, the thought of a book about Cooley was something that Doc Baker was disgusted by. That disgust was, dear reader, understandable.

"I understand that—" I said to him.

"You understand?" Doc Baker laughed. "What do you understand, mister bestselling author? What do you understand, exactly? If you're writing about Cooley—like you did with Silas Rondo—you don't understand very much, I would say. Not very much at all—all you do is glorify these murderers."

The young man seemed speechless mostly, but managed to say, just under his breath, low enough for only me to hear, "But, I liked the Silas Rondo book."

"I really don't know what to tell you," I told Doc Baker. "But I'm not glorifying murderers, as you say. I'm a writer—a biographer. I'm only interested in facts and telling stories."

"Facts," Doc Baker scoffed. "Telling stories."

"Cooley's story is a story that needs to be told," I told him. "If we don't know our history, as they say, we are doomed to repeat it."

Doc Baker laughed, "Is that what you tell yourself? So you can sleep at night? All that about history and—what did you say—and being doomed to repeat it and all of that malarky. Such wonderful words for someone that's never been on the wrong end of Cooley's gun. You don't know what that's like—do you?"

"No, I don't," I told him.

"Of course, you don't," he said.

There were a few beats of silence

"Well," Doc Baker continued. "I know—I know all too well, sir. And—" He pointed at the young man. "Frankly, his pa knew—Jebediah knew too."

All I could do was look at Doc Baker, since I didn't know what else to say. I didn't know what else there was to say that hadn't been said already. It was clear to me that he wasn't happy with my writing a book on Cooley, and there was very little, if anything, I could do to change his opinion. Quite simply, he was more than just a critic—every writer has critics and, though I have a lot of fans, dear reader, I do have my fair share of critics—he was a detractor. Doc Baker, I saw, was someone that was completely against Cooley being immortalized in anything—the thought of a book on a person that caused so much pain and suffering for so many people was something that Doc Baker, and plenty others of that sort, couldn't bear.

"Your book," Doc Baker said. "will only give Cooley life—he doesn't deserve that, sir."

"So, however horrible he is, his story doesn't deserve to be told?" I asked.

To me, dear reader, this seemed like a perfectly fair question, when looking at the whole thing objectively. But, no sooner than the question came out of my mouth, I knew it was probably a horrendous thing to ask, even if it didn't sound all that horrendous in my head beforehand.

Doc Baker took a long look at me, with his eyes sweeping up and down the length of my body—his eyes settled in on my eyes with a kind of disdain that seemed, to me, reserved for those that kill rather than those write. He said, "No, it doesn't—nothing about that man deserves to be told. He's dead and that's all that matters now—that's it. And the world is much better for it—much better, if you ask me. Jeb, you think so, too—right?"

The young man—who, it appeared, went by Jeb for short—stood frozen behind me. It wasn't that he was scared to say anything—it was more about not knowing what to immediately say, after having been put on the spot by Doc Baker.

"Jeb?" Doc Baker asked. "You think so, too—right? Right?"

The young man shifted his feet on the floor and wrung the back of his neck with a hand. He didn't look at Doc Baker. Instead, he locked his eyes on a spot on the hardwood floor.

Doc Baker said to him, "I guess you have forgotten yourself and what Cooley did to your pa. Yeah, I know—he didn't kill Jebediah, but he killed that man's spirit, though. I'm sure of that. Just as sure as if he'd shot him dead—he killed your pa's spirit, and that's why he died the way he did."

The look on the young man's face certainly told me that he believed what Doc Baker said. It also told me that it wasn't the first time Doc Baker had spun that thread of narrative either.

Doc Baker threw up his hands, and said, "What's the point?"

Then, Doc Baker bolted up from his chair and moved towards the door. He looked back at the young man, then at me. He said, "It's people like you—people like you. That's what's wrong with this world, you know. It's people like you and how you make money off of other people's pain and suffering—all their pain and all their suffering. You don't care, do you? Of course, you don't—why would it matter to you? Call it whatever you want to—that book. Call it whatever you want—all you're doing is keeping Cooley alive with it. Cooley's dead—finally dead—and your book is going to resurrect that bastard. Your book is going to immortalize a man that doesn't need to be immortalized— it's people like you that will make life hell for the rest of us."

Doc Baker stormed out the door—it was then, more so than before, that I noticed he had a lame right leg and a limp. He favored that side of his body when he walked, so that each right step was heavier and more labored than the left.

The young man had been watching me watch Doc Baker, and he said, "That's what's wrong with him, you know."

"What do you mean?" I asked.

"His leg—" the young man said. "Cooley nearly blew his leg off—Doc almost lost that leg. That's what he said—he almost lost it. If he had, he said he would have lost his whole business."

Doc Baker's footfall receded away until I could hear him go into his building next door and slam the door.

I asked the young man, "Do you know how it happened?"

"Cooley did it," the young man said.

"No," I said. "I mean—do you know why it happened? How Cooley came to shoot Doc Baker?"

The young man shrugged his shoulders.

"Doc Baker didn't tell you why?" I asked.

The young man said, "Sure, he told me—he said there wasn't no reason for it. He said he didn't do anything to Cooley. He said Cooley didn't have a reason—it just happened because Cooley wanted it to happen."

"That doesn't make any sense," I said—and it didn't make sense to me. "There must have been something—something must have happened. Maybe, a disagreement of some sort—maybe it had to do with a woman they both wanted, or some argument perhaps."

"Nope," The young man said.

It didn't make sense to me.

"Cooley didn't need a reason, you know," the young man said. "That's what they always say—it wasn't about a reason, most of the time."

I continued to try to make sense out of it.

"Didn't they say Cooley killed a whole family back in the day?" The young man asked. "The family of six—killed every one of them, even some little kids. Isn't that in the Rondo book?"

It was, indeed, dear reader. It was one of the handful of anecdotes about Cooley that I placed in the Silas Rondo book. And it was probably the single most horrific thing about Cooley that always seemed to be something that readers of that Silas Rondo book would remember—while some readers would ask me if that really happened, others, like the young man here, would have firsthand knowledge about the story and know it was true. As true as it was, it was something that my publishers didn't want me to put in the Silas Rondo book, since it was a story that could only be told in full measure, and not in an abbreviated fashion—that was what I did, dear reader, I made sure that all the facts of what Cooley did to that family of six was written about in excruciating detail, without holding any punches. Some would say that, though the Silas Rondo book was about Silas Rondo and Silas Rondo was the main subject of the overall narrative, what Cooley did by comparison only made Silas Rondo look less like a monster—that was done by design, you see. Yet, what Cooley did to that family—killing the father, killing the mother, killing a teenage girl, and three very small children—was something I wanted to tie to Silas Rondo, who had been there at the time of the murders, and treat the event as a prologue to what I wanted to do on Cooley for another book.

"I take it that you've read the Silas Rondo book?" I asked.

The young man nodded, solemnly.

"I'm sure you don't think it's all that bad," I said. "Not like the good doctor there—Doc Baker. Surely, you don't think I'm all he said I am."

The young man looked at me silently.

"What Cooley did to the family of six," I went on. "is only a small thing compared to all the other things Cooley is said to have done, you know."

"Small thing?" He asked.

I paused.

"It wasn't a small thing," the young man said. "—Cooley killing that family wasn't a small thing, at all."

I tried to say, "I didn't mean it that w—"

He cut in, "It wasn't a small thing—especially for me. You know why? You know why it isn't a small thing for me? Because the teenage girl—the one killed with the rest of that family—the one you write about in your Rondo book—she was my—"

I listened until he paused. I wasn't sure why he paused the way that he had, but I had a feeling that the teenage girl I wrote about graphically in the Silas Rondo book meant something to him. In that book, as you know, dear reader, I wrote about how Cooley didn't just shoot the teenage girl in the face, but he also mutilated her body by cutting off her breasts and some of her fingers. I wrote about how Cooley had treated the teenage girl's mother the same way—but, somehow, it seemed to me, from all the accounts I had about it, and from what Silas Rondo himself is believed to have said, Cooley took a bit more pleasure in completely destroying the teenage girl's dead body after shooting her in the face. As I have said in the Silas Rondo book., Cooley treated the teenage girl in a way that even Silas Rondo that was going too far—as just as I wrote, it remains unclear why.

"—what I mean is—we were to be married," the young man said. "And Cooley knew that. That's why he did what he did to her—all the things you put in that Rondo book."

I didn't know what to say—I didn't know if there was anything that I could say, for that matter. I didn't know if anything I said, then, would have mattered, when I had written so much in that Silas Rondo book.

There was no doubt in my mind that the young man was still in a great deal of pain by what happened to the teenage girl—the woman he was due to marry—and I was certain that how I wrote about her death in the Silas Rondo book only made that pain all the more potent. It didn't matter that several years had passed since Cooley killed that whole family and went much further with the girl—that was how I referred to her—what happened as still fresh for the young man.

"You don't have to say anything," the young man told me. "It probably doesn't matter all that much to you—that's what Doc Baker says."

I told him, "Well, Doc Baker is wrong—it does matter to me. It matters a lot to me, in fact."

The young man looked at me unblinkingly.

I tried to tell the young man—the young Jeb—that I was sorry about what happened to the teenage girl. I tried to tell him that I was sorry that Cooley killed her and her family the way that he did—I tried, dear reader, but I knew that, even bringing myself to say I was sorry for something that Cooley did, was a problem. It was a problem for me, since I didn't kill those people—Cooley did. It was problem because I was simply apologizing for writing about what Cooley did—I was trying to say that I was sorry for recounting the murder of a family, when Cooley had murdered countless others. It was a problem for me, because it placed me in a compromising position—it was as if, in saying I was sorry, I was an accomplice in what happened, just as Silas Rondo was. In a way, telling the young man I was sorry meant something I didn't want it to mean—but, I tried to say I was sorry, nonetheless, and I quickly realized how bad a decision it was.

"You're sorry?" The young man asked—or, more aptly, laughed. "Sorry? Sorry—for what?"

"For any pain my writing may have caused you," I said. "For—"

He cut in, and said, "Any pain—your writing may have caused me? And you're writing a book on Cooley? You don't think that's not more pain?"

I didn't know what to say.

"Look," the young man said, in a voice that seemed just as angry as Doc Baker's had been. "There's no use talking about it anymore. You've got pa's map now—don't know what it means, but you've got it. I think it's best if you were on your way—unless you need a ride out there."

I told him I would need a ride.

"Okay, then," the young man said, with his eyes refusing to look at me. "Let's go—the carriage and team are out here. We'll use Doc Baker's."

I followed the young man outside to where the carriage and team were hitched to the hitching post.

The young man told me, "Let me let him know we're leaving. You can climb up, okay."

As he walked over to Doc Baker's, I climbed up on the carriage and sat in the box seat. The two horses that made up the team were dark brown and sleek—one jerked its head side to side, appearing agitated at something, while the other seemed steadier and calm.

Faintly, I could hear the young man—young Jeb—talking to Doc Baker inside. Mostly, from where I was, all I could make out was the young man's mumblings and what was clearly Doc Baker's agitated voice responding. What seemed clear to me was that Doc Baker didn't want young Jeb to use the team, particularly if it had anything to do with me—I could just make out Doc Baker complaining about how Jeb shouldn't take that writer out there, and that Jeb shouldn't get himself mixed in anything to do with that writer, and that Jeb would be better off telling that writer to walk out there on foot and find it for himself, and that, if Jeb took me out there, Jeb's pa would be rolling over in his grave.

Doc Baker shouted from within, "And he writes about your beloved person—your betrothed, Jeb—like writing about the side of a barn. You know what I mean?"

I couldn't make out what young Jeb was mumbling in response.

Still, just as surely as I figured young Jeb understood, I knew what Doc Baker meant. Doc Baker was referring to a scene in the Silas Rondo book when I write about how Silas Rondo shot up the side of a barn—you know this one, dear reader. It was the barn that belonged to the father of the teenage girl—Jeb's betrothed—and Silas Rondo shot up the barn in the middle of the night to wake up the family. And, of course, it frightened the family awake, causing the father to run outside to see what the matter was. As I recounted, Silas Rondo attempted to spell out his name in gunshots across the side barn, even though Silas Rondo was mostly illiterate. So, as I carefully detailed, Silas Rondo took his time shooting up the barn and trying to spell out each letter of his name, until the side of the barn didn't look at all like his name, or look like anything in particular, other than dozens of gunshots that, to the untrained eye, didn't look particularly organized in any way. The time Silas Rondo took to do that gave the father plenty of time to come out of the house with his shotgun—it was, at that time, when Cooley sneaked up behind the father, who thought he had Silas Rondo at gunpoint, and blew the father's brains out with a shot at close range. I wrote about how the other family members wouldn't be as lucky as the father—while the father received his fatal shot in the back of the head by surprise, the others would get theirs with barrels pressed firmly to their foreheads as either Cooley or Silas Rondo toyed with them.

I thought about all of that—how I wrote all of that—from the Silas Rondo book, and realized just how horrific that scene was described. Then, I thought more carefully about how I described what happened to the teenage girl—young Jeb's betrothed—and how my editor originally didn't want me to be so specific about it. It wasn't that my editor thought it would turn off readers—since it clearly didn't—it was, rather, the idea that such specificity about real events would offend anyone that actually knew the individuals I was writing about.

The door to Doc Baker's place opened and the young man—young Jeb—came out. He glanced at me, unhitched the team from the hitching post, glanced at me again, walked around to the other side of the carriage, and climbed up on the seat next to me.

"I guess," I said. "Doc Baker doesn't want us to use his carriage."

The young man—young Jeb—laughed just a little under his breath, but he held it back as much as he could. He said, "Something like that."

"Look," I told him. "I don't want to get in the middle of you and the doc."

Just then, from the window to Doc Baker's, I could see Doc Baker himself peeking out at us. Once he realized I noticed, he disappeared from the window.

"You ain't getting in the middle of anything," the young man said.

"What I mean is," I said. "I can find my way out there myself, if that helps."

The young man took the reins in his hands and said, "My pa wanted me to take you out there, so that's what I'm doing."

As the young Jeb gave the team commands to giddy-up, we were off.

I didn't know what to say to young Jeb. I thought about thanking him for taking me out, but I thought against it—it didn't seem like such a good idea. He had made it clear that he was taking me out because it was something Jebediah wanted, and it didn't really have anything to do with what young Jeb wanted. What I realized, and quickly, was that I was nothing more—and nothing less—than a promise that young Jeb wanted to keep to Jebediah, and I was quite aware that young Jeb wanted to get it over with as soon as he possibly could, with the sheer speed he had the team galloping.

So, I took another look at the map that Jebediah had drawn for me. I was reminded about what the man named after Cooley had said, and I thought about what Jebediah didn't bother telling me—I kept looking at the spot on the map where the man named after Cooley told me Cooley's dead body is actually buried

37

We didn't say anything to one another the whole way out to Cooley's burial site, since neither of us, it seemed, had anything to say. The silence—only broken with the sounds of the horses wheezing, the steady, rhythmic clopping of hooves, and the occasional squeaking of the carriage—only made the trip seem longer than it really was. But, the silence only reminded me of how young Jeb's father hadn't been at all quiet, when he first took me out to Cooley's burial site some time before—I remembered how Jebediah had talked excitedly the whole way, and how he wanted me to know how close he had come to Cooley killing him, and how he believed he was probably one of only two people that had ever crossed Cooley for one reason or another and lived to talk about it.

"How did it happen?" I asked him, then.

Jebediah smiled this broad smile, which showed just about every tooth in his mouth. He said, "On account of Billie."

"Billie?" I asked.

"Yeah," he said. "You know about Billie, right?"

I said, "Sure, Cooley's waitress."

"Well," he said. "she's much more than that, you know—"

At the time, I didn't know that Billie was more than just Cooley's waitress. In my mind, with the research I had done up to that moment, it had seemed that Billie had only a working relationship with Cooley—I hadn't found any evidence to suggest otherwise. I had my suspicions, true, but nothing I discovered, up to that point, about Billie alerted me to anything else about her relationship with Cooley. So, what Jebediah said, as subtle as it was, piqued my interests.

"She's more than that?" I asked.

"Yep."

"I don't follow," was all I could say.

"You don't know about them?" He asked me.

I shook my head, no. I remembered how I fumbled around in my bag for all the notes I had taken about Billie, wondering if I had missed something, and if Jebediah was really telling me something I didn't already know.

"They were messing around for years," he said. "Cooley was married to—I forget her name—an old, busty kind of woman—what's her name? Ah—it doesn't matter now. Anyway, Cooley was already married, and was messing around with Billie—it was an open secret, you know. All the other waitresses knew about it and some of the customers knew too. Everyone, except my dumb-ass—nobody told me." He laughed heartily.

I asked, "What do you mean?"

Jebediah told me about how he used to go to Cooley's just about everyday. This was before he took over the undertaker business from his father—who he was named after—and when Jebediah said he was still trying to figure out if he wanted to take over his father's business or move west to California for the gold rush.

He laughed, "I figured my answers were at the bottom of a whiskey bottle, you know—so I drank a lot. The place to do a lot of drinking was Cooley's. So, I was there a lot—I was there so much that me and Billie had this running joke for a little while."

I asked, "Running joke?"

"Yeah," Jebediah said. "I would come in, Billie would ask me 'Jeb'—she called me Jeb—she would ask 'Jeb, are you still looking for answers?' And, I'd say, 'show me the questions, Billie' and she would say, 'coming right up,' and she would bring me a bottle of whiskey—one after another until I was finished drinking for the day."

Then, Jebediah told me about how, sometimes, Billie would sit with him and talk when things weren't too busy—she would ask him if he was still thinking about going to California.

Jebediah said, "Billie would ask, 'what're you looking for in California?' And I would tell her, 'well, gold, of course,' and she would say that I was looking for something, but gold wasn't really it—she would tell me that all the gold in the world wasn't going to be enough, unless I figured out what was going on in here. She would point to my chest—right here—" Jebediah pointed to his chest, pointing to his heart, and went on, "—and she would tell me if I didn't figure out what I was missing here—in my heart—all the gold in the world wouldn't be enough."

I remembered listening to Jebediah so closely that I didn't write any of what he had said down—I knew I would remember it, dear reader. Indeed, I still do, as I'm sure you can tell.

"Then," Jebediah said. "one day—it happened."

"What happened?" I asked.

"One day," Jebediah said. "I was sitting there drinking like always, and Billie came over to talk—asking me about what it was I was running from and if that was why I wanted to search for gold in California—and, then, we stared in each other's eyes for a long moment. Then—"

I listened, remembering how bumpy the road had been, as Jebediah guided his team up a soft incline that leveled out just a bit, before the path gradually sloped downward.

"—we kissed," he said.

I remembered how the wheels of Jebediah's carriage dug deep into the well-traveled path, digging so deep it seemed as if the carriage would get stuck—he whipped the team, so the horses would work a little harder and increase their pull.

"Well," he said. "I don't remember if she kissed me, or I kissed her—maybe, it doesn't matter. I just know we kissed—right there in the place, and Cooley saw it. He was mighty pissed off, let me tell you. He comes marching over to the table where I was at—me and Billie had already pulled back from one another. You know what I mean? We were looking at each other—kind of wondering what just happened, and why. But, Cooley comes marching over with his shotgun. Billie screams just then. Next thing I know, Cooley shoves his shotgun right in my face. Cooley says—he goes, 'boy, I'm gonna blow your fucking head off,' and he's pressing the barrels into my face—right here."

I remembered how Jebediah pointed with two right fingers—as if his two right fingers were the shotgun barrels—to his right cheek just below his right eye. His eyes rolled towards me, checking to see if I understood.

Then, he said, "—and I knew—there was no doubt—he was going to kill me— going to blow my head off. Hell, I had seen him do it to some other guy the week before—some guy that happened to look at Cooley the wrong way. It didn't take much, you know. Cooley had a temper and didn't give a shit about killing a man for anything— it didn't take much at all. It could be over the smallest shit—you know, the littlest shit. That guy—just the week before—gave Cooley a look. Nobody knew what it was, but it pissed off Cooley, good enough. We found out later that the guy had had a twitching eye—so, Cooley shot him over a twitching eye. So, I knew Cooley could kill for lesser reasons—I was sure he would kill me for kissing Billie."

"So," I asked him. "why do you think it didn't happen?"

"You mean," he asked. "why he didn't kill me, then?"

I nodded.

He said, "I don't rightly know."

By that point, I remember how Jebediah had brought the team and the carriage to a stop along this long fence-line made up of two rails. It was just a simple fence-line that was more about defining the property line than keeping anyone out. Over it, there was a large field peppered with tombstones.

"I can't tell you why," he said. "I don't mean I can't tell you—like I know but I can't. What I mean is—I can't because it's still a mystery to me."

It was then, when Jebediah pointed to the large field and hopped down from the carriage. The two horses in the team shifted a bit on their hooves, so he guided them to a spot on the long fence-line—he took the reins that looped them through the horizontal railing.

I asked him, "There has to be a reason, right?"

"Maybe so," he said. "Some say that Cooley always did things for a reason. Those that say Cooley never had a reason for what he did—shit, I say there was always a reason."

I remembered how Jebediah had laughed a little when he said that. It was subtle, but it was a laugh, just the same. It was as if his experience with Cooley was humorous in hindsight. I was sure, though, that there wasn't anything funny about being confronted with Cooley. The broad consensus always was that Cooley was a monster and, when being confronted with him, for whatever the reason, it always felt like you were coming face-to-face with devil himself. Yet, knowing that as well as I did, Jebediah's chuckle seemed out of place.

He told me, still softly chuckling, "For Cooley, there was a reason for doing and for not doing—for killing and for not killing. Always a reason for everything."

I asked him, "What did Billie do?"

Jebediah looked at me with a confused look on his face.

"When Cooley confronted you that way," I said. "what was Billie doing?"

"Nothing really," he said. "She stepped aside—and watched."

I asked him if Billie said anything.

"Naw," he said. "She just stepped to the side—didn't say anything. It's like she enjoyed it, you know. It was like she wanted Cooley to do what he did—to threaten me the way he did."

I asked, "What did you do when it happened?"

He asked me, "What did I do?"

I nodded, yes.

"I sat there like a knot on a log," he said. "There wasn't nothing else to do, I suppose. So, I sat there and looked at Cooley—I looked at him down the length of that shotgun and took a long breath."

I asked, "Because you knew he was going to kill you?"

"Yeah," he said. "I knew—so I just stared into eyes, you know. In such a way to tell him I wasn't afraid, to bring it on—that I was ready."

"Then, it never happened?" I asked "He didn't pull the trigger."

"That's right," he said. "He didn't—he put the shotgun down and let out this big laugh. I don't know if he was laughing at me or what he hadn't done—but he just laughed. Then, he told Billie to get me another drink—and that that drink was on the house. And that was that."

I asked, "That was that?"

"Yep," he said.

Jebediah climbed over the fence railings, and a followed him.

He went on, "I don't know—maybe he wanted me to live on to tell the story. That's my guess—and look at me, I'm doing just that, you know."

I remembered thinking how much I wanted to disbelieve what Jebediah was saying, and how I wanted to think that there was no way Cooley would let someone live the way he had let Jebediah live. Up to that moment, one of the most important things I knew about Cooley was that Cooley was a killer—some would say, without hesitation, that Cooley was a cold-blooded, ruthless, remorseless killer, and a killer of killers. I remembered thinking how what happened to Jebediah was completely different than anything else I thought I already knew about Cooley—or, what I had come to believe. If true, Jebediah's account, I remembered thinking at the time, would completely change an aspect of Cooley's mythology—it would say, in some way, that Cooley wasn't as cold-blooded, or as ruthless, or as remorseless as it had been suggested that he was. What happened to Jebediah, if true, placed what I knew about Cooley in a new light—and that new light, dear reader, confused me.

So, I asked Jebediah, "How do I know what you say actually happened?"

I was still following Jebediah out across the large field, until he stopped, turned, and looked at me. He asked me, "You don't have to take my word for it, mister writer man. I ain't nobody. You can ask Doc Baker, if you want—he'll tell you, he was there."

I saw how Jebediah wasn't necessarily taking what I said personally. There was no sign of frustration with my question, or even a glimmer of defensiveness. He wasn't offended—that made me realize that he was certainly telling the truth.

I told him that speaking with Doc Baker—who, at the time, I didn't know who he was—wasn't necessary. I told him I believed him, and I didn't mean to say otherwise. I admitted to him that what he had told me about Cooley was contrary to the kind of Cooley I had come to understand—based on all the interviews I had had up to that time, his account was an outlier. I told him how I knew about Cooley's belief about always being the one doing the killing and making sure that others were always the ones doing the dying.

"Now, he's the one doing the dying," Jebediah said, pointing at a tombstone that sat out in the open, with about ten yards of open space all around it. He said, "Well, there it is—where he is."

I remembered seeing how Cooley's tombstone wasn't really the kind of tombstone I was used to seeing. It was nothing more than a plank of wood, which looked like it had once been the back of a closed back chair. To me, it looked like someone had just taken the chair's back, burned Cooley's name into it what looked like hurried lettering that were misshaped and uneven, and jammed the whole thing into the ground. The earth beneath the chair's back that meant to be a tombstone was noticeably disturbed—the mound had the right dimensions for there to be a coffin of some sort buried there.

"Here?" I asked.

I remembered how I wasn't really asking him that question, but I was more so asking myself—I was asking myself that question, since it was hard to believe that someone like Cooley would be buried in such a simple way.

Jebediah said, "Yep, that's where the bastard's been buried."

I remembered standing there looking at Cooley's grave, feeling as though it was telling me something I couldn't understand. The way his name was burned into the wood—just Cooley's first name—seemed purposefully mysterious. I remembered how I couldn't put my finger on what it was that was so mysterious—all I knew was that, in all of the gravesites I had ever visited as a means of learning about someone I was writing about, Cooley's grave didn't substantively say anything to me. I remembered how I felt, in that instance, like there wasn't anything I could learn about Cooley from his grave—it was, I remembered, as if Cooley could only be unknowable. There was no last name nor birth year, as was customary with tombstones—there was only the current year as Cooley's death year and nothing that brought me any closer to making sense out of how he died, by whose hand, and why.

I remembered that time with Jebediah, as young Jeb brought the carriage to a halt along the long fence-line, and told me, "Well, we're here—there it is."

I jumped down from the carriage, with young Jeb staying behind. It was clear to me that he was only interested in bringing me there, and nothing more.

So, I eagerly walked up to the long fence-line—seemingly in roughly the same spot where Jebediah and I had been years ago. I carefully climbed over the railings, looking in the direction of where Cooley's tombstone was. I stopped to look back at young Jeb and I saw how young Jeb looked disinterested—from about ten yards away, I noticed just how much young Jeb resembled his father, Jebediah.

It was then, dear reader, when I made it to Cooley's tombstone—the one Jebediah had led me to some years ago—with the wood plank that had once been the back of a chair, with Cooley's name burned into it with misshaped, uneven letters. This time, some years later, I noticed bullet holes sprinkled across the wood plank tombstone, appearing as if it had been used to target practice since I saw it last. Even the earth beneath the wood plank tombstone appeared shot-up too. The potent smell of urine told me, too, that someone had pissed on the grave—there were also lumps of feces, from someone that saw fit to shit on the grave, too.

Young Jeb shouted from the carriage, "It probably didn't look like that last time you saw it."

Looking in young Jeb's direction, I shouted back, "No, it surely didn't."

After looking back down at Cooley's grave, which wasn't really Cooley's grave, I turned my attention towards the tree about a hundred yards away on the other side of the large field—so, I took another look at the map that Jebediah had drawn for me, and left with young Jeb, realizing that it was the same tree referenced on the map. I turned and walked in that direction, feeling as though young Jeb was watching me, even if I didn't want to make sure that was so.

Following Jebediah's map to the spot just beneath the only tree in the large field, I crossed the hundred or so yards through a handful of other graves littered here and there. These other graves were all unmarked—some were so shallow and without coffins that it was clear that whoever buried the remains had little respect for them. Once at the tree, dear reader, positioned on the outer perimeter of the property, I stood for a moment in shade cast by the tree's dense foliage. I looked carefully over the ground at the foot of the tree and let the map guide me to the spot—I remembered the man named after Cooley telling me that the spot would be unmarked, but would have a rock marked with black X drawn on it.

When I located the rock—which was much easier than I expected, even in what was high, overgrown grass—and saw that it, yes, had an X marked on it, just as the man named after Cooley had described. I was half-surprised to see the rock there, since I didn't want to believe what the man named after Cooley had said—yet, I wasn't completely surprised, since I was still hoping to make sense out of Cooley's death, and I knew that locating Cooley's actual grave would be the first step in figuring out what I desperately needed to figure out.

I put Jebediah's map away in my bag and stooped down to get a closer look at the ground—grabbing the rock and putting it aside, I noticed that the ground didn't look to be disturbed, which I assumed would be the case if something had been buried there. I reminded myself about what the man named after Cooley had said about this other grave in relation to the one where Cooley is buried—I kept thinking about how this other grave, if it was a grave, didn't seem like one, and the grave marked as Cooley's was prominent, out in the open, and deliberately situated so it could be easily found.

Glancing over my shoulder to where young Jeb was, I realized he was watching me. He had stepped down from the carriage and was standing leaned against one of the horses. I couldn't tell if his face was from keen interest or if it was from impatience— whatever the reason was, young Jeb was watching.

"Everything okay?" Young Jeb shouted.

I told him that it was.

Young Jeb didn't look completely convinced. He took a few steps forward and put his elbows on the fence railings

I was reminded about what the man named after Cooley had said, and I thought about what Jebediah didn't bother telling me—I kept looking at the spot on the map that Jebediah had drawn for me and I kept trying to connect it to where the man named after Cooley told me Cooley's dead body is actually buried. What kept crossing my mind was that both Jebediah and the man named after Cooley were playing games with me—that it was just a trick, and that Cooley really was buried where he was supposed to be.

Looking more closely at the area at the foot of the tree, I still didn't see any evidence that would suggest that the ground had been disturbed—everything looked the way that he was supposed to look, with the exception, of course, dear reader, of the rock with the X marked on it, which was, no matter how I tried to rationalize it away, was something that had been placed there for a reason.

I remembered how the man named after Cooley had told me, "If you go there and look under that rock with the X on it, you'll find Cooley's body."

With the rock with the X on it put aside, I found myself staring at the spot where it had been. Because the grass had become overgrown all around the rock, there was a bald spot of dead grass looking back at me.

"—under that rock with the X on it, you'll find Cooley's body," the man named after Cooley had said. His voice, now, echoed in my head—I could see his face in my mind when he had said that, and I could see just as clear as if he was sitting in front of me again, and I could see, even then, how there wasn't a hint of facetiousness on his face, and only there was only a firm seriousness.

I looked carefully, dear reader, at that bald spot of dead grass until I could just name out the ground. I could see—looking more closely—that the bald spot of grass looked smooth and pale. There was a small round area that looked paler, with the darker brown dirt around it, and with the overgrown grass still further out—staring at the spot, it was increasingly clear to me that I was increasingly looking at something unusual.

Then, I remembered how the man named after Cooley had it very clear to me, saying, "The skull first—I think you'll find the skull first. That skull—Cooley's skull—is what you want to find."

Though I was already stooping down, I went down further on my hands and knees, and touched the dead spot of grass. I carefully touched something that was just barely visible—it was something that wasn't completely submerged in the ground. I wasn't sure what it was, dear reader—all I knew was that it was something that wasn't dirt, and wasn't some kind of bedrock or sediment, and wasn't something that naturally belonged there.

I wiped away the dirt around whatever this thing was, until more of it was exposed—it was something round, hard, smooth, and pale. I took my bag off from my shoulders and sat it on the ground beside me—I leaned closer and used both of my hands to wipe away more of what was surprisingly soft dirt.

I glanced over my shoulder at young Jeb, just as young Jeb nimbly climbed over the fence railing.

Eagerly, I kept wiping away more dirt and digging with my fingernails, until I began realizing that what the man named after Cooley said would be there was.

Young Jeb stood there, just a step or two inside the fencing, looking at me. Judging from the expression on his face, I knew he wanted to say something, but he didn't—perhaps, he couldn't.

As I kept burrowing further into the ground around something that was minimally submerged—pushing the dirt away and out, until I had made a trench all around it—I could hear myself laughing uncontrollably. I don't why I was laughing, but I couldn't stop. They were hysterical laughs—the laughs of someone that had gone insane, perhaps. But, I didn't care, dear reader—it was impossible to care, at that point. I didn't even care how loud those laughs were, nor that those laughs were echoing across the open field, nor if young Jeb could hear how crazed I sounded, nor if young Jeb was gradually making his way to where I was, one careful footstep at a time, nor that I found myself laughing at what I was pulling from the ground, nor that I was holding up what I had retrieved from the ground as if it was wholly made of gold.

Approaching, young Jeb asked, "What is that?"

I turned to him, with it in my hands.

"Is that a skull?" Young Jeb asked, realizing right away that what he was seeing was self-explanatory. His face went blank and flush, as he rattled off, "It is, isn't it? A skull? Who's skull? What's it doing there? That's not a grave—there isn't supposed to be a grave there. How did it get there?"

I didn't answer any of young Jeb's questions. I had heard them well enough, but there wasn't anything that I could say—there wasn't anything I wanted to say.

Standing up with the skull in my hands, I faced young Jeb, who had stopped about five yards away from me. I turned the skull around so I could face it—and it face me—and I looked closely at the eye holes, the nose hole, the thin batch of white hair clinging fragilely to the scalp, and the teeth. Though the jawbone wasn't attached or missing—

though probably still in the ground—I could tell that all of the teeth that were still attached to the skull were all different shapes, colors and sizes. Where gums once were, there was a wooden plate—though rotted, I could see that all the teeth were attached to this bridge like dentures, and all the teeth had probably belonged to other people. Right away, that reminded me about what the man named after Cooley had said.

I remembered how the man named after Cooley had laughed, "You want facts. Right? So, if you want facts, mister biographer man, you will want to check the skull's teeth. You know what I mean? You know what it is about Cooley's teeth—do you know about this fact?"

Now, I was looking at these teeth—for the first time, I was seeing something irrefutable, and there was no denying what I was looking at. These were the teeth that I had heard about, which, initially, seemed like part of Cooley's mythology. Like many other things about Cooley, Cooley's teeth—whether they were dentures or not, or whether they were made up of other people's teeth or not—was a piece of evidence that I figured would be impossible to see. I figured there would be no way to prove or disprove anything about Cooley's teeth without a body—and I was sure that there was no way to fully know if one actually was looking at Cooley's remains. Even when I first visited the grave marked as Cooley's with Jebediah, I remembered asking Jebediah if there was any way I could dig up Cooley's grave and see the body for myself.

Back then, I remembered Jebediah telling me, "Oh—I'm afraid not. There's not much of a body there, you see—there's been graverobbers. So, the body's been dug up and buried, and dug up and buried so many times, there's only a handful of bones still there."

I remembered asking him, "What about the skull? Is the skull still there?"

I remembered how Jebediah's face changed just a little, but he changed his face when I thought I noticed the difference. I remembered his saying, "That's been long gone—the skull. It's been missing for a while."

I remembered looking at the ground around the tombstone marker, which, even then, was just the back of a chair. I remembered how the ground didn't look as if it had been disturbed as many times as Jebediah claimed it had. To me, it looked as if the ground had only been disturbed for burial and, since burial, the ground didn't show any soil that had upturned and re-upturned. I'm certainly far from a geologist, or a soil expert, but, to the untrained eye, nothing about the grave that had been marked as Cooley's grave appeared to have been ransacked as much as Jebediah claimed. Yet, I took his word for it, and didn't ask any more questions about Cooley's remains or what was—or wasn't—in the ground.

Then, the man named after Cooley piqued my interests again about Cooley's body, and confirmed what I already knew—from so many interviews of those that knew Cooley—about Cooley's teeth. I knew Cooley's teeth could be the way to identify Cooley's body and put to rest any of the mythology about Cooley.

I remembered how the man named after Cooley told me, "Cooley's teeth—that'll show you. That's a helluva fact."

Now, I was looking at what the man named after Cooley called "a helluva fact"— what I was looking at was Cooley's teeth, and what I had in my hands, dear reader, was none other than Cooley's skull. These were the kinds of facts that I told the man named after Cooley that I was interested in.

"This is Cooley's skull," I told young Jeb. "That's who's skull this is—it's Cooley's. And—"

Young Jeb asked, "Cooley's skull?" He looked confused. "Wait—what?"

I pointed at the ground from which I had retrieved the skull, and told him, "This—here—is where Cooley's body has been buried. Not over there—here."

Young Jeb still looked confused. Obviously, he was having a difficult time processing what I was saying.

He said, "I don't understand—what do you mean?"

"Cooley's remains are here," I told him. "Right here—unmarked, under this tree, where Jebediah said they would be."

"Pa, said," young Jeb said—it wasn't so much a question as it was a matter of fact. Then, he asked in a way that wasn't just directed at me, but asking himself, "Pa, said?

Pa—said?"

"The map," I told him. "That's what the map is for—Cooley's grave."

Young Jeb rubbed hand over the back of his neck, then swiped both hands down the front of his face. "I don't understand. Then, why is Cooley marked over there—" He pointed at the marked grave, and said, "—if he ain't? I don't get it. Why here? Why would pa—" He cut himself off, watching me.

I stared carefully into the face of the skull, trying to imagine Cooley's face having once been there. Looking at the nose hole, I thought about how Cooley's nose was described as wide and flat, with the bridge slightly crooked from having been broken so many times in fistfights in Cooley's youth—this was before, some say, Cooley realized that using a gun to solve his problems was a much better way to go. In those open eye holes, I imagined Cooley's eyes looking into mine. I brought together all of the things I had learned about what Cooley looked like from all the people I was able to interview, so I could envision what the face was like that terrorized so many people—the last face some saw just before Cooley killed them. I thought about all the women Cooley mistreated, abused, raped, and ravaged, and I thought about many of those women looked into this face and believed that they were seeing the face of the devil himself—the last face some women saw before they lost all hold of reality, like Billie and Ann. I thought, too, about how this was the last face that the teenage girl, who had once been young Jeb's betrothed, saw before Cooley ripped her from this world so soon—the last face she saw when she realized she wasn't going live to see herself get married nor see herself have children.

Without realizing it, I said, "Alas poor Yorick—I knew him well, Horatio."

Young Jeb said, "Huh?"

I went on, "—a fellow of infinite jest, of most excellent fancy—where be your gibes now?"

"I don't know what you're saying," young Jeb said.

I continued unincumbered, speaking to the skull, in my best imitation of one of the Booth brothers, "—your gambols? Your songs? Your flashes of merriment—"

Rolling his eyes up to the sky, young Jeb said out loud to himself, "I think he's lost it—" Then, directed at me, he asked, "Have you lost it?—you're speaking gibberish."

"It's not gibberish—" I told him.

"It sounds like gibberish to me," he said.

I said, "—it's Shakespeare."

Young Jeb questioned, "Shakespeare?"

I continued looking at Cooley's skull, turning it to look at one profile, then turning it again to look at another profile. I thought about how Hamlet did the same thing with Yorick's skull with Horatio watching—I thought about how absorbed Hamlet was in doing that, and how I was becoming just as absorbed. The longer I looked at the skull, young Jeb grew all the more anxious—I was sure, too, that Horatio was just as anxious about what Hamlet was doing.

"Hamlet with Yorick's skull," I said. "You know—from Shakespeare. What Hamlet says when he's holding Yorick's skull. You know—the play, *Hamlet.*"

Young Jeb looked confused.

"Do you know Shakespeare?" I asked.

Young Jeb asked, "Know him? Not personally, no—ain't he from the old country, though?"

I laughed, "England—and he died almost three hundred years ago."

With a confused look still on his face, all that young Jeb could manage to say was, "Oh."

I explained to young Jeb that Shakespeare's play, *Hamlet* is about a young man seeking to revenge is father's untimely death.

Young Jeb asked, "Untimely?"

"When someone dies too soon," I said. "When they die before they should."

"Like Pa?" He asked. "—he died too soon. That's what Doc Baker always says—that my pa died too soon."

I nodded.

Young Jeb asked, "Does this Shakespeare fellow—does he write the kind of stuff you write?"

"No," I said. "Shakespeare wrote poetry and plays."

"I know about poetry—a poem is poetry," he said. "But, what's a play?"

I told him that a play is a story told mostly in dialogue between characters. In a play, I explained, the story unfolds through what the characters say to one another and all the action that the characters perform is provided to the audience in stage directions. "That's because," I told him. "—a play is performed by actors, on a stage, and in a theater of some sort."

"So," he said. "A play is different from what you write."

I nodded—I thought about going a bit further than a simple head nod, but I decided against it.

When I nodded, it was the first time when I realized that what I did was different than what Shakespeare did. It wasn't that I didn't know that already—not exactly. What I had come to believe about myself and my work, dear reader, is that what I was doing was just as important as what Shakespeare did—while Shakespeare wrote comedies, histories, and tragedies, I had come to think of my work as encompassing all three. To me, the book on Silas Rondo was a history and a tragedy, but also contained a great deal of comedy—I thought about how I chose to detail all most of Silas Rondo's daily experiences, as a way to show the folly of his life outside of all the crimes he committed in so many different states. I wanted to show, with the Silas Rondo book, that there was a history to what Silas Rondo did, and a tragedy to it for those that were Silas Rondo's victims—still, I wanted to show that there was a comedy to the way that Silas Rondo viewed his place in the world and what he believed the world owed him. That comedy, dear reader, was Silas Rondo's tragedy. The same can be said about Cooley, insofar as Cooley's life is, in itself, a kind of tragedy, marked by a kind of history, and grounded in a kind of comedy. Just as I have often been told by readers that the Silas Rondo book is a Shakespearean tale, I knew I wanted my book on Cooley to be another kind of Shakespearean tale, so I approached the research and planning process of the project the same way.

I say this, dear reader, to say that I had a broad vision of what I wanted the Cooley book to be—I didn't just want it to go much further than what I accomplished in the Silas Rondo book, but I also wanted it to speak to the same themes about the human experience that Shakespeare's work predominantly does.

Yet, when I realized I was standing there holding Cooley's skull in my hands like Hamlet held Yorick's, and I became increasingly aware how young Jeb was looking at me the same way Horatio looked at Hamlet in that scene, I realized that Cooley was still an unknowable person. It was, of course, something that Silas Rondo himself is believed to have said once—that Cooley was unknowable—when Silas Rondo realized Cooley had double-crossed him and had had Silas Rondo setup to be killed. As I recount in the Silas Rondo book, when Silas Rondo realized that Cooley was the reason why he—Silas Rondo—was going to die, some say that Silas Rondo said that he—Cooley—would always be unknowable. That always struck me, as I say in the Silas Rondo book, as a significant thing to say when one knows they are about to die—to say that, knowing he was the one that would be doing the dying and Cooley would continue doing the living, always told me something more significant about Cooley. He would always be unknowable and there wasn't anything I do to change that—I couldn't change that any more than all of the characters in the world of *Hamlet* could about Hamlet himself. I thought about how Hamlet was unknowable to Claudius, Ophelia, Laertes, Polonius, Gertrude, and even poor Rosencrantz and Guildenstern and how never fully knowing Hamlet was one of the reasons for each of the character's downfall—I often thought that, if Horatio had been around Hamlet any longer, the fact that Hamlet was unknowable to Horatio would have led to Horatio's own downfall. I thought, too, about how the ghost of Hamlet's dead father was just as unknowable to Hamlet as Hamlet probably was to King Hamlet, when Hamlet's father, the King, was alive.

Reciting some Hamlet's lines to Yorick to Cooley's skull reminded me that there would always be silence coming from it, which was certainly what Hamlet realized too about the silence coming from Yorick's skull.

The longer I looked into the eye holes of Cooley's skull, the more I thought about what some say was the very last thing Silas Rondo said before he died. Sure, dear reader, there was what Silas Rondo said about Cooley being unknowable—which was certainly profound enough for a man like Silas Rondo—but there was also what Silas Rondo said when he stared into Cooley's eyes down the length of shotgun barrels Cooley had pointed into Silas Rondo's face.

"There ain't nothing in that man's eyes," was what Silas Rondo said. "His eyes are as dead as a skull's."

As you know, dear reader, just as I write in the Silas Rondo book, once Silas Rondo said those words, Cooley didn't respond—Cooley went silent and shot Silas Rondo point blank in the face. Then, Cooley turned the shotgun on other members of the gang that Silas Rondo assembled—one by one Cooley shot six of the other seven, leaving the seventh guy alive, so he could tell the story about what happened. That seventh guy was a very young man at the time—he was, as I write, the youngest member of Silas Rondo's gang—and, as he made clear to me, when he recounted how Cooley let him be the only doing the living when everyone else was doing the dying, he said Cooley's eyes were cold, as he was dead inside.

That seventh guy—who I would like to keep anonymous—once told me: "You know, they say Cooley always cared a shitload more about being the one doing the living as long as everyone else was doing the dying—it was always about Cooley being the one doing the killing. But, I don't know anymore—I just don't see it that way anymore."

I remember asking him, "What do you mean?"

That seventh guy, leaning back in a rocking chair, once told me, "I think he's already dead—I think he was dead from the beginning of everything, and Silas couldn't do nothing about that. None of us could."

"Dead from the beginning," I had asked him.

"I think—" That seventh guy once said—one of just a handful of men that Cooley decided not to kill. "—Cooley's always been the one doing the dying. He has been all along."

Those words came to me when I looked closely into the eye holes of Cooley's skull. As you know, dear reader, you won't find those words anywhere in the Silas Rondo book. Somehow, when I went about recording that seventh guy's experiences, what he had said about Cooley always being the one doing the dying didn't make that much sense to me—and, for the Silas Rondo book, those words didn't seem to fit all that well with what I was doing for the book, for that matter.

Those words became some of the throw-away pieces of information I had, which remained outside of the scope of what the Silas Rondo book was meant to be—when I thought against using those words from the seventh guy for the Silas Rondo book, I immediately thought that those words would be better suited for a book on Cooley. Though those words arose in the context of Silas Rondo, there was no doubt in my mind that they would better contextualize a narrative in which Cooley was at the center, rather than in the periphery of Silas Rondo's narrative. Quite frankly, those words—and just a handful of other accounts—were what drew me into the possibility of writing a book on Cooley himself, since I knew that Cooley had become even more mythologized than Silas Rondo.

Yet, once I thought about those words, and saw what I saw in the eye holes of Cooley's skull, those words brought a new meaning that I hadn't considered was possible. It even made me reconsider something that the seventh guy said about Silas Rondo being a surrogate father to all the guys in the gang, including Cooley.

It had been said, not just by the seventh guy, but by others familiar with the inner hierarchy of Silas Rondo's gang, that Silas Rondo fashioned himself as a father-figure to all the guys in the gang. This was especially so for Cooley—some say that Silas Rondo thought of Cooley as the second-in-command of the Silas Rondo gang. Cooley, on the other hand, didn't think of himself as second-in-command, or think of Silas Rondo as a father-figure—for Cooley, Silas Rondo, as I have argued in the Silas Rondo book, was simply a means to a certain end. That end, as you know, dear reader, came when Silas Rondo realized that Cooley was going to kill him and take over the gang. That was only part of the whole thing, since, we know, Silas Rondo was killed first—killing Silas Rondo was Cooley's first priority, but taking over the gang was never a priority. In fact, as I write in the Silas Rondo book, Cooley wasn't concerned with any of the men that made up the Silas Rondo gang, and Cooley certainly wasn't concerned with any of the things that Silas Rondo wished to do with that gang—the fact that Cooley killed just about all of the other members of the gang, one by one, and stacked the bodies all around Silas Rondo's dead bodies suggests to me, just as I argue in the Silas Rondo book, that Silas Rondo was expendable.

The idea that someone like Silas Rondo—a man that lived his life always being two to three steps ahead of everyone else—didn't have the forethought that Cooley was something of a Judas in the midst of the Silas Rondo gang remains a mystery to me. As I write in the Silas Rondo book, if we view Cooley as a Judas that turned against Silas Rondo with an ultimate betrayal of monumental proportions, I don't mean to say that Silas Rondo himself is a Jesus figure—some say Silas Rondo thought of himself as a messiah, and that all the horrible things he did to so many people was just a way for him to bring about God's kingdom on earth—because, as I have often explained to readers of the Silas Rondo book, I don't know if Silas Rondo had that broad of a vision. I think Silas Rondo lived his life day to day, and survival was moment by moment—that was, perhaps, Silas Rondo's problem in the end: he didn't realize how unknowable Cooley was.

So, when I think about Silas Rondo's last words, you can see, dear reader, what Silas Rondo eventually realized, before he was killed. The same can be said about the seventh guy and what he had come to realize himself, before he was let go. Both of them saw something in Cooley that was always dead—it was the same thing I found myself seeing in the eye holes of Cooley's skull.

It struck me, dear reader, that Cooley had killed the only man that had been a father-figure to him, because Silas Rondo didn't realize how unknowable Cooley actually was. Some say that Silas Rondo's father—whoever he was, since there seems to be no existing records about his identity—was also unknowable to Silas Rondo, and that was why, as I write in the Silas Rondo book, Silas Rondo started killing for a living. Some say that Silas Rondo killed so many because he was searching for something about himself—

something unknowable—even if each person he killed only made what he was searching for all the more unknowable.

Perhaps, Cooley killed Silas Rondo to make sense of something unknowable to Cooley—something that filled the blank spaces. Perhaps, Cooley killed so many people, because he was searching for the same unknowable thing that Silas Rondo never found. I'm afraid I can't say for sure, dear reader.

But, the same can be said about Cooley being killed by his son, the man named after Cooley—or, someone that just as well could be referred to as the younger Cooley—because that son believed that Cooley, as a absentee father, was unknowable enough to kill. Maybe killing Cooley, for the younger Cooley, was a way to fill in the blank space, even if, in the end, the blankness only enlarged and what is unknowable remained just as it was. That's the impression I had from the younger Cooley—the man named after Cooley. It was the sense that, even in killing Cooley, what was largely unknowable about Cooley remained that way—I imagine Cooley was unknowable to the younger Cooley all the way up to the very end. I could see it in There was no victory, nor closure in the younger Cooley having killed Cooley—all there was, I believe, was the same emptiness he had beforehand.

Though Cooley was unknowable to Jebediah, Jebediah was just as unknowable to young Jeb.

"I don't understand—" Young Jeb said, though it was hard for me to determine if he was saying that to himself or to me. "—why he would be buried here. I don't understand—Cooley's supposed to be buried over there. I don't understand why—why here? Why would Pa—"

Young Jeb cut himself off intuitively, either realizing that he couldn't answer himself or that I couldn't answer him. Either way, it was clear to me that he couldn't wrap his mind around what he had come to realize—it wasn't just the reality of Cooley, but it was a reality about his father, Jebediah. His face showed how confused he was—the fact that young Jeb still had problems processing the truth that Cooley wasn't buried in the grave marked as his, but was, instead, actually buried somewhere else all along showed me that Jebediah kept himself unknowable to young Jeb. There was something about that, dear reader, that clearly bothered young Jeb in a way that only intensified the more he thought about it. As young Jeb realized what my retrieving Cooley's skull from that unmarked grave meant in a narrow sense, more broadly, it seemed that young Jeb realized the whole mystery meant something to what he knew about Cooley, what hew knew himself, and what he knew about his father. Even in taking over Jebediah's undertaker business, whatever the blank spaces were that young Jeb hoped to fill would always remain blank spaces.

For me, too, I was wrestling with the blank spaces, and the idea that, even with Cooley's skull in my hands, none of the blank spaces I figured would be filled actually were—holding Cooley's skull, as surely as I was, and looking into the eye holes, as surely as I was, didn't mean anything for me nor for the Cooley book that I had hoped to write.

I thought about how Cooley was just as unknowable to me as he was to Silas Rondo, and to all of the members of Silas Rondo's gang that Cooley eventually killed, and to the seventh guy that survived to live to tell what happened. I thought about Bille and Ann, and how neither of them, by the time they died, never really knew Cooley as well as they believed they once had—in the end, Cooley was unknowable to both of them. And, I thought about all the interviews I conducted with a wide range of people that had encountered Cooley at one point in time or another—all the people that had something to tell me about Cooley, something that their individual experiences explained about Cooley—and how Cooley remained unknowable to all of them. Even when I compiled all the interviews and began thinking about what help they would give me, each of their experiences didn't really shed any light on Cooley, since Cooley was always either obscured or distanced. I thought about how I was only able to track down information on three men that self-identified themselves as Cooley's sons, including the man named after Cooley—though two of these men had died before I was able to interview them, the man named after Cooley, being the only one I could locate and speak with, was someone that still didn't know Cooley. Though the man named after Cooley never fully admitted it to me, I was sure that Cooley was unknowable to him, which only made more sense when

What I had come to realize was that, while Cooley was unknowable enough for some of his children to want to kill him as a way of filling in the blank spaces in their lives from Cooley's absence and what, at times, Cooley did to their mothers, Cooley was unknowable enough to other children for them to want to stay away from him altogether, as a means of filling in their own blank spaces from Cooley's absence.

The more I looked into the eye holes of Cooley's skull and came to terms with the fact that Cooley would be remain unknowable to me, and that I couldn't possibly write a book on Cooley if he was so unknowable, I thought about Shakespeare again. Shifting from some of Hamlet's final lines in the play, I thought about *The Tempest*, another play by Shakespeare—I thought about how Prospero's lines more realistically take me further than what Hamlet says to Yorick's skull.

"Graves at my command have waked their sleepers," I said out loud, not the skull, nor to young Jeb still standing there, but to myself. "—opened, and let them forth by my so potent art."

Young Jeb asked me, "What are you saying—is that more Shakespeare?"

I ignored him, without realizing that I was—without meaning to do so, as I thought through what I remembered from Prospero's lines .

"Sounds like it," young Jeb said, mostly to himself.

I went on, remembering the rest as best as I could, "—But this rough magic I here abjure—and when I have required some heavenly music—which now I do—to work mine end on their senses that this airy charm is for, I'll break my staff—"

I turned towards the spot where I retrieved Cooley's skull and placed it back into the small hole I dug.

Young Jeb asked me, "What are you doing?—you're putting it back?"

I didn't say anything—I didn't know what to say, exactly. I began gathering the dirt clumped in mounds all around the hole carefully back into the hole, so I could re-submerge the skull and I cover it back up.

I went on, remembering more of Prospero's lines, "—bury it certain fathoms in the earth, and deeper than did ever plummet sound."

"Fathoms?" Young Jeb asked. "—what are fathoms? Is that like a ghost?"

I still didn't respond. Still, I didn't know what to say to young Jeb that would have made sense to him—and to me, for that matter. In my mind, nothing really made sense anymore. It wasn't just that nothing about Cooley truly made any sense anymore, but it was also that nothing about myself made sense anymore, either—I wasn't sure which of the two scared me the most. All I knew was that, somehow, in some way, what I was doing was all I could do to make sense out of the senselessness, and to make something knowable out of everything that had become so unknowable.

As I pulled the last of the dirt over Cooley's skull, re-burying it, I wanted to make sure that what I had found wouldn't be found by anyone else.

"So, you are—" Young Jeb started off, watching me. "—you are putting it back into the ground? I don't understand—we came all this way—all this trouble."

I didn't respond. I was more concerned with making sure Cooley's skull was re-buried, taking the rock with the X marked on it, and tossing it out and away from the unmarked grave as far as I could. Then, I took out the crude map that Jebediah had drawn for me—I gave it another look, then proceeded to rip it up into as many pieces as I could and scattered the pieces over Cooley's unmarked grave, so it would be impossible for anyone else to reassemble the pieces into anything decipherable.

"So," Young Jeb whined. "—you don't want the map anymore, either?"

I continued to crouch down on the unmarked grave, looking at the ground and realizing that I was doing so much more than just re-burying Cooley's skull with the rest of his remains—I was burying some part of myself. After finishing and publishing the Silas Rondo book, there was no doubt in my mind that I would write a book on Cooley, given the way that the narrative on Silas Rondo ended and what Cooley, ultimately, meant to what happened to Silas Rondo. What I knew, dear reader, was that I had to continue that narrative beyond Silas Rondo, if I wanted to do justice to what happened to Silas Rondo and what Cooley became. The only way to do that, I knew, was to devote a book to Cooley—eventually, what I had come to understand was that there was no Cooley book to write, and that where I ended with Silas Rondo wasn't the beginning of another book, but the ending of something larger. What I realized, then, was that Cooley would still be the one doing the killing—Cooley would be the one killing my life as a writer, with all that remained so unknowable about Cooley. In the end, if I ever expected to be the one doing the living on the other side of the writing life, I would have to do as Shakespeare did, if we are to say that what Prospero did is a representation of Shakespeare's thoughts.

All the years I had spent researching, interviewing, and working on the Cooley book would be figuratively buried with the rest of Cooley—all of what I had gathered would be put into the ground, somehow. Whatever book I had hoped to write on Cooley would be better off, I thought, buried with whatever was left of Cooley himself.

Remembering more of what Prospero says in Tempest, which, some say, represent Shakespeare's autobiographical musings on the end of his own career as a playwright, I said to myself, "—I'll drown my book."

Young Jeb asked, "Huh?"

"Take me back to town," I told him. "There's nothing left to see here."

Young Jeb said, "Okay, sure thing."

I stood up and walked back towards the carriage, with young Jeb following closely behind me. Once at the railing, I climbed back over it—young Jeb did the same. As a climbed up into the carriage, and young Jeb did the same and took hold of the team by the reins, I clutched my bag tightly, thinking about what Prospero did, and thinking about what they say Shakespeare did after writing *The Tempest*.

Just as the team began pulling the carriage and we were about a hundred yards away from the field of Cooley's two graves—one real and one imagined, one private and one public—young Jeb asked me, "You know a lot of that Shakespeare stuff, right?"

I looked at him, curiously.

He went on, "I mean—you've committed to memory all of Shakespeare's stuff. So, you must know a lot of Shakespeare, right?"

I paused, and told him, "Just the things that matter—just what matters."

What mattered to me, then, was going back home. With Cooley re-buried, home wasn't writing a book on Cooley, home was, instead, re-writing the life that was more meaningful than any biography I had ever written. What mattered was working on my own biography, so to speak—what happened was sorting through all the things that made me who I was, and all the things that I began realizing I wasn't. The fact that Cooley was so unknowable brought me the realization that I was making myself more unknowable, not just to myself, but to my wife and son—I wondered what either of them could say about me, if I couldn't say anything about Cooley.

I told young Jeb, "Take me to the station."

Young Jeb asked, just to be clear, "The station?"

"Yes," I said, looking out over the fields we were passing through, which was open with possibilities. "The station—I'm going back home."

Young Jeb nodded, clearly not understanding what I meant.

38

After bidding farewell to young Jeb, while trying to ignore how Doc Baker saw me off with a scowl on his face, I settled into my window seat on the train, and prepared myself for the long way home from Arizona.

Out of the window, I caught sight of the telegraph office window—the same one I went to when I first arrived—and saw it was closed. I thought about the young telegraph operator that I met there—though the telegraph window was closed, I wondered about the young man that had been so excited to meet me and he was so excited he needed to send word to his father, who was also a telegraph operator, and I wondered, again, how close the two men must be for something like that to be shared so easily between the two, between a son and a father, between two men on either side of a telegraph, between two readers that thought so well of me. I thought about how something as insignificant as the son wanting his father to know he—the son—had met me spoke volumes about what kind of son the son was and what kind of father the father was. The two were knowable to one another—it seemed to me that there was probably nothing unknowable between them. Then, I thought about myself, as both someone's son and someone's father, and how, as someone's son, my father was unknowable and, as someone's father, I, myself, was unknowable—I thought about how increasingly unknowable my father had become to me and how, once he died, I stood at his grave, feeling as if I was looking at the tombstone of a stranger—there wasn't anything but this distanced feeling, I remember, seeing my father's name with the dates of his birth and death, and realizing just how strange it was to even call him my father. I thought about how little I knew about him, and how, because he was unknowable, there was a part of myself that I didn't know as well as I should.

I thought, too, about how unknowable I have always been to my own son, and how, as much as I told myself that I wouldn't be like my father was to me, I eventually turned out into him, just the same. I thought about how I had been so focused on my career that I didn't have anything left for my son—and I thought about how my career was what brought my wife and I together and how, at some point in time, my career was what separated us. I thought about how my wife always warned me about how my career was tearing us apart, and I thought about how I believed she was always exaggerating or, in some way, was just jealous of the success my writing career—I thought about the last conversation we had before I left home to go on the speaking tour for the Silas Rondo book, and I remembered, quite vividly, how displeased she was to know that, after the speaking tour, I would begin researching the book I planned to write on Cooley, and I remembered, too, how she told me that she felt like I was married to my work and not her. I thought about how I laughed at her then, and how I told her she was being silly, and how I told her that she was making this whole thing into a choice between my career and my family. She had said that she wasn't, but told me, in no uncertain terms, that, if decided to be away for an unknown amount of time to research a book after already planning to be on the road for several months promoting the Silas Rondo book, there wouldn't be a home for me to return to.

Sitting there on the train that was just leaving Arizona, there was no doubt in my mind that I was returning home. I was returning, even if my wife believed I couldn't—or, perhaps, that I wouldn't. Yet, I was sure—if there was anything I could be certain of—that I didn't know what kind of home awaited me.

I was on my way home knowing I hadn't communicated with my wife in about a year, at least. That was when I received word—from my publisher—that my wife wanted me to know that her mother had passed. My wife had sent word to the publisher, since she knew that they would know how to pass the news along to me—it was an odd but sad thing to admit to myself: I had had more steady contact with my publisher than my own wife. What was more odd and even sadder was that I didn't bother making my way home for my wife's mother's funeral—I didn't know, I would tell myself then, if I was even welcomed home for something like that. The point, though, is that I didn't try—I didn't wire any condolences to my wife, even if it had been, to be honest, impossible for me to return to New York from the other side of the country in time for the funeral.

A year later, there I was, realizing how impossible it would be to write a book on Cooley, but, somehow, possible to repair my marriage. And there I was, dear reader, remembering how I once believed that Cooley was knowable enough person to write about for my readers, when I was becoming an unknowable person to my family. There I was, believing that what I had given up chasing something else was now something worth chasing, in exchange for giving up what I once chased—I had given up the idea of family to chase the idea of Cooley, and I was now giving up the idea of Cooley to chase the idea of family.

The trip back to New York is mostly a blur now—I spent time looking out of train windows, or reading through the notes I had taken for the Cooley book, feeling as if I was reading things written by someone else, or occasionally having brief conversations with fellow passengers that recognized me from the Silas Rondo book, or thinking how much suffering my mother endured to a man as unknowable as my father, or wondering if my son harbored any resentment against me for being absent from so much of his life, or imagining what my wife would say when I told her I had given up the Cooley book, or trying to find the right words to tell my publisher that, even though I had received a large advance, there would be no Cooley book as I had promised, or just thinking what I was going to do once I retuned to New York and was back at home.

And above all, I thought about Cooley—I thought about how Cooley had always been the one doing the killing, so he could always be the one doing the living. I thought about all the lives Cooley had destroyed—all the meaningless violence he had inflicted— and I thought about the lives I destroyed, with all the meaningless violence I had, too, inflicted. In a way, like Cooley, I was also always the one doing the killing, so I could always be the one doing the living.

I thought about how Cooley generally believed that it was best to always be the one doing the killing, so one could always be the one doing the living. Some say Cooley adopted that idea from Silas Rondo, but I tend to disagree with that. It wasn't that Silas Rondo didn't believe in that philosophy—rather, in my opinion, if Silas Rondo had believed such a thing, it is clear to me that Silas Rondo would have anticipated what Cooley eventually do. If Silas Rondo would have imagined that Cooley wouldn't always be loyal, or that there would come a time when Cooley would want more than what Silas Rondo's gang had to offer, Silas Rondo would have approached the incident with the killing of the sheriff differently—instead of taking what Cooley did in stride, and making sure that Cooley understood that only he, Silas Rondo, would be the one doing the killing, Cooley would have never imagined that Silas Rondo's authority could be usurped.

The whole idea about always being the one doing the killing is more than just making sure you are the one always doing the living—it's also about making sure you're the one that's not doing the dying. So, in a way, I see Cooley's philosophy grounded on the relationship between killing and dying. In other words, for Cooley, it's always about what you do and what is done to you—it's about the act you perform and what act is performed on you, and that's the difference

Yet, the whole idea about being the one doing the living isn't really about living, dear reader. It's not about what you build up for yourself at the expense of what you have taken away from someone else—it's about what kind of world you build up for others.

That was what Cooley didn't understand: all the killing and all the dying may have ensured that Cooley was always the one doing the living in the short run, but, in the long run, all the killing and all the dying only made the kind of life Cooley was living all the more complicated. That was complicated, as you know, by the sheer number of people that wanted Cooley dead, or wanted to kill Cooley—not just men, but also women. It seems to me that, though Cooley always wanted to be the one doing the killing, while others were the ones doing the dying, there was always someone that wished, when it came to Cooley, they would be the one doing the killing. Nowhere is that truth more evident than in the man named after Cooley—or Cooley's son—and how he wanted to be the one doing the killing and wanted to make sure Cooley would be the doing the dying, for a change.

It remains impossible to precisely know all the circumstances surrounding Cooley's death. That's the only knowable thing about it. Even when speaking with the man named after Cooley, I realized that he wouldn't tell me the whole story—for whatever reason, he was either unwilling or unable to tell me.

I thought about how much satisfaction the man named after Cooley had on his face when he let me know how I could find Cooley's body. There was this bliss there, in his eyes, when I made sure that I knew what to look for in the remains that would identify Cooley—there was a happiness, there, that told me that, when the man named after Cooley killed Cooley, he found some kind of salvation in Cooley's death. Something that could even be described as freedom—it was as if, in killing Cooley, the man named after Cooley found freedom. That freedom, when looking at it through Cooley's philosophy, is a freedom invested in being the one doing the killing just as much as it is a freedom in being the one doing the living. But, for the man named after Cooley, knowing he would be dying soon—though he never told me he was dying—there was a certain amount of freedom in being the one doing the dying.

When I think about Cooley dying, in whatever way he died, I wonder if he, too, felt some kind of happiness, or bliss, or even freedom in being the one doing the dying. There are plenty of accounts, as I write in the Silas Rondo book, about Silas Rondo dying with a smile on his face—some say it was a smile from being relieved about not having to continue living the kind of life he was living, while others say it was a smile from realizing what Cooley had done to him. Whichever way, as I argue, Silas Rondo was happy to be dying—in his mind, being the one doing the dying was a worthwhile experience and, perhaps, Silas Rondo himself understood that there was something poetic in Cooley being the one that killed him, Silas Rondo.

I began to think, too, that the same thing held true for the man named after Cooley—there was something poetic in his being the one that killed Cooley. In a similar way, there was something poetic in my finding where Cooley was actually buried, something poetic in holding Cooley's skull in my hands—just as Hamlet holds Yorick's skull—and something poetic in no longer lying to myself about writing a book on Cooley, and, for that matter, something poetic in returning home.

Thinking about what was poetic about returning home, I remember being reminded of how Odysseus, the hero of Homer's *Odyssey*, returns home after the Trojan War, and how this theme, as Homer presents it, recurs in Ancient Greek literature at large. Thematically, it's how the epic hero returns home by sea, as something that was viewed as the highest level of heroism, showing a hero's greatness. The hero's journey home, then, is typically arduous and marked by enduring a series of trials that test the hero—but, in the end, the return is never just about returning physically, but it's more about how the hero retains or enhances who they are once arriving home.

All told, my hero's journey home, if I can call myself a hero, even if I am far from heroic, wouldn't be by sea, but would take the A&P to New Mexico, and transfer to the Santa Fe to make my way east into Kansas, then transfer to the Union Pacific and go east into Illinois, and eventually, transfer to the New York Central to reach New York and, then, a short train trip from Albany south to New York City. Once in New York City, after what felt like a hero's journey home, I took a cab to my brownstone in Manhattan— after enduring the trials I experienced in researching and thinking about the Cooley book and, in the end, realizing how writing such a book would test everything I believed I was as a biographer, I had come home wondering if anything about myself had been retained or enhanced since being away for so long.

Stepping out of the cab, letting my eyes wander around the neighborhood, and standing there looking at the brownstone, I felt like I had arrived in a foreign land. I had been away for so long—during the several years it took to research and complete the Silas Rondo book, the speaking tour I went on after the publication of the Silas Rondo book, and the few years I had been occupied with researching and thinking about the book on Cooley—that I felt like a stranger. I felt as if the life I had lived here, before being away for almost ten consecutive years, was now unknowable—it was as if whatever I thought I knew about myself was now something that was so unknowable I couldn't make any sense of myself anymore.

I remembered looking at Cooley's skull, believing that there was something meaningful that I would discover in its eyeholes, and realizing—disappointedly—that finding Cooley's skull only situated me further away from knowing him, rather than closer. His remains didn't reveal any truth for me, if, by truth, I mean: there was something in the remains that would make Cooley knowable to me—all there was, dear reader, was a truth that continued to point back at me in a blatant bright light that only revealed how little I knew about myself and, for that matter, and only revealed how little I knew about what made home a home.

As much as I wanted to feel that I was indeed coming home, I still felt as I wasn't really coming home at all, and that there wasn't anything about this place—this home—that seemed welcoming anymore. I was physically coming home to a place I didn't physically recognize anymore. Nothing about this place spoke to anything I knew about myself anymore, which I had become undone over all those years away—undone in all the ways of being the one doing the living, as I wandered through the lives of Silas Rondo and Cooley. I had spent so much time making sense out of someone like Cooley, who had spent so much time in his life being the one doing the killing, until I had become another one of Cooley's victims without realizing I had become one.

I remember standing there, still looking at my brownstone, focusing on the front door and the windows to either side. I remember standing there, imagining that—on a

Saturday afternoon—my wife and son were surely home.

I remember standing there, thinking about what things were like, now, inside, after all those years of being away—I thought about my little library of books, including some of my own authored books that I kept on display in what served as an office for me. I thought about all the hours I would spent writing longhand on my desk and how I would type out what I written on the typewriter my wife bought me on a Christmas that, now, seemed like a lifetime ago—I thought about the small couch that sat across the room from my desk, and I thought about how my wife once liked to sit there and read while I worked on whatever book I was writing at the time, and I thought about how, over time, she would sit on that couch less frequently, until she began to read by herself in some other part of the house away from me.

I remember thinking about how, in those days, we didn't say very much to one another, and how, at some point in time, I would use that couch as a bed, and eventually use that study as a place to shave and get ready in the morning, so I wouldn't be required to speak to her—my wife would stay in bed upstairs, with the bedsheets pulled over her head, and wouldn't emerge from the bedroom until she knew I was gone for the day.

I remember standing there, outside what was just as much mine as my wife's, thinking about how my wife and son had become, in their own way, a better family without me, and I was just someone that labored on some book in a room that may as well have been miles away from them.

I remember standing there, being reminded of the expression on my son's face when he watched me leave all those years ago, and how my wife stood behind him with her arms draped around him, as if she was protecting him from me, with her own expression telling me that what I was leaving wasn't my home anymore—there was nothing I could do, after all this time, to change things.

I remember standing there, dear reader, thinking about how I had walked away from the Cooley book—how I had come to cold realization that there was no book there for me to write, despite what I believed to be true after writing the Silas Rondo book— and how I re-buried Cooley's skull. I remember standing there, feeling that same feeling and coming to the same cold realization, which would require me to re-bury something else that was just as unknowable as Cooley.

Just like everything about Cooley was an impression in a wandering sky, so, too, was whatever my home was. If home was only an impression in a wandering sky, I decided to re-bury it too—I left for good, for the best, this time, without looking back.